Murder
Most
Catholic

Murder Most Catholic

Divine Tales of Profane Crimes

Edited by
RALPH McINERNY

Cumberland House
Nashville, Tennessee

MYS
Sh. stories

Published by
    Cumberland House Publishing, Inc.
    431 Harding Industrial Drive
    Nashville, TN 37211
    www.cumberlandhouse.com

Cover design: Gore Studio, Inc.

Library of Congress Cataloging-in-Publication Data

Murder most Catholic : divine tales of profane crimes / edited by Ralph McInerny.
        p. cm. — (Murder most series)
    ISBN 1-58182-260-X (pbk.)
    1. Detective and mystery stories, American. 2. Detective and mystery stories, English. 3.
Catholic Church—Fiction. 4. Clergy—Fiction. I. McInerny, Ralph M. II. Series.
    PS648.D4 M87525 2002
    813'.08720938282—dc21

2002006532

Printed in Canada
1 2 3 4 5 6 7 8 — 07 06 05 04 03 02

Contents

Introduction

Ralph McInerny

It may be something of a commentary on our post-Christian times that authors asked to write stories with a religious motif or background should set them in the past, usually the Middle Ages. Has faith become as arcane as the astrolabe? Doubtless it is because monks and nuns and unselfconscious devotion were then as common as the air people breathed that belief is dealt with more easily in a medieval frame. It is the whole period that is strange and exotic to us, and transplanting the devices of the modern mystery story into it underscores the differences between then and now while providing a common measure of appraisal. In a modern setting, there is something countercultural about religious belief.

When Chesterton introduced his Father Brown, he seemed to have two ends in view. One, to counter the rationalism of Sherlock Holmes, whose rigorous deductions from observed facts made the discovery of the criminal a scientific accomplishment.* The cocaine habit and the violin softened that, of course, but when Holmes was Holmes, reason was in the ascendancy. Father Brown, by contrast, was bumbling, intuitive, a poet rather than a scientist of crime. Deductive reasoning gives way to intuition, and intuition is made possible because the priest, like the criminal, has the capacity for wrongdoing. Father Brown imagines himself into the malefactor's shoes and becomes a kind of participant in the crime.

---

*See *Murder Most Divine*, p. vii.

The second reason for choosing Father Brown was to have a symbol of religious faith as the opposite of modern materialism. Chesterton entertained romantic thoughts about the past and achieved some of his most memorable effects by translating the mores and codes of the past into modern England. *The Napoleon of Notting Hill, The Man Who Was Thursday*. Father Brown's great foil is Flambeau, the master criminal with a flair for the poetic, a worthy foe for the otherwordly cleric. Chesterton once said that the madman has lost everything but his reason. Father Brown and Flambeau stand in stark contrast to Holmes and Moriarity. The latter are mad by the standards of the former.

All this may be vague enough to carry my point as to the attraction the Middle Ages have for writers who wish to meld murder and the religious. And of course the reader will be quick to point out the counter examples in this collection to my suggestion. Peter Tremayne's Sister Fidelma mystery, "Whispers of the Dead," will seem to transport the techniques of the deductive mystery into the past and to satisfy in the way that a Sherlock Holmes story does. Lillian Stewart Carl's "The Rag and Bone Man" contrasts with Tremayne's, evoking in a completely convincing way a world of faith and providing us with historical background for the Shroud of Turin. P. C. Doherty's "The Knight's Confession" sweeps us along, and while one might think that, with confessions as long as the one in the story, there would be little time left for sinning, the prolonged confrontation is essential to the story and its satisfying ending. Margaret Frazer's "Lowly Death" uses a medieval setting for color, yet remains a thoroughly modern deductive mystery. The success of the story is in no way diminished by saying that it could be set in modern Budapest or Laramie with important but inessential alterations. T. S. Eliot said in one of the Four Quartets that "the poetry does not matter." In a similarly mystifying way we can say of Frazer's story that the medieval setting does not matter. "A Clerical Error" by Michael Jecks may seem similarly abstractable from the medieval setting, but its surprising denouement suggests otherwise. Anne Perry and Malachi Saxon give us a memorable story that transposes the Salem witch trials into the Middle Ages.

From Stephen Dentinger comes "Cemetery of the Innocents," a marvelous tale of medieval Paris and of the outlaw poet Francois Villon. The attraction of the story lies in its historical evocations more than in its plot, and the few anachronisms do not detract from its power.

From this story, we turn to stories set in the present. Ed Gorman's "Bless Me Father, For I Have Sinned" has the expected master touch, and the late Chuck Meyer's "Divine Justice" is a somber tale of euthanasia with an electronic twist. Kate Charles takes us to Venice with Callie Anson, her Anglican deacon, the evocations of the city firmly tied to an intricate and satisfying plot. In "Arrow of Ice," Ed Hoch works a variation on Roald Dahl in a thoroughly American parish setting. Kate Gallison sets her story in the Episcopal parish of St. Bede's in Fishersville, New Jersey, and provides a satisfying murder mystery. Monica Quill's novella "Veronica's Veil" deals with the return of a nun who had left the convent decades ago and Father Dowling in "The Shorn Lamb" turns up a surprising murderer on the local campus.

It is a great pleasure for a writer to have an occasion to see new work by other writers. As the contributions to this volume came in, I found myself marveling both at the skills of my colleagues and at the resilience of a genre that is easily the most popular with the majority of readers. Mystery fiction, just because of the expectations we have of it, requires the author both to meet and to fairly thwart the reader's expectations. To surprise within the familiar is the recurrent task. The stories in this volume pass with flying colors.

Murder Most Catholic

Whispers of the Dead

Peter Tremayne

Abbot Laisran sat back in his chair, at the side of the crackling log fire, and gazed thoughtfully at his cup of mulled wine.

"You have achieved a formidable reputation, Fidelma," he observed, raising his cherub-like features to his young protégée who sat on the other side of the fireplace, sipping her wine. "Some Brehons talk of you as they would the great female judges such as Brig or Dari. That is commendable in one so young."

Fidelma smiled thinly. She was not one given to vanity for she knew her own weaknesses.

"I would not aspire to write legal texts as they did, nor, indeed, would I pretend to be more than a simple investigator of facts. I am a *dálaigh*, an advocate. I prefer to leave the judgment of others to the Brehons."

Abbot Laisran inclined his head slightly as if in acceptance of her statement.

"But that is the very thing on which your reputation has its foundation. You have had some outstanding successes with your investigations, observing things that are missed by others. Several times I have seen your ability firsthand. Does it ever worry you that you hold so much responsibility?"

"It worries me only that I observe all the facts and come to the right decision. However, I did not spend eight years under instruction with the Brehon Morann of Tara to no avail. I have come to accept the responsibility that goes with my office."

"Ah," sighed the abbot, "'Unto whomsoever much is given, of him shall much be required.' That is from—"

"The Gospel of Luke," Fidelma interrupted with a mischievous smile.

Abbot Laisran answered her smile.

"Does nothing escape your attention, Fidelma? Surely there must be cases when you are baffled? For instance, there must be many a murder over which it is impossible to attribute guilt."

"Perhaps I have been lucky," admitted Fidelma. "However, I do not believe that there is such a thing as a perfect crime."

"Come now, that must be an overstatement?"

"Even when we examine a body with no evidence of who he, or she, was in life, or how and when he, or she, died, let alone by whose hand, a good observer will learn something. The dead always whisper to us. It is our task to listen to the whispers of the dead."

The abbot knew it was not in Fidelma's nature to boast of her prowess; however, his round features assumed a skeptical expression.

"I would like to make a wager with you," he suddenly announced.

Fidelma frowned. She knew that Abbot Laisran was a man who was quick to place wagers. Many was the time she had attended the great Aonach Life, the fair at the Curragh, for the horseracing and watched Abbot Laisran losing as well as winning as he hazarded money on the contests.

"What manner of wager had you in mind, Laisran?" she asked cautiously.

"You have said that the dead whisper to us and we must have ears to listen. That in every circumstance the body of a person will eventually yield up the information necessary to identify him, and who, if anyone, is culpable for the death. Have I understood you correctly?"

Fidelma inclined her head in agreement.

"That has been my experience until now," she conceded.

"Well then," continued Abbot Laisran, "will you take a wager with me on a demonstration of that claim?"

"In what circumstances?"

"Simple enough. By coincidence, this morning a young peasant woman was found dead not far from this abbey. There was no means of identification on her and inquiries in the adjacent village have failed to identify her. No one appears to be missing. She must have been a poor itinerant. One of our brothers, out of charity, brought the body to the abbey. Tomorrow, as is custom, we shall bury her in an unmarked grave." Abbot Laisran paused and glanced slyly at her. "If the dead truly whisper to you, Fidelma, perhaps you will be able to interpret those whispers and identify her?"

Fidelma considered for a moment.

"You say that she was a young woman? What was the cause of her death?"

"That is the mystery. There are no visible means of how she died. She was well nourished, according to our apothecary."

"No signs of violence?" asked Fidelma, slightly bemused.

"None. The matter is a total mystery. Hence I would place a wager with you, which is that if you can find some evidence, some cause of death, of something that will lead to the identification of the poor unfortunate, then I will accept that your claim is valid. So, what of the wager?"

Fidelma hesitated. She disliked challenges to her abilities but, on the other hand, some narcissistic voice called from within her.

"What is the specific wager?" she asked.

"A screpall for the offertory box of the abbey." Abbot Laisran smiled. "I will give a screpall for the poor if you can discover more about the poor woman than we have been able to. If you cannot, then you will pay a screpall to the offertory box."

A screpall was a silver coin valued to the fee charged by a *dálaigh* for a single consultation.

Fidelma hesitated a moment and then, urged on by her pride, said: "It is agreed."

She rose and set down her mulled wine, startling the abbot.

"Where are you going?" he demanded.

"Why, to view the body. There is only an hour or two of daylight left, and many important signs can vanish in artificial light."

Reluctantly, Abbot Laisran sat down his wine and also rose.

"Very well," he sighed. "Come, I will show you the way to the apothecary."

A tall, thin religieux with a beak of a nose glanced up as Abbot Laisran entered the chamber where he was pounding leaves with a pestle. His eyes widened a little when he saw Sister Fidelma enter behind the abbot. Fidelma was well known to most of the religious of Abbey of Durrow.

"Brother Donngal, I have asked Sister Fidelma to examine our unknown corpse."

The abbey's apothecary immediately set aside his work and gazed at her with interest.

"Do you think that you know the poor woman, Sister?"

Fidelma smiled quickly.

"I am here as a *dálaigh*, Brother," she replied.

A slight frown crossed Brother Donngal's features.

"There is no sign of a violent death, Sister. Why would an advocate have an interest in this matter?"

Catching the irritable hardening of her expression, Abbot Laisran intervened quickly: "It is because I asked Sister Fidelma to give me her opinion on this matter."

Brother Donngal turned to a door.

"The body lies in our mortuary. I was shortly to prepare it for burial. Our carpenter has only just delivered the coffin."

The body lay under a linen sheet on a table in the center of the chamber that served as the abbey's mortuary where bodies were prepared for burial.

Sister Fidelma moved toward it and was about to take a corner of the sheet in her hand when the apothecary coughed apologetically.

"I have removed her clothing for examination but have not dressed her for the coffin yet, Sister."

Fidelma's eyes twinkled at the man's embarrassment, but she made no reply.

The corpse was that of a young woman, perhaps no more than twenty years old. Fidelma had not entirely hardened herself to premature death.

"She is not long dead," was Fidelma's first remark.

Brother Donngal nodded.

"No more than a day and a night, I reckon. She was found this morning and I believe she died during the night."

"By whom was she found?"

"Brother Torcan," intervened Abbot Laisran, who was standing just inside the door observing them.

"Where was she found?"

"No more than a few hundred paces from the abbey walls."

"I meant, in what place, what were the conditions of her surroundings?"

"Oh, I see. She was found in a wood, in a small clearing almost covered with leaves."

Fidelma raised an eyebrow.

"What was this Brother Torcan doing there?"

"Gathering edible fungi. He works in the kitchens."

"And the clothes worn by the girl . . . where are they?" Fidelma asked.

The man gestured to a side table on which clothing was piled.

"She wore just the simple garb of a village girl. There is nothing to identify her there."

"I will examine them in a moment and likewise will wish to speak to this Brother Torcan."

She turned her gaze back to the body, bending forward to examine it with careful precision.

It was some time before she straightened from her task.

"Now, I shall examine the clothing."

Brother Donngal moved to a table and watched while Fidelma picked up the items. They consisted of a pair of sandals called *cuaran*, a single sole of untanned hide, stitched together with thongs cut from the same hide. They were almost worn through. The dress was a simple one of wool and linen, roughly woven and threadbare. It appeared to have been secured at the waist by a strip of linen. There was also a short cape with a hood, as affected by many country women. Again, it was obviously worn and fringed with rabbit fur.

Fidelma raised her head and glanced at the apothecary.

"Is this all that she was wearing?"

Brother Donngal nodded in affirmation.

"Was there no underclothing?"

The apothecary looked embarrassed.

"None," he confirmed.

"She did not have a *ciorbholg*?"

The *ciorbholg* was, literally, a comb-bag, but it contain all the articles of toilet, as well as combs, which women carried about with them no matter their rank or status. It served women in the manner of a purse and it was often tied at the waist by a belt.

Brother Donngal shook his head negatively once more.

"This is why we came to the conclusion that she was simply a poor itinerant," explained the abbot.

"So there was no toilet bag?" mused Fidelma. "And she had no brooches or other jewelry?"

Brother Donngal allowed a smile to play around his lips.

"Of course not."

"Why of course not?" demanded Fidelma sharply.

"Because it is clear from this clothing, Sister, that the girl was a very poor country girl. Such a girl would not be able to afford such finery."

"Even a poor country girl will seek out some ornaments, no matter how poor she is," replied Fidelma.

Abbot Laisran came forward with a sad smile.

"Nothing was found. So you see, Fidelma, this poor young woman cannot whisper to you from her place of death. A poor country girl and with nothing to identify her. Her whispers are silent ones. You should not have been so willing to accept my challenge."

Fidelma swung 'round on him to reveal the smile on her face. Her eyes twinkled with a dangerous fire.

"On the contrary, Laisran. There is much that this poor girl whispers; much she tells us, even in this pitiable state."

Bother Donngal exchanged a puzzled glance with the abbot.

"I don't understand you, Sister," he said. "What can you see? What have I missed?"

"Practically everything," Fidelma assured him calmly.

Abbot Laisran stifled a chuckle as he saw the mortified expression on the apothecary's face. But he turned to her with a reproving glance.

"Come now, Fidelma," he chided, "don't be too sharp because you have been confronted with an insolvable riddle. Not even you can conjure facts out of nothing."

Abbot Laisran stirred uncomfortably as he saw the tiny green fire in her eyes intensify. However, when she addressed him, her tone was comparatively mild.

"You know better of me, Laisran. I am not given to vain boasting."

Brother Donngal moved forward and stared at the body of the girl as if trying to see what it was that Fidelma had observed.

"What have I missed?" he demanded again.

Fidelma turned to the apothecary.

"First, you say that this girl is a poor country girl. What makes you arrive at such a conclusion?"

Brother Donngal regarded her with an almost pitying look.

"That was easy. Look at her clothing—at her sandals. They are not the apparel of someone of high rank and status. The clothes show her humble origins."

Fidelma sighed softly.

"My mentor, the Brehon Moran, once said that the veil can disguise much; it is folly to accept the outside show for the inner quality of a person."

"I don't understand."

"This girl is not of humble rank, that much is obvious."

Abbot Laisran moved forward and peered at the body in curiosity.

"Come, Fidelma, now you are guessing."

Fidelma shook her head.

"I do not guess, Laisran. I have told you," she added impatiently, "listen to the whispers of the dead. If this is supposed to be a peasant girl, then regard the skin of her body—white and lacking color by wind and sun. Look at her hands, soft and cared for as are her nails. There is no dirt beneath them. Her hands are not calloused by work. Look at her feet. Again, soft and well cared for. See the soles of the feet? This girl had not been trudging fields in those poor shoes that she was clad in, nor has she walked any great distance."

The abbot and the apothecary followed her instructions and examined the limbs she indicated.

"Now, examine her hair."

The girl's hair, a soft spun gold color, was braided behind her head in a single long plait that reached almost to her waist.

"Nothing unusual in that," observed Laisran. Many women in the five kingdoms of Eireann considered very long hair as a mark of beauty and braided it in similar style.

"But it is exceptionally well tended. The braiding is the traditional *cuilfhionn* and surely you must know that it is affected only by women of rank. What this poor corpse whispers to me is that she is a woman of rank."

"Then why was she dressed as a peasant?" demanded the apothecary after a moment's silence.

Fidelma pursed her lips.

"We must continue to listen. Perhaps she will tell us. As she tells us other things."

"Such as?"

"She is married."

Abbot Laisran snorted with cynicism.

"How could you possibly know that?"

Fidelma simply pointed to the left hand of the corpse.

"There are marks around the third finger. They are faint, I grant you, but tiny marks nevertheless which show the recent removal of a ring that has been worn there. There is also some discoloration on her left arm. What do you make of that, Brother Donngal?"

The apothecary shrugged.

"Do you mean the marks of blue dye? It is of little importance."

"Why?"

"Because it is a common thing among the villages. Women dye clothes and materials. The blue is merely a dye caused by the extract of a cruciferous plant *glaisin*. Most people use it. It is not unusual in anyway."

"It is not. But women of rank would hardly be involved in dyeing their own materials and this dye stain seems fairly recent."

"Is that important?" asked the abbot.

"Perhaps. It depends on how we view the most important of all the facts this poor corpse whispers to us."

"Which is?" demanded Brother Donngal.

"That this girl was murdered."

Abbot Laisran's eyebrows shot up.

"Come, come, now. Our apothecary has found no evidence of foul play; no wounds, no bruising, no abrasions. The face is relaxed as if she simply passed on in her sleep. Anyone can see that."

Fidelma moved forward and lifted the girl's head, bringing the single braid of hair forward in order to expose the nape of the neck. She had done this earlier during her examination as Brother Donngal and Abbot Laisran watched with faint curiosity.

"Come here and look, both of you. What, Brother Donngal, was your explanation of this?"

Brother Donngal looked slightly embarrassed as he peered forward.

"I did not examine her neck under the braid," he admitted.

"Well, now that you are examining it, what do you see?"

"There is a small discolored patch like a tiny bruise," replied the apothecary after a moment or two. "It is not more than a fingernail in width. There is a little blood spot in the center. It's rather like an insect bite that has drawn blood or as if someone has pricked the skin with a needle."

"Do you see it also, Laisran?" demanded Fidelma.

The Abbot leaned forward and then nodded.

Fidelma gently lowered the girl's head back onto the table.

"I believe that this was a wound caused by an incision. You are right, Brother Donngal, in saying it is like a needle point. The incision was created by something long and thin, like a needle. It was inserted into the nape of the neck and pushed up hard so that it penetrated into the head. It was swift. Deadly. Evil. The girl probably died before she knew that she was being attacked."

Abbot Laisran was staring at Fidelma in bewilderment.

"Let me get this straight, Fidelma. Are you saying that the corpse found near this abbey this morning is a woman of rank who has been murdered? Is that right?"

"And, after her death, her clothes were taken from her and she was hurriedly dressed in poor peasant garb to disguise her origin. The murderer thought to remove all means of identification from her."

"Even if this is true," interrupted Brother Donngal, "how might we discover who she was and who perpetrated this crime?"

"The fact that she was not long dead when Brother Torcan found her makes our task more simple. She was killed in this vicinity. A woman of rank would surely be visiting a place of substance. She had not been walking any distance. Observe the soles of her feet. I would presume that she either rode or came in a carriage to her final destination."

"But what destination?" demanded Brother Donngal.

"If she came to Durrow, she would have come to the abbey," Laisran pointed out. "She did not."

"True enough. We are left with two types of places she might have gone. The house of a noble, a chieftain, or, perhaps, a *bruighean*, an inn. I believe that we will find the place where she met her death within five or six kilometers of this abbey."

"What makes you say that?"

"A deduction. The corpse newly dead and the murderer wanting to dispose of it as quickly as possible. Whoever killed her reclothed her body and transported it to the spot where it was found. They could not have travelled far."

Abbot Laisran rubbed his chin.

"Whoever it was, they took a risk in disposing of it in the woods so near this abbey."

"Perhaps not. If memory serves me right, those woods are the thickest stretch of forest in this area even though they are close to the abbey. Are they that frequented?"

Abbot Laisran shrugged.

"It is true that Brother Torcan does not often venture so far into the woods in search of fungi," he admitted. "He came on the corpse purely by chance."

"So the proximity of the abbey was not necessarily a caution to our murderer. Well, are there such places as I described within the distance I have estimated?"

"An inn or a chieftain's house? North of here is Ballacolla, where there is an inn. South of here is Ballyconra where the lord of Conra lives."

"Who is he? Describe him?"

"A young man, newly come to office there. I know little about him although he came here to pay his respects to me when he took office. When I came to Durrow as abbot the young man's father was lord of Ballyconra but his son was away serving in the army of the High King. He is a bachelor newly returned from the wars against the Ui Neill."

"Then we shall have to learn more," observed Fidelma dryly. She glanced through the window at the cloudy sky.

"There is still an hour before sunset," she reflected. "Have Brother Torcan meet me at the gates so that he may conduct me to the spot where he found the body."

"What use would that be?" demanded the abbot. "There was nothing in the clearing apart from the body."

Fidelma did not answer.

With a sigh, the abbot went off to find the religieux.

Half an hour later Brother Torcan was showing her the small clearing. Behind her, Abbot Laisran fretted with impatience. Fidelma was looking at a pathway which led into it. It was just wide enough to take a small cart. She noticed some indentations of hooves and ruts, undoubtedly caused by the passage of wheels.

"Where does that track lead?" she asked, for they had entered the clearing by a different single path.

It was the abbot who answered.

"Eventually it would link to the main road south. South to Ballyconra," he added significantly.

The sky was darkening now and Fidelma sighed.

"In the morning I shall want to see this young lord of Conra. But it is pointless continuing on tonight. We'd best go back to the abbey."

The next morning, accompanied by the abbot, Fidelma rode south. Ballyconra itself was a large settlement. There were small farmsteads and a collection of dwellings for workers. In one nearby field, a root crop was being harvested and workers were loading the crop onto small carts pulled by single asses. The track twisted through the village and passed a stream where women were laying out clothes to dry on the banks while others stirred fabrics into a metal cauldron hanging over a fire. The pungent smell of dyes told Fidelma what process was taking place.

Some paused in their work and called a greeting to the abbot, seeking a blessing, as they rode by. They ascended the track through another field towards a large building. It was an isolated structure which was built upon what must once have been a hillfort. A young man came cantering towards them from its direction, sitting easily astride a sleek black mare.

"This is young Conri, lord of Conra," muttered Laisran as they halted and awaited the man to approach."

Fidelma saw that the young man was handsome and dark featured. It was clear from his dress and his bearing that he was a man of rank and action. A scar across his forehead indicated he had followed a military profession. It seemed to add to his personality rather than detract from it.

"Good morning, Abbot." He greeted Laisran pleasantly before turning to Fidelma. "Good morning, Sister. What brings you to Ballyconra?"

Fidelma interrupted as Laisran was opening his mouth to explain.

"I am a dálaigh. You would appear to be expecting visitors, lord of Conra. I observed you watching our approach from the hill beyond the fortress before you rode swiftly down to meet us."

The young man's eyes widened a little and then he smiled sadly.

"You have a sharp eye, dálaigh. As a matter of fact, I have been expecting the arrival of my wife during these last few days. I saw only the shape of a woman on horseback and thought for a moment. . . ."

"Your wife?" asked Fidelma quickly, glancing at Laisran.

"She is Segnat, daughter of the lord of Tir Bui," he said without disguising his pride.

"You say you have been expecting her?"

"Any day now. I thought you might have been her. We were married only three months ago in Tir Bui, but I had to return here immediately on matters pertaining to my people. Segnat was to come on after me but she has been delayed in starting out on her journey. I only had word a week ago that she was about to join me."

Fidelma looked at him thoughtfully.

"What has delayed her for so long?"

"Her father fell ill when we married and has only died recently. She was his only close kin and she stayed to nurse him."

"Can you describe her?"

The young man nodded, frowning.

"Why do you ask?"

"Indulge me for a moment, lord of Conra."

"Of twenty years, golden hair and blue eyes. What is the meaning of these questions?"

Fidelma did not reply directly.

"The road from Tir Bui would bring a traveller from the north through Ballacolla and around the abbey, wouldn't it?"

Conri looked surprised.

"It would," he agreed irritably. "I say again, why these questions?"

"I am a *dálaigh*," repeated Fidelma gravely. "It is my nature to ask questions. But the body of a young woman has been found in the woods near the abbey and we are trying to identify her."

Conri blinked rapidly.

"Are you saying that this might be Segnat?"

Fidelma's expression was sympathetic.

"We are merely making inquiries of the surrounding habitations to see if anything is known of a missing young woman."

Conri raised his jaw defiantly.

"Well, Segnat is not missing. I expect her arrival any time."

"But perhaps you would come to the abbey this afternoon and look at the body? This is merely a precaution to eliminate the possibility of it being Segnat."

The young man compressed his lips stubbornly.

"It could not possibly be Segnat."

"Regretfully, all things are possible. It is merely that some are more unlikely than others. We would appreciate your help. A negative identification is equally as helpful as a positive one."

Abbot Laisran finally broke in.

"The abbey would be grateful for your cooperation, lord of Conra."

The young man hesitated and then shrugged.

"This afternoon, you say? I shall be there."

He turned his horse sharply and cantered off.

Laisran exchanged a glance with Fidelma.

"Was this useful?" he asked.

"I think so," she replied. "We can now turn our attention to the inn which you tell me is north of the abbey Ballacolla."

Laisran's face lightened.

"Ah, I see what you are about."

Fidelma smiled at him.

"You do?"

"It is as you said, a negative is equally as important as a positive. You have produced a negative with young Conri, so now we will seek the identity of the murdered one in the only possible place."

Fidelma continued to smile as they turned northwards back towards the abbey and beyond to Ballacolla.

The inn stood at a crossroads, a sprawling dark building. They were turning into the yard when a muscular woman of middle age driving a small mule cart halted, almost blocking the entrance. The woman remained seated on her cart, glowering in displeasure at them.

"Religious!" She almost spat the word.

Fidelma regarded her with raised eyebrows.

"You sound as if you are not pleased to see us," she observed in amusement.

"It is the free hospitality provided by religious houses that takes away the business from poor people such as myself," grunted the woman.

"Well, we might be here to purchase some refreshment," placated Fidelma.

"If you can pay for it, you will find my husband inside. Let him know your wants."

Fidelma made no effort to move out of her way.

"I presume that you are the innkeeper?"

"And if I am?"

"I would like to ask you a few questions. Did a young woman pass this way two nights ago? A young woman who would have arrived along the northern road from Tír Buí."

The big woman's eyes narrowed suspiciously.

"What is that to you?"

"I am a *dálaigh* and my questions must be answered," replied Fidelma firmly. "What is your name, innkeeper?"

The woman blinked. She seemed ready to argue, but then she compressed her lips for a moment. To refuse to answer a *dálaigh's* questions laid one open to fines for obstructing justice. A keeper of a public hostel had specific obligations before the law.

"My name is Corbnait," she conceded reluctantly.

"And the answer to my first question?"

Corbnait lifted her heavy shoulders and let them fall expressively.

"There was a woman who came here three nights ago. She merely wanted a meal and fodder for her horse. She was from Tír Buí."

"Did she tell you her name?"

"Not as I recall."

"Was she young, fair of skin with spun gold hair in a single braid?"

The innkeeper nodded slowly.

"That was her." Suddenly an angry expression crossed the big woman's face. "Is she complaining about my inn or of the service that she received here? Is she?"

Fidelma shook her head.

"She is beyond complaining, Corbnait. She is dead."

The woman blinked again and then said sullenly: "She did not die of any food that was served on my premises. I keep a good house here."

"I did not specify the manner of her death." Fidelma paused. "I see you drive a small cart."

Corbnait looked surprised at the sudden switch of subject.

"So do many people. I have to collect my supplies from the outlaying farms. What is wrong with that?"

"Do you also dye clothes at your inn?"

"Dye clothes? What games are you playing with me, Sister?" Corbnait glanced from Abbot Laisran back to Fidelma as if she considered that she was dealing with dangerous lunatics. "Everyone dyes their own clothes unless they be a lord or lady."

"Please show me your hands and arms?" Fidelma pressed.

The woman glanced again from one to another of them but seeing their impassive faces she decided not to argue. She sighed and held out her burly forearms. There was no sign of any dye stains on them.

"Satisfied?" she snapped.

"You keep your hands well cared for," observed Fidelma.

The woman sniffed.

"What do I have a husband for if not to do the dirty work?"

"But I presume you served the girl with her meal?"

"That I did."

"Did she talk much?"

"A little. She told me she was on the way to join her husband. He lives some way to the south of the abbey."

"She didn't stay here for the night?"

"She was anxious to reach her husband. Young love!" The woman snorted in disgust. "It's a sickness you grow out of. The handsome prince you thought you married turns out to be a lazy good-for-nothing! Take my husband—"

"You had the impression that she was in love with her husband?" cut in Fidelma.

"Oh yes."

"She mentioned no problems, no concerns?"

"None at all."

Fidelma paused, thinking hard.

"Was she alone during the time she was at the inn? No one else spoke to her? Were there any other guests?"

"There was only my husband and myself. My husband tended to her horse. She was particular about its welfare. The girl was obviously the daughter of a chieftain for she had a valuable black mare and her clothes were of fine quality."

"What time did she leave here?"

"Immediately after her meal, just two hours to sunset. She said she could reach her destination before nightfall. What happened to her? Was she attacked by a highway robber?"

"That we have yet to discover," replied Fidelma. She did not mention that a highway robber could be discounted simply by the means of the poor girl's death. The manner of her death was, in fact, her most important clue. "I want to have a word with your husband now."

Corbnait frowned.

"Why do you want to speak with Echen? He can tell you nothing."

Fidelma's brows drew together sternly.

"I will be the judge of that."

Corbnait opened her mouth, saw a look of steadfast determination on Fidelma's face, and then shrugged. She suddenly raised her voice in a shrill cry.

"Echen!"

It startled the patient ass and Fidelma's and Abbot Laisran's horses. They shied and were skittish for a few moments before they were brought under control.

A thin, ferret-faced man came scuttling out of the barn.

"You called, my dear?" he asked mildly. Then he saw Abbot Laisran, whom he obviously recognized, and bobbed servilely before him, rubbing his hands together. "You are welcome, noble Laisran," before turning to Fidelma and adding, "You are welcome, also, Sister. You bless our house by your presence. . . ."

"Peace, man!" snapped his burly wife. "The *dálaigh* wants to ask you some questions."

The little man's eyes widened.

"*Dálaigh?*"

"I am Fidelma of Cashel." Fidelma's gaze fell on his twisted hands. "I see that you have blue dye on your hands, Echen."

The man looked at his hands in bewilderment.

"I have just been mixing some dyes, Sister. I am trying to perfect a certain shade of blue from *glaisin* and *dubh-poill* . . . there is a sediment of intense blackness which is found in the bottom of pools in bogs which I mix with the *glaisin* to produce a dark blue. . . ."

"Quiet! The sister does not want to listen to your prattling!" admonished Corbnait.

"On the contrary," snapped Fidelma, irritated by the bullying woman, "I would like to know if Echen was at his dye work when the young woman was here the other night."

Echen frowned.

"The young woman who stayed only for a meal and to fodder her horse," explained his wife. "The black mare."

The man's face cleared.

"I only started this work today. I remember the girl. She was anxious to press on to her destination."

"Did you speak to her?"

"Only to exchange words about her instructions for her horse, and then she went into the inn for a meal. She was there an hour or so, isn't that correct, dearest? Then she rode on."

"She rode away alone," added Corbnait, "just as I have told you."

Echen opened his mouth, caught his wife's eye, and then snapped it shut again.

Fidelma did not miss the action.

"Did you want to add something, Echen?" she prompted.

Echen hesitated.

"Come, if you have something to add, you must speak up!" Fidelma said sharply.

"It's just . . . well, the girl did not ride away entirely alone."

His wife turned with a scowl.

"There was no one else at the inn that night. What do you mean, man?"

"I helped her onto her horse and she left the inn but as she rode towards the south I saw someone driving a small donkey cart join her on the brow of the hill."

"Someone joined her? Male or female?" demanded Fidelma. "Did you see?"

"Male."

Abbot Laisran spoke for the first time.

"That must be our murderer then," he said with a sigh. "A highway robber, after all. Now we shall never know who the culprit was."

"Highway robbers do not drive donkey carts," Fidelma pointed out.

"It was no highway robber," confirmed Echen.

They swung 'round on the little man in surprise.

"Then tell them who it was, you stupid man!" yelled Corbnait at her unfortunate spouse.

"It was young Finn," explained Echen, hurt by the rebuke he had received. "He herds sheep on Slieve Nuada, just a mile from here."

"Ah, a strange one that!" Corbnait said, as if all was explained to her satisfaction. "Both his parents died three years ago. He's been a recluse ever since. Unnatural, I call it."

Fidelma looked from Corbnait to Echen and then said, "I want one of you to ride to the abbey and look at the corpse so we can be absolutely sure that this was the girl who visited here. It is important that we are sure of her identity."

"Echen can do it. I am busy," grumbled Corbnait.

"Then I want directions to where this shepherd Finn dwells."

"Slieve Nuada is that large hill you can see from here," Abbot Laisran intervened. "I know the place, and I know the boy."

It was not long before they arrived at the shepherd's dwelling next to a traditional *lias cairach* or sheep's hut. The sheep milled about over the hill indifferent to the arrival of strangers. Fidelma noticed that their white fleeces were marked with the blue dyed circle that identified the flock and prevented them from mixing into neighboring flocks during common grazing.

Finn was weathered and bronzed—a handsome youth with a shock of red hair. He was kneeling on the grass astride a sheep whose stomach seemed vastly extended, almost as if it were pregnant but unnaturally so. As they rode up they saw the youth jab a long, thin, needle-like *biorracha* into a sheep's belly. There was a curious hiss of air and the swelling seemed to go down without harm to the sheep which, when released, staggered away, bleating in irritation.

The youth look up and recognized Abbot Laisran. He put the biorracha aside and came forward with a smile of welcome.

"Abbot Laisran. I have not seen you since my father's funeral."

They dismounted and tethered their horses.

"You seem to have a problem on your hands," Abbot Laisran said, indicating the now transformed sheep.

"Some of them get to eating plants that they should not. It causes gas and makes the belly swell like a bag filled with air. You prick them with the needle and the gas escapes. It is simple and does not hurt the creature. Have you come to buy sheep for the abbey?"

"I am afraid we are here on sad business," Laisran said. "This is Sister Fidelma. She is a *dálaigh*."

The youth frowned.

"I do not understand."

"Two days ago you met a girl on the road from the inn at Ballacolla."

Finn nodded immediately.

"That is true."

"What made you accost her?"

"Accost? I do not understand."

"You were driving in a donkey cart?"

"I was."

"She was on horseback?"

"She was. A black mare."

"So what made you speak to her?"

"It was Segnat from Tir Bui. I used to go to her father's fortress with my father, peace on his soul. I knew her."

Fidelma concealed her surprise.

"You knew her?"

"Her father was chieftain of Tir Bui."

"What was your father's business in Tir Bui? It is a long journey from here."

"My father used to raise the old horned variety of sheep which is now a dying breed. He was a *treudaighe* and proud of it. He kept a fine stock."

The *treudaighe* was a shepherd of rank.

"I see. So you knew Segnat?"

"I was surprised to see her on the road. She told me she was on her way to join her husband, Conri, the new lord of Ballyconra."

Finn's voice betrayed a curious emotion which Fidelma picked up on.

"You do not like Conri?"

"I do not have the right to like or dislike such as he," admitted Finn. "I was merely surprised to hear that Segnat had married him when he is living with a woman already."

"That is a choice for the individual," Fidelma reproved. "The New Faith has not entirely driven the old forms of polygyny from our people. A man can have more than one wife just as a woman can have more than one husband."

Abbot Laisran shook his head in annoyance.

"The Church opposes polygyny."

"True," agreed Fidelma. "But the judge who wrote the law tract of the Bretha Croilge said there is justification for the practice even in the ancient books of the faith for it is argued that even the chosen people of God lived in a plurality of unions so that it is no easier to condemn it than to praise it."

She paused for a moment.

"That you disapproved of this meant you must have liked Segnat. Did you?"

"Why these questions?" countered the shepherd.

"Segnat has been murdered."

Finn stared at her for some time, then his face hardened.

"Conri did it! Segnat's husband. He only wanted her for the dowry she could bring into the marriage. Segnat could also bring more than that."

"How so?"

"She was a *banchomarba*, a female heir, for her father died without male issue and she became chieftainess of Tir Bui. She was rich. She told me so. Another reason Conri sought the union was because he had squander much of his wealth on raising war bands to follow the High King in his wars against the northern Ui Neill. That is common gossip."

"Gossip is not necessarily fact," admonished Fidelma.

"But it usually has a basis of fact."

"You do not appear shocked at the news of Segnat's death," observed Laisran slyly.

"I have seen too many deaths recently, Abbot Laisran. Too many."

"I don't think we need detain you any longer, Finn," Fidelma said after a moment. Laisran glanced at her in astonishment.

"Mark my words, you'll find that Conri is the killer," called Finn as Fidelma moved away.

Abbot Laisran appeared to want to say something, but he meekly followed Fidelma to her horse and together they rode away from the shepherd's house. Almost as soon as they were out of earshot, Abbot Laisran leaned forward in excitement.

"There! We have found the killer. It was Finn. It all adds up."

Sister Fidelma turned and smiled at him.

"Does it?"

"The motive, the opportunity, the means, and the supporting evidence, it is all there. Finn must have killed her."

"You sound as if you have been reading law books, Laisran," she parried.

"I have followed your successes."

"Then, tell me, how did you work this out?"

"The *biorracha*, a long sharp needle of the type which you say must have caused the girl's mortal wound."

"Go on."

"He uses blue dye to identify his sheep. Hence the stain on the corpse."

"Go on."

"He also knew Segnat and was apparently jealous of her marriage to

Conri. Jealousy is often the motive for murder."

"Anything else?"

"He met the girl on the road on the very night of her death. And he drives a small donkey cart to transport the body."

"He did not meet her at night," corrected Fidelma pedantically. "It was some hours before sunset."

Abbot Laisran made a cutting motion with his hand.

"It is as I say. Motive, opportunity, and means. Finn is the murderer."

"You are wrong, Laisran. You have not listened to the whispers of the dead. But Finn does know the murderer."

Abbot Laisran's eyes widened.

"I fail to understand . . ."

"I told you that you must listen to the dead. Finn was right. It was Conri, lord of Ballyconra, who murdered his wife. I think the motive will be found to be even as Finn said . . . financial gain from his dead wife's estate. He probably knew that Segnat's father was dying when he married her. When we get back to the abbey, I will send for the local bó-aire, the magistrate, to take some warriors to search Conri's farmstead. With luck he will not have destroyed her clothing and personal belongings. I think we will also find that the very black mare he was riding was the same the poor girl rode on her fatal journey. Hopefully, Echen will be able to identify it."

Abbot Laisran stared at her blankly, bewildered by her calmness.

"How can you possibly know that? It must be guesswork. Finn could have just as easily killed her as Conri."

Fidelma shook her head.

"Consider the death wound. A needle inserted at the base of the neck under her braid."

"So?"

"Certainly, a long sharp needle, like a biorracha, could, and probably did, cause that wound. However, how could a perfect stranger, or even an acquaintance such as Finn, inflict such a wound? How could someone persuade the girl to relax unsuspecting while they lifted her braid and then, suddenly, insert that needle? Who but a lover? Someone she trusted. Someone whose intimate touch would arouse no suspicion. We are left with Segnat's lover—her husband."

Abbot Laisran heaved a sigh.

Fidelma added, "She arrived at Ballyconra expecting to find a loving husband, but found her murderer who had already planned her death to claim her inheritance."

"After he killed her, Conri stripped her of her clothes and jewels, dressed her in peasants' clothes and placed her in a cart that had been used by his workers to transport dyed clothing. Then he took her to the woods where he hoped the body would lay unseen until it rotted or, even if it was discovered, might never be identified."

"He forgot that the dead can still tell us many things," Fidelma agreed sadly. "They whisper to us and we must listen."

Bless Me Father for I Have Sinned

Ed Gorman

Except for his Roman collar, you would not have known Gary Brackett was a priest. He looked much more like the brawny tow-headed football player he'd been twenty years ago when we were friends here at this small coed midwestern Catholic college.

I stood on the edge of the two hundred people milling about beneath the big WELCOME WILDCATS OF '62 banner strung between two white birch trees on the east side of Smiley's Lake, one of those small bodies of blue water too small for any sort of commercial exploitation but big enough to go rowing across.

Or to drown in.

There was breeze on the lake now, carrying with it the natural scents of the June afternoon, wildflowers such as bloodroot and ginseng and wild ginger, and the smell of sunlight on newly born grass.

Most of us were strangers to each other now, working hard at pretending otherwise of course, but the years had changed us in many ways, not just physically. The one-time class clown seemed inexplicably melancholy these days; the golden girl looked tarnished now, two bad marriages, the whispers went; and some of the invisible ones, the ones nobody had ever paid any attention to, swaggered about with the air of conquest, a couple of them multimillionaires.

The spouses had it worst of all, dragged along unwillingly and then forgotten when some of the old cliques reconvened.

The ninety-two degree midwestern heat curbed a lot of appetites, including mine. Hot potato salad not being my favorite. Or heat-soggy ham, for that matter.

For the past twenty minutes I'd done my explaining to at least two dozen classmates, some of whom I could identify without a glance at their name tags, some of whom, even with the name tags, were still mysterious figures.

Why hadn't I been at the dance last night? Well, my job as a CPA in Cleveland had forced me to work most of the night and grab a plane only this morning. *What happened to that beautiful wife of yours, Gwen?* Oh, you know, 50 percent of marriages end in divorce and all, and she just found other things and other people, and now with the kids in college there's even less reason to keep in touch. *So how is good old foursquare Robert Anderson doing (I'd played chess instead of baseball, preferred Tony Bennett to the Beach Boys, liked girls shy as myself)?* Well, besides my hair thinning a bit, and the woman I date saying that I can't seem to stay awake past ten o'clock, and even my boss saying I should take time off to "have myself a gosh-darn ball" (my boss being as square as I am and rarely using swear words), well, I guess I'm doing fine. I drive a new Buick, own a DVD player, have a few dollars in the bank, and did pretty well with my last physical check-up.

I was getting melancholy myself. In a practical sense, our lives were over. Most of us were nearing sixty years old; we'd had our chances and we'd had to settle for very mixed results. I felt this most of all with the pretty girls. The really pretty ones should be immortal somehow. But they weren't. And it wasn't because their looks had gone. Most of them were still pretty, still graceful, still winsome and fetching. And yet you could see that they were carrying death just like the rest of us mortals. And it wasn't fair to them. And it wasn't fair to us.

I finished with my mingling and got myself ready to do what I'd come here to do.

Which was why I was watching Gary Brackett. Or rather (I'd never been able to get used to this), *Father* Gary Brackett.

The priesthood had made him no less popular with women. There was a virtual receiving line that wound around a wide elm tree and stretched to a picnic table set off by itself next to the lake's edge where half a dozen aged green rowboats sat bobbing in the blue water. The laughter of women has always been musical to me, and it floated on the air now, graceful as one of the monarch butterflies so prevalent here.

A woman named Trudy Carrington (her name tag I had to check out quickly) came up and took my arm and said, "Isn't it wonderful, Robert? I mean, really inspirational, I mean, of all of us who would have a voca-tion—that dreamboat Gary Brackett?" She winked at me. Even in her fleshiness you could see the cute girl she'd been, especially in the mis-chievous green eye. "And I know I shouldn't be saying this, but he's *still* a dreamboat."

Then she drifted back to her group—the old social cliques were indomitable, the popular with the popular, the outcasts still cast out—and I edged closer to where Father Gary held court.

One thing Trudy had been right about—Gary was certainly the most unlikely of us to "find a vocation," as the priests of the older generation say. As his roommate, I knew just how many of the coeds he'd gone through, and it was an astonishing number. Not that he'd been a braggart, but I'd heard enough plaintive phone calls, seen enough plaintive notes, glimpsed enough plaintive visits to know how in demand he was. Good looks, enough promise as a quarterback that the pros even sent out a few scouts from time to time, a steady three-point-five scholastic average, and a genuinely decent soul—never mean the way some jock-types got after a few beers, and never given to making easy fun of people obviously less fortunate. He'd put up with me, hadn't he?

"Robert!"

My head snapped up as I heard my name and then there he was, looming over me as he'd always loomed over me, putting both hands on my shoulders and saying, "You know, I was really afraid you weren't going to show up. I've been asking everybody about you. Gosh, it's good to see you. Why don't you come over and have a beer?"

I laughed, "I knew it was a fake."

"What?"

"That Roman collar."

Now he laughed. "Oh, I see. You're one of those Catholics who want all of your prelates to be in the Barry Fitzgerald mold. Pious and saintly with twinkly eyes and an unending supply of patience." We were at the table now and he deftly reached out, grabbed a can of Bud from a white styrofoam ice container, and popped it open. "Well, to ruin your image of the modern day priest completely, Robert, I not only have an occasional beer, I even smoke cigars from time to time, and have even been known to watch TV shows where a pretty woman can be seen now and then. And I find many of my flock to be a pain in the rear, overdemanding, intolerant, and indifferent to the real concerns of life." He laughed again. "Now does that sound like Barry Fitzgerald?"

"No, it doesn't," I said. "But I don't believe it, either."

From other classmates with whom I'd kept in touch, I knew that Father Gary Brackett had been a missionary for several years in Africa, working with the most downtrodden and famine-stricken of the lost souls there, and then had put in an equal number of years back in the States working in ghettos of every description, taking jobs that even most priests, no matter how dedicated, would shun.

He looked at the lake. "We spent a lot of hours out there, didn't we, Robert?"

"We sure did," I sighed. "It was all ahead of us."

"What was?"

I had some beer. It tasted as good as liquid gold. The breeze came off the lake again, scent of water, stench of outboard motors. "Oh, everything, I suppose. When you're twenty-one and looking ahead, everything seems possible. The most beautiful women. The most important position. Kind of a James Bond fantasy." I looked at him and smiled. "Then you find yourself forty-two and divorced and lonely and a CPA in Cleveland."

"You're unhappy, Robert?"

"Oh, not really, I guess."

He was a priest now, even if he did have a Bud in his hand, watching my face, searching me out for what I really wanted to say.

I glanced back at the lake. "You remember a girl named Stephanie Moore?"

"Sure. She came here our senior year. A transfer from somewhere in Minnesota." For a moment a curious sadness came into his eyes. For the first time his laugh seemed strained. "She led us all on a merry chase, that's for sure."

"She sure did," I said. Then I looked at the lake again, remembering. Cautiously, I said, "That's the only part that bothers me. Standing here, I mean."

"The lake?"

"Right."

He turned and stared at the lake, too. On the other side, a quarter mile across, the shore was lined with birches blazing white in the afternoon sunlight.

"She drowned there," he said.

"Yes."

"You were one of the people Father MacReady asked to dive for her body, weren't you?"

"Yes." Swimming had been the only sport at which I'd shown any prowess.

"I wonder what she'd be doing today."

"Probably two kids. A housewife. She'd have married well. That I'm sure of."

"You think so?" he said. "I'm not so sure. She took her beliefs very seriously. I suppose that's why she was so frustrating for all of us." He looked at me and smiled. "It wasn't exactly a secret that most of us were in love with her, including you and me."

"No, not exactly a secret."

"But we'd never met anybody like her before," he said.

And we hadn't. Her parents had sent her out here from the University of Minnesota in hopes of taming her. She'd been beautiful, red hair reaching the small of her back, and given to challenging everything you believed in, from the existence of God to the veracity of capitalism (her father was a millionaire many times over). What she was, of course, was the first of her breed—a very early model of the hippies much of our generation would become. But we didn't know that then. That was 1962 and the presumption was that we were all going to be good little boys and girls and go, respectively, right into life insurance and housekeeping as soon as we graduated. No, all we knew then was that she was possessed of a beauty and grace that almost hurt the eyes, a beauty that could hold you in its reckless sway until you thought you'd suffocate or go mad.

"No," Father Gary Brackett said. "I really couldn't see her in suburbia. She'd be working in the women's movement or running some avant garde theater somewhere or being a reporter for one of the networks. Something like that."

She was becoming a living presence for me. I could almost see her that last day, running shoeless in jeans along the beach, hollering for me to catch her, those child-like games she loved to play. I stared out at the lake where I'd taken her that night and I knew then that at last, after all these years, I needed to unburden myself.

"Father."

"Yes?"

"See those rowboats?"

He smiled. "Look inviting, don't they?"

"I'd appreciate it if you'd row across to the other side with me."

For a moment our eyes held and I knew he sensed that something much more important than reliving old memories was going to happen.

His years as a priest had given him an instinct for people, and his instinct was properly reading me now.

"Sure," he said, softly. "Why don't I take a couple more beers for us?"

I nodded and while he went to get the beers, I went down to get the oars ready and the boat pushed away from the muddy shore.

☥

St. Michael's College is six gray stone buildings that resemble a fortress tucked into the side of a long sloping hill topped by pines and hardwoods. Seen from the center of the lake, and especially on a beautiful day, the college resembles one of those Shangri-las tucked away in a rugged Alpine forest.

"We had good days here, Robert," Father Gary said as I rowed us toward the far shore. I worked slowly, liking the feel of the wooden oars and the pull on the long muscles of my arms.

"Very good." I paused, nodded to the two beers that sat between us in the old wooden rowboat, which needed a paint job and some patching. "Mind if I stop rowing for a while and just have a beer?"

"Not at all, Robert." As he popped it for me and handed it over, he said, "There's something you want to say, isn't there?"

"Yes."

"Well, we're certainly good enough friends to say anything to each other, Robert."

"I don't want you to be my friend."

"You don't want me to be your friend?"

"No. Not for the next few minutes."

"Then what do you want me to be, Robert?"

"I want you to be my priest."

"I see."

"I want to go to confession."

He sipped some beer. "Maybe you'd be more comfortable going to another priest."

I shook my head, watched the surface of the water for a time. There'd just been a minor splash. Occasionally, if you were so inclined, you could catch catfish and smallmouth bass and northern pike in this lake. Water bugs of various kinds sewed intricate and inexplicable patterns, inches above the water.

I lifted my head and said, "This is something I should have confessed our senior year. I've tried to confess it many times. Many times. But somehow I never go through with it. I get in the confessional and I—I lock up. Tight. I make my usual rote confession—but I never say what I really want to say. What I really need to say." I stared at him directly. "Father Brackett, I want you to hear my confession."

"All right, Robert. I'll be glad to." He set down his beer. "Are you ready?"

"Yes, I am."

"Why don't you begin, then."

I nodded. "Bless me, Father, for I have sinned. It has been one month since my last confession. But a long, long time—twenty-five years—since my last truthful confession."

So I began.

☥

"I can't tell you what it was like. I couldn't sleep. I couldn't eat. I couldn't concentrate. In one semester my grade point went from a 3.9 to nearly flunking out. I lost fifteen pounds. I started drinking beer to the point that I'd vomit.

"I had no idea what to do. In the past, of course, I'd had crushes on various girls. Puppy love, as my parents called it. Maybe if I hadn't been a virgin the feeling wouldn't have been so intense—but Stephanie was all I could think of. I'd see how other boys—even you, Father—were wrapped up in her but somehow I knew that my feelings for her were even more disastrous than yours. You, at least, had other women to fall back on. I didn't have anybody, and I was going crazy.

"Then one night I convinced her—I was pleading with her—to go rowing with me. I had to be near her. I had to tell her face to face how much I loved her and how much I needed her. I had this insane sense that somehow once she saw how hopelessly smitten I was, she'd change her mind about me, see how much I really loved her.

"She surprised me by agreeing to go. I suppose I sounded so pathetic, she took pity on me. I picked her up at the dorm. I can still remember how I felt—some crazy kind of optimism, as if she were really my girl and this was just one of our regular dates.

"I thought rowing was an especially romantic idea so we went down to the lake and then, in the middle of it all, I told. Everything that was in my heart. Everything. I can still remember how the moonlight made the water golden and how green everything smelled and how even at night her hair was fiery red and her face was beautiful beyond description.

"She heard me out, Father. I have to say that for her. She heard me out. She even touched my hand a few times when what I was saying became very painful for me. Even when I started to cry she didn't ask me to take her back to the dorm, she just kept stroking my hand, trying to calm me down the way you try to calm down an animal that's in pain. I suppose she'd been through this with a lot of boys.

"And when I was finished she just said, 'I'm sorry, Robert. I don't love you and I never could. I wish I could. I genuinely do because I can see how deeply you care for me. But I can't help my feelings, Robert. I really can't.'

"And then, Father, despite her kindness and her pity, I went crazy. I realized then not only how foolish I'd been but how hopeless my life would be without her. So before I knew what I was doing, I grabbed her and pushed her over the side of the boat and held her under by her beautiful red hair until her thrashing stopped and I knew she'd drowned.

"Then I rowed back to shore and went directly to the chapel and sat there praying all night for what I'd done. In the morning Father MacReady organized a search for her and chose me as one of the people to look in the lake.

"I found her body and drug it to shore and ever since I've been living with the terrible thing I did.

"There is not a single day that goes by, Father, that I don't think of her and think of my sin. And now I am confessing my sin and asking God for forgiveness."

During all of this I'd kept my head down, the way you do in a confessional, not seeing how he was reacting, indeed almost afraid of how he would be reacting to his former friend who had turned out to be the killer of a beautiful young woman.

Finally, when I raised my eyes, I saw something that convinced me instantly that the stories of his goodness and kindness were true.

For he sat watching me with tears filling his eyes and his head shaking in pity for me.

"You've suffered so much," he said.

"Yeah, I have. But I didn't suffer as much as she did."

"And it's ruined your life."

"Yes, Father, it has. I'm afraid my guilt took its toll on my first marriage and on every relationship I've tried to have since then."

"I need to talk to you, Robert," he said.

"You can't grant me absolution?"

"Would you mind rowing again, Robert?"

Startled by his strange reaction, I put my hands on the oars and started the boat once more toward the far shore.

He sat back on his elbows, sipping his beer, and said, "Have you ever wondered why I became a priest? I was a pretty unlikely candidate."

"Everybody's wondered that, Father."

"It came on suddenly. My vocation."

"Yes, it did, now that you mention it."

I still had no idea why we were having this conversation.

"Senior year, it was," he said. I turned down a very good chance to try out for the Bears. I turned down a great job offer from General Electric. I even turned down an opportunity to become a model in TV commercials. In order to become a priest."

"I remember. And I remember being surprised."

"Had you ever known me to be particularly religious before?"

"No. That's why it was all so surprising, I suppose."

He smiled. "Father MacReady always complained that he could scarcely get me to go to Sunday mass let alone weekday mass. Yet I became a priest. And do you know why?" His eyes were fixed on mine.

"No."

"To atone."

"Atone?"

"Yes. For a sin I committed."

"What sin?"

"Killing Stephanie."

"But I killed Stephanie!"

He sighed, stared at the lake. "No, you didn't. Apparently she managed to swim to shore after you thought she'd drowned. That's when I found her. And I went through much the same thing you did. Just seeing her there—wet, helpless—I went crazy, too. I didn't ask her what had happened to her. Seeing her so vulnerable I thought it would be a good time to tell her how I felt—how, despite the fact that I could have any other woman I wanted, I could not get her to show me any interest whatsoever. How she literally had ruined my life, never answering my calls or letters or treating me with any kind of interest at all.

"But she only started crying. Now, given what you've just told me, I can see why. She was frightened and confused about having nearly been killed. But I took her tears as yet another rebuff of me—so I pushed her backward into the lake and held her under until I was sure she was dead.

"After the body was discovered the next day, the impact of what I'd done overwhelmed me. I didn't have the courage to step forward and say that I was the guilty party. The police called it an accidental drowning and obviously that's how it was going to go into the record books. But I knew I was still guilty so I gave my life to Christ. All these years I've performed good works as atonement for what I did to poor Stephanie."

He shook his head. "I'm sorry, Robert. You suffered for nothing. You're an innocent man."

☥

He said he'd drive me to the airport instead of me having to take a cab. I needed to be back in Cleveland the next morning early.

On the way, I said, "You've paid for your sin, Father. The work in Africa. The ghettos."

"Oh, no," he said. "No, you can never pay for a sin like that. Cold-blooded murder. And if I'd confessed to the police, you wouldn't have had to waste twenty-five years of useless guilt."

I smiled. "You became something the world needs, Father. A truly selfless man, one who has devoted himself to helping others. Do you think you would have otherwise?"

"No," he said. "No, I guess I wouldn't have."

At the airport he waited with me till the big silver United plane eased into view and then we shook hands and he said, "Thanks for hearing my confession. Now I think I'm going to go see the police."

I shook my head. "You owe me something, Father."

"What?"

"Twenty-five years of needless guilt."

He averted his eyes, ashamed. "I know," he said, softly.

"So I'm calling in my debt. I want you to do what I tell you."

"All right."

Then I smiled again. "The world doesn't need one more lonely prisoner behind stone walls. But it does need somebody who goes out and helps the poor and tends to the sick and the dying. Keep doing your penance, Father, because that way the whole world benefits. I want you to promise me that, all right?"

Five minutes later the plane was arcing east toward Cleveland.

☥

A classmate called me about it, a fellow I knew who was in constant touch with the alumni association. Father Brackett had turned himself in and confessed to the police. The district attorney was now preparing for trial. This was a month after the class reunion.

A few days later I got a call from Father Brackett himself.

"I take it you've heard."

"Yes, I did."

"I want to thank you for hearing my confession that day," he said.

"I thought you agreed not to turn yourself in."

"Render unto Caesar," he said. "I owe a debt to society. I need to pay it."

"If that's what you think is best, Father."

"Take care of yourself."

"You, too," I said.

Father Brackett was found guilty of manslaughter and is serving five to ten. I plan to visit him next week.

DEATH BY FIRE

ANNE PERRY AND
MALACHI SAXON

THE OLD WOMAN WOKE WITH A START. It had been a bad dream, very bad, and unlike the other nightmares that occasionally tormented her. The dreams had started following her pilgrimage to Jerusalem after it had been restored into the hands of the Crusaders in the days of Richard the Lionheart. They had been attacked by bandits, and the Knights Templar, pledged to protect the pilgrims, showed no mercy to anyone who threatened them. It was the first time she had seen men slashed and hacked to death with swords, and the images still came back to haunt her.

This dream, however, was different. It was no random attack of half-starved hill men setting on a group of alien travelers. It was set here at home in the heart of England. She was alone in the meadow at dusk. Peace drenched the air, the dying sun still touched the sky with gold. She was standing knee-deep in grasses at the edge of the woods, wild herbs in her arms.

A flight of starlings swirled up into the air and her eyes followed them until she half saw the movement to her left—that was the moment the unease overtook her, and suddenly she was cold.

It was only a ram, a big heavy animal with a thick fleece. It was not grazing, but standing four-square, its head a little lowered, staring at her.

She was fascinated, unable to remove her gaze from the animal's, as a wild, malicious, almost human intelligence looked back at her out of eyes as red as blood.

She tried to turn away, but she could not move.

It took a step toward her.

This was ridiculous. It was only a ram. She had known sheep all her life. She had shorn them and woven their wool.

It took another step toward her and she tried to move away, but her feet were stuck fast to the earth. Its eyes seemed to impale her.

It lowered its head, the mighty horns pointing at her body.

Moving faster, it seemed to grow as it charged her.

Just before impact she awoke. She almost expected to find her flesh had been gored, but there was no pain, only the pounding of her heart and a sweat that left her clammy and cold. She was shivering beyond control, and far from daylight dispelling her fear, upon awakening the sense of foreboding, if anything, increased.

She rose slowly from her bed and put on her clothes. She must remember to take her infusions of herbs. These were remedies she had learned many years ago, to ease the pain in her aging joints and to stop her ankles swelling—the dropsy.

Her daughter would be at the door soon. She always called in the morning to prepare breakfast and do a bit of tidying in her small house. She was a placid unquestioning soul, with no desire to look at what might be over the horizon. In that respect, she took after her late father. She had a little understanding of the healing powers of some of the herbs and plants, but no comprehension of what could be read in the stars and planets. She was healthy in body, a dutiful wife and daughter, and had borne her husband many children. Be grateful for that.

There was a noise outside now, footsteps, the door opening. It was she. The old woman turned to face her.

"Good morning, Mother. How are you?"

As always she was cheerful, matter-of-fact, seeing nothing beyond the practical, sensing nothing in the air.

"There is a bit of winter chill in the air," she said, coming into the room. "I wouldn't be surprised if we are not in for a shower or two of rain." She said it without even looking at her mother, as she gazed around, wondering what might need washing, sweeping, or putting away.

The darkness of the mind intensified, the shivering heaviness in the air. There was no time to waste.

"I'm well," the old woman replied, moving toward her. "Don't argue with me. Just do as I tell you, and do it quickly. Take these books, the charts, and these instruments and keep them carefully in your house out of sight, Jane!"

"But Mother, these are yours," Jane protested, her eyes wide, her fair face a little pale. "They are—"

"I know what they are." The old woman cut across her. "They are all my books on herbs, on the stars, astrological charts, instruments, everything. Take them and hurry. Do as I tell you. Someday, I hope you will know of someone who will value them. When you meet such a person, you must give them these things. . . . *Give,* do not sell, do you hear me? To those who understand, these are beyond money. Now hurry!"

"Mother, you look troubled. What is it?" Now Jane was frightened too. "You sense danger, don't you?"

The old woman could not explain. "Do as I tell you, then come back and we will talk," she commanded. "Go!"

Jane knew better than to argue. Quietly, she lifted the front of her apron to make a basket out of it, and the old woman put her treasured belongings in.

She felt a slight sense of relief as she watched her daughter walk down the street to the village square and turn the corner toward her own house. She followed slowly, in the same direction, her mind lost in a jumble of thoughts. She sat down on a bench, overlooking the pond, just downstream from the mill. She watched the sunlight sparkle in the drops of water that fell from the wheel. In some ways, life flows like the stream, she thought, in others, it goes round and round like a wheel, lifting water and letting it go again, holding nothing.

The heavy hand on her shoulder startled her. She could see—she could smell—it was Nathaniel, the village reeve, but what sent a shudder through her body was the man next to him, the priest. He was tall, thin, and his black robe was tied tightly around his waist. His hollow cheeks made his hooked nose even more prominent. There was a satisfaction in his face as he stared straight at her. It was almost a leer.

"Witch, I have spent many months, even years, hunting for you," he said in a hard, low voice. "Now at last I have you. You shall not escape the wrath of God. Your body shall be consumed by fire in this world, and your soul shall be tormented by hell fire for eternity in the next." He leaned on his staff, and thrust his face toward her. He continued, "Your only chance of salvation is to renounce the devil and all his works," he continued. "And throw yourself upon the mercy of our One True Saviour."

She had always dreaded a moment like this, when the full weight and majesty of the Church would descend upon her. They feared anything they did not know and understand. Even as a girl she realized that she had special gifts, an ability to understand the herbs and plants that could heal sickness or relieve pain, and how the constellations and the configuration of the planets influence a person's life.

She had sought out every wise man, and woman, to learn the secrets of these arts. She had sat at the feet of Jews and Moors, to glean whatever gem of wisdom she could find. And repeatedly they had warned her to beware of those whose hearts and minds were hardened by the narrow dogma of the Church. She could see them if she closed her eyes. The rattle of the stream in this quiet English village became the crackle of campfires in the desert night, and she could smell the spices of the east again and hear the faint music of church bells in the darkness.

At first she had not understood their fears. They judged out of their own persecutions, their ignorance of her land and people. She had been brought up in the light of the Christian gospel, and she believed devoutly in the resurrection of Jesus, the Son of God, and in his saving grace. She remembered the intense joy she had felt when she came to understand with her heart, not just her mind, what it meant that sins could be forgiven, because of the love and compassion that God had for his creatures. Jesus had walked amongst us and healed the blind and the lame. Surely those who had the power to heal and relieve suffering were following in the footsteps of Christ?

Why then did the Church of Christ persecute them? It took her many years to appreciate the ways of the world and how supposed men of God could still fall prey to such jealousy of a power they did not understand.

Now she was feeling more composed. The darkness was still present in her mind, but the initial shock was over. She looked at the ground in front of the priest and slowly raised her eyes. "Who is my accuser? Who will bear witness against me?" she said calmly. "Would it be Nathaniel here?" She heard Nathaniel's hiss of inhuman breath and ignored it, keeping her eyes on the priest's.

"Many years ago, after my husband died, he paid suit to me, but I rejected him. He married a shrew who made his life a torment. And then he put about the rumor that I had been chasing him!" She looked straight at Nathaniel, who could not hold her gaze and turned the other way.

By now a crowd of villagers had formed. The old and the young were there, the idle and those who should have been busy. But this sort of spectacle did not happen every day and was not to be missed. She saw Alice, with her babe in her arms—the burn on his small arm still red where she had put salve on it yesterday—and the sunlight bright on the flame red hair of Lizzie, the miller's daughter.

"Or would it be Zeb over there?" she went on, her eyes returning to the priest. "I told him not to graze his cattle in the bottom field, because the poison weed would make them miscarry. But he wouldn't listen to me, and of course his cows all aborted their calves. The silly man accused me of putting a spell on them."

The priest smiled, showing his teeth.

"So, witch, you know how to brew up concoctions to produce an abortion!" he said with malevolent pleasure. "How many women with child did you practice your evil art on, so that they could destroy the evidence of their carnal lust?" He threw these words at her and waited for her reply, leaning forward a little, eyes bright.

"Just because I know of these potions does not mean I have used them for evil," she responded with disgust. "I am sure that you, too, Priest, have all the necessary bits and pieces of your body to have carnal knowledge of a woman, but that does not mean that you commit fornication, does it?"

A snigger came from somewhere in the crowd. Unable to identify whence it came, the priest gave the crowd a haughty glare.

"And I presume you know how it is done?—or maybe you don't," she added.

Now there was open laughter, the most boisterous coming from Daft Johnny, the village idiot. Though slow at the best of times, he always managed to catch the jokes with a sexual implication and go into fits of raucous, honking laughter, all the while making obscene gyrations of his body. Now the crowd was laughing at him.

"Silence!" the priest shouted.

Respectfully, they fell silent.

"And by what devilish art, *witch*"—he spat the word—"do you look into the heavens and predict a man's future?"

"I do not look to the heavens to see the devil." She knew, as surely as if the ram's eyes had bored into her soul that she had nothing left to lose now. "What I have learned is the mathematic skill to predict something of a man's character from the position of the stars and planets at the time of his birth. From that, I can make some foretelling as to his future."

The priest was more composed now. He had heard what he needed. He ran his tongue over his dry lips. "It seems, daughter of Eve, that you have eaten plentifully of the fruit of the tree of knowledge of Good and Evil, like your forebear in the Garden of Eden. And you have chosen the

Evil . . . which shall now be your reward."

"Eve—and Adam—are forebears to us both, Priest," she answered him. "If you understand how these things happen."

Daft Johnny started his raucous laughter again, and the priest turned and scowled at him.

Johnny stopped laughing and looked ashamed of himself, staring at the ground, his face flushed.

The old woman was angry. A man of God did not mock or curse those already afflicted. "We all have the Original Sin in us, but we all have the chance to be redeemed, if we so choose," she said sharply.

The priest straightened himself up. He was beginning to relish this theological debate, in which he had no doubt he would emerge victorious. In due course, one more witch would be brought to trial and burned. His reputation, considerable already, would be enhanced, but more importantly, he would have removed a wolf from among the flock of faithful sheep. An evil chancre would be wiped off the face of Christendom, and he would be the instrument of it. He felt a deep sense of joy, in doing God's work. But he must be on his guard. This old woman had the devil's cunning in her.

"If a man's destiny is written in the stars, what freedom of choice does he have?" he challenged her. "If he is destined for Hell, can he still be saved by our Redeemer? How do you answer that, witch?" He leaned forward on his staff, his face closer to hers. "And for all your devilish powers, did you not foresee my coming? Why did you not flee? Surely you know I bring you death, death by fire, and soon—very soon?"

She did not move away from him, even so much as by a gesture.

"Did I foresee your coming?" she said with affected innocence. "Perhaps. But no one can flee from death. It will catch us all. And no one can flee from the Day of Judgment. If I face death by fire in this world, it will be but a fleeting moment. I have faith that I will not face that eternal fire of the next."

The priest threw his head back in laughter. The crowd looked slightly puzzled, almost embarrassed, but no one moved. They did not want to miss any of this exchange. The blacksmith folded his arms and changed his weight from one foot to the other. Lizzie grinned, standing with one hand on her hip.

"When was the day of your birth, Priest—if I may be so bold as to ask?" the old woman said.

He looked surprised, but he answered. "I was born on the Feast Day of Saint Dismas, thirty-two years ago. So what will you tell me of my future, witch? We know *your* future!" He turned to the crowd, letting them see how he was enjoying this combat.

"Saint Dismas," she said slowly. "The good thief, who was crucified with Our Lord at Calvary, and his feast day is on the 25th March."

"You well know your saint's days, old woman," he granted. "Tell me more."

Now her dream made hideous sense. There was almost a relief in that. "You were born under the sign of Aries, the Ram," she answered. "Your good qualities are that you are a man of strong beliefs, assertive, quick to act, and without fear. You wish to do good, but you can be impatient and arrogant."

What she said seemed to please him, until she came to the final statement, which touched a raw nerve.

He leaned forward, and with the end of his staff he lifted up her chin and said to her, "And what do you see of the future?"

"Death by fire," she replied. "Soon—very soon." She spoke more by intuition than calculation from the charts she knew by heart.

The priest withdrew his staff, turned to the increasing crowd, and then back to her.

"Yes, witch, your own death by fire, and soon, very soon!" he mocked. "We do not need to look to the stars and signs of the zodiac, or the works of Beelzebub, to come to that conclusion, do we?" He laughed.

There was nervous movement among the onlookers.

"I was not predicting my own fate," the old woman said. "It is yours. Death by fire, and soon—very soon."

Anger swelled up inside the priest. He raised his staff to strike her, but stopped abruptly and instead laid it gently on the shoulder of Nathaniel. "Take this woman back to her hovel and keep her in," he commanded. "Fasten the doors so she cannot escape and make sure she is guarded day and night. Tomorrow morning I will take her to the nearest town where they can lock her away in a proper jail until she is put on trial."

Nathaniel beckoned two other men to come with him, and they escorted the old woman back to her house. With ropes and boards they barricaded her house, then stood guard outside.

The villagers dispersed, murmuring and unhappy, and went about their daily tasks.

Inside her house the old woman lay down on her bed. There was nothing to do but wait and think about all that had gone on in her life up to now. It seemed so short now that she knew it was drawing to a close, but it had felt never-ending when life was in full flow. As evening came, she drifted off into sleep.

She awoke to a frantic banging on the door, as the ropes and boarding were removed. Nathaniel came in brusquely and said, "You had better come with us, now." He was forceful, but polite, and the priest was no longer with him.

"Follow me," he ordered, avoiding her eyes.

She rose to her feet with difficulty, her bones aching, no herbal infusion to ease their stiffness. He gave her no time and no chance for such a thing.

He turned and went out and she limped after him. The morning was bright, the sunlight sharp and clear. In another few weeks there would be frost on the grass and the leaves would turn gold and flame, and the hawthorn berries would be bright as blood.

They went past the mill and up along the stream, where they reached a path of stepping-stones that led out of the village. It seemed everyone in the village had gathered there, a respectful distance from what was holding their attention. She saw him immediately, a dark mound in the water, the current billowing his skirts. There was no question in her mind that the priest was dead. She knew it as surely as if she had touched the cold flesh or looked into the sightless eyes.

"Well, Beth, you were right when you said that he would die soon, very soon," Nathaniel said with a strange smile, victory and fear in it at once. "But you were wrong when you predicted death by fire. It looks like the whole village just had to come and witness this."

It was only then that she noticed that the bank was lined with people, so still in their awe that they had seemed inanimate until now.

"I'm glad you have remembered that I have a name, Nathaniel," she said as she waded slowly into the water to take a closer look at the dead man. He was lying face down in the shallows; a gash on his right temple seeped blood and turned the water crimson. His staff had floated a few feet down the stream. The old woman picked up his right hand and slowly uncurled his fingers.

"It looks like he slipped on the stones and banged his head as he fell, and then drowned. Death by water—you were wrong," Nathaniel said with triumph.

"No, Nathaniel," she said slowly—"Death by fire."

"The whole village is here, Beth." He waved his hand at the crowd. "They can all see it is death by water," he said with a smirk.

"No, Nat," she corrected, her eyes scanning the crowd. "Not the *whole* village. Lizzie is missing."

Without having meant to, Nathaniel looked around, then back at her. "That means nothing!"

She went down to the dead man again. "Look here, in his right hand," she directed. "Hairs. Who in the village has hair this color?"

His face blanched.

"Only Lizzie," she answered for him. "She was always a flirt, a tease who liked to say no at the last moment. So tell me, Nat, how much of your home-brewed ale did you give the priest last night?"

Nathaniel looked sheepish. "He had come a long way. And after giving us a sermon on not straying from the straight and narrow, he was very thirsty, so . . . well, I suppose we all had a bit to drink, and then I don't remember where the priest got to after that. I'd hardly follow him, would I?"

"Death by fire, Nathaniel," she said softly. "As I predicted. The fire of lust, ignited by the flame red hair of Lizzie. She won't have run far. Only to the next village. Someone go and fetch her. Tell her it is not her fault; she is not guilty of the death of this priest. He carried the seeds of his own destruction within him. . . . Perhaps we all do."

The pallor in his face increased.

"You had better send someone into town to tell the sheriff," she instructed. "Leave the priest there. What is done is done."

Her daughter came to her side and quietly the two made their way back to the village, leaving the crowd murmuring and whispering, huddled tighter now that they stood in the presence of death.

She went back to her small house and at her insistence Jane left her at the door.

Inside she sat down on the bed. She felt tired deep inside herself and sad that a man who would walk in the light, and try to bring that light to others, should succumb to the forces of darkness.

The day passed and no one came. The evening wore on, and the wind began to pick up. A storm was on its way. The most comfortable place to be was in bed with the wool blankets around her.

Suddenly there was a commotion outside. She could hear voices, the sound of boards being thrust against her doors and windows, and rope securing them. Jane's voice rose above the others, desperate, pleading, and then a loud slap, and silence.

So the villagers did blame her for the death of the priest after all. More wood was being stacked up against her walls. Then the smell of smoke. So she, too, would suffer death by fire, and soon, very soon. How silly of the villagers to waste the wood they had gathered for winter, just to burn an old woman.

She felt very tired. Very tired indeed. There was no will to resist. She dimly heard the rumble of the thunder and the first heavy patter of the rain. Perhaps it would put out the flames; perhaps not. It did not matter. She was at the end of one journey and at the start of a new one.

How foolish to worry about the vehicle for it.

THE ARROW OF ICE

EDWARD D. HOCH

THE FIRST THING FATHER DAVID NOONE noticed when he awakened and peered out his window at the Holy Trinity rectory, other than the light dusting of overnight snow, was the demonstration taking place in the parking lot across from the church. A large oilcloth banner had been painted to read LEAVE OUR CHURCH ALONE! He recognized Pat Fitzpatrick kneeling by it, cutting the oilcloth with a sharp blade so it would fit between two poles. It was only seven o'clock, barely daylight on this Sunday in late February, and already they were out there in the cold.

Pat Fitzpatrick was leading them, of course. Pat was always out in front in parish events, whether it was volunteering for bingo or organizing a campaign against reconstruction of the church. He was a good and holy man, but not one to accept the necessities of change. The demonstrators would be there through all three of the Sunday morning masses, possibly lasting into the afternoon's Mardi Gras festival and exhibition of the ice sculptures.

He showered quickly and threw on his black pants and sweater, then hurried through the passage connecting the rectory with the sacristy. He was into his vestments and onto the altar at exactly seven-thirty. The early Sunday mass never filled the church, but there were about a hundred people present, mainly widowers and bachelors who lived alone. Couples and family groups seemed to prefer their services at a later time. Holy Trinity's Sunday masses were at 7:30, 9:30 and 11:30, regular as clockwork, with a 5:30 mass on Saturday afternoon.

There was no organist at the early mass, and without music he was finished by 8:10. Outside of church he waited in the cold to shake a few hands and then walked across the street to confront Pat Fitzpatrick. "Pat, you're at it again!" he said with a rueful smile.

Fitzpatrick shook his head apologetically. "Sorry about this, Father Dave, but we just can't let them tear apart Holy Trinity no matter what the bishop wants."

Pat was in his late fifties, in the first year of retirement from the glass factory, with a wife who still worked as a bookkeeper. It hadn't been an easy life for them, with a daughter who'd gone to New York, made a bad marriage with an older man and ended up a divorced alcoholic whom they never saw. Somehow the bishop's plans for a remodeled church, with a gathering place for worshippers and the altar moved out a bit so pews could surround it, had seemed a desecration of the church he'd attended all his life. Perhaps it was his way of fighting back at a life that had gone wrong.

"I wish you'd come in tomorrow and chat with me about it," David Noone told him. "Nothing is final yet and demonstrations like this only serve to harden positions."

"If nothing is final yet how come you've got an architect coming this afternoon?"

"The word really gets around, doesn't it? He's only coming for a first look at the church, Pat. It doesn't mean a thing. If you're going to be here for the Mardi Gras festival and ice sculptures I'll even introduce you."

He shook his head and finally said, "I'll drop by tomorrow, Father Dave. Just for you. But the demonstration goes on."

And so it did. After the nine-thirty mass, usually the most popular, the demonstrators were still out there. Happily, so were the ice sculptors who'd agreed to take part in the day's Mardi Gras festival activities. Six-foot-tall blocks of ice had been delivered to the parking area behind the rectory, and each of the sculptors had already begun work, chewing away at the ice with chain saws before getting down to the finer details of their work.

"How's it going?" Father Noone asked Angie O'Toole, a second-grade teacher at Holy Trinity's school. It was she who'd suggested the exhibition of ice sculpturing in the first place and he could see why. Wearing bright red ski pants and a down-filled vest, she was working on the block of ice with real vigor.

"Fine, Father Dave. Can you tell what it's going to be yet?"

"Well, I can see the outline of a tree," he answered a bit uncertainly.

"Oh, Father, it's going to be a fish, for Lent! See, it'll be leaping out of the water. I might even make it a swordfish. Come back after the last mass and you'll be able to see it better." She added with a laugh, "I hope."

Young Phil Boyle, a star high school basketball player before he went off to college, was working next to her on his block of ice. He was home on his spring break, and David Noone was surprised that he'd agreed to spend time on ice sculpturing. "Mine is going to be a swan," he explained, and already the bird was beginning to take shape.

The third person, Luke Stevenson, was newly retired, an usher at the 9:30 mass. His talent at ice sculpture was news to Father Noone. Though he'd just started work on it, his block of ice was already beginning to assume the form of a kneeling archer, the bow and arrow only hinted at thus far.

As he returned to the rectory Father Noone paused to glance across the street at Fitzpatrick's people. They were handing out fliers to the parishioners. He wondered what they said and he found out soon enough. Awaiting him in the rectory living room was a tall middle-aged man with thinning hair and a thick briefcase. "Father Noone? I'm Porter Macklin. The bishop asked me—"

"Of course, Mr. Macklin. No one told me you were here and I wasn't expecting you until after the next mass. You're the architect for our renewal project."

Porter Macklin smiled. He had thin lips and the ability to curve them up without even showing teeth. "I will only make preliminary recommendations. Whether they are acted upon is the decision of the bishop and your parish council."

"Did you have a good flight in from New York?"

"Very good. I rented a car at the airport and came directly here."

David Noone nodded. "It's a busy day at Holy Trinity, with our festival and all, but I can show you around now between masses, if you'd like."

The architect nodded. "That would be helpful. I'm only in town for the day. I became aware of your demonstration while I was parking my car." He held out one of the handbills. The heading read: DON'T LET PORTER MACKLIN RUIN ANOTHER CHURCH! "I'm lucky the papers didn't run my picture or they'd have been on me like hounds!"

"I'm sorry about that, Mr. Macklin."

"Why? It's a free country. And believe me, Father, this isn't the first time I've encountered criticism. Many people dislike change."

He followed Father Noone through the passage from the rectory and strode through the sacristy to the altar. "A fine old church," he decided after a few moments' silent inspection. "I was here once some years back. Those pillars might present a problem, and of course this altar will have to go."

"Why is that?" David Noone asked.

"You want the new altar to be moved out, into the midst of the worshippers. That's the way it's done now."

"The way it's done in many new churches. This church was built in 1912."

Macklin opened his briefcase. "Let me show you something, Father. These are aerial views of your church and the surrounding blocks. It gives a nice feel for the density of population here."

"I don't need aerial photos to tell me that."

"And here are two photos from the local press showing the interior of Holy Trinity through the years. You can see that minor changes have been made from time to time."

The old pictures of the sanctuary as it was nearly ninety years earlier and forty years earlier brought back memories. He'd seen the first photo in the church's own faded scrapbook, lovingly kept by the parish's first pastor. The second photo was the way he remembered the church as a boy, when he attended mass on weekends with his grandmother who lived a few blocks away. He never thought of being a priest in those days, much less of one day being pastor of Holy Trinity.

"Well, minor adjustments are always necessary with the changing times, Mr. Macklin. You can see since this last picture that we've removed two rows of seats opposite the transepts so we can better accommodate short processions before the Sunday masses."

The architect had produced a small digital camera from his briefcase and began taking pictures of the church interior from various angles. "I think we can do better for you, Father. We can bring your congregation together in a whole new way."

A flash of morning sun entered the rear of the church as early parishioners began arriving for the 11:30 mass. By its light David saw Pat Fitzpatrick watching them intently from the last pew.

✝

After the day's final mass David Noone was outside greeting parishioners as usual. The days were long gone when he had assistants to take
over the load of some weekend masses. Now, unless he could get help
from a retired priest or one of the Jesuits at the nearby high school, he was
on his own. But in truth this Sunday morning mingling with worshippers
was one of his favorite times of the week. And just at that moment it was
delaying his return to the rectory where Porter Macklin was making notes
while he awaited further conversation about the renovations.

When the last of the churchgoers had drifted over to the festival in
the school hall or the rectory parking lot where the ice sculpting was in
progress, Father Noone went to join them. Angie O'Toole and Phil Boyle
had completed their swordfish and swan, while Parker was carefully
putting the finishing touches on his archer. "This is the tricky part," he
explained to David. "I have to cut away the inner ice while leaving the
shape of the bent bow and the arrow. Of course if I cut away too much,
the arrow might break."

The other events of the Mardi Gras festival, consisting mainly of raf-
fles and games of chance, were in the school hall. He was glad to see they
were attracting a good number of people too. The carnival would last
through Tuesday evening and Holy Trinity needed every penny that could
be raised. He only hoped Pat Fitzpatrick's protest wouldn't dampen his
flock's generosity. With the end of the last mass, some of the protesters
had drifted away and only a handful remained. Pat didn't seem to be
among them and Father Noone hadn't noticed him in the school hall
either.

He walked back to the rectory and entered through the side door.
Porter Macklin was seated at the kitchen table, his photos and notes
spread out before him. His head was back and a long sliver of ice was protruding from his bloody throat. He was dead.

The arrival of two police cars brought people out of the hall and the
parking lot to see what was going on. Father Noone spoke quietly to the
officers, showing them what he'd found. Presently an unmarked detective's car pulled up outside and David saw that it was Sergeant Dominick,
a detective he'd encountered previously, with a woman partner he didn't
know.

"Not another killing at Holy Trinity!" the sergeant said by way of
greeting. "Tell me it isn't so, Father Noone."

"It's in the rectory this time, Sergeant. And there's no doubt about the cause of death. An architect from New York, working on our renovation plans, has been killed." He led them into the kitchen where a couple of uniformed cops were watching the body.

Dominick nodded. "The lab boys are on their way. Was he alone at the time?"

"Except for his killer. I was saying Mass. He'd taken a look at the church and was making some notes. We were to continue our preliminary discussion when I returned."

He looked around the kitchen. "How many entrances are there to the rectory, Father?"

"You came in the front door, but we usually keep that locked on Sundays because there's no one in the office. The other two entrances are this side door to the parking lot and the passageway to the church."

He glanced out the kitchen door, where the ice sculptors and spectators had turned their attention to the kitchen. "They would have seen anyone who entered this way," he observed. Turning to his partner, he realized he hadn't introduced her. "Father Noone, this is Detective Marcia Harcourt."

"Nice to meet you," she said with a pleasant smile. She was in her twenties, with brown hair and gray eyes that were almost green. "Sergeant, maybe I should get some Polaroid pictures of the body before we lose the murder weapon."

"What?" he asked, not comprehending for a moment.

"The murder weapon. It's melting," she said.

"So it is. All right, take a few shots. I hate to remove it before the lab boys get here."

She went to work quickly and efficiently, and by the time she'd finished the kitchen was becoming crowded. The medical examiner pronounced Porter Macklin dead and carefully removed the remains of the ice sliver from his throat. Bending to call a detective's attention to something bloody on the floor, he said, "This looks suspicious. I'll know more after the autopsy."

"Give us a report as soon as you can, Doc," Sergeant Dominick requested. "This is going to be one hot case. Victim's a New York architect."

David Noone saw the technicians dusting for prints. "You're probably wasting your time here. There are people in and out all day, even when we don't have Mardi Gras. The women who work in the rectory office, my housekeeper, visitors—they all park out here and come in through the kitchen."

"We're just doing our job, Father," one of them said and kept on dusting.

He went out to the parking area where work had halted on the ice sculptures. Luke Stevenson's archer still wasn't finished. In fact it had taken a step backward. The arrow had vanished from the archer's bow. "What happened?" he asked Parker.

"Broke off. I went in the kitchen to get a glass of water to freeze it back on, but it didn't work."

"Was Macklin there at the time?"

"There was a man working at the kitchen table. I didn't know who he was. We said hello, that's all."

"Did you notice anyone else go in through this door?"

He gave it some thought. "Angie used your restroom once, and I think Phil went in looking for a Band-Aid after he cut his finger."

"Was this before or after you went in?"

"I'm not sure. We were all working on our sculptures." Suddenly he seemed to realize where these questions were leading. "Father Dave, you can't think one of us killed him!"

"I'm just trying to figure out what happened, Luke. That sliver of ice in his throat was about the length of your arrow."

"I told you it broke. I threw the pieces into that snowbank."

Angie O'Toole had overheard the conversation and joined in. "None of us are too happy with the renovation plans, Father, but no one would kill him over it. That wouldn't have stopped anything. And why would it have to be one of us three? The rectory was open on the church side, wasn't it?"

"That's right."

"Anyone could have come in after mass."

David Noone sighed. "But a person coming in from the church after mass wouldn't have been carrying a long sliver of ice."

Bishop Martindale arrived at the rectory the following morning just after the early mass as David was finishing breakfast. He was a stocky, red-faced man known as a skilled administrator. It was no surprise that he turned up early, wanting to get to the bottom of things. "Father Noone," he said, walking into the kitchen unannounced. "I got back from Boston last night and heard what happened. Is there any new information?"

"I'm afraid not, Bishop. The autopsy results are due today, but I doubt if they'll tell us much."

"Mr. Macklin was stabbed in the throat with a sliver of ice?"

"Apparently."

Bishop Martindale made himself at home, finding a cup and saucer in the cupboard and pouring himself some coffee from David's percolator. "You understand this is serious business, Father." He sat down at the table. "Where was he found?"

"Here in the kitchen. He was going over his notes while I said the 11:30 mass. He died in your chair." A flicker of distaste crossed the bishop's face but he made no effort to rise. "I administered the last rites, though I don't even know if the man was Catholic."

"Fallen away, I suspect. He was divorced, though he still wore a wedding ring. What about this man who's been causing all the trouble? Was he here yesterday morning?"

"You mean Pat Fitzpatrick? He's at the 11:30 every Sunday."

"Was he leading his demonstration?"

"Yes."

"Do you think he's enough of a fanatic to have killed Macklin over this renovation business?"

"I don't believe Pat is a fanatic at all. He's a good Catholic who's clinging to the past. You'll find them in every parish. I don't agree with what he's doing, but he has a right to be heard."

Bishop Martindale put down his coffee cup and frowned. "These people have to realize that change is coming to Holy Trinity and to the other old churches in this city. We're in a new century, Father."

"I believe Pat will be dropping by later to see me. I hope we can find some common ground for discussion."

"In the meantime, what about this killing?"

All David could say was, "It's in the hands of the police."

Pat Fitzpatrick came by to see him shortly before noon. "That detective, Sergeant Dominick, was questioning me, Father. Does he think I killed the poor man?"

"Of course not, Pat. Come into my office and we'll talk." It was a cluttered little room with a desk, two chairs, and overflowing bookcases. Never large enough to accommodate David's needs, it had become even more crowded with the necessary addition of a computer on a side table that left him with little space to maneuver.

"I saw him, you know," Pat told him when he was seated in the worn green leather chair reserved for visitors. "The architect. I saw the two of you talking up on the altar before the 11:30. I recognized him from the picture in the paper."

"I noticed you in the last pew," David admitted. "You could have come up and spoken with him."

They talked at length about Holy Trinity, about the conflict between maintaining the old traditions and appealing to a new generation of worshipers. When they parted an hour later, David Noone felt they'd both learned something from the encounter. He promised to convey Pat's thoughts to the bishop.

A short while later, Sergeant Dominick phoned. "I thought you'd be interested in the autopsy report, Father. The medical examiner says that sliver of ice didn't inflict the fatal wound. He was killed by a knife with a serrated edge, some sort of kitchen or hunting knife. His ring finger was hacked off too, possibly when he tried to defend himself. I'd like to come out and see if you have any knives that might have been used."

"I'm sure we do, but I doubt if the killer would have returned the weapon to a drawer. He'd have taken it with him, wouldn't he?"

"Let me have a look."

While he waited for their arrival, Father Noone went outside to examine the three ice sculptures that had been created for the Mardi Gras festival. It had been a cold night and all three were intact, though the archer still lacked his arrow. He ran his hand over the delicate swan and the leaping fish, feeling the chill of ice on his flesh. Staring up at the kitchen windows, he tried to determine whether any movement could be seen through the curtains. No, he decided, the killer would have been safely hidden.

"Hello, Father," a voice behind him said. He turned to see young Phil Boyle standing there with his camera.

"How are you, Phil? The swan still looks good."

"I forgot to get a picture yesterday. I thought I'd take one before it melts."

"Good idea."

"Would you stand next to it, Father?"

"Do you really want me in it?"

"Sure!"

David Noone took up his position and smiled for the camera. Then he asked, "You went in there yesterday, didn't you? Before the body was discovered?"

"Into the kitchen? I was looking for a Band-Aid, but then I just washed off this cut and the bleeding stopped."

"Phil, did you speak to Porter Macklin?"

"No. I told the detective he wasn't in the kitchen then. He may have been in your downstairs bathroom. I heard the toilet flush. That's why I gave up on the Band-Aid."

"So you didn't see him at all?"

"Nope."

"No idea who might have killed him?"

"None, Father."

He was just leaving the parking area when Sergeant Dominick arrived with Detective Harcourt. Phil nodded to the sergeant and Dominick glanced back at him. "He was one of the ice sculptors, wasn't he?"

"That's right, Sergeant. He came over to take a picture of his swan."

David led the way into the kitchen and watched while the detective examined a variety of knives. Some he hardly remembered seeing before, no doubt left there by a variety of cooks and housekeepers during past years. Dominick held a couple up to the light, imagining possible bloodstains, but then returned them to the drawer. "Do you notice anything missing?"

"Not really," David replied honestly. "But I don't keep that close a count of the kitchen knives."

Dominick closed the drawer. "I think we can safely assume the killer took the weapon with him."

"The knife thrust killed Macklin?"

"Yes. The autopsy report was clear about that."

"Then why was that sliver of ice necessary?"

The detective shrugged. "I have no idea."

At the early mass on Tuesday morning, Father Noone was preaching a brief sermon on the day's gospel when the truth came to him, as clear and blinding as the morning sun through the stained glass window above the altar. There was only one point that needed clarification, the damned arrow of ice, and after mass he drove over to Luke Stevenson's house.

Luke was scraping up some ice from his driveway. "Morning, Father. I'm trying to give the sun a helping hand here and get rid of some of this ice today."

"Sometimes we just have to let nature take its course, Luke. You put that arrow of ice in Porter Macklin's throat, didn't you?"

He stopped his work and stared at David Noone. "I swear to God I didn't kill him, Father."

"I didn't say you killed him. I'm saying you put that ice in the wound after he was already dead. It couldn't have been anyone else but you, Luke. No one would have carried a sliver of ice into the kitchen to use the rest room or find a Band-Aid, but if you'd just broken the arrow off your archer you might have taken it in with you while you went for a glass of water to freeze it back in place. That was when you saw Porter Macklin seated at the table."

His voice was almost a whisper. "He was already dead, Father."

"I know that. Even before the autopsy report I doubted a sliver of ice could have penetrated his throat without breaking. Ice isn't as sharp as a knife blade. You were afraid that Angie or Phil had done it and you wanted to mislead the police."

He shook his head sadly. "Both of them are so young. It was a crazy thing to do, to take another human's life to save our church. It was almost like those fanatics who kill the abortion doctors."

"Which one did you think it was?"

"Angie O'Toole, I suppose. She went in second, ahead of me."

David Noone nodded. "Perhaps there's another possibility, Luke. We'll see."

He went back to the rectory and called a friend at the newspaper. There was one more bit of information he needed, and the reporter got back to him within thirty minutes. "You were right, Father Dave. I just got the word from Macklin's sister in New York. But how did you know?"

"I pretty much guessed," David Noone told him. "Wasn't Father Brown an intuitive detective?"

After that he telephoned Sergeant Dominick and told him that he needed to see him. "Could you be out here this afternoon around four?"

"I can't, Father, but I'll send Detective Harcourt. She'll handle whatever you need."

"Well, all right. That will be fine."

It was shortly after four when Pat Fitzpatrick arrived at the rectory. "What's up, Father?" he asked, slipping into the familiar visitor's chair. "Not more guff about the protests!"

"No, Pat. I'm afraid this is much more serious. You never told me your daughter was married to Porter Macklin."

"What?" He half rose from his chair. "What business was it of yours? Why did you need to know?"

"It would have helped explain why you killed him on Sunday."

He was halfway out the door when Detective Harcourt blocked his path while she read him his rights.

Pat Fitzpatrick sat stony-faced, moistening his dry lips with his tongue, while David Noone spoke. "I had a reporter friend check with New York. Porter Macklin and your daughter Jennifer were married nine years ago and divorced three years ago. I knew that your daughter was divorced. I just never knew her husband's name. The bishop told me Macklin was divorced too, though he still wore a wedding ring. I didn't connect those two facts at first, even though they were both in New York and I'd known your daughter married an older man. He even told me he'd visited this church once years ago. And I hadn't noticed that the killer had hacked off Macklin's ring finger until the autopsy report mentioned it. It didn't seem like a defensive wound to me. It seemed more like someone trying to remove that ring. Then I remembered other things. I'd seen you cutting that oilcloth sign with a blade of some sort on Sunday morning. And most of all I remembered you saying you'd recognized Macklin from his picture in the paper. But the paper didn't run a picture of him."

Pat turned his sad eyes toward David Noone and spoke for the first time. "Do you know about Jennifer? Do you know she's an alcoholic? He drove her to that, and then he dumped her. He came here to ruin my church the same way he ruined her life."

"That's enough, Pat," I told him, glancing at Detective Harcourt. "You need a lawyer."

He stood up to accompany Marcia Harcourt. "You know," he told her, "my daughter must be just about your age." Then he turned back to David. "Father, before I leave, would you hear my confession?"

THE RAG AND BONE MAN

LILLIAN STEWART CARL

AGITATED VOICES ECHOED OFF THE WALLS of the forecourt. Anselm shook his head in disapproval. More than the usual number of pilgrims had passed through the priory today, the feast of St. Anne, and he was only too aware that not all of them came with pious motives.

He turned his face to the late afternoon sunshine. Even though the days were dwindling, July was still the best of the summer. Anselm supposed he could find a lesson in that, something about the waning days of one's life being the richest. But he was tired after the day's sacred labors and was content merely to bask in the warmth and light and the subtle scent of incense. Inside these walls was an enclave of peace, not quite of this world, on the threshold of the next. What better symbol could there be of that than the Holy House of Nazareth in the Lady Chapel behind the church, the replica of Our Lord's childhood home?

The sound of running steps shattered his reverie. He opened his eyes to see young Brother Wilfrid bobbing before him. "Father Prior, one of the pilgrims has been found dead in the chapel of Mary and Martha."

"May he rest in peace," Anselm returned, wondering why Wilfrid was so disturbed. Every few days an ill pilgrim gave up the ghost here in

Walsingham, if unable to find healing in this world, then more importantly easing his passage into the next.

"Father, he was murdered."

Oh, thought Anselm. Yes, that was a problem. "Tell Brother Porter to
shut all the gates and allow no one in or out," he ordered Wilfrid, and he
ordered his own aching body across the forecourt to the church.

Several people stood outside the door. All voices bar one, a woman's
in full lamentation, fell silent as Anselm approached. Glancing at the
group, he assessed them as a motley collection of pilgrims no different
from any other—save for my lady the king's mother, who was bending
solicitously over the howling woman. Sorry to see the dowager queen
involved with such an unseemly matter, Anselm offered her a brief nod of
sympathy.

The interior of the church was dark and cool. A double row of pillars
led to the high altar and its crystal reliquary containing a few precious
drops of Our Lady's milk, bright as a star in a constellation of candlelight.
Anselm bowed before it, then turned toward one of the chapels.

The room was small as a hermit's cell—or a tomb. A man lay prone
before the altar, but not in an attitude of prayer. A runnel of blood crept
out from his body to puddle amongst the scattered rushes. Anselm knelt
down and with an effort—the man was fleshy, Anselm was not—turned
him over.

He knew this face, pale and distorted though it was. Hubert of
Gillingsoke, a merchant who came to Walsingham more to peddle his
wares to the pilgrims than to pay his respects at the shrine.

Hubert's tunic was soaked with blood from the gaping wound in his
throat. Anselm saw no blood trail, no smudges, no scattered drops—like
a slaughtered cow, Hubert had dropped where he stood. The small knife
he carried was still in its sheath. He had neither defended himself nor
attacked another. The murder had been the work of only a moment. Had
Hubert even seen his murderer's face? Probably not, if the killing stroke
had come from over his shoulder. His vacant eyes were already glazing
over, drained of life and its passions, good or ill.

The odors of profane blood and profane body thickened uneasily in
Anselm's throat, almost masking the faint aroma of—smoke? One of the
tall beeswax candles on the altar had been knocked over and extinguished. The cloth below it was singed. Worse, one end of the cloth was
blemished with a crimson smear swiftly darkening into brown. The murderer had wiped his blade on it.

And the reliquaries? Anselm rose to his knees, frowning. The gold-rimmed crystal displaying one of St. Martha's hairs was lying on its side. The jeweled casket containing St. Mary Magdalene's finger bone was gone. . . . No, thank God and all His saints, there it was, on the floor behind the trailing end of the cloth. Reverently Anselm picked it up.

"Father Prior," said Wilfrid's voice behind him.

Anselm looked around and up. "It was your place to conduct the group of pilgrims about the grounds and keep watch over the relics."

"And so I did, Father. Although this group was the last of the day, I didn't hurry them at all—we stopped by the chapel of St. Lawrence, and the holy wells, and the wicket gate. At the Lady Chapel each pilgrim passed through the Holy House and then each placed a coin in the collection box. . . . Well no, Hubert groped in his purse but offered nothing—instead he hissed angrily at his wife and she opened her purse. Until we came here to this chapel, nothing was different from any other day."

"So how, then, did this evil deed happen?"

The young monk retracted his stricken face into his black-cowled shoulders like a turtle retreating into its shell. "Ah—well—you see, Father, the old sister swooned and the young one asked me to bring cool water to bathe her brow. So I ran to the well."

"Sisters?" Anselm did remember seeing two Benedictine nuns amongst the pilgrims outside. "Did everyone remain here in the chapel whilst you fetched the water?"

"No, Father. When I returned they were walking into the porch, the old nun supported between the young one and Hubert's wife, and everyone else gathered close. We got her outside and set her down. Once the color came back into her face—it looked like bleached linen, it did—Hubert's wife asked where her husband had gotten himself off to. I went with her to search him out and here he was. Like this. Murdered."

"Was anyone else in the church when you left to fetch the water?"

"No one save our lady the king's mother. After she paid her respects to Mary and Martha she returned to kneel before the high altar, as always. . . ."

"Yes, yes." Queen Isabella had established her own patterns of devotion over the years. The relic of St. Mary Magdalene, the beautiful sinner, was her favorite, but she paid most of her attentions to the Blessed Virgin Mother. If anyone needed to pry open heaven's gates, it was Isabella. But then, if prayer could pry open the gates of heaven then hers would do so.

When Isabella took up her usual lodgings at the prior's house last night, she'd told Anselm she wanted to ask his advice on the disposition of a relic. Several times during the day he'd wondered just what she meant. Could she, with her connections in France, have come by another relic of the Magdalene to add to the Holy Mother's treasury?

He put his speculations aside. The matter of Hubert's death, while hardly more important, was more pressing." And our lady Queen Isabella followed the pilgrim group outside?"

"She was with the others when I came back with the water, Father, and right helpful she was, too, first with the sister, then with the wife."

"So the church was empty when you came in search of Hubert here."

"Yes, Father."

"You should have made sure it was empty before you left. You should have summoned help for the sister instead of . . ." He stopped. No need to rub the boy's nose in his folly. The deed was done. "Fetch a hurdle and several strong backs to carry him to the infirmary. And gather the entire group of pilgrims—including my lady the king's mother—in my parlor."

"Yes, Father." Wilfrid hurried away.

Anselm listened to the slap-slap of the young brother's sandals receding across the chancel of the church. The sacristy door creaked open and shut with a thud. He turned back to the inert flesh that had once been a man.

The flesh was weak, Anselm told himself. Pilgrims were often overcome by exhaustion and emotion, especially if they'd been fasting and walking barefoot—as well they should, if they wanted their prayers to be answered.

And then there was Hubert, his feet shod, his protruding stomach rarely, if ever, purified by hunger. Along with linen, wool, and silk, he dealt in bits of rag and bone which he claimed were relics of the blessed saints but which, for all Anselm knew, he'd "discovered" in the midden behind his house.

If Hubert had tried to steal the reliquaries, all one of the other pilgrims needed to do was raise the alarm. And since, manifestly, neither reliquary had been stolen, the matter could hardly be a falling out of thieves. . . . Thieves. Anselm felt along Hubert's belted waist and found two trailing ends of leather. That was it, then. His purse had been cut clean away. It was justice, perhaps, that a less-than-honest man should fall victim to one even worse.

Reminding himself that it was not his place to pass verdict on the dead, Anselm closed the staring eyes. For a long moment he knelt, listening, as though the man's ashen lips would open and speak a name. But no. His silence was absolute. With a groan Anselm stood up, removed the altar cloth, and set the candle upright on bare stone.

Which was worse, the defilement of this sacred space or that Hubert had died unshriven? If he'd said his prayers properly in front of our Lady's shrine, though, surely she'd hear his confession even now and intercede on his behalf. "May God have mercy on his soul," Anselm murmured, and turned toward the door.

The western front of the church shone brightly in the light of the setting sun. But Anselm was no longer aware of the light. Neither did he smell incense. He twisted his nose at the ripe reek of summer and mortality, smoke, cooking food, offal. He'd never felt so much under siege from the town, its high street crowded with inns and shops breeding sin and disease.

He turned to Brother Nicholas, the infirmarian, whose stooped figure in its black robe looked like a raven. "Yes, Father, I'll clean the man's body and bind up his throat, make him decent so his wife can take him home. Gillingsoke is on the road to Castle Rising, isn't it?"

"Yes," replied Anselm, "but Hubert's house and manufactory are in town, in Norwich. He held his property free of any lord. Such times we live in, Nicholas, such times!"

Clucking his tongue, Nicholas went on, "Here is Hubert's purse—see the sprinkling of blood? It was lying behind a pillar in the church. The thief must have emptied it out into his own purse."

So as not to be discovered holding it, Anselm told himself. The small leather pouch in Nicholas's hand was flaccid as Hubert's body.

The porter, Brother Simon, stood waiting his turn. His nose and the shaved crown of his head were both sunburned—he didn't hide inside the gatehouse, he was faithful to his task. "Yes, Father, I saw the pilgrims fussing about on the porch of the church. Soon after I heard the woman scream inside. No one had left for some time. I sent Brother Peter to close the meadow gate and then he and I searched the enclave. No pilgrims are inside the pale now, bar the ones waiting in your parlor."

"Thank you," Anselm told them both, and told himself that their observations were probably useful but he was at a loss to say how.

He supposed he should send to the earl for a sergeant at arms—which would be yet another trespass by the outside world. Unless, Anselm thought suddenly, he solved this crime himself. Then all he'd have to do was turn the culprit over to the sergeant, shut the gate upon them both, and set about cleansing the sacred precinct.

He walked across the forecourt, bent beneath the weight of his task.

But as crosses went, this one in no way approximated the poundage of our Lord's. Summoning the iron into his soul, Anselm opened the door to his house and stepped into his parlor.

The room, already small, seemed claustrophobic, warm and still. Pilgrims were ranged along the walls, some standing, some sitting on benches and chests, both his own and Isabella's. Wilfrid stood guard over the one high-backed chair, trying to redeem himself after his earlier dereliction of duty. Anselm lowered himself down, only too aware of the dust dabbling his feet and the hem of his black robe and of the sweat trickling down his back. But he couldn't ask Wilfrid to bring him a cool drink, not when all these people had none.

Every face turned toward him, every eye focused on him. One of these people, Anselm thought, was a thief and a murderer. He could ask to inspect their purses, but each coin looked like another—how to tell which ones had begun the day in Hubert's pouch?

The room was so quiet he could hear the concerted breaths of the pilgrims and the whimper of a baby. . . . And a combination of the two, the quick gulped breath of a woman who'd been sobbing. Yes, there she was, Hubert's young wife, Alianor, small, sleek, her eyes like smoldering coals. She wore a headdress and a cote-hardie of an elegance beyond her station, not to mention her surroundings. The trailing end of one sleeve was stained a brownish crimson. It must have touched her husband's wound when she and Wilfrid discovered his body.

"I'm sorry for your loss, Madame," Anselm said.

She parted her compressed lips. "I've lost my husband, my livelihood. I don't know where to turn."

In truth, Anselm told himself, she hadn't lost her livelihood—since Hubert's property and business were free-held they would come to her. But now, in the throes of her grief, was no time to mention such legalities.

The king's mother stood close beside Alianor, one supporting hand on her shoulder. "You may come to me at Castle Rising, you know the way."

"My thanks, my lady," said Alianor. "I shall indeed throw myself on your mercy. But—oh, Father Prior, you must find the evil man who deprived me of my lord and husband!"

"If God so wills it." Anselm turned to Isabella. "My lady, you and your retainers were the last to leave the church before the discovery of the murder. Did you see or hear anything?"

"Not at all, Father Prior." Isabella's voice was still inflected by the language of her youth, even though her youth—and her infamies—had occurred many years ago. Supposedly she'd once had a remarkable worldly beauty. Now her face was like fine marble eroded by time and repentance. "The murderer must have passed close behind us," she said, "but lost as I was in veneration I saw and heard nothing. Sir Raynald?"

Isabella's steward was a thickset man, freckled of face, red of hair. He smiled shamefacedly. "I confess, my lady and Father Prior, to woolgathering as I knelt, estimating expenditures and the like. I'll be sure to beg our Lady's pardon for my inattention. Walter?"

"I was praying very passionately that my trespasses be forgiven." The rawboned man-at-arms smiled tightly and a flush brightened his sallow cheeks, making Anselm wonder how many of his trespasses were hedonistic ones.

Raynald asked, "James?"

Isabella's squire stepped forward, his jaw square, his blue eyes steady, his broad shoulders set beneath his flowing sleeves. "I heard my lady's voice, Father, and the footsteps of the other pilgrims. Perhaps one set came late, behind the others—it's hard to say, the space is filled with echoes and drafts and my mind was centered on my prayers."

Isabella turned to her ladies in waiting. "Maud, Blanche, did you see or hear anything?"

While dressed less soberly than the queen herself, who wore the habit of a Franciscan nun, still the women's clothing lacked the frills and furbelows of Alianor's. They were both of a middling age and ordinary countenance. "I knelt beside you, my lady," said the one, "and repeated the Psalter of our Lady as you spoke it. Blanche?"

The other said, "The church is dark. After several moments staring into the altar candles strange shapes and shadows moved in the corners of my eyes, as though the pillars themselves came forward to kneel."

"Yes," said one of the nuns suddenly, "I saw them too, the shapes of angels and ministers of grace, of the Holy Blessed Virgin and her mother, blessed St. Anne."

"I beg your pardon?" asked Anselm.

The older nun's thin face was almost as colorless as the wimple surrounding it, and yet a subtle glow in her flesh made Anselm think of a fine painted window shining with the light of heaven. It was the younger sister, wider than she was tall, round and rosy of cheek, who answered. "Father Prior, I am Sister Margaret and this is Sister Juliana, from the priory at Little Aldersthorpe. Mother Prioress gave Juliana permission to come to our Lady's shrine on this, the feast day of St. Anne, our patron saint."

"And you came as Sister Juliana's companion."

"Yes, Father. I am infirmaress, and she has been—infirm."

And hadn't long to live, Anselm concluded. Yet Juliana came here in celebration, not to plead for healing.

"I'm afraid I saw and heard nothing this afternoon," Margaret went on. "My attention was to Sister Juliana. Mother Prioress has excused her from fasting, but still. . . ."

"The incense," said Juliana with a beatific smile. "The relics, the spirit of a blessed soul lingering in their physical remains, working miracles. Shape and shadow and our Lord made flesh, out of Mary by the spirit of God."

This one was a bit wander-witted, Anselm told himself, and turned to the gangly young man who hovered over a drawn and pinched young woman. She crouched on one of Isabella's small chests, holding a child of perhaps two years of age. The simplicity of their garments reminded Anselm of the Holy Family, and yet their expressions, worry shading into despair, had nothing holy in them. "Who are you?" he asked.

"I am Thurstan, a plowman of Fakenham," said the man, politely enough but with little deference. "This is my wife, Hawise, and our son, who we named Edward after your son, my lady."

The corner of Isabella's mouth tucked itself into a rueful half-smile, perhaps remembering that her late husband and his imperious father had also been named Edward. She peered at the child's face. His lips were blue, his skin tinted with lavender. "He is ill?"

"He was taken ill in the spring," answered Thurstan, "choking and wheezing, and now wastes away before our eyes."

"And we thought ourselves fortunate to be spared the plague this last year." Hawise rocked the child in her lap and it whimpered again.

"May the Holy Mother have mercy," Anselm said. Of all the pilgrims who flocked to Walsingham he liked the children best. It was sad when one died, yes, and yet it was also a blessing for their souls to be taken up into heaven before they were contaminated. . . . The desolation in Hawise's face made Anselm realize she was seeing matters from a very different perspective. Somehow he'd never asked himself how the Blessed Virgin felt upon seeing her son's bloodied corpse lowered from the cross. Strange, to think that everything was not as it seemed. Stranger still, to find that thought less discomforting than stimulating.

"We saw nothing in the church," Thurstan said.

Anselm forced himself back to the issue at hand. "You went outside with all of the others?"

"Our lady the king's mother knelt before the high altar," Hawise said, then glanced at the man standing to one side, half obscured by the ray of sun just creeping into the narrow window. "But this man, here, he came behind us."

"Well then," said Anselm.

The man was tall, dressed in a simple wool tunic and mantle. Rough dark hair streaked with gray framed a patrician face, high-browed, hawk-nosed. "I am Geoffrey de Charny, knight," he said in the accents of France.

The others glanced at him in surprise and even resentment. Several inched away. Isabella did not. Her eyes lit up. "Ah, *un chevalier francais.*"

"*Je vous en prie, Madame.*" Geoffrey bowed, his shadow on the oppo-site wall bending and straightening as well.

Well, well, thought Anselm. A Frenchman. An enemy. "You were the last to go outside?"

"No," replied Geoffrey. "The merchant, Hubert, he stayed behind."

"Of course he did, we know that. But you were the last of the group that did go outside?"

"Save my lady the king's mother, yes."

"You, then, were the last person to see Hubert alive."

"So it seems."

Anselm leaned forward like a hound on the scent. "Why are you here? Were you a captive?"

"I was captured at Calais. My king has paid ransom. I stop here on my way to take ship at King's Lynn."

Raynald's sandy brows rose. "If King Jehan has paid your ransom then you must be a great knight indeed. An honorable man," he added to Anselm.

"The truly wise man gives thanks to God and to the Virgin Mary for any successes he may achieve," Geoffrey said.

Amen to that. Anselm deflated a bit, suddenly uncertain. France and England might be at war, but a warrior turned pilgrim, a man of honor trusted by his captor, always had safe conduct. And was hardly likely to go about murdering merchants.

"A Frenchman who can't afford to pay his own ransom," Alianor said scornfully, "might think a bit of thievery wouldn't come amiss. He has killed many Englishmen, no great mischief to kill one more who stood between him and a holy reliquary."

"Is the relic missing, Father?" asked Geoffrey.

"No," Anselm replied.

"Perhaps," suggested James, Isabella's squire, "he dropped it on the floor as he fled."

"Why do I steal a finger bone of the blessed Madeleine when her body already lies in my country?" Geoffrey returned.

"More than one body," muttered Walter. "Those French monks either create relics or steal each other blind."

Geoffrey quirked a brow but said nothing.

"If the holy thief succeeds in his purpose, then the blessed saint herself wants to move," Juliana pointed out. "And some relics have the power of self-replication, like the holy Eucharist itself."

Anselm had heard Hubert expressing similar rationalizations, although from a very different viewpoint. Not that it mattered—Walsingham's reliquary of St. Mary Magdalene was safe in its chapel. "Only Hubert's money was stolen," he said. "And his life."

"Hubert had no money," said the lady in waiting named Blanche. "I overheard at the door of the Lady Chapel, he reached into his purse, found it empty, then muttered a curse at his wife for keeping their coins herself."

Alianor shrugged. "He'd forgotten he gave me the coins to carry. He was always short-tempered."

Behind Anselm's back Wilfrid nodded agreement. He'd already mentioned the quick exchange between man and wife before the collection box.

"Even though the thief didn't know Hubert's purse was empty," said Anselm, grasping at a quickly receding straw, "the motive remains the same."

"And perhaps this man here," Alianor went on, "the plowman with the ailing child, needs money badly enough to kill for it."

Hawise frowned, but Thurstan drew himself up and shook the mop of flaxen curls from his brow. "I'm not a wealthy man, far from it. But I've no need to steal. After the black plague killed so many in our village I have more work for my hands than ever before, and higher wages and a bit of respect as well."

What is the world coming to? Anselm asked himself. Although he saw where he himself was going. He wouldn't be giving thanks for achieving any successful criminal investigations, not at this rate. He sank back even further in his chair, sent a prayer for assistance heavenwards, and tried to concentrate his mind.

Had this crime gained nothing for the murderer, then, and accomplished no end whatsoever? No money stolen, no relics stolen—had Hubert died for a mistaken perception, because everything wasn't what it seemed?

Anselm envisioned Hubert in the chapel, between the group with Alianor, Juliana, and the others on the one hand and Isabella and her retainers on the other. He must have died after the former left the church but before. . . .

Impatiently Alianor looked right and left and then stepped forward, shaking her becrimsoned sleeve at Anselm. "My husband's blood cries out for justice, Father Prior! If you can't find his killer here, then send these people about their business and look amongst your own brethren. Who's to say which of them entered the church, privily, through the sacristy door?"

"That door creaks," Anselm explained, trying to keep the indignation from his voice. "My lady Queen Isabella would certainly have heard it, even if the guilty party had waited to cross the chancel until she'd turned away. . . . What is it, Sister?"

Margaret was looking closely at Alianor's forearm, exposed as the sleeve of her cote-hardie slid back. "You've been injured, Madame. Five bruises, four on one side, one on the other, like the violent grasp of a man's hand."

"It's no matter, please don't concern yourself." Alianor quickly dropped her arm and the folds of cloth covered it.

Anselm sat up, suddenly seeing the murder from a different viewpoint, and answered his own question. What had been accomplished by Hubert's murder was Hubert's death.

Alianor might have tired of her husband knocking her about—that much Anselm could understand. But she hadn't broken her vow of obedience, not to mention the sixth commandment, and murdered him. When she'd left the church with Juliana and the others, her husband was still alive.

Juliana, Anselm saw, was staring at the shadow play on the wall, Alianor's sleeves billowing like smoke in the brilliant sunlight, Geoffrey's figure like an upright effigy. Was it Sister Juliana who'd said something about shadows? No, it was Isabella's lady in waiting Maud who said she'd seen moving shapes while she knelt at the altar. And someone else, one of the men, had also said something very interesting. . . .

The room was so silent Anselm could hear the child's labored breath and the shuffle of feet as several people shifted impatiently. Shoes, he thought. He and his brethren wore sandals, but everyone else here wore soft leather shoes. Isabella and her retainers heard no footsteps because there had been none to hear. They themselves had been the only people in the church save Hubert.

Everyone spoke of the king's mother as though she and her retainers moved together like soldiers in formation. But if Maud saw a shadow moving before her, what she was seeing was a shadow cast by the light of the candles in the chapel behind her, the shadow of one of her own colleagues as he stepped cat-footed through the door, did the evil deed, and returned. All he had had to do was station himself in the rear of the group and wait until Isabella, in a voice that had once commanded armies, began speaking the Psalter.

Abruptly Anselm stood up. The man had done two evil deeds—he'd murdered Hubert and he'd wiped his blade on the altar cloth, knocking the reliquary to the floor. Yes, he saw the way now, as clearly illuminated in his mind as the mottled plaster wall of his parlor was illuminated by God's holy and revealing light. "Wilfrid, gather every knife in this room and bring them to me."

Wilfrid stepped out from behind the chair, puzzled but knowing better than to ask questions. He collected blades from Geoffrey, Thurstan, Raynald, James, and Walter. When Margaret proffered a tiny knife Anselm shook his head. "Thank you, Sister, but so small a blade as that could not have cut a man's throat in one stroke—nor could you, I think, have reached over his shoulder to make that stroke."

Turning away from them all and yet aware of every eye upon him, Anselm walked into the hot glow of the sunbeam which shone through the window bright as the Holy Mother's crystal reliquary. He beckoned Wilfrid, his arms bristling with knives, to his side. Picking up the first knife, he drew it from its sheath and held it to the blazing ray of sun.

Geoffrey's dagger was long and plain, but the hilt was cunningly wrought. The blade was pristine, polished to a silvery gleam. Thurstan's knife was well-worn and stank of onions, but it, too, was clean. Not that Anselm suspected either man, not any more. It was simply appropriate for him to inspect all the knives.

He picked up the third one, a fine blade with a jeweled hilt. Raynald's, he guessed. He drew it from its sheath and turned it back and forth in the dazzling light. Clean. That left two, both simple, very similar, knives.

Feet shuffled behind him, but he didn't glance around. He plucked the next knife from its sheath and held it close, squinting in the glare. Yes, there, a streak of rust-red forming a thin crust between shining blade and dull guard. Wetting his fingertip, Anselm touched it to the crust. It came away red. If not for the sun he'd never had seen it.

"This knife has blood on it." He turned back toward the watching people, blinked away several bright shapes floating in his vision, and asked, even though he knew the answer, "Who does it belong to, Walter or James?"

For a long moment none of the eyes watching him blinked. Then James exclaimed, "Walter! Have your debts grown so great you coveted Hubert's money? One sin begets another and yet another, it seems."

Walter's jaw worked—he'd have spat on the floor, Anselm assumed, if he'd been anywhere but in a prior's parlor. "I have gambling debts, yes. But I didn't kill the man. Look to your own knife and your own sins, Sir Squire."

Raynald caught James's arm and pulled him into the light. The squire, his lower jaw outthrust, shook him away. "I tell you, that's Walter's knife, not mine."

One lingering shape in Anselm's eye resolved itself into a vision of a flaccid leather pouch, spotted with blood. Blood will tell, yes. Blood will confirm. Between thumb and forefinger he picked up the loose fabric of James's sleeve and spread it before the all-seeing light of God.

Bending close, he smelled the young man's acrid sweat. He saw a delicate spray of brown droplets fanning across the cloth. The drops drew an ugly picture—James's left hand grasping Hubert's shoulder or hair, his right arm reaching around and drawing the knife across his throat in a smooth, quick stroke. Hubert's last breath, expelled through the wound, sprinkling his lifeblood over James's stylishly long sleeve.

And it was James himself who'd uttered the words that damned him. "You knew that the reliquary had fallen to the ground," Anselm said. "Only the murderer could have known that."

"You killed my husband!" Alianor shrieked.

James turned on her with a snarl. "It's what you wanted, you daughter of Eve! Isn't that why you seduced me there at Castle Rising, when you and your husband came to peddle your wares? He's old, you said. He's vile-tempered, you said. Hold me, you said. And then when you'd had your way with me you told me that our passion was sinful, that it would be better to marry than to burn, and that I had no choice but to kill him and take you as my wife."

"No." Alianor took a step back and collided with Isabella, who laid a firm hand on her arm. "No, you're lying."

"You and Hubert did visit Castle Rising," Isabella said quietly. "I bought a length of baudekyn from you, but none of your collection of relics, false or otherwise."

Maud stared from Alianor to James and back. "I heard you talking, the both of you, about a relic. I thought that to be evidence of your piety."

"Is he lying, daughter?" Anselm asked Alianor. "Or is he confessing his guilt? What of you? Confess your disobedience and purify your soul."

"No," Alianor said again, her voice stretching thinner and thinner.

"We made our plans," James said between clenched teeth. His glare at Alianor was filled with passion, yes, but with hatred, not lust. "She told me her plans, rather, that I, fool that I am, agreed to put into effect. Her old husband, who was no great loss, by the by, wanted to steal the relic of St. Mary Magdalene. A holy theft, he named it. He'd told Alianor to feign a swoon there in the chapel, but in the event she didn't need to."

"It was I who swooned," Sister Juliana said, not at all shamefaced. "And among those female voices I heard in my dream was one whispering, 'now, do it now'. I thought the saint was speaking to me, and although I didn't understand, I didn't question, as God's mysteries are beyond human comprehension."

The color drained from Alianor's face. "God and the Holy Virgin help me," she murmured, and swayed like a broken reed. Maud and Blanche stepped forward to ease Alianor's sagging body to the floor. She wasn't feigning a swoon, not now.

Anselm regarded her sadly. The flesh was weak, and no flesh was as weak as a woman's. . . . Well, neither Hubert nor James were male exemplars, were they?

All Hubert had had to do was attach himself and Alianor to the dowager queen's party. Then, when—someone—provided a distraction and drew the others away, he would steal the reliquary. But Alianor and James had their own plot, parallel to his. All Alianor had had to do was guide her husband to Walsingham on St. Anne's Day, when Isabella would also be there. Perhaps Alianor and James intended all along to throw suspicion onto Walter. Or perhaps they took advantage of his presence—and his failings—as they took advantage of having a peasant and a Frenchman in the party.

James took Hubert's empty purse to make it appear as though robbery was the motive. And he knew that whilst Hubert could have slipped out of the priory with the reliquary beneath his tunic, the hue and cry over a murder would never permit James himself to do the same. So he'd left the reliquary lying on the floor of the chapel, where it'd fallen, most likely, after he wiped his blade on the altar cloth.

Why then, Anselm wondered, should James and Alianor have been discussing a relic at all? Because they could hardly avoid discussing Hubert's business?

Margaret patted Alianor's cheeks, bringing her round. James watched stone-faced. Wilfrid handed back the knives, giving James's to Raynald. Thurstan inspected his and then used it to clean a bit of food from his teeth. Geoffrey tucked his into his belt abstractedly, as though feeling he had little to do with the events taking place before him.

Isabella met Anselm's eyes with a remote, rueful expression. For just a moment he could read her mind. Her own husband had been no exemplar, either. Her rebellion against him, while wrong, was not inexplicable. Like Alianor she had discovered one very effective tactic: There was no need to wield a weapon yourself if you could beguile a man into doing it for you.

Isabella had had years to pay penance, humbling herself and showing compassion even for those like Alianor. Especially for those like Alianor. . . .

And suddenly Anselm saw the plot entire. What else had Hubert's murder accomplished? It had left Alianor in possession of his property and his business, dealing not only in cloth but in relics. She had no need to plead poverty in front of Isabella and ask for her succor at Castle Rising.

But Isabella possessed a relic, one she wanted to discuss with Anselm. While Hubert might have lusted after a relic from Walsingham, Alianor lusted after the one from Castle Rising. Perhaps she'd learned of it from James. Perhaps she'd merely used James as a means to her end—not only to dispose of her husband but to claim Isabella's compassion in her bereavement and thereby gain access to her relic.

The sunbeam faded, filling the room with twilight. With a quickly muffled groan, Anselm sat back down in his chair. James's life would end on the gallows, no doubt about it. As for Alianor—well, unlike Isabella, the earl was not known for his compassion. "Wilfrid, have Brother Simon send for the earl's sergeant at arms. Sir Raynald, if you'd be so kind— ladies. . . ."

"My pleasure, Father." Raynald and Walter marched James across the room and out the door. He stepped out proudly, as though on parade.

Maud and Blanche came behind with a stumbling Alianor. "Is there any justice for me, Father? A young woman married against her will to a violent old man—why shouldn't I look to my own provision?"

"We shall all stand before the judgement of Christ," Anselm told her, "and each one of us shall render account of himself to God. All the church can offer you is forgiveness, if you ask for it."

Perhaps she would ask, as Isabella had. Perhaps she'd never find humility. Anselm watched the two young people disappear out the door and felt old and weak and empty.

The child, Edward, was fretting, making little cries of discomfort. Hawise bent over him and Margaret knelt beside them. Suddenly he sat up in his mother's lap, coughing violently, his entire body spasming. "Blessed Virgin," exclaimed Thurstan, "as you loved your own son, help mine!"

In one great paroxysm the child spat something into Margaret's hand and lay back, breathing deeply. Isabella set her hand on his face, watching in amazement and, Anselm thought, gratification, as Edward's skin flushed a rosy and healthy pink.

"It's a miracle," said Juliana, crossing herself.

Margaret inspected the damp object in her hand. "It's a bit of nutshell. It must have been lodged in his chest."

Tears of joy were running down Hawise's fragile cheeks. "The day he took ill I was cracking walnuts and he was playing at my feet. Children will put anything and everything into their mouths."

"God be praised," said Anselm, and he surprised himself with a smile.

"Yes, indeed," Isabella said. "And God be thanked for giving me such a clear and unequivocal sign."

"My lady?" Anselm asked.

"We were all brought here together for a purpose—the child, Sir Geoffrey, all of us. I see it plain as you saw the blood on that knife, Father Prior, illuminated by God himself."

Geoffrey tilted his head quizzically. "Madame?"

"I wished to ask your advice about a relic, Father."

"Yes," Anselm replied. "I was just thinking of it. If you'd rather wait until some better time. . . ."

"This is the time." Isabella raised Hawise from the chest she'd been sitting on. Thurstan wrapped wife and child in one long arm and stepped aside. Margaret went to stand beside Juliana.

Isabella reached into her belt, withdrew a key, and unlocked the chest. Leaning forward, Anselm saw a length of baudekyn, its silk and gold threads shining in the last gleam of light from the window.

Reverently Isabella rolled back the end of the precious cloth. Inside it lay folded linen. She grasped one end of the linen and pulled it from its wrapping, higher and higher, until she held it unfurled to the height of her own body. Still part of the cloth lay concealed in the chest.

At first Anselm thought it was ordinary linen cloth such as Hubert sold. Then, very faintly, he began to make out the impression of a man's body, a bearded face bedaubed with blood, crossed arms wounded in the wrists. The linen seemed to emit a pale light of its own as well as a subtle fragrance. He rose to his feet, slowly but painlessly, drawn by the soft but radiant glow of the cloth and that elusive scent of—myrrh, he realized. The unguent which anointed our Lord's corporeal body. . . .

"It is the burial shroud of our Lord himself," Isabella said.

"What?" Chills ran down Anselm's back.

Juliana gasped and fell to her knees, Margaret at her side. "Look, it is the image of our Lord, wounds and all. Thurstan called upon the Virgin in the name of her son, and through his spirit dwelling in the relic the child was healed."

"I doubted whether this cloth was the genuine relic," said Isabella, "having seen many false bits of bone and rag and such over the years. But here, in this moment, God has shown me—shown us all—the truth."

No, Anselm told himself, the miracle was not a matter of perception or a difference in viewpoint. The cloth was exactly as it appeared.

One by one everyone sank slowly to his knees, save the little boy, who burbled happily in his mother's arms. The child, made in the image of God, the image now displayed before them. The image of a mortal man, his body like Anselm's own. What would have been the point of our Lord's sacrifice, had he had no body to suffer?

Anselm felt dizzy, as though a wind was blowing through his skull and sweeping his old perceptions away. Automatically he made the sign of the cross over them all, and then traced the sign again, more slowly, for the first time fully aware of—and taking joy in—its physicality.

Isabella's voice was a note of music. "I was sent from France to marry Edward the year after my father, King Philippe, charged the Order of the Temple with heresy. He purged them with blood and fire and took their treasure for his own. One of my bride-pieces was a jeweled chest from the Paris commandery. It was years later, long after my son exiled me to Castle Rising for my sins, that I found the false bottom in the chest and this cloth, folded so that only the face of the image could be seen."

"The Templars were charged with worshipping a face," said Geoffrey. "A face with a beard."

Isabella folded the linen back into the chest. Its glow vanished into the shadows like the sunbeam disappearing from the wall. Its fragrance lingered, now smelling less like myrrh than like baking bread. After all, Anselm told himself, while man might not live by bread alone, bread was necessary to life. He bounded to his feet like a spring lamb, refreshed, and reached out to assist Juliana and Margaret. But they too, stood effortlessly. Every face was turned to the chest, and every face glowed rosily as though turned to the sun, even in the now-dark room.

"This is the so-called idol of the Templars," said Isabella. "They didn't worship it, they venerated it. I believe they saved it when Constantinople was looted by their own brethren, the Crusaders, and kept it so secret that even my father's treasurers didn't know where—or what—it was. The irony of the most sacred of relics falling into the hands of she who was once named 'the she-wolf of France,' her father's daughter, has not been lost on me."

"God so willed it," stated Juliana.

Isabella nodded. "I could, I suppose, present this relic to our Lady's shrine here at Walsingham, buying my way into heaven with it."

For a long moment Anselm's mind filled with the image of Walsingham as the greatest shrine not just in England but in the world, drawing pilgrims and their offerings. . . . The thought came to his mind as though a voice whispered it in his ear: I can't have it both ways. I can either disdain the world or welcome it to my doorstep.

"And yet," Isabella went on, "I see that today's events are a sign from God himself, that my own penance is only a small part of a much greater one. France and England have seen war, plague, famine, death these last few years. This most holy of relics must be returned to the place whence it was stolen, to redeem both my and my father's pride and to heal both my homelands. Sir Geoffrey, you must take it with you back to France."

"My respect to your nephew, my liege Lord Jehan," said Geoffrey with a frown, "but he would destroy the *suaire*, the shroud, as evidence of the Templars. I could give it to the holy father, the pope."

"Who is captive in Avignon, in my nephew's domain, without hope of ransom. He wouldn't dare accept such a gift. No, Sir Geoffrey, find some small church that will hold the holy shroud in trust until such time as its presence can be revealed and appreciated for what it is."

"I shall give it, then, to my own church at Lirey and conceal its origins."

"Thank you," said Isabella, and, turning to Anselm, "I beg your pardon, Father Prior. I know what this relic would have meant to you here within these walls."

"But we can see only part of God's plan from within these walls," Anselm told her. "Our Lord himself opened the door of his mother's house and went out to meet the world."

"If there were no outside world," said Margaret softly, "why should there be need for places like Walsingham?"

Yes, thought Anselm, without pilgrims there would be no priory. Without the world there would be no pilgrims. Without the body and blood of Christ—the actual, physical body and blood—there would be no faith. That's why relics exist. How long, he wondered, had he himself been no more than a rag and bone man, never seeing the true significance of his charge?

Geoffrey brushed the chest with his fingertips, then with a low bow accepted the key from Isabella's hand. "Thank you for your trust, Madame."

"I have learned," said Isabella, "to trust in God."

"Amen," Anselm said with feeling. "Who would have thought that a rag and bone man like Hubert would be an instrument of God's will?"

"God works in mysterious ways," said Hawise. Edward was squirming. She set him down and he toddled toward the chest, where he started beating its top with crows of delight. Grinning, Thurstan pulled him away.

A bell rang outside. "It is the hour of compline," said Anselm, "the completion of the daily cycle of prayer. Please, come to the church with me, so that we can pray for James and Alianor, and give thanks, and prepare ourselves to begin again tomorrow."

"Yes, Father." Thurstan gathered Hawise close. Margaret supported Juliana. Geoffrey bowed Isabella out the door.

Anselm waited a long moment, eyeing the room now empty of people but never empty of faith. Then he turned and went out into the twilight, grateful to be part not only of his canonical community, but of the greater community of mankind, saint to sinner and everyone between.

HISTORICAL NOTE:
The artifact now known as the Shroud of Turin can be traced back to 1355, when it was owned by the de Charny family and displayed at the tiny church of Lirey in France. How it got there is anyone's guess. Since Isabella the Fair (or the She-Wolf, take your pick) had good reason to make her pilgrimages to Walsingham, and Geoffrey de Charny, who was in England in 1351, was known to be an exceptionally pious knight, this particular guess is only slightly less probable than some.

✝

Divine Justice

Chuck Meyer

New York Times Headline:
UNANIMOUS SUPREME COURT APPROVES RIGHT TO DIE

THE COURTROOM WAS SURPRISINGLY SMALL, considering the magnitude of decisions made there and the personalities of the people making them. But it seemed especially cramped today as the decision was read. The decision no one expected. No one but me.

In the old days the reporters would have made a mad dash out of the courtroom to the bank of phones in the marble lobby. But today they stayed put. Only their fingers hurriedly dashed out the story for immediate upload to their newsrooms on wireless modems.

I noted the expressionless faces staring down from behind the high bench like ghosts on a graveyard wall. Breaking with the usual restrained decorum, the winning doctors and attorneys were ecstatic, shaking hands and hugging, undoubtedly thinking of the patients who would benefit from this incredible decision to acknowledge their right to die. The eight Supreme Court justices were pale and stoic as the Chief Justice lowered his gavel to end the day's session like any other.

I left the courtroom and was about to step into a cab when a television reporter stopped me. She had interviewed me many times in the last year and knew my sentiments, but she asked for the camera anyway. I told her, as on every other occasion, that it was a complex issue but that I was happy for those who would no longer be required to suffer the indignities of American high tech death. I got into the cab and came here to Bethesda Naval Hospital, where I am Chief of Chaplains, to finish what I began eighteen months ago—manipulating a landmark decision of the highest court in the land.

I conceived the idea the day Oregon passed its Death with Dignity Act, permitting physicians to prescribe lethal medication for the terminally ill. I knew it was only a matter of time before the right-to-lifers challenged the constitutionality of the law and began their slow trek to the Supreme Court. So that very day I sat in front of this same computer (on which I am recording these events for future historians) and began to gather the data that would lead to today.

My passion for the issue has burned for the thirty years I have been a hospital chaplain. I have sat at the bedside of hundreds of dying people, watched them waste away, descend into the incredible indignities of a hell worse than Dante could dream. Their immune systems weakened either by debilitating disease or excoriating treatment. Some develop sores from lips to anus, unable to eat, swallow, or defecate without rasping pain; others, emaciated to a hollow aged shell, try to die but are sustained by hard plastic breathing tubes stuck down their throats and taped tightly to their mouths, IVs thrust into ancient purple veins, and slimy tubes slipped up their urethras by twenty-year-old techs. Still others, comatose or demented, will have their fetally contracted sticks of legs broken or amputated so their abdomens can be cut open to insert a nutrition tube to prolong their horrid existence.

What were war crimes at Nuremburg are now the standards for high tech death in this country. And, like the Nazis before us, we do not limit our terminal torture to the old; we inflict it with equal vehemence on the newly born, especially those anomalous infants who would otherwise quickly and mercifully die. We use our same instruments of torture with the self-serving disclaimer that neonates feel no pain, regardless of all outward appearances to the contrary. Then we drench ourselves in the champagne of self congratulations when we produce an end product that will require a lifetime of invasive procedures, none of which we will have to witness, comfort, or financially support, often to the emotional detriment of other family members.

I must admit that, in recent years, things had gotten somewhat better. The aging of the population, particularly the Boomers, coupled with media attention to other right-to-die cases and advance directives, seemed to have resulted in more willingness on the part of the medical system to withdraw aggressive treatment in favor of comfort care. But the conservative backlash in the country made it clear that nothing would progress further until the Supreme Court dealt with the issue. And now they have. Unanimously. Slam dunk. It's over.

At first I thought it unimportant to try for unanimity, did not even think I could arrange it given the various ages and backgrounds of the justices. I planned a modest split decision by picking only the five I thought would respond favorably. But then I became worried that they might not react the way I expected and knew I would have to engage the entire court to assure a majority opinion in favor of the right to die. This must be not just an academic exercise for them, mere legal pontifications of nine uninvolved non-participants, voyeuristically examining the torment of the dying from the lofty safety of their tenured perches. It must be something they experience in their very bowels. They must be made to stand face to empty face, black robe to black cowl with Death itself to know the consequences of their decision and make the right one.

It was relatively easy, really, to arrange. I knew I could not enlist the help of anyone in my circle of friends, though I'm sure they would have been willing to assist. There are literally thousands of us out there with the same experiences with our patients and their families, the same sense of helplessness at the end, the same frustrated anger. It would have been easy to motivate a small group to rally behind the idea, but the chance for discovery or a sudden attack of legal conscience multiplied geometrically with each person I would add. As Ben Franklin said: "Three can keep a secret if two are dead." So I had to do most of it alone, with the help of my computer and my years of privileged and unquestioned access to various hospital departments and systems.

My job was made easier by the court's idiosyncrasies. Though they all had different physicians, they all came for free care to Bethesda Naval for anything other than routine prescriptions, including the annual government physical. The health of each justice was a matter of the utmost privacy. They never socialized privately and never talked of anything so personal as illness or medical conditions. Such information could easily have national political as well as social and legal repercussions, depending on the cases before them that year. I knew that, even if a justice was given three months to live, he or she would continue showing up at the court until death prevented it, without so much as a good-bye to the others along the way. They were all known to be fanatic about their health, even in the midst of ten-dollar cigars and single malt Scotch. They gulped handfuls of vitamins, exercised when convenient, and balanced stress by yelling at subordinates. With the exception of the lone bachelor who lived in a highly secure and manicured condo in Chevy Chase, they all had spouses and gardeners. Even the bachelor had the required government-provided maid.

Through a combination of experience with physicians and net search, I learned which substances would produce the symptoms I wanted. To succeed I had to acquire those substances and get the justices to ingest them. For that I needed help.

Many years ago a well-known senator came to the hospital after his car was riddled with gunfire. The FBI investigation unearthed circumstantial connections with organized crime, though it could never be proven. When he thought he was about to die, the senator—a good Episcopalian—confessed to me his sins in vivid detail.

When he survived he said he either had to trust me or kill me. Now it was my turn to trust him.

With no questions asked—and grateful that he now was privy to one of my sins—he used his underworld connections not only to obtain the chemicals and drugs I needed, but to package and mix them into the usual medications or food ingested by each justice. Servants were either threatened or bribed into providing a direct route to kitchens and medicine bottles. Within weeks symptoms appeared and sent the justices to their physicians—and to Bethesda for tests.

Although they demanded "confidential" status, there is no such thing in a hospital; literally everyone has access to any information on the chart, from the physician's progress notes to test results. It took only a small computerized intervention on my part between the time the lab processed the blood, urine, and tissue samples and the appearance of results on the chart. With a little rearranging, the figures for blood gases, hemoglobin, hematocrit, white and red blood cell counts, and pathology findings for tissue samples were easily made to corroborate symptoms brought on by the substances they were ingesting at home.

One by one, the justices of the U.S. Supreme Court were given death sentences by their physicians.

I actually enjoyed fitting the disease to the person.

Chief Justice Leonard Campion had markers in his blood that indicated metastatic prostate cancer. The eighty-five-year-old man already had trouble peeing. Now he had red urine and pain all over his body.

Forty-seven-year-old bachelor John Holman had a suppressed immune system and nonexistent t-cell count, all consistent with end-stage AIDS. The black constituency he represented would be stunned.

Right-sided intermittent aphasia and total left-sided numbness led Deborah Ellman, the court's first woman, to be diagnosed with a stroke that could extend at any minute and take her life. At fifty-eight, it was consistent with her family history. Her father had died of a stroke at sixty.

An ebullient Felix Murphy, known for running marathons at age seventy-nine, suddenly had attacks of disorientation and dizziness. A switched brain scan at the hospital revealed a slow-moving astrocytoma in the brain that would kill him within a year.

Pancreatic cancer brought the sixty-eight-year-old Jake Neff to tears, according to his physician's notes. Usually killing within three months, his case might take as long as eighteen.

The only Hispanic member of the court, seventy-two-year-old Martin Martinez, ignored the increasing shortness of breath and chest pains he felt walking up the stairs to his palatial home in Fairfax County. Forced by his wife to call his physician, he was furious at the diagnosis of an expand-ing—and inoperable—aortic aneurism that would eventually burst and cause him to exsanguinate.

Lou Gehrig's disease (ALS) would end Leah Michals's career with her brilliant mind mercilessly locked into a flaccid fifty-year-old body as she suffocated to death with useless lungs.

Eighty-one-year-old Carl Fredericks asked the same question to an attorney three times in fifteen minutes, left the courtroom, and went to his doctor. Two days and several painful tests later he was given the sen-tence of advanced Alzheimer's. In a little over a year he would forget who he was.

Post-menopausal bleeding on her sixty-first birthday was Joanne Miller's first indication that something was definitely wrong. The usually energetic black woman became depressed and lethargic when her doctor determined she had ovarian cancer.

Of course I could not guarantee how they would internally deal with their diagnoses, but I did make sure that each disease was in such an advanced stage that little could be done other than symptom alleviation. I also directed an increase in the substances being supplied to them so that the disease would flare just as they thought they were doing better.

My timing was nearly perfect, though I did worry that someone in a moment of weakness would tell another about his or her misfortune. But it never happened. They were consistently stolid politicians to the end, avoiding speculation about their health, which would have led to the president nudging the court in his direction once more before leaving office. If the word had gotten out that the president could appoint the *entire* court, political havoc would have reigned. But it didn't.

In fact, fortune smiled on my plan, expediting it considerably in the form of the two federal district court decisions striking down anti–assisted suicide laws. With such a heady issue facing an interested nation, the Supreme Court would be urged to offer an opinion this session.

I upped the ante by ignoring the No Visitors sign when any of them came to Bethesda for tests or treatment. It is hard to be discourteous to a collar, and I always promised not to stay long. By offering a listening ear—and a confidential one—I proved a benign source of companionship they could find nowhere else. I never acknowledged their illness, but talked generally about "people" with terminal diseases and the issues facing them.

What did they think about pain? Was there some pain they were unwilling to endure? How was suffering different from pain? What of the suffering Alzheimer's patient who no longer knows who he or his wife is? Or the ALS patient who gradually watches her body deteriorate, lose function, lose control until she is a mass on the bed to be moved and toileted? And if we have an ethical obligation to quell pain—which we can do with our incredible pharmacology—then do we have an ethical obligation to quell suffering? Or should we make humans suffer and prolong their existence so they can deteriorate "naturally," unlike our more benevolent attitude toward cats and horses and dogs? What if the pain or the suffering was intractable, unable to be relieved or affected? If it forced patients to exist at an unacceptable quality of life, should they have a right and the legal means either to obtain the necessary substances to end their lives or to designate another to do so once they lost the capacity to do it themselves?

Sometimes I wondered if they knew what I was doing. Always I left with a smile and a promise to return on their next admission, if there was one. Always they seemed pleased I had visited, appreciative of the reasoned consideration of their mortality. But underneath our intellectualizing, I could see their emotions surface as they faced the knowledge they would die extended, debilitating, sometimes disfiguring deaths. I obliquely implied that more prominent people experience more complex, painful, and expensive medical intervention than the average American.

During the months they checked in and out of the hospital they became increasingly outraged, not only at the futility of such treatment and the resulting wasted allocation of care, but at the coercive nature of the system that demands it. Riding roughshod over individual liberty rights and the pursuit of happiness, the system demands patients stay existing, not alive, until the last ounce of medical intervention has been exhausted. Eventually each justice came to see there are things worse than death, conditions of life that are intolerable, suffering that is only able to be relieved by death.

So I was not surprised by the decision of the court today that citizens with terminal conditions have a right to die when, where, and how they choose. I was surprised it was unanimous, pleasantly surprised because it will send such a strong message to those who would prolong suffering and dying. It is interesting to me that those who shout the loudest to impose their values on the ill are never ill themselves.

But the entire court thought they were ill, and facing that possibility steered them in the direction of siding with those who are too weak to take their lives back into their own hands.

I am archiving this document so it will send itself via email to the *Washington Post* and the *New York Times* exactly ten years from today. By then the country will have seen the long-term result of this ruling and the boon it has been to those who are waiting to die but wish to wait no longer.

Starting tomorrow the symptom-causing substances will be discontinued. Starting tomorrow the justices will miraculously begin to go into remission and their test results return to normal. Starting tomorrow the patients and families I deal with will have another door opened to them when all others have closed—the door to a welcome, hastened, assisted death with peace, comfort, and whatever remaining dignity can be found.

My last task is to program this summary into the memory of the system and punch "Enter" twice.

Oh, my God. This cannot have happened. They must have installed a new program I did not know about. It automatically date-corrects before saving. It "corrected" the year from ten years hence to now—and sent it. The whole plan to coerce the court will be revealed tomorrow.

As will my *own* terminal illness. But thanks to them I will be gone.

✝

Cemetery of the Innocents

Stephen Dentinger

In the days of François Villon's youth, shortly before his banishment from Paris in 1456, the poet could often be found near the Cemetery of the Innocents. It was not only the city's most desirable burial place but also a popular meeting spot for both bourgeois and street people. Located off the Rue St. Denis, a few miles north of Notre Dame Cathedral, it boasted shops of every sort that had sprung up around the Holy Innocents cloister. Villon marveled at the way prostitutes and alchemists seemed to work side by side. He moved among them freely but was always on his guard. As did most young men, he wore a dagger on the belt of his tunic.

Dogs wandered among the crowds, ready to yelp if kicked or stepped on, and Villon tried to incorporate the rhythm of their whines into his poems written in the slang of the underworld. The dogs and the dance, those were two of his favorite topics. All around him, on the walls of the cemetery cloister and in the adjoining Church of the Holy Innocents, were depictions of the danse macabre, with skeletons risen from the graves to tempt the living into joining the dance that would bring them finally to death. There were verses of a long poem too, sometimes read aloud by the Parisians who came daily to tour the place.

On this afternoon in early June, among the usual crowds that had come to view the charnel houses, Villon was attracted by a comely young woman of perhaps twenty who stood in awe of the mural's dancing grotesques. He took her to be a prostitute newly arrived in Paris from the provinces and fearful of the wandering dogs. "Fair maiden," he said on approaching her, "let me take you to my rooms, away from these snarling beasts."

She turned, startled at the sound of a male voice so close to her. "It is not the dogs that I fear but this terrible depiction of the dancing dead. What meaning does it hold?"

"I am told it was painted here a generation ago in response to the great sufferings from warfare and the recurring Black Death. It is merely a reminder of the fate that awaits us all. You will see dancers almost daily, depicting these scenes for the populace."

"And these bones? This skull?"

It was true that growing piles of skulls and bones had collected under the cloister arches. Even as they watched, a grizzled gravedigger was adding to the nearest pile, pausing only to shake some of the dirt free from the bones. "There are forty-eight arches in the cloister surrounding the cemetery proper," he explained, "each of them donated by wealthy bourgeois and nobles who expect to be interred here. The problem is that twenty parishes have the right of burial as well, and the old dead must be constantly disinterred to make room for the newly departed. The bones are piled here, and their tombstones sold to others."

"How awful!"

"It matters not to the dead. I have not seen you before. What is your name?" he asked, anxious to shift the conversation to a more personal basis.

"I am Isabeau, newly arrived from the south. I seek employment here in one of these shops."

"A woman of your beauty can earn more than they will pay," Villon told her, but before he could continue Friar Giles interrupted.

The cloister priest was a large man, with muscles powerful enough to handle any troublemakers who might wander into the area. He sometimes counted Villon among them. "Do you have any business with this man?" he asked Isabeau, perhaps taken with the freshness of her skin. He must have guessed she had not been long in Paris.

She shrugged. "He has simply befriended me."

"Francois Villon befriends no one without a reason. Tell me, Villon, were you about to rob the lady of that purse she wears on her belt?"

"I am a poet, not a cutpurse," he answered. "Rather I would compose a sonnet to her beauty."

"You have been warned," the friar told Isabeau, whose hand had gone instinctively to her purse. "Do not be deceived by the promises of a brigand." He turned back toward the cloister. "I must go now to give my afternoon sermon. It is nearly time for the Dead One."

They watched him mount the small balcony that served as a pulpit. "What did he mean?" the young woman asked Villon. "Who is this 'Dead One'?"

"You will see soon enough. Do not be frightened."

Friar Giles launched into a dour sermon on the wages of sin, and within ten minutes he was interrupted by the blowing of a horn from the Rue St. Denis. Isabeau gasped and gripped Villon's arm as a robed figure with a death's head for a face led a procession of awful dancers into the cemetery grounds. He blew on his horn again, then stuck it through the cord of his robe. Some of his followers were grotesques and beggars, others were common people likely atoning for their sins. They danced in a maddening display that verged on the obscene, often attempting to drag others with them. Villon struck out at one wrinkled crone who fastened a withered hand on Isabeau's wrist.

"Take me away from here!" the young woman begged, almost in tears. For others in the crowd of spectators, though, the scene was one of some merriment. They laughed and even threw pieces of ripe fruit at the dancers, perhaps attempting to ward off death.

Villon placed a protective arm around Isabeau's trembling shoulders and guided her out of the Cemetery of the Innocents, finding refuge in a tavern in the next block of shops.

"There is nothing to be frightened of," Villon assured her.

"Nothing but death!"

"You are too young to harbor such fears. Tell me, do you have a place to stay this night?"

"I left my few possessions at a nearby bake shop. The woman said I could stay with her for one night."

"Come to my rooms instead," he urged. "I promise you safety."

She wiped the beginning of tears from her eyes and nodded in assent. "You are a good man, Villon. I will trust you."

He smiled. "Even after what the friar told you?"

"Yes."

They picked up the cloth bags with her few possessions at the bakery and Villon bought a loaf of bread. Then he led the way to the place where he was staying, a two-story house much like its neighbors. They passed a blind fiddler playing in the street and Isabeau paused to give him a coin, but Villon urged her on. "The man is no more blind than you or I. When he collects enough coins he will squander them at the tavern."

"How do you know that?"

"I have squandered my coins with him on more than one occasion. Come, when we have eaten I will take you to meet my neighbor, the alchemist."

"Bernard claims he was a count back in Venice," Villon explained as they walked across the road to his room. "He must be close to fifty years old now and still trying to turn base metals into gold."

"Is he one of those with a shop near the cemetery?" she asked.

"Sometimes." He pounded on his neighbor's door and presently a wiry man with a wisp of a beard opened it. "Good Bernard, Count Bernard, I must introduce you to Isabeau, newly arrived in the city. I met her today at the Cemetery of the Innocents, where she was frightened by the death dancers."

"And no wonder!" Bernard said with a smile. "They are enough to frighten anyone. But come and meet Friar Philippe, a new friend."

The city seemed filled with priests these days, but Villon was gracious as he shook the friar's hand. Philippe was a slender man with a clerical tonsure and a monastic manner. He explained that he was presently a disaffected mendicant monk seeking a new position. "Are you at the chapter school of Notre Dame?" the friar asked.

"I have completed my education," Villon replied.

"No man ever does, in this world."

Bernard laughed, perhaps to lighten the tenor of the conversation. "We are not all as wise as you, Friar Philippe. The priests of Rome are a special breed."

The tonsured cleric turned his attention to Isabeau. "And who might this be?"

"Fair Isabeau," Villon said, "newly arrived here from the provinces. She may enter a nunnery." She shot him a startled glance that he ignored. "But tell me how the experiments go, Bernard. Are you any closer to your golden dream?"

The wiry alchemist shrugged, gesturing toward a pile of papers covered with arcane formulas. "It is not something to be achieved in a single lifetime, however much I might desire it. Friar Philippe says I must open myself to the Lord and accept the certainty of death."

The priest nodded. "Perhaps in a new life all will be easier."

Villon could see that Isabeau was hardly enjoying this talk of death. After a bit more discussion of turning base metals into gold he cut short the conversation so they could return to his rooms.

"What people are these?" she asked when they were back across the road. "All this talk of death and gold! Is this what Paris has become?"

"Sometimes. But there are pleasures too."

Isabeau stayed the night with him and the following day they strolled in the bright sunshine as he showed her around some of the shops in the neighborhood of the cemetery. She was gaining confidence with all that she saw, no longer frightened by the beggars and cripples who seemed to be everywhere. One legless man offered carvings made from bones, and Villon imagined the artist scouring the bone piles after dark in search of just the right sizes.

Isabeau was taken with some of the women she saw on the streets, and she poked him to ask, "Is that one a prostitute?"

Villon chuckled. "Her name is Esmeralda. She comes here from Spain, as do many of the girls. Come! I will introduce you!"

Esmeralda was a young, black-haired beauty with a gold tooth that glistened when she smiled. She wore hoop earrings like a gypsy and perhaps that was her true identity. She eyed Isabeau up and down like the competition and said, "You are very pretty. Are you on the street?"

"I—no, I'm not," Isabeau answered a bit uncertainly. "I hope to work in one of the shops."

Esmeralda shook her head in disapproval. "I worked in one at first too. The man who hired me expected my favors to be given free. I told him I could make more on the street."

"I'll be careful," Isabeau replied.

Friar Giles had been conducting a tour of the cemetery and now he came over to them. "Esmeralda, if you are on cemetery property I assume you have come to pray over our latest unfortunates and not to conduct your business."

She bent to pick up a dirt-encrusted skull from a nearby pile of bones. "I come to collect the unfortunates and give them a better home than this."

"Where are you taking that skull?" he demanded. "Put it down!" When she refused, he reached out and grabbed it away from her. "The danse macabre will be starting soon. Your soul would be better served if you were to join in their procession and contemplate the fate that awaits you."

"It is a dancing mania like those in other countries," she said, spitting out the words, challenging the priest to his face. "The dancers are no more than our flagellants back home in Spain, wandering the countryside as they scourge themselves with whips. And your church encourages such things!"

They heard the Dead One blowing his horn then, signaling the dancers' entrance from the Rue St. Denis. The hooded figure led the procession as before, mimicking the bizarre parade depicted in the murals of the Holy Innocents Church. There were perhaps ten people in line, each holding tight to the hand of the person before and behind, forming an unbreakable chain. Villon was startled to recognize the alchemist Bernard at the end of the line being pulled forward in this mad dance, and as the dancers passed near them, Bernard reached out his free hand to grasp Esmeralda's. She went with him willingly, but with a smirk on her face, and in turn grabbed the hand of one of the street beggars who frequented the area. The chain of the dance doubled in length even as Villon watched. It twisted in upon itself, led by the skull-faced man, and some of those joining now, like Esmeralda, seemed to regard the whole thing as a joke on death or the clergy or both.

As the dance grew wilder, spectators retreated, fearful of being added to the line. Villon heard the sounds of a lute in the background, coupled with the eternal yelping of the dogs and the rhythm of these awful dancers. The line twisted upon itself once more like a serpent in the sun, and then the hooded figure of death led them into the cemetery itself. Villon saw his neighbor Bernard lurch forward and seem to stumble. Suddenly Esmeralda screamed and let go of his hand.

Villon saw the blood soaking through Bernard's tunic and ran to him, but it was already too late. Bernard was dead.

While Esmeralda knelt by Bernard's body, the others in line had quickly linked hands, closing the gap. Either not knowing or caring what had happened, the danse macabre continued on its way.

"He is dead," Esmeralda said, cradling the alchemist's head in her hands.

"Yes," Villon confirmed.

"It is almost as if they knew it, as if the dance itself was too much for his heart."

"It was a blade that was too much for his heart. He was stabbed in the chest with some weapon." Villon uncovered the bloodied tunic to show her the wound.

"Do you mean someone killed him?" Isabeau asked as if unable to grasp the idea.

Friar Giles had arrived to kneel and administer the last rites to the victim. When he finished, he stood up and asked, "Did anyone see who did this?"

Esmeralda shook her head. "I was right next to him, holding his hand, and I saw nothing. The people were afraid to come near us."

"And yet there is no weapon in the wound," the priest murmured. "What do you make of this, Villon? You are privy to the techniques of the street ruffian. Is there any weapon that could have killed him from a distance and then disappeared?"

"None that I know of," he answered. "But I am neither a ruffian nor their confidant. For all I know he might have been killed by an arrow of ice that melted at once."

"There would have been traces of such a weapon," Friar Giles argued, accepting the suggestion as serious. "And he could not have killed himself since his hands were held by the dancers on either side. It is a puzzle, enough to make one summon up the supernatural."

"Did you know Bernard?" Villon asked the Spanish girl.

"Everyone knew the alchemist," she replied. "He changed copper into gold for me. I still have the coin."

"Bernard did that? Show me!" he challenged.

Esmeralda reached into the little purse on her belt and produced a gold florin such as Villon had never seen. "He asked for a copper coin and the following day he returned it like this."

"Let me keep this for a time. I will return it to you later." Villon slipped the coin into his pocket.

Friar Giles had watched all this with some interest. "I know the man as an alchemist and a fraud. I cannot allow his burial in consecrated ground."

That did not set well with Esmeralda. "Who would you allow in your Cemetery of the Innocents, Friar? Those fools who parade through the streets in death masks? Our ruler Charles, crowned by Jeanne d'Arc, whom he repaid by allowing her execution?"

"She was burned by the British for heresy."

"But Charles did nothing to save her."

The muscular priest gave a sigh. "Even now he is moving to right that wrong. We expect she will be rehabilitated by year's end."

"Then it is too bad she has been dead for twenty-four years."

"Mistakes are made," the friar admitted. "I will not make another by allowing the alchemist to be buried here." He turned and walked away.

Later, while Isabeau prepared a light supper in Villon's rooms, he examined the florin Esmeralda had given him. A single scratch with his dagger across the fleur-de-lis on the back of the coin quickly revealed what he had suspected. The gold coating was merely painted on. The coin had not really been turned to gold at all.

He told Isabeau of his finding but she merely shrugged. "The alchemists are charlatans, as everyone knows. I have learned that much from you in just a few days' time."

"Friar Giles knows it, but Esmeralda does not. She attributed some sort of real power to Bernard." He wondered if someone's belief in Bernard's power might have led to his death. Later, while Isabeau slept, he crossed the road to the alchemist's rooms. Entering easily with the aid of his dagger in the simple lock, he planned to search the room by candlelight. But he saw at once that someone had arrived before him with the same idea. The place had been ransacked, and Bernard's meager belongings were heaped in the center of the floor. It was impossible to tell what, if anything, had been taken.

On the morning of the alchemist's funeral some said the rising sun turned the sky to gold. Perhaps that was as close as he would come to his dream. The funeral had been intended as a small affair, held on the grounds of a non-denominational cemetery a mile or so from the Innocents.

There were no priests in attendance, not Friar Giles or even Friar Philippe. But the denizens of the area had turned out to honor one of their own. There were jesters and jugglers, painters and poets and prostitutes, street performers of every sort, and the eternal dogs had followed along with their mournful howling. But somehow the time of sorrow soon became one of celebration. Esmeralda was there as well, and at one point she climbed atop a tombstone to lead them in singing a hymn, one of joy and hope. Then she led them on a procession of her own, in mockery of the dance of death they had become so accustomed to seeing.

The city authorities had little interest in Bernard's death; no one had even come 'round to investigate. That did not bother Villon, who had no use for organized government. When the funeral ended and the plain pine coffin was left in the care of the gravediggers, Villon and Isabeau walked through the dirty streets back toward his rooms. "Where did Esmeralda go?" Isabeau asked, glancing about for the young Spanish girl.

"With her friends, the street people."

"Could she be the one who searched Bernard's room, seeking more gold like the coin he gave her?"

"Anything is possible." A stray dog scampered at his heels and without thinking he kicked it away.

"Do you do that to people too?" she asked.

"Do what?"

"Kick them when they tag along behind you."

He laughed and reached out to grab her. "This city is no place for you, dear Isabeau. Perhaps it is no place for me, either. Its ways are too rough, and too soon they become our ways as well."

"Then let us go back to the countryside. You can write your poems anywhere."

"There is one matter I must clear up first. Bernard's death."

"The alchemist? He meant nothing to you."

"But the way in which he died did. He was struck down during the danse macabre, as if the Lord himself had hurled a thunderbolt at his chest."

"Do you believe that is what happened?" she asked.

"No. The Lord of the Old Testament might have hurled thunderbolts but not the Lord of Friar Giles."

"What of the Lord of the danse macabre?" For there ahead of them on the Rue St. Denis were the dancers led by the personification of Death itself, returned to claim more victims.

Villon watched them, a solid line of penitents in an unbroken chain, and as they moved closer he knew what he must do. "Stay here," he told Isabeau. "Do not move, whatever happens."

He walked forward, straight toward the line of dancing figures. The hooded leader with the skull for a face had to have seen him coming, but he still pulled the dancers forward. Villon dropped a hand to his dagger.

Once he was facing Death head to head, he said to the masked man, "I come in vengeance. I come for the killer of Bernard the alchemist."

And Death reached out his hand.

Villon saw the dagger coming from the hooded man's sleeve, but he was an instant faster and thrust quickly to find his mark. The skull-faced man let out a sigh as he dropped his weapon and slowly collapsed in the road.

✝

When they removed the mask, revealing the face of Friar Philippe, Villon sent someone running for Friar Giles to administer the last rites. The priest came and shook his head sadly as he knelt by the dying man to hear his confession.

Later he told Villon, "You have killed a priest. It is a serious offense."

"It was he who murdered the alchemist Bernard. You heard his confession yourself. I struck out at him in self-defense."

"What he confessed can go no further. There is no way that I could repeat it to the authorities."

"He came at me with his dagger."

"According to witnesses, you accused him of killing the alchemist."

"I did. I believe he killed him then ransacked the man's rooms, hoping to find some hidden gold, of which there was none."

"What made you so sure of his guilt?" the priest asked.

"The line of dancers always clasped hands. It was an unbroken chain, which meant that only the leader and the last person in line had a free hand. Yet no one else ventured close to the dancers, not after they grew so wild. The last dancer in line was too far away to have stabbed Bernard, but we saw the skull-faced leader twist the line in upon itself at least twice, once just before Bernard stumbled and went down from his wound. Only the leader could have stabbed him. The face of Death was just that for the alchemist."

"But why kill him? Just on the chance of finding gold?"

"Philippe visited him recently, perhaps more than once. I think Bernard convinced him it was there, that he could create it. And that proved to be his downfall."

The friar shook his head sadly. "Even though Philippe was disaffected from his order he was still a priest. By killing him, even in a fight, you have committed a grave offense."

Villon nodded. "Perhaps I should think about leaving the city for a time, before I am banished."

"You are a creature of Paris, Villon. You will never leave it for long."

Within a week, the danse macabre had returned to the Cemetery of the Innocents. From somewhere, perhaps a grave, a new leader had arisen to summon the dancers. But by that time Francois Villon and Isabeau had found a measure of temporary peace in the countryside.

✝

Veronica's Veil

Monica Quill

I

When Kim got out of the VW bug and walked toward the entrance of Elm Grove Care Center, she tried to put a spring in her step but could not. These weekly visits to the aging woman who had been Sister Veronica were the hardest task Emtee Dempsey had ever given her.

"She is still one of us, Sister Kimberly. Our sister in religion. And we are all she has."

A repressed groan had come from the hallway when the old nun said this, and then there was the sound of Joyce returning to her kitchen. Sister Veronica had been mistress of novices when Joyce and Kim joined the Order of Martha and Mary—the M & M's. From her they had learned the rudiments of the religious life, an ideal that seemed to be almost perfectly realized in Sister Veronica. Of course it had been Emtee Dempsey who had first stirred in Kim the idea of joining the order. Not that she had ever suggested it. She was anything but a recruiting sergeant for the convent. But she was what she was and Kim had been struck by an admiration and awe she still felt for the old nun. Emtee Dempsey represented a life dedicated to the spirit but one that included the life of the mind as well. By contrast, Sister Veronica's vision of the life that lay before them if they survived the novitiate was ethereal. A life of prayer and abnegation, turning one's back entirely on the lure of the world. Twenty years younger than Emtee Dempsey, Veronica became lyrical and there were tears in her eyes when she spoke of the joys of kneeling in silent adoration before the tabernacle. Sister Veronica had been one of the first to go over the wall when the years of madness struck the order.

Vatican II meant different things to different people. For most of the members of the Order of Martha and Mary the mandate to update and renew the spirit of their founder, the Blessed Abigail Keineswegs, making it appropriate to modern times, had suggested a 180-degree turn. Soon their ranks were thinned, the college the order had run west of Chicago was sold, along with most of the other property, the proceeds distributed, and the exodus was all but complete. Thanks to the efforts of Benjamin Rush, an attorney and trustee of the college, the house on Walden Street in Chicago and the lake place in Indiana were saved. Emtee Dempsey, Joyce, and Kim had moved into the house, a lovely structure designed by Frank Lloyd Wright, a gift of an alumna to be held in perpetuity by the M & M's. A once flourishing order had been reduced to three members.

None of their former sisters in religion had visited the house on Walden Street, although a steady stream of alumnae came to their door to see the ferocious professor of history whom the passage of years invested with nostalgic magnetism. Sister Veronica had never visited. They knew nothing of her until the call had come a month before from Elm Grove.

"Sister Veronica is with us," a fruity voice said. When Kim understood the significance of the call, she passed it to Emtee Dempsey.

Without hesitation, the old nun accepted the claim on them that the former Sister Veronica now made. Nor had Mr. Rush balked when they were asked to take over the expense of the former nun's stay at Elm Grove. Emtee Dempsey visited Veronica, who had dissolved into tears and wailed about the dreadful mistake she had made. Thus the weekly visits had devolved upon Kim.

"Did she cry?" Emtee Dempsey would ask warily when Kim returned.

"Not much."

"The gift of tears," Joyce mumbled. A phrase from the novitiate. Sister Veronica had cried before the tabernacle during her devotions and considered it a special grace.

"Are you alone?" Veronica asked when Kim came into her room. She moved her head on the pillow in order to see around Kim. The former nun apparently had just given up, declared herself ill and threatened by dementia and other ills she had read about in the *Merck Manual*. She checked in at Elm Grove and told them to call Walden Street.

"How are we today?"

Kim winced as she said it. Why did one fall into condescending baby talk with the ailing?

"Every day is the same." Her lower lip trembled.

Kim went to the bedside table and moved the stack of books to its center. They did not seem to have been touched during the intervening week. It was impossible not to feel the boredom of Veronica's life or to ignore the haunted looks of the other inmates who looked out of their rooms from the ashes of hope whenever anyone passed.

"Did you ask Sister Mary Teresa? Oh, I wish she would come."

"Why don't we go for a spin?"

This entailed getting Veronica into her wheelchair, no easy task. Inaction had made her gain weight, and she was unable to help in the transfer from bed to chair. And then they were off, down the hallway toward the nurses' station, past the large room where several old people slept open-mouthed in front of the television. There were tables there where meals were served. The itinerary was the same, up and down identical corridors in the other wings and then, before pushing Veronica outside into the sunlight, a stop at the little chapel, where Veronica's weeping seemed self-pity rather than the gift of tears. Finally, they were out on the patio, where Kim pushed the chair next to a bench and sat.

"Isn't it a lovely day?"

"Why doesn't Sister Mary Teresa come see me?"

"Veronica, you know how old she is."

"I heard she is as active as ever."

Apparently Veronica had kept tabs on her old order. It seemed impossible that this collapsed old woman with milky eyes and brushed thin hair was decades younger than the vigorous old nun who seemed never to age.

"Mr. Rush has spoken with the cardinal."

"There is more joy in heaven over the sheep that was lost . . ." But sobbing interrupted the reference.

It was a beautiful late April day, the sun bright, the smell of early flowers, the twitter of birds. But what difference did the weather make to the old people spending their last days in Elm Grove?

"I want to be buried in the habit," Veronica said pathetically.

"Everything will work out."

The door pushed open and a nurse's aid came blinking into the sunlight, pulling a cigarette from a pack. She hunched over it while she lit it, sheltering the match from an imaginary wind. She inhaled deeply and then smiled at Kim while smoke escaped between her teeth.

"What a day!"

"Come sit in the sun."

Her name was Penelope and her cross was Mrs. D'Antonio, a very old woman whom age had not mellowed. Mrs. D'Antonio was the terror of Elm Grove; she spoke with a bark and complained about everything. She had retained the idea that there was something important she should be doing, but she could not remember what it was.

Penelope collapsed on the other end of the bench, ignoring Veronica, holding one elbow so her cigarette was inches before her face, for easier access.

"And how is Mrs. D'Antonio?"

"Don't ask."

"Does she ever have visitors?"

"Never."

"You should take turns with her."

"Tell it to Alice."

Alice was the head nurse of the section in which Veronica and Mrs. D'Antonio had their rooms.

"She must have family. How else could she afford being here?"

"She's a ward of the state."

Penelope tried unsuccessfully to get contempt into her voice. Even at Elm Grove there were social stratifications, and being a state ward put one at the bottom of the ladder.

"I used to love this job," Penelope said with feeling. "Now I would willingly take a job at McDonald's."

"Mrs. D'Antonio was sleeping when we went past her room."

"Drugged." Penelope added, "Doctor's orders. Everyone is on something, to make the time pass."

"What a good person you are," Kim said with sudden feeling.

Penelope looked at her sharply, perhaps suspecting sarcasm, but Kim meant it. Whatever Penelope's complaints, she stayed with the job, coming day after day, and her treatment of Mrs. D'Antonio did not betray her feelings toward the old terror. No wonder she had been assigned to Mrs. D'Antonio. No one else had her calm firmness with the old woman.

"It's a job."

"If it were only a job, you'd be at McDonald's."

Penelope threw her cigarette onto the lawn and laid a hand briefly on Kim's arm. "You've discovered my secret. The thing is, she reminds me of my mother."

The door opened and Alice called to Penelope. "It's worn off."

Penelope was on her feet and heading for the door without hesitation. Watching her disappear inside, Kim said to Veronica, "What wonderful help they have here."

In the doorway, Penelope looked back at Kim. "Maybe I'll bring her outside." She paused. "That way I can have another smoke." And she disappeared to the hissing closing of the door.

2

That night Katherine Senski came to dinner at the house on Walden Street, dressed flamboyantly, as usual. Compared with Benjamin Rush, a study in chiaroscuro—black suit, snow white shirt and hair, silver tie— Katherine looked almost tropical. If her plumage was meant to interest the elderly lawyer, her cause was hopeless. She held her glass of sherry at arm's length, as if about to take the pledge, then brought it toward her lips, stopping halfway.

"Did you say D'Antonio?" She might have been looking at Kim over the rim of her glass.

"Mrs. D'Antonio." Kim closed her eyes. "I know the first name but I can't think of it. Not that it matters. She is the terror of Elm Grove."

Katherine cried out. "I would rather be placed on an ice floe and pushed into the Arctic Ocean than live in such a place as that."

"It has an excellent reputation, Katherine," Benjamin Rush said, almost defensively. After all, he had arranged for the order to underwrite Veronica's expenses at Elm Grove.

"Why does the name D'Antonio ring a bell?"

Sister Mary Teresa, seated in her brocade chair in the living room, had been following rather than directing the conversation, but now she intervened.

"The armored car robbery in Rockford. D'Antonio was the only one arrested."

"He confessed," Katherine remembered.

"But would not reveal the names of his fellow thieves, nor where the money was."

"It was millions!"

"An interesting case, legally," Benjamin Rush said. "The evidence was all circumstantial. The guards, of course, had been murdered."

"Did D'Antonio confess to that?"

"There was no need to. If an accomplice murders in the course of the crime, all are held responsible for it."

"I wondered at the time whether his supposed gang was real or imaginary. What if he had done the deed all by himself."

"Katherine, that would have required bilocation if not ubiquity."

Katherine leaned forward, an expectant look on her face. "Go on. I love to have my vocabulary enriched."

"He would have had to be in three places at the same time," Emtee Dempsey said. "Which word caused you difficulty?"

"I think I doped out the meaning of *bilocation*."

"The Latin word for where or whereabouts is *ubi*. An adverb. It is made a substantive by adding *-itas*. The *q* is added for phonetic purposes. Its meaning makes it synonymous with *omnipresence*."

"Are you taking notes, Sister Kimberly?" Katherine asked. "First my brain is fuddled by this marvelous sherry and then I am made a school girl again, receiving a Latin lesson."

"We were talking about William D'Antonio, the bank robber," Benjamin Rush reminded them. Kim sometimes thought that the two old women performed for the equally aged lawyer. But his call to order got them back on track.

Kim would verify the account of the Rockford robbery the next day, checking the files of the *Tribune*, downloading the coverage in national magazines and far-off papers. Ten years before, an armored car, having made stops at all the major banks of Rockford, Illinois, just west of the city of Chicago, came up the ramp of the interstate to begin its homeward journey. The ramp was blocked by a highway crew, doing temporary repairs. Vehicles were let through one at a time. This had been the testimony of two truckers who had preceded the armored car. The driver, apparently lulled into credulity by the ordinariness of the repair site, entered into conversation with the maintenance worker who was directing him through the narrow passageway to the interstate. He had been shot once, literally between the eyes. Simultaneously, a cloud of gas had been released into the armored car. The driver's companion was shot four times. There were two bullets missing from his gun, but he must have fired as he fell backward, since the bullets both hit the ceiling of the cab. The bogus repair crew then scrambled aboard the armored car and drove away. The bodies of the guards where found thrown into the brush behind an oasis parking area. The armored car itself was eventually recovered from the Fox River.

It was months afterward that William D'Antonio confessed to the crime. Voluntarily. The investigation had then reached an impasse. Kim's brother Richard, Detective Lieutenant in the Chicago police, provided them with an update on the prisoner William D'Antonio.

"How could a confession of guilt make sense without revealing where the money is?"

Richard smiled as if others too had considered and then rejected this difficulty. But Emtee Dempsey was perfectly prepared to be docile and play to Richard's male pride if she could get information out of him. Kim could have wrung her brother's neck for being so smug.

"The general view is that there was a falling out of the thieves and that D'Antonio confessed because he wanted the safety of prison." Richard laughed. "He is almost as vulnerable in prison as he would be on the street. He was viciously stabbed once and has been beaten several times. His age makes that twice as bad."

"How old is he?"

"He will be eighty on his next birthday. If he makes it."

"No one has a guarantee of reaching his next birthday, Richard."

"Maybe not. But not many people need the special protection D'Antonio gets in Joliet."

"Richard," Katherine said. "Did you say he will be eighty?"

"That's right."

"Then he must have been pushing seventy when he engaged in this robbery."

"The theory is that the younger people cut him out after the job was done."

"Why would they work with such an old man in the first place?"

"D'Antonio had the knowledge. He had been a bank guard ever since getting out of the army and knew the routine of the armored car pickups to the minute. Recognizing his face might have been what led the driver to feel at ease when he was stopped."

"And once his usefulness was done, he could be disposed of?"

"That's right." Richard was every bit as condescending to Katherine as he was to Emtee Dempsey.

"Why the attacks in prison?" Emtee Dempsey asked.

"What do you mean?"

"How long is his sentence?"

"It might as well be life. He will never outlive it."

"So what danger does he pose?"

"Sister," Richard said after a moment, "you have to understand the criminal mind."

"No doubt, no doubt. But I am having as much difficulty understanding the police mind. On your theory, D'Antonio's former associates have nothing to fear from him. Yet you say attempts on his life have been made."

"I don't think they tried to kill him."

"I should think not!"

Katherine said, "All right. Out with it. What do you think, Sister Mary Teresa?"

"What anyone would think. That D'Antonio betrayed his associates, that he gave himself up to get out of their reach, and that he knows something they don't know."

"What?" Richard asked.

"Where the missing millions are."

Richard laughed. "If he is the only one who knows where that money is, it sure won't do him any good. The only way he will leave Joliet is in a box."

Sister Mary Teresa nodded. "That is a complication of course."

3

The turnover at nursing homes was a plague that had not spared Elm Grove, at least at the lowest rung of the ladder. When Penelope first noticed Harry, her breath caught because he was so handsome, even pushing along his bucket with one foot while the graceful sweep of his mop went on, but she warned herself to think of him as a visitor. Harry looked so out of place in his janitorial role that she was sure he would not be at Elm Grove long. But that had been a month ago and he was still on the job, always ready with a smile for her.

"You do that as if you enjoy it."

"It's the rhythm that does it. I learned that in the navy."

"A swabbie?"

"You got it."

Harry seemed to time his own breaks to coincide with hers, and they often found themselves enjoying a cigarette together on the patio.

"You been here long?"

"Long enough."

"Nice place."

"I like it."

Exchanges like that, nothing much, but Penelope became sure that he was interested in her. And he commiserated with her about Mrs. D'Antonio.

"Who knows what I'll be like when I'm her age," Penelope said.

"About a century from now."

Harry was more or less her age, she guessed.

"Janitors don't stay here long."

He made a face then smiled, wrinkles forming at the corners of his eyes. His work clothes were immaculate and somehow he managed to make them seem something other than a uniform. The collar of his shirt was turned up and he wore it open, the top three buttons unused. Penelope took her eyes away from the hair on his chest.

"In the navy I was a medic."

"You should be an aid here."

"Maybe I'll get promoted."

From the open door of her room came the barking discontent of Mrs. D'Antonio.

"She ever happy?"

Penelope smiled. "When she's asleep."

That night he called.

"How did you know my number?"

"You're in the book."

"So how did you know my name?" Identification at Elm Grove used only first names.

"I asked."

Penelope had dashed from the shower to get the phone and now stood wrapped in a towel and shivering as she spoke, but she could not keep the smile from spreading across her face.

"I suppose it's too late to ask you out."

"Tonight?"

"So how about tomorrow night?"

She had been ready to say yes to tonight, but in a way this was better. More time to look forward to it would be best.

"Tomorrow night? Sure."

"Want to just go from work?"

"I'd rather come home first."

He read her address to her. "Is that it?"

She hung up and drifted back to the bathroom where she wiped steam from the mirror and looked at herself. Her hair was soaked, her contacts were out, but the reflection was of a young woman much happier than she had been when she ran to answer the phone.

At Elm Grove the next day, he gave her a little conspiratorial smile, and that was all. It was enough. Penelope's white gym shoes might have been double-soled as she went about her task. She was standing by Mrs. D'Antonio's bed when he looked in and gave her a high five.

"She asleep?"

Penelope held up the little paper cup which had held the medication that explained Mrs. D'Antonio's repose.

"You bowl?"

"I'm no good at it."

"I'll coach you."

She hurried out to her car a minute before her shift was done and got home in good time, despite the afternoon traffic. She closed the door of her apartment and looked around. What would it look like to a stranger? She'd had few visitors during the year she had been in the apartment. And no dates. She ran to her bedroom.

Six-thirty came but no Harry. The bell did not ring until a quarter to seven, and those fifteen minutes were agonizing for Penelope. But then there he was.

"Traffic," he explained. "Ready?"

He was in jacket and Levis, maybe the same shoes he wore at work. So she had guessed right about what to wear.

"Nice place."

"I like it."

"So let's go bowling."

How long had it been since she was in a bowling alley? The clatter of pins, the sudden shouts and groans, the great echoing arch of the ceiling, the rumble of balls down the varnished lanes—it all seemed familiar. Bowling alleys must be all alike.

Harry had called and reserved a lane. He insisted she go first and when she paused, adjusting her fingers in the heavy ball, Penelope felt awkward. She started to move, praying she did not trip or get a gutter ball or make a fool of herself. But her ball rolled slowly down the lane, too slowly, she half feared it wouldn't even get to the pins. But then it curled to the left and there was a clatter. Only two pins were left standing. She got only one of those and Harry was entering her nine on the sheet.

"Good beginning."

His first roll was a strike. All the grace he showed with mop and pail were now put to the task of zinging the ball toward the ten pin and sending it and its companions flying. Her score crept over one hundred, but Harry's was more than twice that.

"You didn't tell me you were a pro."

"I bowled a lot in the navy."

"On shipboard?"

He laughed. "There I was bowlegged. No. San Diego. Ever been there?"

California might have been the moon so far as Penelope's travels went. She shook her head.

"It's overrated. I'm glad to be back in the Midwest."

They bowled another line, and she had the sense that he was holding back on his game. And he gave her pointers, standing close to her as he advised her on how to bring the ball back when she moved forward. She turned to look at him and his face was inches from her own. She turned back, followed his instructions, and after the dust settled all ten pins were down. A strike!

"I never did that before in my life."

"Let's quit while you're ahead."

They went into the bar then and had beer and she asked him about himself.

"Tell me about Penelope."

Her life sounded almost interesting as she told him. The small town east of Madison, coming to the big city with a small-town girl's dream. "And I ended up in Elm Grove."

When did the conversation turn to Mrs. D'Antonio? Even the terror of Elm Grove seemed an interesting subject. And Harry could not have been more interested. Did she have family? No visitors at all? Is her mind completely gone? She from around here? That name sounds familiar. How do you stand her?

"With medication she calms down almost immediately, and before she drifts off, she talks, almost making sense. I suppose it would make sense if I knew more about her past. Her husband's name is Bill, that much is clear."

"She talks about him?"

"A mile a minute. And then she conks out."

"What kind of medication is it?"

"I don't know. The nurse doles it out."

"Red, pink, what?"

"Yellow. Little yellow pills in the shape of stars."

He brought her to her door and the moment of truth. When he put out his hand she gave him hers. He took it, hesitated, then raised it to his lips. "Thanks for a great date." He kissed her cheek then and was gone. Inside, door shut, Penelope stood with her eyes shut and felt she was off on an astral journey.

4

Kim was surprised to find Richard talking with the nurse when she arrived at Elm Grove. Alice had one hand on her cart of medicines. Richard glanced at her and that was all. She marched up to him.

"What are you doing here?"

"Someone's missing."

Alice the nurse looked at Kim with a tragic expression. "Mrs. D'Antonio."

She had to say it twice, since no sound emerged on the first try. Then Kim saw Penelope standing down the corridor, outside Mrs. D'Antonio's room, her expression devastated. Kim went to her.

"What happened?"

"I don't know!"

But something in her manner indicated that she did know. Kim took her arm. "Let's get some coffee."

They went into the dining area where large thermoses of coffee were kept. Kim filled a cup and handed it to Penelope. The aid looked at it as if she had never seen a cup of coffee before, but finally she took it. Kim poured another and led Penelope to a far table where she could keep an eye on Richard at the nurses' station.

"When did it happen?"

"I don't know. After lunch maybe. I saw she wasn't in her room. She wasn't on the patio either."

"Had you taken her out there?"

Penelope had the look of someone about to lie. What she did instead was cry.

"Tell me about it."

It didn't make much sense. Kim had to ask who Harry was. Penelope had wheeled Veronica out on the patio and come back for Mrs. D'Antonio. She had just gotten Mrs. D'Antonio into her chair with other patients clamoring for attention when Harry had offered to take the old woman outside.

"I should have gone with him. I tried to go with him."

He had brushed away the offer. Take a break. She was in good hands with Harry.

"Harry is gone too?"

A stiff little nod and the tears came once more.

"Penelope, it's not your fault. Harry worked here, didn't he?"

"He was a janitor."

Richard came across the room to the table. He looked down at Penelope like the God of the Old Testament. "You, Penelope?"

"Richard, she's told me what happened."

His mouth became a line. "Good. Now she can tell me. Why don't you leave us alone?"

Veronica was still in her wheelchair and Kim's visit was the usual thing, but she found herself more impatient than she had ever been before with the woman's whining. Why didn't Sister Mary Teresa ever come? Was there any word from the cardinal? Kim tried to remember Veronica as the mistress of novices, explaining the religious vocation to her and Joyce. But that beautiful ideal was what she had deserted and now, in the throes of hypochondria and some real ailments, she wanted to undo what she had undone.

"So do we all, Sister Kimberly," Emtee Dempsey had said. "'It is the blight man was born for.' You remember the poem?"

"Her name is Veronica, not Margaret."

Emtee Dempsey ignored this. "We all stand in need of mercy. It is the human condition."

"I wish you would come out to Elm Grove and tell Veronica that."

"She knows it as well as I do."

Today, Veronica was blissfully unaware of what had taken place just down the corridor, an elderly woman wheeled out the door by a helpful janitor and probably into an awaiting vehicle. How easy it would have been. The kidnapping of inmates was one contingency Elm Grove had never dreamt of guarding against.

When Kim left Veronica's room, Richard was no longer in evidence. Neither was Penelope.

"He took her away to talk with her," Alice said. "Oh my God, why did this have to happen on my shift?"

"Kidnapped!" Emtee Dempsey sat at her desk, fountain pen in her chubby hand, before her a sheet of paper on which she had been writing with her perfect hand her daily stint on the history of the twelfth century that would be her masterpiece.

"Wheeled out the door and away."

The old nun closed her fountain pen, laid it on the desk, placed the sheet of paper on the pile to her right, and settled back. "Tell me everything."

'Everything' proved to be elusive. What Kim had learned from Penelope was part of it, certainly, but the great question was, *Who was Harry?* Richard had no doubt. He had come to warn Emtee Dempsey that he would brook no interference with his investigation.

"You learned about it just by chance, Kim. If it had happened yesterday or tomorrow, you wouldn't have been there. Pretend you weren't. I don't want you thinking you have any business poking into this." He still resented her talking with Penelope first.

"You must tell us what you have learned, Richard," Emtee Dempsey said in her most conciliatory tones.

"It looks pretty simple."

The people who had been putting the pressure on D'Antonio over the years had decided belatedly to get at him through his aged wife.

"So you now think he knows something they don't," Emtee Dempsey said sweetly.

"It looks that way." He seemed to have forgotten previous conversations. "Harry, if that's his name, is either one of them or working for them."

"You don't know who he is?"

"We know he didn't even live at the address he put on his application form at Elm Grove. His name is probably as phony as the address. Harry Brown. He sweet talked one of the aids into letting him just roll that old woman out the door."

"The wife of William D'Antonio."

"She won't be able to tell them a thing," Kim said.

Richard looked at her. "She is of use to them in other ways."

"To put pressure on the husband?"

"He's sitting down there in Joliet wondering what they'll do to her."

"Have you talked to him?"

"Not personally yet. I'm going down there tomorrow. I'm here to tell you to just leave things to us. I don't want you pestering that nurse's aid."

"Richard, I would never interfere with an official investigation."

Emtee Dempsey said this with a straight face. But before Richard had come, the old nun had given Kim instructions about Penelope.

"Sister Kimberly, don't you think it would be more comfortable for her if she came to stay with us until this is over?"

"She won't."

"I realize she will be unwilling at first. But I know your powers of persuasion."

Perhaps Emtee Dempsey would consider what she had said to Richard the truth because her interference had already been put under way.

The following morning, when Kim came to Penelope's apartment, she found Officers O'Connell and Gleason on guard outside the door.

"Your brother said to expect you."

"Is she home?"

"You can't go in."

Kim pressed the bell. "I don't see why not."

"Sister, we have our orders."

"Is a court order among them? You can't stop me from talking to a friend."

"You don't even know her."

The door opened then, and Penelope cried out, "Oh, I'm so glad you've come, Sister."

Kim passed between the bewildered O'Connell and Gleason into the apartment.

"Close the door, Penelope."

The poor girl had been made to feel like a pariah and was all the more grateful for Kim's tender concern. It was clear that Penelope felt both foolish and innocent.

"He seemed so nice."

"How long had you known him?"

"Since he came to work at Elm Grove. A month ago."

"And you saw him only at work?"

"We had one date. The night before last. We went bowling." That innocent pastime now seemed the height of folly and Penelope wept on. Kim could scarcely blame her. It was clear that Harry, or whatever his name was, had come to Elm Grove with the specific purpose of spiriting Mrs. D'Antonio away. Richard was right. He was either one of Bill D'Antonio's fellow thieves, or employed by them to kidnap their silent partner's wife. Threatening her would probably break his silence at last.

Or would it? Men ruthless enough to kidnap a demented old woman from a nursing home were unlikely to return her in the condition in which they had taken her. Once their captive had served their purposes . . . Kim stopped that line of thought, lest Penelope should detect it.

"His name wasn't Harry."

"He said he had been in the navy. He mopped floors like a dancer."

"Where did you go bowling?" Kim committed the name to memory, no need to let Penelope know that she was here to learn anything useful the nurse's aid could supply. And console her, of course. She would do that even if Penelope knew nothing.

"He could have been a professional bowler. He had strike after strike."

That sounded like baseball to Kim. Joyce would understand. If Harry lied about his name he could have lied about other things, but can anyone tell nothing but lies? It was important to know any and everything the man had told Penelope. But had he been in the navy? One thing he could not have faked was his prowess at bowling. And his graceful way with a mop.

"I feel so foolish," Penelope said.

"Had he shown interest in Mrs. D'Antonio, before. . . ."

She nodded her head. "I thought he was just being nice. He even wanted to know what kind of medication she took, the kind we gave to subdue her."

"What did you tell him?"

"I don't know what it is. Alice, the nurse, doles out the medicines. I just knew the color and shape."

"So you told him that?"

5

Alice, the nurse, when asked by Richard, found that the medication given Mrs. D'Antonio was missing. She had readied her cart for the distribution of medicine when she saw the janitor pushing Mrs. D'Antonio toward the door. Down the corridor, Penelope was looking after the disappearing wheelchair with a dreamy look.

"I left the medicines and went to talk to her. What she had done was unwise. I cannot have janitors taking care of patients, as I told her, forcefully. Then I went back to my cart."

"Did you notice anything missing?"

Alice just looked at Richard.

"Was Mrs. D'Antonio the only one who took that medication?"

"Each patient's medication is kept separate. They are billed for it, of course."

Veronica was billed for several, but her favorite was the little orange and black capsule. Since Mrs. D'Antonio was presumably out on the patio sitting in the sun, Alice had gone by her room to the next.

"Why would he take her medicine?"

"Another is missing too. Your friend Veronica's. He must have known which one subdued Mrs. D'Antonio when she got very bad."

"What would it do to anyone else?"

Alice hesitated. "I am told there is a black market in it. Youngsters take it for the thrill."

"And do they get it?"

"If they can stay awake."

There was indeed a street market for the drug, and its users were not suffering from dementia, at least not in the same sense. Harry could have made quite a profit from it.

"Nonsense," Katherine Senski said. "He took it so the old woman wouldn't be a nuisance."

"Penelope said that it made Mrs. D'Antonio almost rational. It was the only time she said anything that made sense." Kim looked around the living room of the house on Walden Street. "Until it put her to sleep, that is."

"Did Penelope tell the young man that?"

"Yes, Sister."

6

Any number of people at Elm Grove could have identified the janitor who had called himself Harry, but of course the task fell to Penelope.

"They treat me as if I were his accomplice,' she said to Kim when the nun arrived at police headquarters in answer to her call. She needed moral support as she was shown photograph after photograph by a very large lady in uniform who looked like "Before" in a Weight Watcher's ad.

"They're desperate. They haven't a clue."

The bored lady on the other side of the table looked at Kim and then subsided into indolence.

"They call it routine when they subject people to this sort of thing."

"They all look alike."

"Probably the same photographer."

Kim sat there as Penelope dutifully looked at the pictures shown her. Routine could be mocked but it made some farfetched sense that the man Penelope had known as Harry would be in the police mug book. His mop handle had been taken downtown in the hope that it would contain fingerprints, but the very nature of mopping insured that they would be blurred.

"That's him!"

The fat lady did not actually sing, but she lurched in her chair, at first annoyed by the disturbance, but then almost as excited as Penelope.

"You sure, honey?"

"Of course I'm sure. That's Harry."

Harry, it turned out, was Eugene Schmidt, recently released from Joliet, where he had been serving a sentence for dealing in drugs. Penelope was given these facts along with Kim in Richard's office. Her brother was suffused with triumph. Routine had produced what routine was meant to produce. The large lady cop who had shown Penelope the photographs had come to Richard's office too, but was not asked to take a chair.

"Good work, Hazel. I appreciate it. Take a break."

The information on Eugene Schmidt suggested a double reason for making off with all Mrs. D'Antionio's medication. He could sell what was left over.

"We'll get him," Richard said.

"Wouldn't he have a parole officer?"

Richard observed a moment of silence, then picked up his telephone.

"I won't keep you ladies."

Kim rose and so did Penelope. "Keep us posted, Richard."

"I'll tell you what I tell the newspapers."

If he was insufferable now, what would he be like when they arrested Schmidt and recovered the old woman? Richard acted as if he had single-handedly recovered the missing millions from the Rockford robbery.

"Penelope, you're welcome to stay with us until things settle down."

"In the convent? I'm not even Catholic."

"You don't have to take the veil. We have a lovely apartment you'll have all to yourself."

"I already have an apartment."

"Emtee Dempsey would very much like to talk to you."

"Emtee Dempsey?"

"My boss. Come on, she's worth seeing. I'll take you to your place after we visit her."

Emtee Dempsey seized on the mention of bowling, something Kim had thought was simply a device to get talking with Penelope, but the old nun went on and on, as if her secret wish was to haunt bowling alleys. They might put her to work as a pin.

"They've identified the janitor. I mean Penelope did."

"I feel like a rat."

"My dear, he betrayed your trust."

"He was so nice."

"I'm sure he was. Was he left-handed or right-handed?"

Penelope peered across the desk at Emtee Dempsey. To her enormous credit, Penelope had not mentioned the massive headdress the old nun wore, part of the order's traditional habit, but of course she couldn't keep her eyes off it. Its movement suggested that the old nun might take flight at any moment, lifting into the air, borne aloft by the great starched wings that seemed to sprout from her head. This was the habit Veronica wanted to be buried in. ("She would have been better advised to live in it," Emtee Dempsey had commented. "But that is unkind, however true. What kind of truth is kind?" Kim knew enough to avoid such gambits.)

"Left-handed! That seemed to make his bowling more amazing."

"And he mopped the same way?"

"No. No, he didn't. That's why I was so surprised by the way he bowled."

An ambidextrous kidnapper. What difference did it make? But Emtee Dempsey was far from through. "What is a strike? What is a spare? Are there actually ten pins? They have numbers?"

"Yes."

"Painted on them."

"Oh no. It's their place in the triangle." Penelope turned to look at Kim. "Listen to me. You'd think I was an expert. I didn't know these things until Harry took me bowling."

Penelope at least was determined to keep calling him Harry. That is how she had known him. She had never known Eugene Schmidt.

"If only they would find Mrs. D'Antonio. No matter what I tell myself, I'm to blame for that. The poor old thing."

"She's nearly eighty," Kim said, and the old nun scowled.

7

Eugene Schmidt was arrested in Midway Airport, a once great terminal now resembling a bus depot of the 1960s. He was scheduled to fly to Cancun but, as the arresting officers said, he was going to the "can can" instead. Schmidt actually laughed at the bad joke.

"I've been there before."

"Cancun?"

"Where you said."

This and hundreds of other biographical items emerged over the next forty-eight hours while Schmidt was interrogated by rotating teams. The fact that he could represent the recovery of all those millions missing from Rockford banks made him an object of special interest. And it was fun interviewing him. He was cooperative, intelligent, without shame. He had been in and out of trouble all his life, but it was trafficking in drugs that had led to his extended stay.

"With the crooks and criminals," he said, making a face. "Me? I was just trying to insure my supply when I agreed to deal. Guess how long before I was picked up? One week."

"Maybe you were set up?"

The thought that someone might treat him unfairly was not what bothered Schmidt, but that he had been too dumb to think of the possibility. "Naw," he said finally. "I wasn't important enough."

"Tell us about Rockford."

"My shoes?"

"Funny."

"What are we talking about?"

He was a moderately good actor, but no one who had spent time at Joliet would be unaware of William D'Antonio and the heavy security he was under. The authorities were determined that he should not fall again into the hands of his former accomplices, or inmates working for them, who had tried to beat out of him the secret of the missing millions. The state had an equally intense and more justified interest in those same millions.

"Sure I heard of him. Everyone heard of him."

"But not everyone shows up as janitor in the rest home where his wife is gaga and wheels her out the door. Where is she?"

His story was simple and implausible, but he stuck with it. He had pushed the old lady outside as a favor to Penelope, parked her in the sun and then went around the corner of the building to have a smoke.

"You can smoke on the patio."

The story altered slightly when missing medication was found in the room he had rented.

"What a fizzle. That stuff does nothing for you."

"So you did steal her medication?"

"It was just sitting there asking to be taken along. The way Penelope talked about it, I had to try it." He shook his head. "I've gotten higher on aspirin."

He had gone around the corner of the building from the patio to hide the medication, but there was no nook or niche.

"So I come back to the patio. The old lady's gone, I figure the nurse came for her, so I decide to take the pills out to my car. I did. I tried one then and there, waiting for a big kapow. Nothing. I figured one wasn't enough. I had a cigarette instead. I'm sitting there when I see Penelope and then Alice come roaring outside and looking around. I figure they've missed the medication already. I duck down and wait. Even after I started the car, I stayed there. Then I drove away."

"And decided to go to Cancun?"

A wide sunny smile. "On the profits. I sold those nothing pills one at a time, talking up what they did."

His manner was so engaging that many wanted to believe him, but of course it was an incredible story. Richard mentioned the susceptibility of some other interrogators with a touch of contempt.

"It's bunk. It's a pure accident that a week after he gets out of Joliet he just happens to apply for a job swabbing floors in the rest home where D'Antonio's elderly wife is kept? Under a false name? And sweet talks the nurse assigned to the old lady into letting him take Mrs. D'Antonio for a spin?"

Emtee Dempsey's great headdress dipped in agreement. "A string of improbabilities."

"He must have pushed her right to a waiting vehicle, say a van, and they lifted her, chair and all, into it, and off it went, slick as a whistle."

"They?"

"The ones he's working for."

"Any leads on who they are?"

"We'll find them," Richard said grimly.

Finding them was not the problem. The problem was to link the half dozen men the investigation of the Rockford robbery had turned up as likely accomplices of William D'Antonio.

"None of them was arrested?"

"Sister, D'Antonio would be walking around free if he hadn't turned himself in and confessed. He double-crossed the rest of them, and they will get him or the money or both or die in the attempt."

"What does William D'Antonio tell you? Hasn't he been asked who those accomplices were?"

Richard pulled on his earlobe. "Silent as the tomb. What do you make of guys like this? They take millions of other people's money, D'Antonio double-crosses the others and seeks safe haven in prison. His life is threatened several times, but nothing can induce him to give up the names. These are people who are hiring inmates to kill him or beat him, and he is mum as an altar boy about who they are."

"Maybe things would be worse if he told you."

"Worse than dead?"

Eugene Schmidt recoiled from the suggestion that he had anything to do with kidnapping the wife of William D'Antonio. His only interest had been to do a favor for Penelope. And to get hold of that medication. He was pressed on what had happened to the old woman, but free as he had been to acknowledge his role in stealing her pills, he insisted that he was innocent of the kidnapping.

That denial came before the body of Mrs. D'Antonio was discovered, a huddled bundle thrown by the side of the road, presumably from a moving vehicle, given the way the body had rolled to its final resting place. She had been dead at least twelve hours before her body was discovered. Eugene Schmidt's reaction was a crescendoing claim to innocence.

"When did a criminal ever admit to a crime?" Richard growled.

8

"I will come with you today," Emtee Dempsey said, avoiding Kim's eyes. Was the old nun ashamed of her cowardice in neglecting Veronica at Elm Grove?

"She'll want news."

"That's why I am going with you."

"What news?"

"The good news."

"Oh, for heaven's sake."

"Yes, indeed."

All this was quite predictable repartee, meant to keep Emtee Dempsey in the moral ascendancy. Kim wanted to tell her that she understood perfectly the old nun's reluctance to visit Elm Grove. Veronica's whining apart, who knew what bugs and germs to which Emtee Dempsey would be susceptible floated around? On the other hand, it could be bracing to realize that most of the old women in Elm Grove were younger than she was.

"After we visit Veronica, I want to go downtown."

"To shop?"

Emtee Dempsey did not consider this worthy of an answer. "To the jail. I want to talk to Harry."

"You mean Eugene Schmidt?"

"A rose by any other name."

"For heaven's sake."

"Sister Kimberly, a pious sentiment endlessly repeated loses its efficacy."

"I wasn't being pious."

"More's the pity."

Veronica rose up from her bed to a sitting position like the son of the widow of Nain when Sister Mary Teresa entered her room. The nun had created a sensation from the moment she entered Elm Grove, and with swishing skirt, clacking rosary, and aerodynamic headdress progressed majestically after Kim, smiling benediction at the astonished inmates. And now she confronted her former sister in religion. Veronica threw up her hands.

"Thank God you're still wearing it."

And so the conversation went immediately to Veronica's great hope. Despite having left the order and lived apart for decades, up to God knows what, as Joyce put it, now in her decline she wanted to undo all that and be reinstated.

"If I could only be buried in it, that would be enough."

"Veronica, that is why I've come. It's perfectly all right. The cardinal has been very understanding. He himself will come to receive the renewal of your vows. . . ."

There are many cries and screams heard in Elm Grove, but the shrill expression of inexpressible joy that emerged from soon to be once more Sister Veronica was a first.

Kim left the two old women to their reminiscing and went in search of Penelope. Alice the nurse looked warily at Kim when she came up to the nurses' station.

"Penelope? She has been transferred to section B."

"Is she working now?"

Alice leaned toward Kim. "Would it sound awful if I said I am almost glad that they found Mrs. D'Antonio?"

Kim realized what agony it must have been for Alice to have one of her wards kidnapped and not to know for days whether she was alive or dead.

"I understand. May she rest in peace."

"God knows what she must have been like without that medication."

Penelope was now working in a section where patients were completely bedridden, indeed who might never leave their beds again. There was no question here of taking a patient for a spin in her wheelchair. Was this Penelope's punishment?

"It's quiet." She glanced toward the woman on the bed. She had been in a coma for nearly a year and lay there, mouth open, face restless with who knew what thoughts or images that seemed to keep peace at bay.

"You've heard of Mrs. D'Antonio?"

"I'll never forgive myself."

"Penelope, it was not your fault."

"The police think so. They think I was Harry's accomplice. I mean Eugene. Whatever his name is."

"He says he had nothing to do with it."

Several expressions flitted across her face. Hope, doubt, despair. "But how would anyone else know she was on the patio?"

The assumption that Harry/Eugene was innocent as he claimed demanded improbabilities and chance happenings. But he would take the blame only for stealing Mrs. D'Antonio's medication. Lucky for him, he had been in the Cook County Jail when the body was found, but that did not exonerate him as an accomplice.

"Does he ever mention me?" Penelope said.

"You could go see him."

"Oh, I couldn't."

"I'd go with you."

"When?"

"Today?"

But Penelope thought tomorrow would be better, and of course every today had its tomorrow. But it was her hesitation that permitted Sister Mary Teresa to visit Eugene Schmidt first.

9

"Visit him! In jail?"

Emtee Dempsey smiled at the image Katherine's questions evoked. "It has a solid evangelical ring to it, doesn't it? 'When I was in prison . . .'"

When it became clear to Katherine and Kim and Joyce that Emtee Dempsey was fully serious about visiting the jailed Eugene Schmidt, Katherine supposed that they could spirit the old nun in and out of the jail without creating a media event.

"But that is just what I want to create."

"Sister!"

"And I want you with me, Sister Kimberly."

This was on the Tuesday evening when Kim had returned from Elm Grove and brought up her suggestion that Penelope visit the jailed janitor she still insisted on calling Harry.

"That suggested it to her," Kim said to Joyce, out of earshot of Emtee Dempsey.

"It's good for her to get out more than once a day."

"Then why doesn't she visit Veronica again?"

"That's your job."

"It's not a job and it's everyone's duty. 'When I was sick, you visited me.'" But the fact is that Kim did find it a job to visit Veronica, a duty. Veronica's mood had swung entirely, and she was now so sweet she made Kim's cheeks tingle. The woman who had been mistress of novices had been hidden all along under that whining exterior and emerged now like a ghost from the past. Nothing in Veronica's manner suggested that she had spent most of her adult life in the outside world.

"What did you do all that time?"

"I don't understand."

"After you left the order."

Veronica closed her eyes with pious dismay. "I would like to forget all that, make it as if it had never been."

"You were away what? Twenty years?"

"Have you been keeping count?" Veronica asked sharply.

"Did you work, what? Of course you didn't get married."

"Why 'of course'?"

"Did you?"

Veronica's eyes moved away from Kim's as if seeking something less judgmental. "Let us just say that I was as star-crossed in love as I was in my vocation."

This was too much. The thought of another woman in Emtee Dempsey's entourage with a tragic romantic past was insupportable. Katherine had made her lost love a leitmotif of her life, the more so for mentioning him only obliquely and infrequently. Now Veronica had similar secrets. Of course she could not be married; she could not be reinstated if she were.

Penelope had come to know Veronica and was amazed by her change of condition. "I thought she was bedridden, but now she is up and about, pushing herself around in her wheelchair."

"That's what a vocation does for you."

And so Kim and Emtee Dempsey and Joyce set out in midmorning for the Cook County Jail on a much publicized—thanks to the won-over Katherine—visit to Eugene Schmidt. When the old nun emerged from the Volkswagen bug a cheer went up from the assembled media as if she had just performed a demanding feat. Perhaps she had, given her sidewise measurements and the width of the Volkswagen door. She turned and the full effect of the traditional habit of the Order of Martha and Mary made itself felt. Cameramen darted about for better shots as the print reporters converged on Emtee Dempsey. She lifted a pudgy hand, gave them all a beatific smile and then sailed on toward the entrance, Kim at her side, the chevron of media people following like ducks on a pond. Joyce was left to speak to the reporters while the cameras went on to record every aspect of the old nun's visit to the jail.

Schmidt was more startled than delighted by the apparition that greeted him when he came into the visiting room, but the presence of Kim calmed him.

"You dress like that too?" he asked Kim.

"Young man," said Emtee Dempsey with authority, "please sit down. We do not have time for sartorial exchanges. I am told you profess to be innocent of the kidnaping of Mrs. D'Antonio."

"I had nothing to do with it."

"You wheeled her onto the patio."

"I did. As a favor to Penelope. But . . . Do you know about the medication?"

"Tell me about it."

"I took it because it sounded like a real trip. I was looking for a place to hide the stuff when they must have kidnapped her."

"Did you hide the medication?"

"I had to keep it. I didn't want to dig a hole and bury it. I took it to my car and got out of there. I took one because of all the excitement. Whatever punch it had would have been lost. But there wasn't any punch."

"You tried the medication?"

"He nodded."

"The yellow ones?"

"I took one of those in my car." He made a face. "It did nothing. Nothing." A slow grin appeared. "Think of the poor suckers I sold it to. Maybe I'm lucky to be in here where they can't get me."

"Let us return to the patio at Elm Grove. You pushed Mrs. D'Antonio outside, parked her chair in the sun, then went in search of a hiding place for the purloined medication?"

Schmidt looked at Kim. "Does she always talk like that?"

"Was there anyone else on the patio?"

Schmidt gave it some thought.

"You went around a corner to look for a hiding place. Why? Would someone have seen you otherwise? Someone already on the patio, someone other than Mrs. D'Antonio?"

Eugene Schmidt's head swung to and fro even before she finished speaking and the corners of his mouth descended. "Naw. That wasn't it."

"No one else was out there?"

"No. Just that friend of yours," he said to Kim. "She was out there huddled in her chair as if the sun might hurt her. But no one else. I know what you're after, strangers lurking about. There weren't any. Just me and two helpless old ladies."

"And soon there was only one."

"Yeah. It's a mystery."

Emtee Dempsey went on to quiz him about life at Joliet. ("Not life! Give me a break. Ten to fifteen and I got out in seven.") How did it compare with Cook County Jail? She seemed genuinely interested in his account, that grew and grew, episode feeding on episode, with no end in sight. You would have thought Emtee Dempsey was writing a book on prison life rather than a history of the twelfth century. But who wouldn't have gone on as Schmidt did, with such a rapt audience. D'Antonio? Sure he had heard of him, seen him a couple times, but he was carefully guarded at all times.

"Why?"

"He double-crossed the guys he pulled a bank job with."

"The missing millions?"

"No one knows what he did with it. He confessed to the crime, pleaded guilty but wouldn't identify his pals. They have to figure anytime D'Antonio felt like it he could put the finger on them. So there's that and the missing money. He needs a guard."

"I believe you," Emtee Dempsey said when she rose to go.

"Tell that to these guys, will you?"

"Yes, I will. Come see us on Walden Street when you're released. And bring Penelope."

A flabbergasted Eugene Schmidt was led away and an equally flabbergasted Kim followed the diminutive figure down the hallway and outside where a remnant of the press corps remained. This time Emtee Dempsey stopped to talk.

"As you know, I am Sister Mary Teresa of the Order of Martha and Mary. I have been visiting Eugene Schmidt, a foolish young man who is wrongly suspected of being involved in the kidnapping of the wife of William D'Antonio. He was of course in jail at the presumed time of her death. This is Sister Kimberly, who knew Mrs. D'Antonio when she was a resident of Elm Grove nursing home. It is my earnest hope that Eugene

Schmidt will soon be released. Now I bid you all good day."

And so she sailed away to the awaiting Volkswagen. Joyce was already in the back seat. Kim helped the old nun into the passenger seat, assisted unnecessarily by members of the Fourth Estate. A minute later they drove away.

"Now what was that all about?"

"We shall have to wait and see."

And she would talk no more about it. Perhaps she saw that her grand gesture was only that. Schmidt still stood accused of stealing medication, perhaps a small offense, but with someone of his background, serious enough.

10

Richard came pounding on the front door of the house on Walden Street, pushed past Joyce when she opened it and thumped down the hall to Emtee Dempsey's study. Kim and Joyce remained in the hallway listening to the two of them, exchanging versicle and response in a chorus made up of Richard's angry tones and the soft soothing voice of the old nun. The exchange lasted for ten minutes and then Richard, his expression still angry, emerged from the study.

"I hold you responsible," he growled to Kim.

"For what?"

"For interfering with an investigation, for arousing sympathy for that punk, for . . ."

But he had run out of breath. Joyce opened the front door and smiled sweetly at Richard. He left in a huff.

"Emtee Dempsey goes to jail and holds a news conference and I am held responsible."

"You drove."

Joyce scampered out of reach, heading for the kitchen. Kim went into the old nun's study.

"We're interfering in a police investigation."

"I should hope so. That boy is no more guilty than I am."

"You may be making Richard's point."

"What else have they done but round up innocent young men?"

No wonder Richard had been angry if this had been the line Emtee Dempsey took with him. "They think he's connected with the ones who are guilty," the old nun added and made a face.

"What makes you so sure he isn't?"

"Sister, it is as plain as the nose on your face."

Kim fled. If Sister Mary Teresa were going to make another premature claim to know the answers the police were seeking in vain, allies were needed. From the kitchen she called Katherine.

"She's bluffing, isn't she?" Katherine said.

"Would you like to suggest that to her?"

There was a pause. "She will take refuge in some tautology and I'd feel like a fool. 'I know that the ones who kidnaped Mrs. D'Antonio are the ones who kidnaped Mrs. D'Antonio.'"

"Please come."

Katherine came, asked for a glass of merlot, urged Kim to remain in the study and avoided all mention of the foray for which she had greased the wheels. Emtee Dempsey looked at her with bright blue eyes.

"You are singularly incurious this evening, Katherine."

"Curiosity has killed more than one Katherine."

"I am referring to my triumphant visit to the Cook County Jail. Sister, see if we are on the local news."

The story was the teaser of the newscast. Mentioned at the outset as to come, mentioned again before a break and finally the scene outside the courthouse was shown. Sister Mary Teresa came down the jailhouse steps as if a pigeon had lighted on her head; Kim a step or two behind like the indentured slave she was. Sunlight glanced from the old nun's rimless glasses, reporters hovered, finally came her statement. She sounded as if she were the angel leading St. Paul out of prison, but Eugene Schmidt was still behind bars and was likely to remain there.

"You have painted yourself into a corner," Katherine said. "That young man is guilty as sin. I thought visiting him would convince you of that."

"Guilty as sin, perhaps, but innocent of the crime of which he is accused."

"Surely you don't believe that he pushed that woman's wheelchair outside to where her kidnappers were waiting purely by accident."

"Your statement includes no crime."

"All right, he pushed her out there in order that she might be kidnaped."

"That is not so."

"Because he was hunting around for somewhere to bury the medications he had stolen? How about that for a crime?"

"What he took was a placebo, Katherine. It does not rise to the level of commandeering a bottle of aspirin."

"Is that what he told you, that it was a placebo?"

"He told the police as effectively as he told me. But they had not ears to hear."

"You are being enigmatic."

"I am as simple as a dove."

Katherine groaned helplessly and held out her glass for more merlot.

No one had ever bettered Emtee Dempsey in the art of dialectical fencing. Katherine turned in desperation to other topics, her only consolation the excellent merlot, a gift of Benjamin Rush. The following morning Kim got her marching orders.

I I

She was awakened by Emtee Dempsey at six A.M.

"You drop me at the cathedral for mass, but you and Joyce go to Elm Grove and fetch Sister Veronica."

"Fetch her."

"Tell her the great day has arrived."

"You want me to bring her here?"

"Aren't you fully awake? Of course bring her here. Won't she fit into our car?"

"Not in her wheelchair."

"The wheelchair won't be necessary." The old nun turned and clumped downstairs to the chapel for her morning meditation.

The vow of obedience is a liberating thing. Sister Mary Teresa was her religious superior; Kim had vowed to obey her superiors in all lawful things. Veronica had been wailing to be reinstated in the order and apparently the permission had come from the cardinal. Joyce was still half asleep when they dropped Emtee Dempsey off at the cathedral.

"We'll miss mass," she said drowsily.

"Out of obedience."

"Yeah. Okay." And she put her head back and fell completely asleep in the passenger seat.

When they drove up to the doorway of Elm Grove, a patient in a wheelchair waited on the patio, a nurse beside her. It wasn't until she stopped the car that Kim recognized Penelope and Veronica. Veronica seemed to be asleep.

"Back seat?" Penelope asked.

"How did you know?"

"Sister Mary Teresa called."

"What's wrong with Veronica?"

"She just had medication."

Joyce was awake now and she and Penelope transferred Veronica to the back seat, laying the limp body in the fetal position on the cushions.

"Doesn't she have to check out or something?"

"That's all taken care of. You never told me she was a nun too."

"She's been undercover for years."

Penelope nodded. The doors of the Volkswagen were closed and they set off for the house on Walden Street.

When Kim stopped at the cathedral, Emtee Dempsey came out, looked in at the still inert body of Veronica, and nodded with satisfaction.

"Put her in the basement apartment. I will walk."

Joyce protested, offering her seat, but Emtee Dempsey set off for the house on foot.

"This way she isn't an accomplice," Joyce said.

Kim tried to laugh away the suggestion, but it was all too easy to imagine Emtee Dempsey jousting with an accuser with such a distinction. But of what could they be accused? Taking Veronica to where she had begged to go could scarcely be likened to spiriting poor Mrs. D'Antonio out of Elm Grove.

Veronica was put to bed in the apartment in what Emtee Dempsey called the basement but was simply a floor beneath street level, in all respects like those above. Emtee Dempsey made no allusion to the returned member of the Order of Martha and Mary.

"Aren't you going to thank us?"

"For saving Veronica's life?"

"Hardly that."

"Don't be too sure."

The old nun had set far more in play than bringing Veronica to the house on Walden Street. O'Connell and Gleason, disguised as janitors, were waiting at Elm Grove when two masked men burst into the building, ran down the hall, and shot every shell their weapons held into Veronica's bed. They were soon overpowered by Gleason and O'Connell, reenforcements arrived, and off to Cook County Jail they went. Penelope put through a call to Emtee Dempsey, who received the news calmly, put down the phone, picked up her pen, and resumed the page she was writing, a page which along with several thousand others was part of her history of the twelfth century. Joyce, listening in on the kitchen phone, brought the news to Kim, who after a moment of shock headed for the study.

"What in the world is going on?"

The pen was screwed into its cap and laid upon the desk. "An infinity of things are going on in the world."

"At Elm Grove."

"William D'Antonio's betrayed accomplices tried to assassinate their accomplice."

"Their accomplice!"

"They shot up the room in which Veronica had been staying, destroying the pillows Penelope had artfully arranged beneath the cover."

"Are you saying Veronica was the accomplice of those kidnapers?"

"Better check on her. Penelope said the sedative should be effective through the morning. Then ask Richard and Katherine and Benjamin Rush to please join us for lunch."

12

With a groggy Veronica in the care of Hazel, the very large policewoman, in the basement apartment, Benjamin Rush and Katherine Senski arrived for lunch. They were already at table when Richard bustled in, his expression that of a man who had accomplished his purpose.

"They deny it, of course, but those guys we picked up at Elm Grove were William D'Antonio's assistants in the Rockford armored car robbery.

"Congratulations," Katherine said, glancing at Emtee Dempsey.

"Your job is almost complete," the old nun said.

Richard gave her a tolerant look. "The rest is up to the prosecutor."

"There is another accomplice, I am sorry to say."

"Penelope? We won't prosecute her. She hadn't a clue what was going on."

"Neither did Eugene Schmidt."

"When the others talk, they'll finger him."

"Not unless you encourage them to do so."

"Who is the other accomplice?" Benjamin Rush asked, but his pained expression suggested he already knew.

"A silly woman who is now under guard downstairs. The woman who was the Judas goat, telling the kidnappers that the woman in the other wheelchair on the patio held Mrs. D'Antonio, the poor soul for whom they had come."

"Sister Veronica?"

"Just Veronica," Emtee Dempsey corrected.

"But you said the cardinal was ready to reinstate her," Kim protested.

"I think you will find I said nothing of the kind. Oh, I might have said what the cardinal would do, but that was hypothetical."

"Surely you didn't suspect her when you visited her at Elm Grove!"

"That visit confirmed my suspicion. Why did Eugene Schmidt seem guilty? Because he had recently come to Elm Grove. Quite coincidentally, out of genuine affection for Penelope, he showed an interest in Mrs. D'Antonio. For the same reason, he offered to take Mrs. D'Antonio to the patio."

"While he stole the medication."

"That was merely a target of opportunity. The promise of dulling his mind with drugs made him act on the spur of the moment. Penelope had unwisely told him how powerful Mrs. D'Antonio's medication was. His past addiction weakened his will. But there was someone else who filled all the specifications Eugene Schmidt did."

"Veronica!"

"She was no more ill than I am. But she is an accomplished actress. You may remember her in the role of Joan of Arc at the college when she was given special permission to act in the play she directed. The placebo Eugene took from the nurse's cart was Veronica's medication."

"That is why you wanted the telephone number of Dr. Auslander," Benjamin Rush mused. Auslander was the physician he had asked to look in on Veronica at Elm Grove.

Emtee Dempsey nodded. "He told me she was at best a hypochondriac."

"And at worst?"

"Pretending. Her reaction to the supposed benefits of the placebo was all he needed to know."

"Why didn't he tell us?" the lawyer asked.

"He did. When asked."

When Veronica was brought upstairs, she reacted violently to Sister Emtee Dempsey's account, but the hefty female police officer subdued her easily.

"You are still under the influence of genuine medication, Veronica. Let me now tell you of your assassination."

Veronica sat in silence as Emtee Dempsey described the volleys that had been shot into her bed at Elm Grove. The sad expression of the betrayed betrayer spread across Veronica's face.

"And so, Veronica, I can keep my promise to you. You will soon be back in a cell after all."

The death of his wife unloosed the tongue of William D'Antonio. The stolen money had been lying unproductive in a safety deposit box in one of the banks whose daily deposits had been part of the amount taken from the armored car.

"They killed those men," D'Antonio said in explanation of his silence. "There was to be no violence. There was no need for violence."

The soporific gas introduced into the cab of the armored car would have sufficed to render the guards inert. D'Antonio had preferred that the stolen money be no one's rather than become blood money.

"A good thief," Emtee Dempsey murmured.

"He's as guilty of those murders as if he shot them himself."

"Legally, perhaps."

Richard gave her an impatient look. He was in no mood for theology. And it still irked him that Eugene Schmidt had got off scot-free.

The happy couple, Penelope and the man she persisted in calling Harry, would be married in a month.

"The reward will provide a pretty nest egg."

Richard swore a muffled oath. That Eugene Schmidt was to be the recipient of the reward offered by the Rockford banks infuriated him.

"And what of Veronica?" Katherine asked.

"It all depends on whether the word of those blackguards is believed. Of course, they shot up her room in Elm Grove, and that suggests they thought she knew more than was safe for them. The poor woman was as naive as a novice."

"Novices don't have the gift of tears," Kim said.

Emtee Dempsey observed a long silence. "The lachrymose have a tendency to romanticize their weakness. One thing, Katherine, like yourself she never married."

"It is not the same thing," Katherine said indignantly.

And so Sister Mary Teresa had managed to annoy everyone. Everyone but herself. She was content that, by and large, mercy, if not justice, had been done.

LOWLY DEATH

MARGARET FRAZER

THE BRISK SNOW SLANTED DOWN London's College Hill Street on a mean little wind, blighting the hope a few mild February days had brought of an early spring. On either side the narrow, shoulder-to-shoulder houses rose white-veiled into the blur and all in all Dick Colop would have preferred to be at home behind closed shutters in his father's scrivener's shop where lamps were lighted and a glowing brazier kept both ink and fingers warm enough to work. But, alas, he wasn't, and he hugged his cloak closer to him as he turned in under the low-roofed gateway to Paternoster Passage into Paternoster Yard. The yard, closed in by St. Michael Paternoster church on one side, the row of Whittington's Almshouses on the other, and the Priests' House at the far end, should have been sheltered, but Dick had been schooled here by the priests when he was younger and he knew all too well how some trick of the rooftops brought a wind like today's down into the yard with a cruel swirl of cold and bluster, and he was ready when the expected gust caught him. Head ducked deeper into his hood, he hurried on, into the narrow half-shelter of the Priests' House doorway.

Less concerned with politeness than with being inside, he rapped hard at the door with gloved knuckles, then stood stamping his feet for a while until he heard old Bartholomew's shuffle along the stone-floored passage. By the shuffle he knew Bartholomew's rheumatics were playing up, and Dick put aside his impatience at having to wait, counting himself lucky that Bartholomew must have been at his morning task of polishing the silver in the butlery and therefore close to hand. The priests of Whittington College, well housed and well paid to serve St. Michael's church and almshouses while praying for the souls of the late Sir Richard Whittington, his wife and kin, and the well-being of King Henry VI, lord of England, France, and Ireland in this year of God's grace 1437, could well have afforded some servant other than old Bartholomew and indeed they did, having not only a cook but two others, but Bartholomew had come with the church, as it were, a natural son of the last priest to serve there before it had been purchased by Whittington's executors to carry out his will, and there had been agreement that Bartholomew came with the purchase. Now that Bartholomew grew slower with every year, Sire Thomas, Dick's least favorite among the priests, sometimes spoke of being rid of him, but all the while Dick had been there the other priests had refused the thought and plainly still did, for which Dick was glad because not only had Bartholomew understood a growing boy was a hungry creature and always seen to him having something to eat between meals, Dick always preferred to see Sire Thomas thwarted than not—an uncharitable thought of which Dick was never ashamed, given too many reasons for it when he was his pupil.

With that in mind, he gave Bartholomew a wide smile and greeting when finally he opened the door for Dick to slip inside.

"Dick Colop," Bartholomew said in return. "Decided to take up priesting after all and come back to us, have you?"

Dick answered that old jest between them with a laugh and, "No, but I'm hoping Master Pecock is in. Is he?"

"Upstairs in his chamber. You know the way."

Dick surely did, having had more than enough Latin lessons there. He had been sometimes able to slide out of his other lessons with the other priests but never managed to escape Master Pecock, even when his duties as Master of Whittington College should have been enough, in Dick's opinion, to divert him.

But Master Reynold Pecock was a difficult man to divert in any case, and besides being a priest and upon a time a fellow of Oriel College, Oxford, he had a love for teaching that—often though it had been Dick's bane—kept company with a wit and kindness that had kindled and kept friendship between them even after Dick had left off schooling to apprentice in his father's craft. It was for Master Pecock's wit and kindness that he was here this morning and, having thanked Bartholomew, he went up the stairs alone and was pleased when his light scratching on the closed door to Master Pecock's chamber was answered promptly by, "Come in," because when Master Pecock was far gone in writing or study of something, not only getting his attention but keeping it could be troublesome.

Nonetheless, when Dick opened the door to the small but neatly kept chamber that was Master Pecock's study—his bedchamber lay beyond it through another doorway—he found Master Pecock seated at his tall-legged desk where the light fell best through the glassed, east-facing window with quill pen in hand and a sheet of paper in front of him. From habit, Dick started to apologize for interrupting but Master Pecock, alacritously laying down his pen, said, "Not in the least. You rescue rather than interrupt." He was a man somewhere in his forties, his dark hair graying neatly at the temples and still a trace of his native Welsh in his voice. "I'm trying to find a plain way to show how it is that although there are truths of natural law to which we can come by reason, there are also truths of faith above our reason that must come from the revelations contained in holy scripture."

Looking firmly solemn, Dick nodded as if that had made sense to him, which it had not, while Master Pecock went cheerfully on, "Unfortunately, I've found that perhaps I don't understand the matter so clearly myself and, given choice between you and St. Gregory's commentary on reason's place in God's scheme of things, I gladly choose you. What's the trouble that brings you here?"

Turning to him from closing the door, Dick was brought up short by the question. "How do you know I'd not come merely for friendship's sake?" he asked in return.

For answer, Master Pecock gave a downward look through his wooden-rimmed spectacles, held on by ribbons around his ears, at Dick's shoes, low-topped and of thin leather.

"Ah," said Dick. "The wrong shoes."

"For being out in this weather," Master Pecock agreed, "and without even wooden pattens to lift you up from the wet."

"I only expected to go a little way along to a friend's and then a few doors more to the White Bull," Dick admitted. "Footing it through London wasn't part of my plans."

"Even best laid plans can go down the wind." Master Pecock quoted one of Bartholomew's favorite proverbs with a smile and pointed to the room's other chair. "Now, what's the trouble?"

Dick sat while saying, "I've a friend. John Yonge. He's from Cheshunt in Hertfordshire now because his father was a mercer who made enough to buy land thereabouts and move. The family is from London, though, and John's father and Andrew Bullok were apprentices together when they were young and stayed friends afterwards."

"Andrew Bullok. Would he be the late husband of Mistress Bullok in Horserider Street?" Not far away and part of St. Michael parish.

"The same. She took over the business after he died."

Master Pecock nodded. "That was before I came here but I've heard her speak of him."

"Yes . . ."

"And it was John Yonge who married the daughter Agnes two years ago, wasn't it?"

"Yes. His father and Mistress Bullok agreed a marriage between John and her daughter would suit both families."

Sitting back in his chair to listen, Master Pecock gave a decisive nod. "Of course. John is that reedy, fair young man who comes to church with them and Agnes looks much like her mother. I know them only somewhat. They go to Sire Thomas for preference. Do I remember rightly there's been a child baptized, too?"

"Little Andrew."

"Named for his late grandfather. Very familial. But I must assume you're telling me about them because they're concerned in the trouble that brought you here, and does that trouble spring from the fact that this John Yonge—your friend, you said—and his wife are presently living here in London with Mistress Bullok rather than with his father or some place of their own, although I believe it might well be said that Mistress Bullok has a strong way about her and might not make the most easy of mothers-in-law?"

Used to Master Pecock's extended way with words, Dick ignored most of them and answered, "John is studying law at Lincoln's Inn. It seemed to make good sense they live with her while he does, with Master Yonge paying toward their keep."

"It seemed," Master Pecock echoed. "Meaning that it no longer does?"

"Meaning they no longer can. She's dead."

"Dead? Mistress Bullok? I'd not heard she was ill."

"A servant found her dead this morning. Her heart failed in the night, it seems."

"Seems? You are over-given to qualifying your statements this morning, young Richard. Why 'seems'?"

He was rising as he asked it, and Dick rose, too, while answering,

"John and I purposed to go out together today. I didn't know what had happened and came to his door just as Sire Thomas and the crowner's deputy both did."

"Of course Sire Thomas would be wanted," Master Pecock said, crossing the room toward his heavy outdoor cloak, hanging on a wall peg beside the chamber's door. "There'll be prayers needed, and equally of course the coroner's man had come because it was an unexpected death and he has to say there was no wrong-doing with it." He swung his cloak around his shoulders. "All as it should be. Seemingly." He quirked a small smile at Dick. "And yet you're here, wanting my help. Why?"

There, of course, was the main question and Dick hesitated over his answer before saying, "I went briefly in, to ask if there was aught I could do, for John or anyone. While I was there . . . please pardon my saying it this way but something didn't feel right. I know that's not sound evidence of anything but . . ."

Master Pecock held up a hand. "Given there is no denying that feelings exist, thus far that you felt something is allowable as evidence that something unsettled you. On the other hand, how sound your feeling was remains to be determined. What did you feel and do you know why you felt it?"

"I don't know why I felt it or even what it was, just that something wasn't as it should be. Agnes was weeping and trying to answer the crowner's questions. She was almost as upset because they'd quarreled last night as she was that her mother was dead. She was going on, saying over and over, 'Why did they have to quarrel? Why did they have to be so angry about it?'"

"Quarrels before sudden deaths rarely look good to a crowner," Master Pecock said, leaving the room with a sad shake of his head. "But the quarrel wasn't between her and her mother?"

"No," Dick answered, following him. "It was between her mother and Master Yonge."

"About what?"

"I don't know. Agnes just kept saying that and crying and John kept trying to comfort her."

"And Master Yonge? Why is he in London, as I take it he must be— or at least he was yesterday, since he was quarreling with Mistress Bullok then?"

They had reached the outer door, Dick moving ahead to open it but pausing, his hand on the latch to look back at Master Pecock uncomfortably. "I gather he's in London because of his quarrel with Mistress Bullok."

Master Pecock's rather fulsome eyebrows rose. "Then next you're going to tell he stayed the night at Mistress Bullok's, aren't you? That he and his son and his daughter-in-law were all there when she died."

"Um, yes."

"Hence your uneasy 'feeling,' sufficient unto asking me to come."

"Yes, but there's something else, too. A candle."

He paused and Master Pecock encouraged, "Yes? A candle?" And prompted further, when Dick didn't promptly answer, "Left burning by her bed when it shouldn't have been? Or else not burning by her bed when it should have been? Or burned down a little but not enough? Or . . ."

To stop him Dick said quickly, "She didn't die in her bed."

"You're not going to tell me she died in Master Yonge's, I trust?"

"No! She died in the cellar, it seems."

Master Pecock raised his eyebrows again. "Seems."

"John says she always goes through the house last thing every night, after everyone else is to bed, making sure all is closed and locked and barred before she goes to bed herself. She must have been doing that when she died because John told me the servant found her in the cellar this morning."

"There's no question of a fall down the cellar stairs, I gather?"

"Nothing was determined yet while I was there. The crowner was just beginning to ask questions."

"But this candle that you find unsettling—it wasn't where it should be, I take it."

"It was in the kitchen. A burned down stub of a candle. On the floor, rolled under the table there."

"I assume Mistress Bullok did not keep the kind of kitchen where a candle is likely to be found on the floor?"

"Mistress Bullok did not," Dick said firmly.

"But it could happen. An unlighted candle, lying on the table, could roll off and under the table, unnoted for a time."

"It could," Dick granted. "But there was also a thick splattering of wax on the floor a foot or so away from the table. As if the candle, lighted, had been dropped there."

Master Pecock smiled upon him, immensely pleased. "Now there's something that's more than 'feeling' and 'seeming,' young Richard. Let's be gone."

Relieved, Dick smiled back. He had watched Master Pecock deal with questionable deaths before now. Vague he might be about some things and poor-sighted without his glasses, but no man, once given a problem, was less likely to let go of it until he sorted it through to the end. If there were to be questions about Mistress Bullok's death, Dick wanted him there for John's sake, if nothing else and, still smiling, Dick opened the door and stepped aside to let him go out first. Hunched deeply into their hoods and cloaks and heads down, they crossed the yard with talk paused. Only in the brief shelter of the passage to the street did Master Pecock lift his head enough to ask, "Since Sire Thomas is already there, what excuse do we give for my coming?"

"When I left, Sire Thomas was already in the cellar, praying aloud for Mistress Bullok's soul . . ."

"Sire Thomas does pray most impressively."

". . . and therefore I've brought you to be a comfort to everyone else while he does."

Master Pecock accepted that with a nod as they came into the snow again and they went in silence the brief way to Mistress Bullok's. Her house was of an older sort, broader fronted than most, rising the usual three stories high to a steep roof, each floor more out-thrust than the one below it, but with a stone-walled cellar below that raised what should have been the ground floor six steep stone steps above street level while six other steps led down to a heavy door into the cellar, useful when goods were delivered to be stored. Fewer people than would have been there in better weather were gathered gawking in front, kept somewhat at bay by the crowner's man on the steps up to the front door, but he had seen Dick when he left and greeted Master Pecock by name and, probably supposing that Dick belonged there and that in a matter of death more priests were better than less, he let them go past him without question, into the narrow way that ran between the great hall on one side and the butlery and pantry on the other. Beyond them, Dick knew, were the parlor, stairs to the upper stories and the kitchen. In the usual way of things Dick would have stayed where he was and called for a servant to see them in. Today, instead, he said, "They'll likely be in the parlor," and led Master Pecock into the great hall. It was far smaller and less grand than would be found in a lord's or wealthier merchant's house, and ceilinged above the rafters rather than open to the roof beams, but with the usual low dais at the far end where master and mistress would sit at table to dine on better days than this one while the rest of the household sat at lesser tables below them.

Today, out of keeping with how things should have been with midday dinnertime approaching, the tabletops still leaned against one wall, their trestles beside them. Nor were any lamps lighted or the fire built up and burning in the wide fireplace set in one wall, and among the shadows Dick only belatedly realized John and Master Yonge were standing silently beside the cold hearth when John said, "Dick. I wondered where you'd gone." With surprise he added, "Master Pecock? Sire Thomas is already here. Didn't Dick tell you?"

"John," Master Pecock said in greeting and ignoring his puzzlement, bent his head to the older man. "Master Yonge, yes?"

Master Yonge briefly bowed his head in return. He and Master Pecock were much the same age, Dick guessed, both somewhat balding but Master Yonge red-faced and well-fleshed while the priest was slighter built and tended toward pale, having always given his most heed to the indoor work of books and study, Dick knew; but where they presently most differed was that Master Yonge's baffled and embattled look seemed hardly to take in that they were even there, while Master Pecock's keen considering turned from Master Yonge to John and back again, assessing them even as he greeted them.

To help matters along, Dick asked of John, "Where's the crowner's man? Has he finished?"

"Finished?" John's echo was bleak. "No. He looked to be nearly done and then suddenly he wasn't. He sent us here and has been questioning Agnes in the kitchen ever since."

"About what?"

"I don't know. He found a candle under the table and the next moment told us to come here and wait. So we've been waiting." His wary glance at his father suggested it had not been as quiet a wait as it presently seemed.

"A candle?" Master Pecock asked as if he'd heard nothing about a candle before this. "What sort of candle?"

"Just a candle. Just a plain, damned candle," Master Yonge snapped impatiently.

"There was some candle wax spattered on the floor beside where Agnes was sitting in the kitchen," John explained. "She leaned over and started to scrape it off with her fingernail, not even thinking what she was doing. Just scraping at it for something to do."

He was talking to busy his mind more than for any other reason, Dick thought, as Master Pecock asked, "What then?"

"While she was leaned over, scraping, she saw this candle under the bench," Master Yonge said with greater sharpness than John. "A stupid stub of a candle. She picked it up and said, 'How odd,' and the crowner fellow said, 'What's odd?' She said it shouldn't be there; her mother would have been angry. Then he turned all interested in it and the wax on the floor."

"Well, that's hardly a problem," Master Pecock suggested with an innocence Dick doubted.

"It surely is," Master Yonge returned hotly. "The man was satisfied and ready to leave and instead this past quarter hour or more he's been questioning Agnes and . . ." He looked at his son. "What's the maidservant's name?"

"Ida."

"Right. He's been questioning them and by now knows Mistress Bullok and I quarrelled yesterday and there's no telling what nonsense he will craft out of that."

"You quarrelled?" Master Pecock asked. "Over what?"

"Over money, of course." Master Yonge sounded disgusted. "We made agreement when John and Agnes were married that I'd pay her twenty marks a year for five years, to be spent on their keep and John's training. Now this year she's suddenly short and says she can't give enough for John's needed books. Says the baby has cost so much she's come up short and John must needs make do or I must pay more. Like I was a fool and would just accept that. How much can a baby cost, I ask you! I said I'd see her household book to see how she was misspending things before she had another penny out of me. She said she'd see me in hell first. I said . . ."

"Father," John interrupted, discomfortable. "She's dead."

"What? Well. Yes." Master Yonge fell silent, with grace enough to look abashed.

More as if to end the awkwardness than out of any real interest, Master Pecock asked mildly, "Did you resolve the matter?"

"Humph," said Master Yonge.

It was John who said, with another wary look at his father, "They'd passed the yelling and she was half way to agreeing he could see the accounts. So that was something."

"When she had to, she could be reasonable," Master Yonge grumbled.

With both of them, grief seemed no part of their feelings. Poorly curbed irk on Master Yonge's part and an uncomfortable rue on John's were all they were managing, but their faces shifted to more suitable sadness at the sound of light, slippered footsteps approaching the door. Agnes entered, a slight-built young woman, pretty enough and usually bright-humored. Today, though, her prettiness was damp with tears and all her brightness gone. Her gown was plain and workaday and she had only a headkerchief over her fair hair and no wimple or veil as a married woman with guests usu-

ally would, but had undoubtedly come downstairs this morning ready for
an ordinary day, not this one; and without heed for anyone else she went
straight to John, into his out-held arms, to cling to him and bury her face
against his shoulder and sob there, the words muffled but her pain plain,
"Oh, John, what's going to happen?"

John made comforting noises but Master Yonge asked, "What's the
crowner's man up to?"

Still clinging to John, Agnes turned her head enough to give Master
Yonge a frightened look before she said to John, not his father, "I've sent
Ida to bring down little Andrew. I thought he'd be a comfort to us and
Elynore had to come down anyway. Master Roswell wants to talk to her,
too."

"About what?" Master Yonge demanded.

"I don't know," Agnes sobbed into John's shoulder.

Master Yonge took a step toward her. "What's he been asking that's
kept you in the kitchen for so long?"

She burst into open tears again. "I'm not supposed to say!" she wailed
and turned, turning John with her, to put between her and his father.

Master Yonge made a broad, impatient gesture with both hands, but
Master Pecock forestalled whatever he might have said by saying, "Sir, I
somewhat know Master Roswell. Would you like me to go and ask him
what's toward?"

"Yes!" Master Yonge almost exploded on the word. "By all I saw this
morning, Mistress Bullok died of heart seizure, nothing else. So why all
this . . . this questioning and upsetting?"

"There's blood," Agnes sobbed from John's arms. "On her head!"

"She hit her head when she collapsed," Master Yonge grumbled.
"That's all. She probably never even felt it."

Agnes gave a moan and sagged against John who remonstrated,
almost angrily, "Father!"

Master Yonge subsided slightly, only muttering, "What did she want
to be in the cellar at night for anyway?"

"She *always* went to the cellar," Agnes sobbed. "Every night she went
to every door and the windows, to make certain they were locked or
barred like they should be because she didn't want to leave it to the servants. Don't you dare say anything against her!"

"And was everything locked and barred as it should be?" Master
Pecock asked mildly. "This morning, when you arose, I mean?"

Agnes hiccupped and looked confused. "Yes. Maybe. I don't know. I
suppose it was. Yes."

"Ida was exclaiming a robber had killed Mistress Bullok," John said. "Because of the blood. I went around. Everything was shut as it should be."

Master Pecock nodded, murmured a general, "By your leave," and with another nod for Dick to come with him, left the hall. Once in the passage again, though, he stopped and asked, "Young Richard, you know these people more than I do. Even Master Yonge you've met before this and I haven't. How do they seem to you? Is anything about them other than seems to you it should be?"

Dick had already considered that and answered readily, "No, they're all very much themselves."

"I take it John never had deep affection for his mother-in-law, but did they get on well enough together? Mind you," Master Pecock went on, more to himself than Dick, "I should think affection for Mistress Bullok would be difficult to come by in any case and the more so when living under her very roof."

"He did well enough with her," Dick said slowly. "He did as she wanted and never argued, so there was no trouble." Somewhat unwillingly, he added, "My mother is always saying she's a good woman. Was a good woman," he amended.

"Which is most often said when there is doubt of it, for a reason or reasons. It's often thought that to not be a bad woman—and I think Mistress Bullok was not—is the same as to be a good woman—or man— and on those grounds many people develop a better opinion of themselves or others than in truth is justified, while if it's granted that good should be an active matter rather than a passive one, then the absence of bad actions is hardly the same as actual good actions and . . ."

"Sir," said Dick.

Left uncurbed, Master Pecock could go on that way for long whiles, following thoughts most people would not even bother to have, but reminded of what was to hand, he broke off, cleared his throat and said, "Has Agnes ever shown fright of Master Yonge before this?"

"Not that I've seen."

"And the kitchen is which way?"

Dick led him to it. At the back of the house, it looked out by a single window into a high-fenced rearyard, probably a garden in summer but presently merely full of snow. By this time on any day the kitchen should have been bustling with preparations for dinner, but on the wide fireplace hearth the fire was banked and unburning, and rather than bustle and warmth, all was chill and gray, with pots, pans, and everything else tidily in their places save for a ladle and a candle stub lying on the thick-topped worktable in the room's middle where Master Roswell, the crowner's man, was talking with tearful Elynore, an older woman in what she was fond of saying was her prime of life (though Dick hoped to still have all his teeth when he was in his) who had been Mistress Bullok's maidservant for twenty years and more, as she was also fond of saying. She and her mistress had been always strong-mindedly certain how to run the household and to see her miserably weeping, her headcloth awry and she not caring that it was, made Dick for the first time fully feel—rather than merely know—that Mistress Bullok was indeed dead.

Master Roswell greeted Master Pecock with almost open relief. He was by occupation a chandler, maker of excellent candles, his service as sometimes deputy to the crowner done more for civic duty than desire. As such, he was usually sent to deal with sudden deaths where there was likely to be no difficult questions and no trouble and he looked none too happy that this one was going differently than expected. Or maybe it was simply questioning Elynore he was finding discomfiting because, rather than asking why Master Pecock was there, he followed his glum greeting to him by sending her on her way with suggestion she take food and drink to Mistress Agnes and the others. Very willingly, sniffing mightily on her tears the while, she obligingly filled a tray with a jug of wine, cups, yesterday's bread, some honey, and left. As Dick closed the door behind her, Master Pecock promptly asked, "How goes it?"

Master Roswell had seen Master Pecock sort through questionable matters before now and rather than questioning why he was there answered readily, "Not so easily as I'd hoped when I was called."

"Because of that candle stub," Master Pecock said.

"To start with. Dick has been talking, I take it. You've likewise heard Mistress Bullok and Master Yonge quarreled yesterday?"

"So he said."

"He admits it then." That seemed to make Master Roswell none the happier. "I don't suppose he admitted to killing her, too? To shoving her down the cellar stairs maybe?"

"Was she shoved?"

"No." Master Roswell granted grudgingly. "Not down the stairs anyway. She's not even lying near them but along by the first of the cellar pillars that are holding up this floor. Nor has she any of the scrapes, bruises, or broken bones a fall would likely have given her. What there is . . ." Master Roswell stopped, visibly working over something within himself before he said, "What do you make of this?" He took up the ladle—made all in one piece and of iron, meant to last for decades—from the table, turned it over and pointed to a dark smear on the bottom of its bowl. "That's blood there, if I know anything."

"From something lately cooked?" Master Pecock asked, bland as unsugared pudding.

"We're a little past the year's time for making blood sausage," Master Roswell returned dourly, "and both daughter and Elynore say there's been nothing cooked to leave this on the ladle and, besides, nothing is ever left dirty in Mistress Bullok's kitchen if anyone knows what's good for them. Look." He held it up, closer to the priest. "It's smeared and almost gone. Someone wiped it as well as they could in the dark last night."

"If it was dark, how did they know it was there?"

"Because they'd put it there by hitting the old woman over the head with it, would be my guess."

"How did you come to find it?"

"After Mistress Agnes found the candle where it shouldn't be, I asked her if there was anything else out of place. She looked around and said she thought not but I should ask Ida who'd know even better. When I did, Ida saw right off that the ladle was hanging between the two spits instead of where it should have been, beside the roasting forks. Mistress Bullok always wanted everything kept just right and always the same, Ida says, and that ladle's place had been the same all the fifteen years she'd been with Mistress Bullok so she knew it was wrong as soon as she saw it."

"You've looked for other blood here?"

"I've looked. The only blood I've found is in the cellar, on Mistress Bullok's head where something hit her hard and on the pillar base she's lying by. The pillars are wood but they're set on stone and that's where the blood is."

"She might have hit her head there."

"If it was a heart seizure that took her, the way it first looked, I'd say she collapsed, yes, and hit her head there and there'd be naught more to be said about it."

"But then the candle and ladle came into it."

"Aye. With them in it, I have to think that whatever happened to Mistress Bullok happened here in the kitchen and someone wants me to think differently and therefore there's something wrong about all of it."

"Well thought through. You think someone struck her down here, moved her body to the cellar, and attempted to make it seem she died there and naturally."

"Yes."

"With Master Yonge most likely to have done it."

"They'd quarreled, and he's someone has the strength to move her body."

"Who else was in the house last night?"

"Mistress Agnes and her husband, the two servant-women, and Master Yonge's man, Ralph. The baby, of course, but I'm leaving him out of it."

Matching Master Roswell's half-hearted jest, Master Pecock said, "Because he couldn't have moved the body. Then there were none others? No apprentices or journeymen?"

"The man who runs the shop for her sleeps at his own place and the apprentice stays with him. They've no way to come in once the place is shut for the night."

"As it was shut."

"Elynore goes around and locks up at dark. Later, when everyone else goes up to bed, Mistress Bullok would check everything a last time. The last anyone admits to seeing her last night, that's what she was doing."

"Who slept where and what do they say they did after they went up?"

"The woman Ida has a place at the top of the house. There are two rooms there, I'm told. She has the small back one. Last night Master Yonge and his man had the front one, as he often does when he's in London. They all say that none of them heard any of them moving around in the night. Though that doesn't mean none of them did. She might have slept too sound, and Master Yonge's man might lie for him."

"Too true. Or they might have slept too soundly to have heard her. What of Elynore?"

"She sleeps on a truckle bed in Mistress Bullok's chamber. She says she laid down while waiting for Mistress Bullok to come up and fell asleep. She's torn with guilt she slept right through and didn't wake until this morning to know her mistress never came to bed."

"And John and Agnes?"

"They sleep in a chamber beyond Mistress Bullok's. The only way to it is through hers."

"And Elynore doesn't know whether either of them left it because she fell asleep."

"No, she says right after they'd all come up, Mistress Agnes went back down, but Mistress Agnes had already told me that. Was weeping over it because it was the last time she saw her mother."

"Why did she go down?"

"She and Master John—and he says this, too—were both upset over their parents' quarrel and after they'd talked a bit, she wanted to see how her mother did and went down to her."

"And Mistress Bullok was well, I take it."

"She was putting away her account book in a locked chest in the parlor and still bitter against Master Yonge but settling a bit. She sent Mistress Agnes back to bed, saying she'd be up soon, and that was the last Mistress Agnes knows of her. Master John says that Mistress Agnes was gone only a little time and when she returned they went to sleep until morning. She couldn't have moved her mother's body anyway," he added.

"Thus everyone is seemingly accounted for," Master Pecock said, "but in truth no one is. Elynore could be lying about how soon she went to sleep and could have gone down after Agnes came back. Agnes or John could have gone down when Elynore was so soundly asleep she'd not hear them. Likewise, Master Yonge or his man or Ida. Whoever went, went unheard and beknownst to anyone else. Or else someone is lying for them."

"But, still, Master Yonge is the only one with reason to kill her," Master Roswell pointed out.

"The only one of whom we know," Master Pecock returned, "and even then it's a feeble reason."

"That doesn't mean he didn't do it," Master Roswell cautioned.

"Quite true. Did you, by the way, find a candle or lamp in the cellar such as Mistress Bullok might have been using?"

"There were a candle and candlestick fallen beside her, and spattered wax."

"But no candlestick here, only the candle."

"Because the murderer took that downstairs but had to find another candle to go with it. They're kept there." Master Roswell pointed to a wooden box on a nearby shelf. "So that would be no trouble."

"May I see what's to be seen in the cellar?"

Master Roswell was willing and led the way. From the head of the stairs Sire Thomas could be heard praying in the deep, intensely mournful voice that made him the parish's favored priest for funerals, and they found him kneeling near the stairfoot, his prayer book lighted by four oil lamps burning above him on a shoulder-tall stand. By their light Mistress Bullok's body could be seen lying beside the nearest pillar but beyond it the cellar stretched away in shadows, low-ceilinged, narrow, with crates and bales of goods piled along the walls. At the far end, lost in the dark, was the door to the outside stairs up to the street, whose lock and bar Mistress Bullok had supposedly been coming to check last night. Sire Thomas acknowledged the men with a nod but no pause as they passed him, circling to the far side of Mistress Bullok's body so they would not shadow it. She had been turned over on her back and straightened from whatever untidy way she had likely fallen, Dick guessed, because her eyes were closed, her hands folded on her breast, and her skirts smoothed to cover her feet. But everything about her was so slack and silent—skin already grayed and sinking over her bones, mouth hanging slightly open—that she hardly seemed Mistress Bullok at all, simply a gray-faced stranger who vaguely resembled her. Or maybe it was that her blood-marked headkerchief and wimple had been removed and were lying beside her, leaving her mostly white hair uncovered, unseemly for a widow.

But if she had been alive to care about such things, they'd not be here to see it, Dick thought.

Master Roswell pointed out the small, irregular stain of her blood on the squared stone of the pillar's base. The wound itself was on the shadowed side of her head, difficult to see, but Master Pecock leaned over and touched it, bringing a startled, disgusted gasp from Sire Thomas. On their part, Dick and Master Roswell only watched until Master Pecock, satisfied of something, wiped his fingers on the already-stained headkerchief, straightened and asked of Master Roswell, "Have you felt the wound? You'd be well advised to, I think."

Wry-mouthed, Master Roswell did and Dick saw his expression change, but as Master Roswell straightened, before he could say anything, Master Pecock said, "Shall we return to the kitchen?" and they did, leaving Sire Thomas to his prayers and Dick strangling on curiosity that was not satisfied by Master Pecock asking, when they were in the kitchen again, "So, Master Roswell, from all of this, what do you judge happened?"

Slowly, as if considering as he went, Master Roswell answered, "I'd have said someone—almost surely Master Yonge—struck her down in the kitchen, probably with anger and no forethought, and then thought to make her death look like heart failure. He carried her into the cellar, smeared her blood on the stone as if she'd fallen, and dropped the candle and candlestick beside her. Then he tried to clean the ladle but didn't dare a light in the kitchen and therefore cleaned it poorly and either forgot or couldn't find the other candle and so went back to bed, lucky no one heard him either going or returning."

"And now?" Master Pecock asked encouragingly.

Just as Dick so often had when Master Pecock's pupil, Master Roswell paused, wary of his answer, before saying, "The wound is wrong for that. If she was hit with this ladle, the break in her skull would be rounded. It's not. It's a crack."

"Likewise," Master Pecock said, "I think we should consider other possibilities than merely Master Yonge as murderer. First, it's possible he did indeed kill Mistress Bullok. To judge by Agnes' demonstrated fear of him in the parlor just now, she fears as much. Or possibly what she truly fears—or of which she may be certain—is that her husband is the murderer . . ."

"Not John!" Dick protested.

Master Pecock held up an admonitory hand. "We are naming possibilties and, however unlikely you deem such a thing to be, it is, I think you will grant, possible, with Agnes protecting John by openly appearing to suspect her father-in-law. Third, Agnes perhaps killed her mother."

"Why?" Dick scoffed.

"We are considering how, not why, at this point. Fourth, perhaps it was one of the servants for a reason yet undetermined. Fifth, Mistress Bullok did indeed die of no more than heart seizure as it first seemed and there was no murder at all. Yet."

"Yet?" Dick echoed.

"Think it through, young Richard, think it through. Meanwhile let us turn all the matter that we have around. Would you say, Master Roswell, that the wound is more in keeping with Mistress Bullok having struck the stone base of the pillar than been struck with this ladle?"

"Yes."

"Then let us suppose she did have a seizure in the cellar. It's very possible. She was a choleric woman and had spent an angry evening. Suppose she fell, struck her head, and died either from the hurt to her head or of her heart's failure."

"But there's the candle here in the kitchen and the ladle," Master Roswell protested.

"Suppose someone—we shall shortly consider who—found her dead . . ."

"Agnes," Dick said. "We know she came downstairs last night."

"We do but nothing is certain until fully proved. So let us suppose this someone, seeing there was nothing to be done for Mistress Bullok, saw a chance for something else. A cloth to the wound for blood to smear on the ladle, as if blood had been wiped off it rather than on. A candle lighted and dropped on the kitchen floor to spatter wax, then the candle left as if it had rolled out of sight and the supposed murderer could not find it. By those two simple, quickly done things the happenstance of natural death was shifted to look like murder. Of course Agnes is the most likely to have done all that, but what other proof do we have of her?"

Dick, who had been thinking, said, "The ladle. Of everything that could be used here in the kitchen it would be the least costly." Because anything that was the instrument of a person's death, from a dagger to a falling rock to a kicking horse, was considered *deodand*, a forfeit to the Church, redeemable for money or else lost. "That's something Agnes would think of and Master Yonge likely not."

"But equally something Elynore or Ida might consider," Master Pecock pointed out.

"But we *know* Agnes came downstairs, so we have to consider her first."

"But why would she?" Master Roswell asked, distressed.

Master Pecock nodded at Dick who said eagerly, "Because if there was a murder, Master Yonge would be first and most suspected—" But what followed made him stop short, wrenched by what he suddenly saw. Slowly he said, "And with her mother gone and then Master Yonge, she and Master John would have everything and no one to gainsay their enjoying of it."

Master Roswell put in quickly, "The flaw there is that if Master Yonge is convicted of murder his property is forfeit to the king. There'd be small profit for them in that."

"Master Yonge assigned much of his property," Dick said. A way of insuring against legal mishaps by putting property in the name or names of others so that it was not liable to whatever actions might be brought against the actual owner who nonetheless could remain in control of it. "It was part of the marriage settlement. He and Mistress Bullok both did it, with reversion to their heirs."

"And therefore," Master Pecock said, "Agnes had all to gain if Master Yonge was found guilty of murder."

"Did Master John act with her in it, do you think?" Master Roswell asked.

"John wouldn't, not even to inherit," Dick said. "He and his father get on well."

"From all I've ever heard, Mistress Agnes got on well with her mother," Master Roswell returned, "but that didn't stop her putting by her grief through the night to do this, if indeed she did."

"Love her mother though she seemingly did," Master Pecock said, "she's maybe enough her mother's daughter that, finding her already dead and past help, she was willing to take this chance to have everything."

"That's still no proof Master John didn't agree to it," Master Roswell insisted.

"Why don't we go and ask them?" Master Pecock suggested.

Master Roswell stared at him, startled, then smiled grimly and said,

"Why not? We'll lose nothing and maybe gain."

And gain they did, because only the asking was needed. As Master Roswell laid out their doubts and proofs but naming no names, Master Yonge frowned and then frowned more, while John gaped as if unable to understand what he was hearing, and Agnes ceased crying, her eyes growing large and larger until at the end Master Roswell turned and asked her directly, "So was it you who did all this?"

Her face crumpled. "*Yes!*" she wailed on a fresh flood of tears. "I found her dead and there wasn't anything to do for her and she'd not have minded Master Yonge being guilty if it meant more for me and John and I'm going to buy Masses for her. I'm sorry! It would have been all right!"

Walking back to St. Michael's through the diminishing snow, Dick asked Master Pecock what was likely to be done to Agnes.

With regret and resignation the priest shook his head. "Very little under the law, I suppose, except a fine should the crowner pursue her waste of his man's time. I trust there'll be heavy penance given of course, when she makes confession for disrespect to her mother and seeking Master Yonge's destruction. John may be unpleased with her for a time, too, and surely Master Yonge will, though of that I have some doubt."

"Doubt?" Dick said unbelievingly.

"I thought that after his first dismay he showed something of grudging admiration of her enterprise. After all, when all's said and safely done, he might well prefer a clever daughter-in-law to one who's not. Especially now that she knows she's not so clever as she thought she was."

It was said so seriously that Dick almost failed to hear the gleam of laughter behind the words before Master Pecock went on, still solemnly, "Which leaves only the matter of you being disconcertingly taller than when I last saw you, young Richard, and I must insist that you either cease to increase your height or visit me more frequently, that your growth be not so disparate as to be discomfiting when we do encounter."

And Dick began to laugh.

Ex Libris

Kate Gallison

THE BIRDS OF EVENING were beginning to sing their sundown songs as Mother Lavinia Grey and her parishioners packed away St. Bede's monthly flea market, another successful fundraiser for the ever-needy Episcopal church of Fishersville, New Jersey. Much of the stuff donated by the townspeople had gone unsold, but they had taken in a little over a thousand dollars, amply repaying the work of selling and the inconvenience of dragging the surplus down to the Salvation Army in Trenton. Mother Grey sighed and wiped the dust off her hands. Two more boxes of books and it would all be off the lawn and put away again.

One last customer was poking among the books. Buford Preble, the venerable town drunk, fingered the mildewed spines of some old tomes that had plainly been cleaned out of someone's damp cellar.

"Nothin' left but books, Mother Vinnie?" he said.

"You should have come by earlier, Boofie," she said. "We've put everything away. Come back next month. We'll have a whole new load of stuff."

"Guess I'll take this book, then," he said with a strange little smile. Mother Grey supposed he was bound and determined to buy something. "How much?" he said.

"It's for the church," Mother Grey said, in the new formula the vestry had devised. "You decide." People gave more if you pointed out that it was for the church; they shifted out of the bargain-hunting mode and into the mode of charitable giving. Not that Boofie had a whole lot to give. Mother Grey had heard a rumor that he was living on the street again. Maybe she should have let him have the book for nothing.

He gave her a quarter. "Now I've got something to read," he said.

As he went off down the street with the book in his hand Vera Wells called out to Mother Grey from where she was putting the folding tables away inside the church. "You're not getting rid of those books, are you? I have a customer for those who went to get the car. They're all paid for."

Oops. "Boofie!" she called, but Buford Preble was gone. Surely one little book would not be missed from that huge box. It held such a quantity of books, each one moldier and more mouse-eaten than the last. Mother Grey finished tidying the church lawn and thought no more about it.

The next time Mother Grey saw Buford Preble it was to read the burial rites over him.

✠

To say that the town of Fishersville was devastated by Buford Preble's loss would be an exaggeration, but he was missed. There was an empty chair at the Saturday AA meeting at St. Bede's, where Boofie used to turn up from time to time. There was an empty bench beside the public phone in front of the city parking lot, where the city's port-a-potties were, the bench that used to be called Boofie's office. It was all the same to the tourists, but the locals thought of Boofie when they passed the bench. That he had fallen in the canal and drowned came as no surprise to anyone, since poor Boofie was never sober, and frequently had trouble keeping his feet. Like everyone else in Fishersville he used the canal path to travel from one end of town to the other.

The real hoopla came the week after the funeral, when the *Clarion* got hold of a story about the autopsy. Enough barbituates had been found in Boofie's body to cause the police to call his death suspicious. The *Clarion* put the story on the front page and it became the talk of Fishersville.

"How could you not have known about this?" Sheila Dresner demanded of Mother Grey. "I thought you had your finger on the pulse of the town, Vinnie. I thought the police confided in you."

"Actually they don't," Mother Grey said. "But somebody seems to have confided in Paula Featherston." Paula's stock in trade for the *Clarion* was the shocking story. Not your average feel-good shopper weekly, the *Clarion* gave Paula free rein to tell all according to her lights. If at times her lights were somewhat dim, still it made for good reading. Generally she covered the schools. Her kids brought home stories of minor disciplinary problems and errors in teacher judgement that could always be blown up into epidemics of juvenile delinquency and abuse. The letters to the editor that were printed the following week in outraged agreement or rebuttal made for even better reading.

As a rule, Mother Grey found that she could discount the *Clarion's* more sensational coverage by a factor of 7 percent for reportorial hysteria. As for this murder story, the sinister results of the drug tests on Buford Preble's body seemed to be solid reporting. The 7 percent hysteria factor consisted of Paula's assertion that, since an unknown killer was loose in the town, nobody was safe.

"That's nonsense," Mother Grey said. "Most of us are perfectly safe."

"You and I are safe for certain," Sheila said. "I didn't know any of the same people Boofie knew."

"Yes you did," said Mother Grey. "Boofie knew everybody in town."

"He knew you, anyway," Sheila said. "How well did you know him?"

Good question. Unless one counted the AA meetings at St. Bede's parish house, where Boofie would sometimes turn up too drunk to climb the stairs to the meeting room, and Mother Grey would stumble over him on the bottom step, she hardly encountered him at all to speak to. So on those grounds she was safe. Even Paula Featherston was safe, unless of course she happened to find out who the killer was and threatened to reveal his or her name. Most of the other sober citizens of the town were probably safe as well, since the most likely culprit was one of Mr. Preble's companions in inebriety.

Or not.

"Doesn't it bother you that a murderer is running around loose in Fishersville?" Sheila said.

"Yes," said Mother Grey. "It bothers me a lot. But I have every confidence in the ability of the police to solve the crime. If indeed there was a crime."

"You mean if Paula got the story straight," Sheila said.

"Right. If Paula got the story straight about the lab tests, and Boofie was drugged before he went into the water, then the police can handle it."

"I see that you're not in the mood for crime-solving today," Sheila said.

"Boofie's death is not a crossword puzzle, you know, nor an exercise in mental agility." Mother Grey thought she believed that the meddling of amateurs in police matters was inappropriate, unwarranted, and generally a bad idea. Officer Jack Kreevitch didn't monkey with the spiritual welfare of her parishioners, and she didn't do his police work for him.

Except every once in a while, she thought. Maybe it's time. As soon as her friend left she got out her yellow pad and her good fine-tip blue pen and started crime-solving.

After ten minutes she had a long list of potential suspects, but they were all people she would like to see sent away to jail, not people she really suspected of harming poor Boofie.

"Barbituates," she muttered. "Who would have access to such things?" More to the point, what sort of motive could anyone have for killing that harmless man? Some stupid disagreement between friends. Banal and stupid, as evil often is. But poisoning was not the method a couple of drunks would use to hurt each other if they came to a disagreement, not in Mother Grey's experience. Fists or blunt instruments would be the weapons of choice. Poison implied forethought, a certain subtlety of mind.

Why would anyone poison him? Maybe Boofie was in the way. Maybe someone wanted to use his bench, Boofie's office. To solve the crime in that case would be easy; she would watch the bench and see who sat there now.

Or robbery. But Boofie had nothing worth stealing.

Then suddenly she thought of the book.

What book was it? Could it have been valuable, or have had something valuable tucked inside it? And who could have wanted it enough to kill poor Boofie for it?

Perhaps the person who had bought the box of books at the church flea market had done it, whoever he or she might be. Mother Grey called Vera Wells, hoping Vera would remember. But three weeks had now passed since the flea market, and Vera's memory, never really crisp, failed her completely.

"You can't remember at all?" Mother Grey said. "Young or old? Black or white? Man, woman, or child?"

"I can't even remember the box of books," Vera said. "Is it important?"

"I don't know," said Mother Grey. It's up to me then, she thought, as she hung up the phone. Try to visualize the book. It was about a hundred years old, on the slim side, hard-bound in dull red cloth, faded black lettering of a curly sort, decorated with art-nouveau flowers, too beat-up and mildewed to be worth much as a collectible, and the title was . . . *The Annals* of something.

If the book were still among Buford Preble's effects then it had nothing to do with anything. If not . . . But where in the world were his effects? The man was homeless.

She tackled a friend of Boofie's on the subject, catching him as he came out of the Saturday AA meeting, an old man by the name of Lester Willcox. "Do you know where Boofie was staying just before he died?" she asked him. There were various hideouts in and around Fishersville where a man might lay his head, ranging from the empty boxcars of the abandoned rail line to the Hotel Ford, a group of junked cars in a field on the side of Reekers Hill north of town.

"Gonna solve the murder, are you, Mother Vinnie?" Lester gave her a lewd wink.

"No, no. There was something—I just thought—"

"You and the cops. They think I did it, you know. But I would never hurt Boofie."

"Of course not. What would you gain by it?" she asked, rhetorically. The only thing Lester had gained by Boofie's demise was the mantle of town drunk, which now sat easily on his stooped and tattooed shoulders.

"Boofie slept in a shed by the canal," he said. "Out back of that house that belongs to the gay guys from New York City. They only stay there weekends and they never look in their shed." That should narrow it down; there weren't more than twenty households in Fishersville fitting that description. But, no, backing on the canal. That would be more like five.

"Do you know the address?" she asked, hoping to make it easy on herself.

He did, and he told it to her. "Good luck investigating," he said. "I'll tell everybody you're looking for the killer. In case they have evidence for you."

"Oh, please don't," she said. She expected that he would ignore her. Soon she would have the townspeople after her day and night with clues and advice. No doubt one of these would be the actual killer.

Time passed. It was Monday before Mother Grey could get on with her detecting, Sunday being filled with church chores. By lunch time she figured the gay guys would have returned to their desks or whatever in the Big City, leaving her free to trespass on their property unmolested. The door to their shed was locked, but the window wasn't.

She hadn't got much further than turning over the stained and smelly pallet where Boofie used to sleep, and finding no book under it, before a key turned in the lock and the shed door swung open.

"Well, Vinnie," said Officer Kreevitch.

"Well, Jack."

"Lester Willcox told me you were on the case. You know, you're really going to have to get your compulsive crime-solving habit under control. I would hate to have to arrest you for breaking and entering."

"Yes, Jack."

"Go home."

"Okay, but first let me tell you about the book."

"If you can do it in five seconds. That's how long it's gonna be before the county detectives get here." She noticed he had a roll of crime scene tape under his arm. Good. He was on the case too. Maybe they could cooperate after all.

So she told him all about the slim red book with the flowers, and he helped her search. The book was nowhere to be found in the shed. As the footsteps of the county detectives approached suddenly Jack Kreevitch had a flash of insight, staggering in its brilliance. How glad she was that Jack was on the case. To find out about a book, he said, you go to the library.

"An old red book with flowers on the cover," the librarian mused, nibbling her glasses thoughtfully. "*The Annals* of something. I take it this would not be found in *Books in Print.*"

"Not likely," said Mother Grey. "It looked very old. Ninety, a hundred years. Pre–World War One."

"Have you tried our card catalog?"

"Oh. Right."

The card catalog yielded a number of old volumes whose titles began with "The Annals." One of them was called *The Annals of Fishersville.* It was said to be in the local history collection. Mother Grey wrote down the particulars and returned to the front desk.

The librarian took the key and went to unlock the glass case where the local history books were kept. Mother Grey, looking over her shoulder, saw the spines of many books, but none of them red. It wasn't there.

"That's strange," the librarian said. She called out to her library clerk, busy at the desk with a stack of forms. "Wilhelmina, have you seen *The Annals of Fishersville?* It should be in the cabinet; we don't allow it to circulate."

"That red book," Wilhelmina said. "No, that's been missing for more than a month now. People keep asking us for it."

"What people?" Mother Grey asked.

"Different ones. Jane Foote wanted to see it. She's the one I'm doing all these interlibrary loans for. She's on a big research project. And Bill Warner, for his genealogy business."

"Jane Foote," Mother Grey repeated.

"The mystery writer. You must know her, she wrote those books that were supposed to be about you."

"I do know her. She comes to my church sometimes. And I read one of her books once, but I couldn't see any resemblance to me in her clergy-woman detective." Jane Foote's detective was a hopeless twit who spent her time chasing men and solving unbelievable murders, and none at all on her proper business. She knew nothing of what a real priest ought to know, theology, for instance, or homiletics, and her church had no parishioners and no income. In the real world the Diocese of New Jersey would have closed it down in a month and a half. "Bill Warner, you say? Who is he?"

"A genealogist who lives here in town. He often comes here to look for things to use in his work."

"So they both asked you for the book, but you couldn't give it to either of them."

"No. As I say, it's been missing."

✝

Armed with this new information, Mother Grey went to see Jack Kreevitch. She found him filling out reports at his desk in the new police station, a renovated auto body shop at the edge of town. OSHA had finally forced the city to relocate its police department from the basement of City Hall, whose ceiling was too low for federal safety and health regulations.

"Nice office," she said to him. "How do you like it?"

"Not bad," he said. "Kind of small, but at least I can stand up straight without hitting my head."

"Plenty of parking, too," Mother Grey observed.

"So," he said. "What can I do for you? Tell me you haven't come here to talk to me about Boofie's murder."

"Well, actually . . ."

"Is it the book thing?"

"I found out that the book is an old local history that disappeared some time ago from the Fishersville library."

"I hope you're not going to try to tell me Boofie was killed for a library book."

"Umm . . ."

"Go see if you can find out how the book got into St. Bede's yard sale. Then come back and see me."

"That's going to be difficult. People drop things off at the church all the time, whether anyone is there to receive them or not. Tracing a box of books could take forever."

"Good," Kreevitch muttered. She went home to the rectory in a huff. Waiting for her in the mail slot, folded in three, was a sheet of white paper with cut-out newspaper letters pasted to it:

FORGET ABOUT THE PREBLE CASE OR ELSE I'LL KILL YOU.

She took it straight back to the police station and tried to make Kreevitch look at it.

"Very funny," he said, and sent her home again.

Clearly the trail of the killer was growing hot. Or could it really have been a joke? She called Sheila.

"Did you leave a death threat in my mail slot?"

"No. Why would I do that?"

"No reason. To be funny, maybe."

"You're detecting again, aren't you, Vinnie?"

"Only socially."

"You told me you quit. You ought to be ashamed."

She saw Lester Willcox on the street, and stopped him. "Do you know who left a death threat in my mail slot?"

His answer was evasive. "If somebody is leaving death threats in your mail slot, Mother Vinnie, you should probably quit detecting for a while. I would."

He was warning her off. Maybe he was the one after all. "Do you know where to get barbituates?" she said.

"No, but if you find out let me know. I could use some good drugs." He shambled away. Surely his mind lacked the sneakiness, the quality of crafty malice necessary to poison a person. To say nothing of the fact that he clearly had no use for such a thing as a book.

Her fingers took a short stroll through the yellow pages and turned up a number and a street address for Bill Warner, professional genealogist. The address was right down the street; he must work out of his house. She would go straight over there and see whether she could catch him looking guilty.

A little bronze plaque decorated the front of the building, nothing quite so garish as a sign, announcing Bill Warner's occupation. She knocked on his door. Warner had a heavy brass knocker of the colonial sort, whose sonorous whack reverberated somewhere inside.

He opened the door himself and stood in the doorway, smiling jovially, a tall man with thinning white hair. Before she had time to tell him who she was or why she had come he greeted her by name. Everyone in town knows who I am, she thought. What's the use of trying to dissemble? A whiff of air came out, smelling of mildew.

That smell! It was the box of books! They must be right inside the front door. From where she was standing she could see the corner of the box.

Now for the cat and mouse game. She would not, of course, go charging in and accuse him of murdering Boofie. If she did that he might get rid of the evidence before the police arrived. Or worse! He might carry out his threat to kill her.

But she could get into the house on a pretext and take a look at those books, maybe see whether he had *The Annals* in the house somewhere.

"Mr. Warner, I wonder if I might come in. I was interested in having my family tree traced, and I thought, since you were right here in town—"

He waved her inside. The door hit the box of books as he swung it open, driving clouds of mold spores into the air. Both of them sneezed.

"Ah, those books!" Mother Grey cried, feigning to notice them for the first time. "You know, that almost looks like the same box of books we sold at the flea market the other week."

"It is," Bill Warner said. His cheerful smile did not appear in the least guilty. "I bought them from one of your parishioners there."

He frowned. "But, you know, one of the books was missing when I got the box home, and although all of them are useful, the missing book was the one I wanted the most. I don't suppose you have any idea what happened to it?"

Either the man was a diabolically cunning and clever actor, or he truly had no clue. "What was it called?" she asked him, batting her eyes innocently. Two could play that little game.

"*The Annals of Fishersville*," Warner said. "It's so rare even the libraries don't carry it."

"Was it valuable, then?"

"Only to historians and genealogists," he said. "I don't think it would bring much in the book market; it was pretty badly damaged, and would only be of local interest."

"I see." There was a long silence.

"Well, I guess someone must have just picked it up," he said. "So, about your genealogy. Is there any particular reason why you want to track it?"

"Oh, yes," she said. "Yes. I was thinking of joining the DAR."

It was another hour before she was able to pry herself away from the genealogist's searching interview. She had to leave a considerable sum of earnest money with him to finance the researches he was preparing to undertake. And for what? Mother Grey had no intention of joining the DAR, and Bill Warner was as innocent of murder as anyone she ever knew. She was certain of it. Almost.

Next day Sheila Dresner came over for coffee just after Mother Grey's mail arrived. She brought it in from the box on the porch and handed it to Mother Grey. Amongst the other things was a big manila envelope from a travel agency.

"What's this, Vinnie?" Sheila said. "Taking a trip?"

"Not that I know of," Mother Grey said. She opened it up. A note from the travel agent said, "Here's the material you requested. Call me again if I can be of further help." It was clipped to a sheaf of brochures for Switzerland.

"Switzerland?" Sheila said.

"Reichenbach falls. Someone wants me out of town."

"Vinnie, it's a death threat."

"How do you figure that?"

"Sherlock Holmes . . . detective . . ."

"Oh." She called the travel agent to find out who had asked them to send her the brochures, but nobody answered the phone.

Knowing in advance that he wouldn't take her seriously, but still hoping he might, she called Jack Kreevitch at the police station.

"I don't see how you could call that a death threat," he said. "Somebody sending you travel brochures."

"But—"

"It'll be okay, Mother Vinnie. Trust me. You know, you could use a little time off. Why not take a trip? Sounds like a good idea to me."

"Right, Jack. Thanks." How annoying. Now she was going to have to seriously get busy and find this murderer herself in order to have any peace.

Sheila had been sitting at the kitchen table the whole time, watching her turn red and fume. "So you're detecting again," said Sheila.

"Sure am."

"What's the next step? Can I help?"

"I don't think so. I'm going to talk to Jane Foote."

"That woman who writes the stories about you?"

"Those stories are not about me," she sniffed.

She found Jane Foote enjoying a cappuccino at the the Fishersville Coffee House. Mother Grey placed her own order and sat down at the polished bar next to the novelist.

"So, Jane," she said. "What are you up to lately? Written any exciting mysteries?"

"I don't write mysteries anymore," Jane Foote said.

"My word. Why not?"

"I don't want to. My head isn't in that place anymore. What I'm working on now is a historical novel about the War of 1812."

"Interesting," Mother Grey said. "That's not a period I know a lot about."

"Not many do," Jane Foote said. "It isn't very thoroughly taught in this country. The Canadians are more interested in it because it was during that conflict that they first began to be conscious of themselves as a country."

"My word," said Mother Grey, her eyes glazing over.

"But there were a lot of battles and events that would be interesting to Americans, if they knew about them," Jane Foote said. "I've been reading some marvelous books."

"Anything happen here in Fishersville?"

"I believe that Winfield Scott and his men crossed the Delaware here on their way from Fort Mifflin in Philadelphia to the Niagara Frontier," Foote said. "But they may have crossed in Trenton."

"Would that make a difference to the book you're writing?"

"Yes, I think it would. I'm trying to make it as accurate as I can, so that if my fictional characters had really lived then, they could have seen and done the things I put in the book." She wandered off into rhapsodies about the glory of endless research, the sweet pleasures of finding different views of the same event in different primary sources, the search for the elusive reference work.

"That must be a lot of fun for you," Mother Grey said.

"It is. I'm very excited about it. This book feels like the thing that I was born to do." Jane Foote looked Mother Grey in the face with a curious stare. "Come have a cup of tea with me sometime and I'll read you part of it." She told her how to find her house. "In fact, how about this afternoon?"

"I'd be delighted," said Mother Grey, neglecting to add that her chief delight would be to look around Jane's house for the missing copy of *The Annals*.

✝

Mother Grey had never been in Jane Foote's house. It was comfortable and smelled mostly of freshly baked bread, only faintly of cats. The whole place, however, was messy and cluttered. Books, papers, leaflets and spiral-bound notebooks covered all the flat surfaces in her living room except for the coffee table and the seats of two chairs. The chairs needed vacuuming; they were bristly with loose cat hair. On the coffee table Jane Foote had arranged a tray with a teapot, cream and sugar, and two cups, as well as a plateful of small strawberry jam sandwiches.

"How nice," said Mother Grey. She spotted *The Annals of Fishersville* almost at once in a pile on the floor beside the potted plant, third book from the top.

"One lump or two?"

"Two, please."

"I made the bread for these sandwiches this morning," Jane Foote said. "Don't you love a bread machine?"

"Probably I would," Mother Grey said, "but I don't have one." She boldly slid the slim red book out of the pile. "I take it this is one of your reference works." There were no library markings on the book. This had to be a different copy of *The Annals* from the one that had disappeared from the library. In fact, it almost had to be the book that Buford Preble was killed for.

"Yes," Jane Foote said. "I had to have it. As you can see, it chronicles every event of significance in Fishersville from the time of its founding until 1910."

"When you found that the library didn't have it, you should have bought a copy. I understand these things can be taken as tax deductions."

"There were none for sale."

Mother Grey sighed and put her teacup down. "I know you killed Buford Preble to get this book, Jane."

"Why, so you do."

"Why didn't you just borrow it from him?"

"He wouldn't let me have it. The book was his mother's. That box of books at the church came from his old family home, he told me; the new owners must have dropped it off at St. Bede's for the flea market."

"The book was his mother's?" Mother Grey said. She looked at the cover. "By Fanny Preble," it said. "Buford Preble's mother wrote *The Annals of Fishersville*?"

"No, his great-grandmother wrote it. The old lady was quite the historian." She placed her empty teacup in its saucer with a little clink. "I saved the best part of this whole story for last," she said. "You know those books I've been writing about you?"

"I know the books, but whoever you've been writing about, Jane, it certainly wasn't me," Mother Grey said. "I am nothing like that woman."

"What, not even superficially? Your height, your weight, your hairstyle—"

"Come, now. Surely you don't imagine I'm anything like that trivial, silly—"

"Whatever. In any case, I'm not writing those anymore."

"This is the best part of your story?"

"Yes! I have thrown off the shackles of mystery writing, and now I'm taking up the torch of historical fiction. Naturally I have to kill off my detective. I'm pleased to see you drank up all your tea. I would judge that you have about—"she glanced at her wristwatch—"forty seconds of consciousness left."

"Barbituates again?"

Jane Foote smiled and nodded.

Mother Grey put the slim red book back in the pile. With a long sigh she folded her arms across her chest. "Jane," she said, shaking her head from side to side. "Jane, you're a sick woman."

"No, I'm not. I'm simply taking a realistic approach to managing my writing career."

"That isn't what I meant. You're sick."

"What do you mean?"

"It wasn't I who drank up all of my tea, but you. I switched the cups. I'll call an ambulance," she added, as her hostess slumped slowly over in her chair. After the trial, Mother Grey told herself, when it wasn't needed anymore for evidence, she would see that this copy of *The Annals* went to the Fishersville Public Library to replace the missing one. The cause of scholarship should be supported at all costs.

Almost all costs, perhaps she should say.

✝

A Clerical Error

Michael Jecks

He had broken the law, and right this minute, that was all John Mattheu, novice at the Abbey of Tavistock in Devonshire, in the year of Grace thirteen hundred and twenty-two, could think of. It saved him from considering the body in the stream before him.

Why had he come here? Every day he exercised the abbot's horses, but rarely this way. He could only assume an evil spirit had guided him. If only someone else had found him. Anyone else.

It was the dogs that brought him to his senses again. They were all over the place, panting in the unusually warm weather. Brother Peter, the almoner, had told him with a dry chuckle only yesterday that any weather other than rain was unseasonal on Dartmoor, and John had to agree. Since he had arrived at Tavistock two years ago, he had endured more dampness than he would have thought possible.

That it was a man was obvious from the boots and the outline of the strong shoulders under the black woollen cloak. His tippet was thrown up over his head concealing his features, and it had soaked up water from the little brook into which the man had fallen. At his side a scruffy mastiff stared down at the man forlornly. The brute looked familiar, but John couldn't remember where he'd seen it before; so many people had dogs for their protection, and right now it was the long-legged hunting raches of his abbot's which demanded his attention.

He had broken the law. If he weren't on the moors illegally, he could have ridden back to town, raised the hue and cry, and told the abbot, but the rolling, grassy, rock-scattered moors were legally *forest*, hunting grounds owned by the king, and bringing hounds here was a serious offence that could cost the abbey dearly. The sheriff would not be impressed, nor would the coroner. And Abbot Champeaux had not given permission for John to bring the dogs. Whichever way he looked at it, John was in trouble.

What should he do? He tentatively reached down to the body, curling his lip as he felt the soggy shoulder of the woollen cloak, tugging it away, and then gasped with shock, for he knew the man: Ralph atte Moor, one of the king's own foresters.

"Oh! Dear God!" he moaned. "Why me?"

His journey back to the abbey was a great deal swifter than his casual ride out, and his mind was churning with near panic as he clattered in through the water gate to the court behind, hurling himself from the saddle and landing on the forepaw of one of the bitches, making her yelp with hurt surprise.

"Hey, there, boy! Ware the beasts!" roared a voice, and John looked up to see the grim features of Peter the almoner staring down at him.

Peter was a fearsome looking man. His face was badly scarred by a hideous axe wound that stretched along the line of his jaw from the point of his chin to below his ear. Novices whispered that he had gained it during one of the raids by the Scots, when their false king Robert Bruce had attacked as far as Carlisle, slaughtering and burning as he went. Peter had been a brother in one of the priories put to the torch, and the murderous villains had tried to kill him along with his brethren, but the blow intended to decapitate him had merely shattered his jaw and stunned him. Later he had come to, and a physician in Carlisle had somehow saved his life.

His pate never needed shaving. Although he had the bushiest eyebrows John had ever seen, and his reddish hair showed little sign of greying, there was little left of it, only a fringe that began at one temple and reached around the back of his skull to the other. When the barber came, he only ever asked for a few ounces of blood to be taken, and swore that the cause of his long life was that simple precaution.

Now the fifty-year-old monk was gazing down at him with exasperation in his grey eyes. "Well? What on God's good, green earth is so important that you should leap on to the lord abbot's raches?"

"He's dead! I found him out on the moor, and . . ."

"Quietly boy! Calm yourself!" Peter scowled at him thoughtfully, then took him by the elbow and led him into the gatehouse. There was a great earthenware jug resting by the fire, and he filled a mazer and handed it to John. "Drink this."

The strong, heavily spiced wine warmed his belly and sent shoots of fire to his toes. "Ralph atte Moor, sir. I found him in the stream by the quarries near Dennithorne. He's dead."

"What were you doing up there?"

John flushed. "Exercising the abbot's horse and hounds."

"The raches don't need to go on the moors for their exercise," Peter observed drily. "No matter. The body is more important. Let me answer for the dogs."

He sat staring at the fire while John finished his drink, and John knew what was uppermost in his mind. Ralph was unpopular with everyone. Harsh in language, brutal with those who infringed Forest Law, he was a bully with the power to gaol people. He would strike a man down for any supposed misdemeanor. John knew of Ralph, although Peter knew him better. Peter had the duty of distributing charity to the people at the Abbey's gates and supplying the lepers at the Maudlin, so he could often visit the town's taverns. It made Peter a useful source of local gossip for other monks.

"His dog was there?" Peter asked.

"Yes, sir."

"He is a big bugger, that mastiff," Peter mused. "Was there any sign who could have killed Ralph?"

"Nothing I could see, sir."

"Probably because like all youngsters, you don't have eyes in your head for anything other than women and the nearest wine flagon, eh? Fortunately, I am more observant. Well, I suppose we should tell the abbot and get up there. Come along, boy!"

The abbot did not see John personally, but Peter made it clear that their lord was not pleased with him. John must exercise the hounds, but that didn't mean he had permission to go on the moors, where even the abbot was not permitted. The abbot had himself been rebuked for chasing deer on the moors occasionally, but for a novice to take it into his head to do the same was a different matter.

Reeve Miria was informed, and he arrived on his horse through the court gate within the hour. Robert Miria was a squat, fair-haired man with a face like a walnut, dark and wrinkled. His expression was sour. "What's all this then? I hear Ralph's dead. That right?"

"Aye." Peter led the way through the water gate, over the bridge, through the deer park, then up the hill to the moor. It took little time for him to explain what had happened. "Since there were no vicious marauders there, it seemed pointless to raise the shire's militia."

"Don't be sarcastic, old goat! I'll decide whether to raise the hue when I get back."

Peter shrugged, loping along easily. His pace was clearly comfortable for him, although John found himself growing tired. He had suggested that they should have horses saddled and bridled, but Peter had looked at him from his bushy eyebrows and growled that God gave man legs to use, and horses were only for the vain.

"Can't you move faster?" the reeve demanded again as John lagged behind.

John had not enough energy to respond. It was all he could manage just to keep his legs moving.

At the quarry the two men waited for John, Robert Miria gulping from a wineskin while Peter refreshed himself with a few sips from the stream, drinking from a cupped hand.

Even over his exhaustion, after climbing for at least a mile and a half, John could see that the old monk was alert. He bent one knee at the side of the stream, one hand on the ground, the other in the water, then lifted it swiftly, his eyes ranging over the horizon ahead in case a gang of felons might attempt to attack. John had the impression of strength and power, like a man who could spring up in a moment to defend himself.

John sank down at the water's side and thrust his face into the stream, drinking deeply.

"How much farther, boy?" Peter asked.

"A half mile, perhaps."

"Come on, then," Reeve Miria said. "I have other matters to deal with at Tavistock."

"You always were a busy man," Peter said, scanning the land ahead.

"A merchant needs to be busy. It's people like me who keep the town alive. Without burgesses, there's be nothing. And that would mean nothing to keep your lot in the abbey alive either!"

"Oh, I think we could survive," Peter responded, checking his sandals. "Our manors would keep us going. It's not as though the town shares all its profits with us."

"The abbey gets the rents," the reeve snarled. "And extortionate they can be, too."

"But they are not usury," Peter said.

The reeve stared at Peter as the monk carried on. "What's that supposed to mean?"

"Nothing. I'd heard that someone was charging interest on money loaned, that's all. Illegal, of course, but some folk will try to make money they don't need. It's as bad as a doctor charging money from a poor man: the doctor should value life more highly than money. God in his goodness gave the doctor the skills necessary to save life, so the doctor is charging for God's gift of knowledge—it's obscene! Therefore a merchant shouldn't ask profit from lending money. If he has money to lend, he must have sufficient already; only a thief would demand profit from lending it."

"You're talking crap!"

"Christ's teaching?" Peter asked with apparent interest. His lisp, caused by the crushing of his jaw and the loss of almost all the teeth on one side of his mouth, sounded almost like a laugh, and John wondered what the point of the conversation was. He was convinced that Peter wouldn't have raised the matter had there not been a reason.

"Come on, I don't have time for all this shit!" the reeve said dismissively.

"Of course. Oh, I should warn you: I asked Ivo Colbrok and Eustace Joce to meet us up near the place."

"Why?"

"Oh, I just have a feeling that they might be able to help," Peter said, setting off again.

He was right. At the entrance to Dennithorne a small group had gathered. The men John recognized: Eustace Joce, the tenant who farmed Dennithorne, and Ivo Colbrok, who looked after the abbot's warrens in Dolvin Wood. There was also a woman, whom John did not recognize, but whom he thought must be Eustace's wife, from the familiarity with which he treated her.

Peter stood among the group, looking at them all. "Lordings, I am sorry to have asked you to meet us here, but we have a solemn duty. A man's body has been found, and we must report on it for the coroner when he arrives."

"D'you know who it is?" Eustace asked. He was a large, leathery skinned man, dressed in a strong rather than fine linen shirt, with a leather jacket atop. His massive biceps were as thick as a maid's waist, John thought.

"Ralph atte Moor."

Eustace Joce said nothing, but looked at the woman, who had given a startled cry and raised her hand to her face on hearing the name. "Not Ralph?"

Peter's voice became more gentle as he said, "I am afraid so, maid. He is a little way further up here."

She shook her head and tears began to run slowly down her cheeks.

"Typical of the fool. Dry your eyes, Anastasia! Anyone would think he was close to you, eh?" Eustace watched his wife with small, suspicious eyes.

"It's only right that a man should be mourned," Peter said quietly.

"I don't see why. A fool like him doesn't deserve compassion. He was a shit when he lived, and I don't give a fig what anyone else says."

"That is not a very compassionate attitude," Peter remonstrated.

"He made one enemy too many," Eustace said harshly as he set his face to the hill.

"Was he unpopular, would you say?" Peter asked.

"You know damn well he was!"

"Ah!" Peter said mildly, and Eustace shot him a questioning look, but Peter merely trudged on thoughtfully and didn't speak again until they were at the body.

Ralph had a great swelling on his forehead when they pulled him out of the water where he lay face down.

"Perhaps he simply drowned?" Peter murmured, and asked John to help him roll the body over. When John saw Ralph's face, although he had helped lay out two monks and one lay brother, he felt a deep sadness. It was the sympathetic instinct of one man upon seeing how another had died.

Against the pallor of his face, the ugly, blue mark stood out like the mark of the devil, and all the gathering stood studying it in silence for some little time.

It was Peter who voiced their thoughts. "It, um, looks as though he was struck down."

No one spoke. There was a curious atmosphere which John did not fully understand, as though all the men and the woman were waiting for someone else to say something. Peter was the only person who appeared unconcerned. He stood with his left hand cupping his hideously damaged jaw, his elbow supported by his right hand, a vague smile on his twisted face as he looked down at Ralph. "It would have been a heavy blow," he said.

"To knock that bastard down, it'd have to be," Ivo Colbrok said.

Peter sighed to himself and walked to the mastiff. "Hello, Rumon, old fellow."

The mastiff was apparently aware that his master was beyond help, and somewhere deep in his canine brain there was an understanding that these people were not here to harm his master, but to help if they may. Unlike most mastiffs, he did not threaten the folks about Ralph's body, but sat back and watched with mournful brown eyes. When Peter approached him, the great head turned to him, but listlessly, as though the reason for his existence was ended.

"Why did you ask us to come to this God-forsaken place?" Ivo demanded, looking from Peter to the reeve. "What good can we do here?"

Reeve Miria was watching Peter, who stood patting the dog's head. "We have to record what is here for the coroner."

Eustace sniffed. "The coroner won't be pleased if we've messed the whole area about before he can come here."

"By the time Coroner Roger of Gidleigh can get here," Peter declared, "the body will have been eaten and rotted. I am happy to take responsibility for the corpse, but I must see how the land lay so that I can describe it to the coroner. And then I and my novice here will mount guard until Coroner Roger arrives."

John thought his words made good sense. He watched as Peter walked to the stream and stood gazing down. The waters flowed swiftly here, in a steep-sided and moorstone-lined cleft some three feet deep. Above was a stone clapper bridge, formed of a single flat stone that traversed the stream. It was not broad enough for a cart, but few carts travelled up here. This bridge had been thrown over the stream by the miners, who regularly sent their ponies down to Tavistock to replenish their stores, and it was only some two feet wide. Peter stood on it, bouncing himself up and down a little. "It's solid," he said. "It didn't topple and knock him into the water."

"Of course it didn't!" Reeve Miria said scornfully. "Since when did a moorstone block that size move."

"You haven't told us what you want us here for," Ivo said shrewdly. "If you wanted only those who were nearest to the body, you'd not have called me up here, you'd just demand Eustace and some of the other locals. The coroner's rules demand that the people who are nearest and those who're within the parish should be called to view the body. Yet I am a member of Tavistock's parish, while Eustace is a moorman and comes from Lydford parish. Why?"

He was demanding an answer from the Reeve, but the Reeve himself did not answer. Instead he looked over to Peter, who was now kneeling at the side of the stream, between the corpse and the waters. Hearing the question, he looked up. "You ask why?" he enquired. There was a faint tone of surprise in his voice. "I should have thought that was obvious, my friend. Because here among us is the killer. All of you had a desire to kill Ralph."

There was a grim silence in answer to his words. John felt anxious, aware that his stomach suddenly felt empty. Peter was staring up at the horizon again, seemingly unaware of the upset and annoyance he had caused.

It was curious that nobody questioned his statement. There was a strange stillness, as though all the people there were holding their breath and waiting for him to make another comment, and John wondered for a moment whether Peter was half expecting an outburst, something that might make the murderer declaim his innocence before all. Eventually, Peter dropped his head and turned to face them.

"Ralph died, I think, either from the blow to his head, or from drowning because he had been stunned and could not lift his mouth and nose above the waters. I can't say that I am expert enough to interpret the signs, but I can be sure that he died some hours ago. He is quite chill, isn't he? That means that he died hours ago and it's taken this long for the warmth to flee his body."

Ivo Colbrok gave a great "Hah!" and smiled triumphantly. "Well that means I could have had nothing to do with his death: I was in the Plymouth Inn last night, and stayed there until this morning, when I went home."

Peter gave him a shocked look. "I trust you didn't think I meant you'd killed him, Ivo? The only argument you had with Ralph was about the rabbits."

"Yes . . . Well . . . He would complain about them every few days. Insisted that my rabbits chewed into his crops last year. Absolute crap, of course. I look after my rabbits, I do. There's no need for them to wander, and why he should think that they'd eat his manky peas and beans, I don't know. Anyway, there was nothing the bastard could do about it," he added smugly, "since your abbot is the owner of the warrens. I pay him rent each year to farm his rabbits, but they are still his own and, as I told Ralph, if he had a problem with them, he should go to the abbot."

"Yes," Peter said ruminatively. His chin was cushioned in his hand again. It was a familiar posture, and John had often wondered whether it was an affectation which he used to conceal his scar. "The abbot told me of that. In fact before I came up here today, the abbot told me to ask you about the argument you had with Ralph last midday."

Ivo paled and his voice grew quieter. "I hadn't realized the good abbot had heard."

"Oh, the abbot has good hearing regarding matters which may need to be decided before his court," Peter said cheerily. "I understand that it was some other problem?"

"He accused me of trying to poison his dog," Ivo snarled. "That monster there! Rumon, he called it, after the saint, which is blasphemy in any man's language."

Peter smiled at the mastiff, who chose this moment to scratch laboriously at his pendulous jowls, flicking a thick gobbet of saliva some yards, narrowly missing John. "St. Rumon may be the saint most honored in our church, but Ralph always said it was only fair that the fellow should be given the saint's name, since he was born on the saint's day."

"I didn't try to poison the tawny brute, anyway. That was a lie put about by Ralph to justify trying to thump me."

"I wasn't aware that Ralph required provocation to hit people," Peter said mildly.

John had noticed before that the almoner tended to avoid a man's eyes when he was questioning them. It was a trait that he had exhibited on occasions with the novices, when he suspected one guilty of a misdemeanor, as though by looking away he could hear the truth more distinctly. Only when he was certain of his judgement did he look up and meet his victim's gaze with a firm and determined scowl.

He looked up now, and fixed his stern features on Ivo. Ivo flushed and looked away as though ashamed.

"Did you try to poison his dog?"

Ivo threw his hands out in a gesture of appeal. "What would *you* do? The brute got in among my warren. He loved chasing the rabbits, and it was doing none of them any good."

"So you did?" Peter said sadly, ruffling the dog's ear.

"I would have been justified if I had," Ivo said evasively.

"You say that you have witnesses last night who can confirm you were at the inn?"

"Yes."

"What of when they were asleep?"

"The door was bolted."

"So that it could have been opened from somebody inside?"

"Are you saying I killed him?"

"It's possible. I know you and he had regular arguments."

"That's rubbish!"

"Perhaps. But, you see, this man's body is very cold. What if he died, let us suppose, early yesterday afternoon?"

"I was at the market."

"Ah, that's good!" Peter said with simulated relief. "So you can provide witnesses who saw you at every moment of the afternoon?"

"Well, I don't know about . . ."

"Because otherwise one could wonder whether you and Ralph argued, and then you followed him here and viciously struck him down, leaving him here to die."

Ivo blinked, and although his mouth worked, no sound issued.

Reeve Miria sucked at his teeth. "I find this very interesting. I think I should come with you and speak to the market people. If no one can confirm your story, Ivo, I think you could be in a difficult position."

Ivo glanced at him sideways, when Peter was looking away, and John saw him make a gesture towards his purse. Reeve Miria's expression didn't alter, but John was sure that he moved his head just a fraction, scarcely enough for anyone to have noticed, but John was half expecting it; there were so many stories about the reeve's corruption flying about the town. He reflected that he should warn Peter about the reeve, but then he almost smiled at such a fatuous thought: Peter would already have heard of it.

The reeve cleared his throat. "We should get back to town, then. Try to check this man's story."

"I am glad the matter is resolved so quickly," said Eustace Joce. He snorted and yawned. "I for one have work to be getting on with. I have some sheep with something that looks nasty. I only hope to Christ Jesus that it's not another murrain."

John shivered at the mere word. In 1315 and 1316, there had been a terrible famine which had affected all, the highest and the lowest in the land, and at the same time there had been a disease among first the sheep, then the cattle all over the country. It lasted years, and all farmers were

petrified at the thought that it might recur. Even the abbey's flocks had
been decimated.

"I hope your animals are safe," Peter said earnestly. "It would be awful
to have another instance of disease amongst the animals. I shall suggest a
prayer to the abbot."

"That is good of you, brother," Eustace said, and cast a smug look at
Ivo. "Come, Anastasia. We should return."

"Hmm?" Peter looked up as though surprised. "I should be most
grateful if you could remain a little longer, friend. Or I should say,
"friends." There is much to be considered. For example, I noticed how
sad you were, maid, on hearing that this man was dead."

"I do not like to think of a man dying," Anastasia said with gentle
compassion and a quick look at the corpse.

She was a most attractive woman to John's eyes. Her features were
pleasingly regular like the Madonna's, her complexion sweetly pale and
set off by a clean white wimple which decorously concealed her hair.
Only a few strands of a magnificent chestnut hue escaped, gleaming
auburn in the sun. She looked delicate, with a broad forehead and eyebrows which arched in crescents over large green eyes. Her mouth was
well shaped, if John was any judge, with full and soft-looking lips. As for
the rest of her body, he preferred not to permit his eyes to commit the sins
of lust or covetousness, but it was impossible not to notice the firm,
rounded swelling under her bodice or the swaying of her hips. She was
indeed beautiful, and when she turned her eyes upon Peter, he studied
her with a smile, as though considering her for the first time.

"The world would be a better place if there was a little more Christian
sympathy," her husband said shortly.

He was a good-looking man, John thought. Powerful and well-pro-
portioned, he was a contrast to Peter, with his appalling wound.
Apparently Peter thought the same, for he looked away as though
ashamed.

"Tell me, maid: did you know this Ralph well?"

"Not particularly, brother."

"No? Your accent shows you come from this town, though. Were you
born here?"

"Yes. But what of it?"

"Surely Ralph lived here all his life as well. And you and he were of
an age, weren't you?"

She threw her husband a faintly perplexed smile, as though wondering where this interrogation was leading.

"What are you talking about, brother?" Eustace grated. "My wife is here because you asked her, not for any other reason."

John privately wondered as much. Anastasia was so pretty a thing, it was impossible to consider that she could have wielded a stone heavy enough to smash Ralph's head. Compared to her mild-mannered responses, Peter's questioning sounded harsh and almost cruel.

Peter sighed. "I was only wondering how well your wife knew Ralph. She was surely not acquainted with him for the first time today. Even if one sees a dead body by the side of the road, it would not normally lead to tears, would it? Not unless the dead man was personally known to us. That is why I wished to verify how well your wife actually knew him."

Having stated his piece, he looked away again, but this time John could see that his eyes were not unfocussed, gazing into nothingness, but were concentrating with an almost furious anger on Ralph's head. He was a man possessed by an idea, John thought, and such a pure, perfect idea that it would not admit of any other to enter his head.

"If you demand to know, then yes, I knew him," Anastasia said, with a smile that captivated John. "We grew up together."

"What has this to do with the man's murder?" Eustace demanded. His face was red now, as though he was feeling the barb of an insult.

Peter looked to him. "Why should you feel that it has anything to do with Ralph's death? I have not said that any of my questions are related to Ralph, and yet you seem to feel threatened. Why should that be?"

"I? Threatened? Ballocks to you, my fine brother! I know your sort. You are only a feeble charity-giver, aren't you? Well in my experience, the charity-giver is often the receiver of charity himself! If you didn't have that wound, you wouldn't be here, would you?"

Peter gazed at him directly then, and a blaze of rage, so pure and unfettered that John thought it could have melted lead, leapt from his eyes. Eustace recoiled, a hand rising as though to protect himself, but then, as soon as it flared, Peter's anger dissipated. "You think I am a weakling, generously protected by the abbot against the cruelty of the world, Master Joce? Perhaps you are right. I am a sad old man, when all is said and done."

"My apologies, brother. I didn't think what I was saying," Eustace Joce said.

Liar! John thought to himself. *You said what you thought you needed to distract Peter from your wife, didn't you?*

"That's perfectly all right, Master Joce," Peter said with a sigh. And then he turned back to Anastasia. "Since you knew him so well, maid, when did you last meet him?"

"Brother, I will not have you interrogating my wife like this!" Eustace exploded immediately. "This is ridiculous! A man is found up here, dead, and you leap to conclusions, demanding to conduct your own inquest— well, I won't be a part of it, that's all I can say!"

He spun on his heel and called to his wife. Anastasia threw him a look of . . . what: gratitude? John wondered . . . and was about to follow him, when Peter called to them.

"Master Joce, please do not go now. There are other matters I would discuss with you."

"I don't have time for all this."

"Master, please," Peter sighed. "Speedier to answer questions now than to wait and explain in court."

"What does that mean?" Eustace demanded angrily, spinning to face the old monk.

"The good abbot has asked me to report to him, and I have a duty to weigh all the facts. If someone refuses to answer my questions, I would have to recommend that the abbot had him arrested on suspicion at least until the Coroner arrives."

"You . . ."

"My friend, I have no choice. You must see that," Peter said placatingly. "I am a servant to my Lord Abbot."

Eustace's mouth snapped shut and he took a deep breath. "You already have your man. Ivo had a dispute with him: surely he was the murderer."

"I never did a thing to him!" Ivo declared angrily.

"Enough!" the Reeve said, stepping between the two as they squared up to each other. "Calm down and listen to the monk."

"Although one man might appear to have a motive, so may another, do you not think?"

"I don't understand what you're getting at," Eustace said. "And I don't see why I should waste time listening to this rubbish."

For the first time Peter's voice hardened. "Then stop behaving like a cretin, and listen! You may learn something! Now, maid, did . . ."

"No! If you have any questions, you can ask me," Eustace declared, putting a hand on his wife's forearm.

"Very well. When did you first suspect you were being cuckolded by Ralph?"

Eustace gasped and he shivered, once, convulsively. "Who told you that?"

"It is common knowledge you will not let your wife out of your sight."

"That means nothing!"

"No, but your response here, today, does. Would not a man who thought his wife was sleeping with another seek to end their affair? He might kill the man, his wife, or both, but few men would allow the situation to continue."

"I didn't kill him."

"But you did suspect that he might have captured a small part of your wife's heart, didn't you? That much is obvious."

"I . . ." He threw an anxious look at his wife. "I wondered, that is all."

She smiled then, but this was not the gentle, soft-featured woman whom John had admired only a few minutes before. Now Anastasia wore a harsh expression, and instead of a gentle Madonna, John thought she looked more like a vicious harlot, a cruel and manipulative Herodias plotting a vengeful death.

"So you accuse my husband of killing him, brother?"

"It would not be surprising if he did, maid. You sought to make your husband jealous, didn't you?"

"My husband is a poor fool if he thought I desired Ralph. What would I have done with such a pathetic creature? He was dim, an unreliable fool! The only thing he was good for, or good at, was hitting people. He was a brute, no less a brute than that monster of a dog of his: Rumon! Naming a dog after a saint is as sinful as naming a child after a demon! Both are evil, both are heretical."

"Tell me, maid—St. Rumon. What was he made saint for?" Peter asked in his most courteous voice.

Anastasia blinked, shot a glance at her husband, then squared her shoulders defiantly. "I can't remember."

"Neither can I," Peter confessed happily. "So if we are so heretical as to have forgotten that, perhaps Ralph could be forgiven for naming his dog after the man. At least his dog is loyal," he said thoughtfully, glancing at the dog. He shook his head a moment, then peered back at the woman. "Why do you dislike the man so much, maid? Had he upset you?"

"He was nothing to me," she declared.

"Curious," Peter said thoughtfully. "I once spoke to him, and he told me that he had been married. He wedded for love, although the woman died during the famine. Who would she have been? Reeve, do you remember her?"

"Yes. Cristine, her name was, a pretty, fair-haired girl, as slim and as fresh and as lovely as a small white rose. All the men loved her."

"And she died young, I suppose?" Peter asked.

"Too young. So many died too early in those terrible years."

"Were you jealous of her?" Peter suddenly shot out, staring at Anastasia. She sneered at him. "Of her? Marrying that?"

"Show some respect for the man, woman!" Reeve Miria said. "It's his corpse lying there!"

"Why should I show him anything but contempt? I never liked the man."

"I thought you had once been sworn to marry him," Peter said gently.

Eustace stared at him, and for a moment John thought he was going to leap upon the brother. His face mottled with anger, and his hand rested briefly on his sword, but his wife put her hand on his, stilling the blade in the sheath.

"Yes, it's true enough," she said quietly.

John was shivering with nervous excitement as the little group calmed, but also with a faint fear that Peter was possessed of supernatural powers. It seemed as though Peter was able to guess at people's innermost thoughts and rip from them their darkest secrets.

"Thank you, mistress," Peter said, this time with a bow to honor her confession.

"I did not kill him," she said. "But I hated him from the moment he betrayed me with Cristine. I suppose I should have been grateful to her. She saved me from marrying him. Still, all I knew was, he had given me his word that he would marry me, and he reneged on it. Cristine and I grew up together, and she had been my best friend, and suddenly, he went with her and made his vows at the church door in front of the parson and the congregation. His words to me were conveniently forgotten."

Her husband stared at her. "But I thought you were in love with him again. You spoke much of him when his wife died."

"Yes, we should consider you, Eustace, shouldn't we?" Peter said. "Because you knew your wife had loved this man, didn't you?"

"I still don't see that my family's affairs are any of your business," Eustace returned, but with less anger than before.

"I merely wish to resolve some problems," Peter said with a calm smile.

Eustace studied him in silence for a long moment, then, "I knew she had loved him, yes. I grew up in Tavistock with both of them. It would have been difficult not to notice how fond they were of each other."

"And then Cristine married him, and you saw your opportunity to marry the woman you had adored for years," Peter said, with a wistful tone to his voice, John thought, as though he had experienced the same chance himself.

"Yes. I never had cause to regret my offer of marriage," Eustace stated stoutly.

"Until recently, when you began to suspect that Anastasia might be carrying on an affair with Ralph."

"I wondered, that is all. We have been married seven years now, and I suppose it is natural for a man and his wife to become a little less romantic, but I thought there was a problem."

Anastasia turned her astonished face to him. "You seriously thought I would consider an affair with a rough, dirty fellow like Ralph?"

"I didn't know what to think," Eustace muttered. "All I was convinced of was that you were less affectionate to me."

"Oh, husband! I need affection too. I thought if you were jealous of another man, you might show me more."

"Why? Are you so insecure?"

"I am pregnant!"

Eustace's mouth gaped wide. "Are you sure?" he asked.

A little of the steeliness returned to her face, but only for a moment. Then she smiled. "Yes, husband, I am."

"That's wonderful news," Peter said warmly. "Congratulations! Um. But where were you last afternoon, master Eustace?"

"I? I was at the market, at my stall. I would think that almost everyone in the town could confirm that. Including the reeve here, because you came to buy some eggs and a lamb with your lady, didn't you, Robert?"

Peter looked at the Reeve, and there was a glitter in his eyes that reminded John of the times when the old monk had caught one of the novices with his hand in the biscuit jar. "Is that so, Reeve?"

Reeve Miria shrugged. "Yes. I was there most of the afternoon, apart from a short space when I had to go home."

"On business?" Peter enquired.

"Yes."

"Such as, for example, asking for a loan to be repaid?"

"A man of business has so many affairs it's sometimes hard to remember them all," Miria said loftily.

"Perhaps you should try to exercise your mind, then, Reeve," Peter said. "Could it have been a meeting to talk about calling in a debt, do you think? Perhaps—correct me on this—but could it have been a loan to Ralph, for example?"

John felt his brows leap upwards in surprise as though they were on springs. Turning to face the reeve, he saw that the man had blanched, and he fiddled with the thong that bound his swordbelt.

"He came by at one point."

"Early in the afternoon, wasn't it?"

"I think it might have been."

"So you could have had plenty of time to follow him here, strike him down, and return to town to fulfil your duties as reeve."

"To ride all the way here and back? And I didn't even know he'd be coming up here. How could I?"

"Maybe he mentioned he was coming here. It was part of his bailiwick, and he was always happy to talk about his work."

"I did nothing wrong," the reeve said.

"Nothing? Even though you wanted to make profit from lending money? You were committing usury, Reeve. That is wrong. Jesus taught that it's sinful to make money from money. If you have enough, any spare is God's gift. Using that to make profit is an abuse of his plenty, and that is a most serious crime. You demanded his loan to be returned, even though you knew he couldn't afford it."

"I did what any man of business would have done."

"Perhaps in future you'll consider doing what a man of Christian spirit would do," Peter snapped. His bushy eyebrows had dropped and now they all but concealed his eyes. Only an occasional glitter shone from them.

Then he took a deep breath. "Look at us all. Here we stand: one man who had a perpetual battle with him because of some rabbits; another who feared that Ralph wanted to steal his wife; the wife who hated him and wanted revenge for not marrying her, but who now was more concerned about her pregnancy than her husband; the reeve who wanted profit, and damn any man who wouldn't repay his debts even though the reeve was not himself in need. This is a sad, terrible matter. I must pray and contemplate. John, come with me."

He turned abruptly and crossed the clapper bridge, swiftly putting yards between them and the silent and ashamed group. Without turning, he said, "Have any of them followed us?"

"No."

"Good."

Peter suddenly grabbed John's upper arm and stared at him keenly. "Boy, whatever you do now, do not lie to me! I wanted all those to be here because I thought one of them had killed Ralph. I drank with him yesterday at an alehouse after he had met the reeve, and I knew that each of them hated him. He told me so. After I left him, he came straight to the moors to check on his bailiwick. Some of those back there could have come here and killed him, but it's not likely. However the chance of a lad seeing him, now that is quite possible."

His eyes were intense chips of diamond. They cut into John as he spoke.

"Boy, did you meet Ralph yesterday? Don't lie to me, because if you do, I shall punish you myself, and you'll regret it if I do. You were up here, weren't you? Yesterday, like today, you rode up here to exercise the horse, but also to see if you could have some sport. It's illegal to be up here, we all know that, but if a forester like Ralph saw you, he'd threaten you with immediate exposure to the abbot. Is that what happened? And then you hit him?"

John gaped, and such was the strength of his emotion, he felt the tears begin to fall. He couldn't speak; his tongue was frozen and he was too shocked to deny Peter's words.

"I see, boy. Well, no need to say more. I shan't propose to hold these others any longer. I understand. Come!"

He turned and walked back to the bridge, John following with his mind whirling and eyes streaming.

It was this that prevented him from seeing the disaster. As Peter climbed onto the clapper bridge, John sniffed and rubbed his eyes. Afterwards Peter wondered whether there was a similar command that the forester had used for his mastiff, a signal that could be used silently at night to show Rumon what he wanted; whatever the reason, Rumon caught sight of John's arms up at his face and instantly gave a joyful bark. He sprang up and leapt forward as Peter reached the middle of the bridge, and bounded on, over the bridge, and to John.

"No!"

John heard the cry, but he had no eyes for anyone or anything other than the monster suddenly thundering towards him. He saw huge, pendulous jowls flying in the wind, drool trailing; he saw a slobbering tongue; ripples of sagging flesh moving with each step like waves on the sea; and then the creature was on him, knocking his legs away, and panting happily over him, tongue swabbing his throat and cheeks like pumice.

No one came to help him, and it was some time before he could push, curse, and kick the dog from him and stand again. Realizing at last that this was not a reincarnation of his master, the dog sat again, cowed, and only then could John turn his attention back to the crowd.

He saw Anastasia, he saw the reeve and Ivo, he saw Eustace, but where he expected to see Peter, there was nothing. Only two legs waving in the air near the bridge.

"Will one of you moronic, demented, poxed sons of a Carlisle whore come and help me up?" came Peter's voice, roaring with an entirely unfeigned fury.

"So that was that," Peter said later as he and John sat at their fire. The rest had departed, all strangely muted after their confessions of the afternoon.

"Why did you want all those people up here?" John asked.

"They could any one of them have killed him. It was possible. Yet I wanted to show each that their motives were not good. Ivo wanted to kill the dog—is that justification for murder? He never tried to get on with Ralph. At least now, I hope, he will consider his behavior and moderate it in future. Eustace I know has been jealous of his wife for years and it is about time he grew out of it. She is not so faithless as to throw herself at another man; although she could well seek revenge for a slight. And what worse slight could a woman receive than that the man she sought to marry should take her best friend instead?"

"What of the reeve?"

Peter chuckled. "He's no murderer! But I detest this modern practice of seeking reward for that which God has granted. I tweaked the tail of his pride. Maybe in future he'll charge lower interest."

"And me?"

Peter smiled grimly, perhaps with a faint indication of remorse. "There are times when even the best cleric makes mistakes. I thought that you were up here, and I saw that if you had met the forester you could have been in great trouble, so it was possible that you could have grabbed a rock and stunned him. If he fell in the water, he would drown, but I was prepared to give you the benefit of the doubt and assume you hadn't *intended* to kill him."

"Whereas in fact . . ."

"Whereas in fact it was his faithful dog." Peter reached over and rubbed the mastiff's head. "I wondered about that as soon as we arrived here. If a man had knocked Ralph down, I would have expected a dog like this to defend him. At the least I would have expected to find some material from a man's coat nearby, bitten from him by the brute—but there was nothing! That should have proved it, I suppose, but you never can be sure, and some of the largest beasts I have seen have also been the most mild."

"So how did Ralph die?"

"You saw what happened to me. Suppose Rumon saw a rabbit when Ralph was halfway over the bridge? He is a clumsy, lumbering monster, so, as he passed over the bridge, he clipped Ralph's legs just as he did mine, and Ralph toppled headfirst into the stream. He struck his head and was dazed, so when his head went under the water, he couldn't save himself. That was that."

"Dying here all alone."

"Aye, with his killer: the only creature in the world who loved him without reservation."

Through a Glass, Darkly

Kate Charles

Venice had been a mistake. Callie knew that, without a shade of doubt, before the boat from the airport even reached the Piazza San Marco. Had been a mistake, was a mistake, would be a mistake. Past, present, and future.

It hadn't seemed a mistake just a few hours ago, early that morning when she'd left her flat. Then it had seemed like utterly the right thing to do, for so many reasons. A welcome escape from the untidy chaos of tea chests, the demands of unpacking. An escape, an adventure. And apart from that, it was the culmination of a lifetime's dream. Venice. Beautiful, magical Venice.

And indeed it was beautiful, and even more magical than she had imagined. On the horizon, across the lagoon, it shimmered like a mirage, insubstantial and ephemeral, as though she might close her eyes and, opening them again, find that it had vanished. The spray of the boat, the mist on the lagoon, veiled it slightly, as though it existed in a different dimension from the concrete world in which Callie usually moved.

Beautiful, yes. But it wasn't supposed to be like this. In her dreams of Venice, she had not been alone. For years it had been a shadowy, faceless figure at her side, and then it had been Adam. Adam of the laughing brown eyes, of the sweet, self-mocking smile. She and Adam, approaching Venice together for the first time: their honeymoon, perhaps.

Across the aisle from her sat a young couple who were almost certainly on their honeymoon, the ghosts of wedding confetti still clinging to them as they sat close together, their fingers entwined, starry-eyed. And another couple in front of them, older but clearly in love. Everywhere on the boat they sat, two by two.

All couples. All seeing Venice together.

On the seat next to Callie was her handbag: her sensible black handbag. Not Adam.

Venice had been a mistake.

Half an hour later, Callie was feeling slightly better, as the excitement of being in Venice gripped her in spite of herself. Agog with the sights, with the sounds and the smells of the city, she wheeled her case from the airport boat's terminus along to the nearest stop for the vaporetto—the water bus. If she hadn't been hampered with luggage, she would have just started walking, heedless of destination, and willingly lost herself in the twisting streets and byways. But good sense dictated that first she should find her hotel, get rid of the case, and then find a bite to eat somewhere.

The hotel where she would be staying had been described as being on the Grand Canal, just a few steps from the vaporetto stop. Callie had looked at the map in the guidebook, poring over it on the flight, and had located the street, at the top end of the backwards S of the Grand Canal. As the book suggested, she purchased a three-day ticket for unlimited use of the vaporetti. The woman in the ticket office spoke no English, so this was achieved through a rather painful process of gestures, and involved proffering a wad of lire notes of impossible denominations—thousands of lire, which she had to keep telling herself amounted to only a few pounds—but it would save her from further such ordeals. That accomplished, she waited no more than a moment on the swaying 'bus stop' before the vaporetto arrived, then dragged her case on board in the midst of a shoving mob: no orderly queues like she was accustomed to in England, Callie observed ruefully.

She managed to find a seat, then settled back to enjoy the boat's stately progress along the Grand Canal. It was just as she'd thought it would be, except that it was even more beautiful, shimmering in the autumn sunlight. The opaque water of the canal, reflecting the color of the sky. The majestic palazzi—Byzantine, Gothic, Rococo all cheek-by-jowl, the mellow houses with their crumbling plaster-work and peeling paint, the gondolas with their cargoes of blissful couples. . . .

Adam again, intruding into her thoughts. Spoiling her pleasure.

Callie found the hotel without any difficulty. After the dazzling sunlight outside, the lobby seemed a dark cave. But the man behind the desk gave her a charming smile. "Buon giorno," he said; then, it seemed to her, he sized her up with an expert glance. What was it he was seeing? she wondered. She was alone, she was relatively young, she was wearing no wedding ring. Could he tell from her face, from her clothing, that she was English?

"Signorina?" he said, pulling the register towards him.

"Miss . . . ?"

"Caroline Anson. Miss." Callie smiled back at him self-consciously. "Reverend, actually," she added, unable to resist the temptation to use her brand new title. "The Reverend Caroline Anson."

Now he stared at her. "You are a priest?"

She felt she needed to explain. "Not a priest, no. Not yet, anyway. I'm a deacon. In the Church of England. Anglican." She didn't tell him, though, that she had been ordained for just over twenty-four hours.

"We do not have women priests in our church here." His voice was carefully neutral.

"Yes, I know." Callie's hand went to her neck in an unconscious gesture. His reaction was what she had expected, and it was the main reason she had not worn her new dog collar: Italians, she suspected, were not used to seeing women in clerical dress—apart from nuns, which were a different kettle of fish altogether—and she didn't really want to be stared at in the streets.

The temptation to wear the collar had been great: after all, it was new, and she had worked hard for the right to wear it. She was not ashamed of her calling; on the contrary, she was proud, and wanted everyone to know that she was now in Holy Orders.

But she was on holiday, after all, and she knew that—apart from the fact that this was a Catholic country, and she was a woman—wearing a dog collar somehow set people apart.

Callie preferred to fade into the background, and that is what she did for the rest of the day. She walked the streets of Venice, down to the Rialto and over to San Marco, across little bridges and down tiny alleys, not caring where she was or worrying about getting lost, but just drinking in the flavor of the place. Trying to avoid thinking about all the happy couples who surrounded her, trying to escape from the inevitable memory of Adam.

Eventually, footsore, she returned to her room and made herself a cup of tea. The room was adequate: immaculately clean, but quite small, furnished with a single bed. Its window, though, overlooked the Grand Canal, and that was worth a great deal. The crisp ironed sheets of the bed beckoned to her, and, succumbing, she laid down for what she told herself would be a few minutes of rest before venturing back out again.

Nearly two hours later, she woke in the semi-darkness of an autumn twilight. Time for dinner, then. Dinner, as well as breakfast, was provided at the hotel as part of the package price, so it was just a matter of tidying herself up, brushing her hair, applying a bit of lipstick, and going downstairs.

Callie hovered at the door of the restaurant and waited for someone to notice her and find her a table. The room, although it wasn't large, seemed quite full. Two by two they sat, at every table.

A young man appeared at her elbow. "Signorina?" he said anxiously, then continued in accented but serviceable English. "If you would not mind sitting with the other lady? The lady on her own?" He gestured towards the corner table.

She hadn't noticed the middle-aged woman, sitting alone in the shadows. "Yes, all right," Callie agreed, reluctant to intrude on the woman's solitude, but even more reluctant to insist on a table of her own, especially as there did not seem to be one available. "If she doesn't mind, that is."

"No, she will not mind." He grinned. "She is English, too. And alone like you."

Callie allowed herself a moment of bitterness as he led her to the table: to be lumped together with another inconvenient English spinster, and one with more than a few years on her, seemed the final indignity, scarcely to be tolerated.

But the woman welcomed her with a smile. "Please, do sit down," she invited, indicating the empty chair across from her. Her voice was soft, her accent genteel and not readily identifiable as from any particular region beyond the Home Counties.

Callie sat, warmed out of her bitterness by the smile. "I'm sorry to intrude like this," she apologized.

"Not at all. It's good to have the company. I'm Imogen," the woman added.

"Callie."

"That's an unusual name."

"Short for Caroline. My little brother had trouble saying his Rs." She wasn't sure why she'd said that; she wasn't usually in the habit of sharing such information with total strangers.

Imogen didn't really seem like a stranger, though, as she nodded in understanding. She possessed an ordinary face: unmemorable, undistinguished, and yet not without character. Her eyes spoke of a warm intelligence, and her smile was sweet. It was not the sort of face to attract notice, but it was comfortable, and Callie liked its owner instinctively.

'Is this your first day here?" Imogen asked.

Callie nodded. "I flew in at midday."

"And how do you like it so far?"

"Venice is wonderful," Callie stated. "The most beautiful place I've ever been. But," she added impulsively, her eyes sweeping around the restaurant, "it isn't a very good place to be on your own. I think it might have been a mistake to come."

Imogen smiled, then seemed to choose her words carefully. "Being on one's own has its compensations," she said. "I love to watch people. A single woman on her own—no one notices me, so I can stare quite openly at people and get away with it. And this restaurant is an ideal place for people-watching."

"People-watching?"

Her smile turned into a conspiratorial grin. "I have names for them all," she said. "Those two over there, for instance. The ones looking so soulfully at each other. I call them Romeo and Juliet."

Callie cast a surreptitious glance in their direction, then realizing that Imogen was right about not being noticed, she turned and looked at them more closely.

"Yes," she agreed. "They are a bit like that."

"Italian, I think. Or maybe French. Honeymooners."

"What about the two at the next table?" Callie studied them: a middle-aged couple, the woman well-upholstered and talking volubly, the man thinner and listening with a long-suffering, almost glazed look on his face.

"English, of course. Probably from somewhere like Tunbridge Wells. And I call them Mr. and Mrs. Bennet."

Callie laughed in spite of herself. "That's perfect."

"You see those two over in the far corner?"

They were an oddly matched couple, the man some years older than the woman, and in this case it was the man who was doing the talking. He seemed to be lecturing his companion, who was trying her best to be attentive. 'They're English," Callie guessed.

"Oh, yes." Imogen nodded. "What do you think, then?"

Before Callie could reply, the waiter, who had been hovering inconspicuously nearby, appeared beside their table, pad and pencil in hand. "The ladies are ready to order?"

She hadn't even looked at the menu, Callie realized. She opened it now: all in Italian, of course, and rather too many choices to take on board. "Do you have any recommendations?" she appealed to her companion.

"I usually order the set meal, the daily special," Imogen said. "It's good value, and always tasty, whatever it happens to be. That's what I'll have," she addressed the waiter. "And a glass of the house red."

"Make that two." Callie shut the menu, and thus relieved of decision-making, returned her attention to the couple in the corner. The identification teased at her mind, just eluding her grasp, then suddenly she had it. "Dorothea and Mr. Casaubon."

Imogen gave a delighted laugh. "Exactly. You know your *Middlemarch*, then. As well as your Jane Austen."

"And what about the next table?" Callie lowered her voice, in case she were overheard, but the young couple in question didn't seem to be paying any attention; they were bickering good-naturedly and without pause.

"They're new—I haven't seen them before. Any ideas?"

"Beatrice and Benedick," Callie said promptly.

Imogen's smile expressed her pleasure. "Brilliant. You're good at this game. Are you sure you haven't played it before?"

The waiter arrived with the two glasses of wine. Callie took a sip, then looked around. "What about the others, then?"

Imogen nodded towards a dark recess, where an expensively dressed but paunchy man leaned across the table towards a curvaceous young woman in a clingy frock. "American. They're not married—at least not to each other. She's probably his secretary, and his wife undoubtedly thinks he's at a conference or business meeting somewhere." She paused. "Bill and Monica, of course."

Callie covered her mouth with her napkin to stifle a snort.

"And in the same vein," Imogen continued, indicating another table, "we have Ron and Nancy. Definitely married, this time."

In this case, Callie observed, the middle-aged couple were of around an equal age, though the man, as is so often the way, was better preserved. He possessed wavy dark hair and a trim figure, while his wife had a web of fine lines marking the thin, almost transparent skin of her face. She was attractive enough, and had the sort of bone structure which indicated that she might have been beautiful once—but now she seemed faded, like the bloom off the rose. What identified them with the former president and first lady was the look of rapt adoration which the woman bestowed upon her husband. She never took her eyes from him, though he seemed to pay her merely desultory attention. He refilled his wine glass and drank from it; he applied himself to his food. His wife gazed at him lovingly, proudly.

"And the two over there," said Imogen, lifting her glass in their direction. "Take a look."

Instinctively, Callie had up till now avoided looking at the pair who sat side by side on a banquette. They were young, and they were in love. Food was inconsequential to them. Heedless of everyone else in the room, they sat entwined, nibbling on one another. It verged on the indecent, and Callie found it almost painful to watch.

"The Bunnies," said Imogen dryly. "I call them the Bunnies."

A giggle bubbled up into Callie's throat, dissolving the lump of pain.

Callie enjoyed the meal more than she imagined she would; Imogen, in her quiet way, was good company, and the food was excellent. It wasn't until they'd finished the pasta course and moved on to the chicken that Imogen asked, "So, what brings you to Venice, all by yourself?" She gave a wry smile, adding, "I can say that, since I'm by myself as well. But you don't have to answer if you don't want to."

To her surprise, Callie discovered that she did want to answer. She opened her mouth and it came out: how she had always dreamed of visiting Venice, how she had found herself with a few days to spare between her ordination and the assuming of duties as a curate in a London parish, how she had also found herself in possession of an unexpected sum of money—a generous ordination gift from the congregation where she'd done her parish placement. "I got a great last-minute package deal," she concluded, feeling somehow flat. "It seemed a good idea at the time."

"And now?" Imogen had listened carefully, continuing to eat.

"Now I don't know. As soon as I arrived, and saw everyone so . . . *coupled*, if there's such a word, I realized that I probably shouldn't have come."

Imogen paused, put her fork down, and gave Callie a searching look. "Tell me what happened," she said quietly.

She hadn't planned to tell her this part; she hadn't planned to utter

Adam's name ever again, let alone expose her pain to anyone's scrutiny. But somehow it came out in spite of her resolution. "Adam," she said haltingly. "We were at theological college together. Three years. We were going to get married. Next year, as soon as we were established in our curacies. We were going to be a team." She stopped.

"And?"

"He met someone else. On his parish placement. He told me a fortnight ago." The bald words brought it flooding back. They'd sat in a pub and he'd told her, his brown eyes alight with joy. All of the usual clichés had risen so easily to his lips: a wonderful girl. You'll love her, Callie. I want you to be friends. I want us to be friends.

There had been no ring to give back; at least she had been spared that. Adam was a poor student who couldn't afford the sort of ring he'd wanted to give her; the ring was to have come after ordination, after he started getting his stipend.

Now—soon—someone else would be wearing the ring that should have been hers.

And it wasn't even as if she could expunge him from her life and resolve never to see him again. Their paths would cross often: they were in the same diocese, even in the same deanery. She would see him, would have to be polite to him.

Eventually, she would have to meet her, the wonderful girl. She didn't know how she would bear it.

To her credit, Imogen didn't resort to cliché herself. She didn't say, "You're better off without him," or "At least you've found out what sort of chap he is now, before you married him," or "You'll meet someone else, just you wait and see." She just listened sympathetically, and nodded.

Amazingly, Callie discovered that she felt better for having told her.

Back in her room, Callie spent some time at the window. The Grand Canal, which during the day had mirrored the blue of the sky, was now as black and opaque as ink, but it was a live blackness: undulating, in constant motion. Reflected lights of passing boats and the buildings on either side moved on its surface like colored, animated graffiti.

Callie had not been sleeping well; it wasn't surprising, with the disruptions to her life of late, not least her heartache over Adam. She was not expecting to sleep well that night, especially in a strange bed, and having napped earlier. But she'd scarcely slipped between the crisp, sweet-smelling sheets before she was asleep.

And the next morning, when she awoke, her room bathed in warm Venetian sunlight, it was with anticipation for the day ahead. She spared a moment to lean out of the window and contemplate the scene: already the Grand Canal hummed with activity, with supply boats and water taxis and vaporetti and a few gondolas. Then she showered quickly and went down to breakfast.

She hoped to find Imogen already there, but the table they had occupied the night before was empty, the cutlery and crockery pristine and unused. Throughout breakfast Callie watched and waited for her to appear, but though most of the others put in an appearance—with the exception of the Bunnies, who, Callie surmised, were probably still in their room, breakfasting on each other—there was no sign of Imogen.

On her own, Callie got through breakfast quickly and was soon ready for a full day of sightseeing. She decided to start with San Marco, at the very heart of Venice; she chose to catch a vaporetto rather than walk and risk being distracted by a multitude of other temptations along the way. Some of her fellow guests at the hotel seemed to be bound in the same direction, if not to the same destination: on one side of the boat, Mr. Casaubon lectured Dorothea, pointing out the palazzi as they passed and favoring her with a brief history of each one, while on the other side, Beatrice and Benedick squabbled amicably over their guidebook. And a short time later, crossing the expanse of the Piazza San Marco, Callie glimpsed Bill and Monica sipping tiny cups of coffee at a table outside of Florian's, while Romeo and Juliet were among the throngs of people feeding the pigeons in the square.

What a balm for the spirit San Marco proved to be. It dazzled, it enchanted. Callie had never seen so much gold, such perfection in the melding of soaring dome and majestic marble pillar. And yet it seemed smaller than she had expected, somehow intimate in its concentration of lavish beauty. She wandered around happily for what might have been minutes or might have been hours, so unaware was she of the passing of time.

And she was only dimly aware of the other people, though there were many tourists and sightseers milling about. They seemed somehow inconsequential, insubstantial, in that little heaven between the intricate pictorial mosaics suspended in gold above her head and the equally intricate, but abstract, mosaic patterns of the multicolored marble floor. Then she discovered the gold altarpiece, ablaze with thousands of jewels and precious enamels, and stayed in front of it until she was crowded out by more impatient sightseers.

In the south transept, Callie came upon the entrance to the Treasury and decided to go in. There was an admission fee, which to her pride she managed to count out from her stash of lire without any help from the man at the ticket desk.

Once inside, she was confronted with such a collection of reliquaries—fashioned of precious metals and shaped like various body parts—that, overwhelmed, she moved straightaway into the main room of the Treasury, where glass cases housed items of great rarity and beauty, many of them looted from Constantinople. Few people had penetrated this far, perhaps loath to pay the extra fee, and for that Callie was grateful; it meant that she could take her time without being rushed along.

Callie studied a bowl hewn from rock crystal many centuries ago, and while her eyes travelled over the intricacies of its decoration, she somehow became aware of the people on the opposite side of the freestanding glass case. Perhaps it was something in the intensity of the voices that caught her attention, but whatever it was, she looked through to the other side of the case, and recognized the man: it was Ron, he of the adoring wife.

But the woman with him was not his wife. There was no mistake about that, even through the glass. This woman was much younger, vibrant, and beautiful. She had dark hair and full red lips and was dressed stylishly in a short dress that displayed her long legs to advantage.

She was standing very close to Ron. She was touching his hand, covering it with her own.

Callie strained to hear what they were saying.

"When?" whispered the woman. "When is it going to happen?" Her accent, in keeping with her appearance, was Italian.

"It will," said Ron, his vowels those of an upper-class Englishman.

"You say that, but …"

"It will," he repeated, more forcefully. "Don't you understand, Gabriela? The timing has to be right. Not too soon."

Gabriela removed her hand and seemed to withdraw from him slightly. "How did you get away from her today?"

"She had a headache. Went back to the hotel."

"But what if she had not had a headache? You have to plan these things."

"Torcello," he said. "It's planned."

Fascinated, but suddenly ashamed of her eavesdropping, Callie moved towards the door, out of the Treasury and back into the body of the basilica. She tried to put the overheard conversation out of her mind, but the word *Torcello* reverberated: an intriguing, resonant word. Who, or what, was Torcello? Was it perhaps a variety of pasta? An exotic dessert? A local wine? An arcane musical instrument? Finding a seat in the transept, she got out her little Italian dictionary and looked the word up.

Torcello, she discovered, was an island in the lagoon, a few miles from Venice. That sent her to her guidebook, which informed her that Torcello was once a thriving center of population but was now in great decline. Its main glory was its splendid Byzantine cathedral, said the book, and that alone made it worth a visit.

On impulse, Callie checked the map that showed the vaporetto routes and realized that she could be on Torcello within an hour.

Why not? she told herself. The guidebook said that it was well worth a visit, and this would be a beautiful day to spend some time on the water—and make good use of her three-day vaporetto pass. She emerged into the sunshine and walked the few yards to the vaporetto stop, studying the more detailed map posted there for the route and the timings.

From the Fondamente Nuovo, the boat would call at several islands, of which Torcello was not quite the last. Then it would double back and reverse its journey.

That, Callie calculated, would give her an hour on Torcello, before the boat returned. If an hour wasn't long enough, she could catch the next boat.

It was indeed a lovely afternoon on the lagoon, the sun striking sparks off the water and just a few low clouds scudding on the horizon. Quite a few people had boarded the vaporetto at the Fondamente Nuovo, so seats were at a premium; Callie took the opportunity to go outside of the enclosed cabin and look over the prow as it cut through the water. But most of the passengers got off at Murano or Burano, so by the time the boat reached the stop for Torcello, Callie was nearly alone. She was the only one who disembarked there, and just two people got on.

To her surprise, the cathedral was at some distance from the vaporetto stop, about a quarter of an hour's walk along a stagnant-looking canal with improbably green water. Walking along, Callie realized that she was hungry: she hadn't eaten anything since breakfast, and it was now well past lunch time. But any hopes she had of finding a bite to eat were dashed by the "closed" signs hanging on the two restaurants she passed.

The rumblings of her stomach were forgotten as soon as she reached the cathedral. It was very different from the gorgeous exterior of San Marco, built of weathered red brick and looking rather unprepossessing from the outside.

Inside, though, were splendors which made the trip all worthwhile. A soaring curved apse at the east end, with an attenuated and serenely beautiful Madonna and Child mosaic hovering amidst the pale gold, dominated the vast interior space. There were other fine mosaics as well, and a vivid depiction of the Last Judgement filled the west wall.

After some thirty minutes of exploration, Callie looked at her watch with the realization that if she didn't make a move quickly, she would be in danger of missing the vaporetto. Emerging from the cathedral, she discovered that the weather had altered during her time inside: the few scudding clouds had moved in, multiplied, and now filled the sky, appearing to press down on the tower of the cathedral, oppressive and chill. The green of the canal had taken on a dark opacity that seemed somehow sinister, and Callie hurried along beside it, anxious now to leave Torcello behind her.

The boat was approaching as she reached the landing, and she boarded gratefully. Only a handful of people were aboard, none of whom paid her any attention.

Callie shivered. What, she thought, if she had lost her footing and slipped into the mossy green water of the canal? There would have been no witness, no one to help, and no one to miss her.

The lagoon now seemed an inhospitable place, its choppy water mirroring the sky, transformed to the color of tarnished pewter. All Callie wanted was to get back to the hotel, to a nice hot cup of tea.

Callie had looked forward to seeing Imogen at dinner that night, but the other woman was not there. "Gone," said the waiter with a shrug. "Gone home today."

She was unexpectedly dismayed by this news, but she resolved to enjoy her meal and follow Imogen's practice of people-watching. Surveying the couples at the other tables, she surmised that Mr. and Mrs. Bennet had also departed—back to Tunbridge Wells, or wherever it was they came from—to be replaced by a well-groomed and even glamorous middle-aged woman in the company of a much younger man. Her toy boy, Callie decided, mentally naming them Mrs. Robinson and Benjamin.

Apart from that change, everyone else was the same as the night before. The Bunnies still nibbled, Beatrice and Benedick continued their bickering, and Mr. Casaubon lectured on. Callie, from the security of her virtual invisibility as a solitary woman, her interest piqued by what she had accidentally observed and overheard earlier in the day, paid special attention to Ron and Nancy.

Nancy looked, if anything, rather more drawn than she had before, with dark smudges under her eyes and a certain tightness in the corners of her mouth. That, Callie supposed, was attributable to the headache. But still she gazed at her husband, following his every move with her eyes, speaking little.

Ron wasn't doing much talking either, Callie observed. He concentrated on his food, chewing each bite carefully, and was rather knocking the wine back.

Callie finished before they did, and passed by their table on her way out, taking her time.

As she went by, Ron spoke. He took a sip of wine, and without looking at his wife, said casually, "By the way, I thought we might do Torcello tomorrow."

By the time Nancy replied, Callie was out of earshot. But somehow she doubted that Nancy would have disagreed.

The weather on the next day—Callie's last full day in Venice—had worsened from the afternoon before, with a chilly fog now sitting firmly on the city. From her window that morning Callie could scarcely see the Grand Canal, the boats disappearing in and out of tiny clear patches between the shreds of mist.

Outside she found that everything seemed muffled, the cheerful clamor of the streets now stilled beneath the grey blanket of fog. If she were here on her honeymoon, or with a lover, Callie reflected, it would seem terribly romantic and beautiful. But she wasn't, and it didn't.

Dispirited, she decided to visit the church nearest to the hotel, the one whose dome she could see from her window.

It proved to be the church of San Geremia and Santa Lucia. St. Lucy, the patron saint of eyes—and according to Callie's guidebook, the relics of St. Lucy herself were on view in the church. Anglicans are not, as a whole, into relics, so Callie wasn't quite sure what to expect. She certainly wasn't expecting the electric candles that burned cheerily in front of various statues, their bulbs switched on by means of dropping money into a slot. Evidently then, someone—faithful and devout—had been here before her, though there was no sign of anyone else in the church. She passed through the shadowy building, starting when a spotlight sprang to life and illuminated a vast and murky canvas on the wall, and she paused to read a sign—in several languages, including English—which promised her a partial indulgence from her sins through the blessing bestowed by viewing the relics of St. Lucy.

She wondered whether the relics had anything to do with eyes: Lucy had supposedly had her eyes torn out rather than lose her virginity, and she was often depicted proffering a plate on which reposed a pair of eyes, like two gruesome marbles.

But the relics were even stranger than that, and certainly not the sort of thing one would have found in an Anglican church of any description. Stretched out in a free-standing glass case, almost like a crystal coffin, was the emaciated figure of a very small woman, swathed in splendid damask vestments, her face covered by a heavy silver mask. Through the glass, Callie could make out the only thing remotely human about the figure: the tiny withered feet poking out from the bottom of the vestments, the skin shrivelled like ancient leather on their bird-like bones. Callie found it depressing, and worse—inexpressibly sad.

"He who has eyes . . . ," she said softly to herself.

Suddenly she realized how cold the empty church was, and with a shiver, she retraced her steps and made for the door. On the way, she discovered that the church wasn't in fact empty, as she passed a figure kneeling in prayer before a statue in a dim corner. A young woman, dark-haired. For just an instant, Callie thought that it was the woman she'd seen in the Treasury at San Marco—the woman called Gabriela. But of course it wasn't, and she shook her head at her own fancifulness.

"She who has eyes," she chided herself.

Callie, glad that she'd seen San Marco in the sunshine, passed much of the day indoors, looking at Renaissance paintings in the Accademia and the Ca' d'Oro. Then she browsed along the Rialto, searching for one or two suitable souvenirs to take back with her. Venice's most popular souvenir, the carnival mask, was available everywhere, in every imaginable style and color, bejeweled and beribboned, suitable for hanging on a wall, but they left Callie cold. She found them hideous and even faintly sinister, especially the plague doctor, with his black tricornered hat above a beaked and bird-like white face. Adam would probably like one, she thought with a small pang: his parents had been missionaries, and he had had several African tribal masks on the walls of his room at theological college.

Second only to the masks was the proliferation of blown glass items from Murano, and for her mother, who collected china cats, Callie selected a suitable feline specimen. She wanted something for herself as well; after considerable deliberation, she chose a small notebook covered in marbled paper, its blank pages thick and creamy. And in an out-of-the-way shop she fell in love with a tiny etching of the city, seen from the lagoon, mirage-like, just as she had first experienced it. It was expensive, but she had a bit of money, which she'd been given as an ordination present from her mother, and she struggled with her conscience only briefly before succumbing to temptation.

That evening she went down to dinner early, one of the first to arrive in the restaurant. But she took her new notebook with her and began to write down her observations of Venice. She tried to find the words to describe San Marco, looking up in time to see Ron entering the restaurant on his own, without his wife. The waiter showed him to his table, then listened gravely to him and shook his head.

Callie couldn't quite hear what was said, but few minutes later when the waiter brought her pasta, she inclined her head towards Ron's table and remarked casually, "He's on his own tonight?"

The waiter nodded. "His wife is not well. She suffers from very bad headaches, he says. Tonight she will rest, as they leave in the morning."

"So do I," said Callie, as much to herself as to him. "So do I."

By morning the fog had lifted, and Venice was once again bathed in a golden glow, making it all the more difficult for Callie to leave. She packed her suitcase, took a last look out of her window at the Grand Canal, and went down to the reception desk to check out.

Ron was there in front of her, signing his credit card receipt.

"*Grazie*. Thank you, Mr. Hawkins," said the desk clerk. "You have enjoyed your stay with us, I trust?"

"Yes, very much."

"And Mrs. Hawkins?" The clerk looked over his shoulder, as though expecting to see Nancy rather than Callie, who hovered close enough to hear the conversation.

"Oh, yes indeed." Ron shrugged, then added, "She's meeting me at the airport. She had some last-minute shopping that she just had to do, something she didn't think about until this morning." He gave a brusque little laugh. "You know how women are. I told her it would be a rush, but . . ."

The clerk waved his hand and shared in the joke. "Yes, my wife is the same. I just hope that your wife does not miss the plane."

Ron put away his credit card, picked up two bags, and departed.

A few minutes behind him, Callie headed for the bus station and was soon on her way to the airport. Ron was not on the bus, she observed: he had probably taken a water taxi. She wondered whether he and Nancy would be on her flight.

Though she kept her eyes open at the airport, she didn't see anything of them until she was boarding the plane, at which time she had a glimpse of what she was sure was Ron's wavy hair, somewhere in the queue to board. Not a sign of Nancy, though she told herself that didn't necessarily mean anything. Once on the plane, she didn't see either one of them: they were probably travelling first class, she concluded.

It was a full flight. Callie had a window seat, hoping for a final view of Venice as they took off, but to her disappointment she was on the wrong side of the plane.

A young man occupied the seat beside her. Young, she observed, but not too young—around her age, in fact. Curly black hair. And when he turned to her, smiling, passing her a bag of peanuts from the flight attendant, she saw that he had lovely brown eyes.

Callie got out her marbled notebook and began to write. But instead of describing the joys of Venice, she found herself enumerating:

1. Nancy adores Ron.
2. Ron talked to a young woman called Gabriela in San Marco.
3. Nancy has not been seen (by me) since yesterday morning.

It was not a lot to go on, she concluded ruefully. Suspicious, perhaps, but scarcely conclusive. She should just let it go. Callie shut the book and stuck it in her handbag.

The young man beside her opened a newspaper. It was in Italian, she saw. He must be Italian, then.

But a few minutes later, when the flight attendant brought their drinks, he folded up his newspaper and spoke to Callie in an accent as English as her own. "Did you enjoy Venice, then?"

"I loved it," she responded honestly. "It's wonderful. Not like anywhere else on earth."

"I love it, too," he said, then introduced himself. "I'm Mark."

"The patron saint of Venice. San Marco."

She'd blurted the first thing that came into her head, and it sounded pretty fatuous to her. But he turned a bit in his seat and gave her a warm smile. "Well, actually my name is Marco, though in England I'm usually known as Mark. My parents were born in Italy, you see. They're Venetian. My grandmother still lives in Venice. I visit her whenever I have a chance."

"Hence the Italian newspaper," said Callie. "You speak Italian, I mean."

Marco laughed ruefully. "I'm not fluent, much to my parents' disappointment. But I get by well enough."

Over the next few minutes she learned more about Marco: that he'd lived in London all his life, that he was a policeman. Those were the things he told her. She learned, also, that he was a very good conversationalist and had the knack of making her feel that she was as well. He drew her out, got past her initial shyness; she found herself telling him about her impressions of Venice, about her favorite books, even about her calling to the ordained ministry.

As the plane neared Gatwick, circling for landing, Callie had a moment of regret that the journey was over so quickly, then was overcome immediately with embarrassment and a huge wave of shyness. "I'm sorry," she said. "I've been talking, and I've kept you from your newspaper."

"Oh, that." Marco laughed, securing his tray table and putting the paper on his lap. "Talking to you has been much more interesting than struggling through an Italian newspaper."

Unwilling to meet his eyes, Callie looked at the folded paper. A word in a small headline at the bottom of the page leapt out at her: Torcello.

"Oh, what does that say?" She pointed at the story, little more than a paragraph.

Marco scrutinized it, his brow creased. "Well, it's about a body being found. In a canal on Torcello."

"A body?" Callie could hear her voice rising in pitch.

"Apparently it was found last night. A woman's body. Not identified."

She leaned back in her seat, pushed back by the gravitational force as the plane descended. No, she thought. It couldn't be. She was letting her imagination run away with her again.

But she couldn't help remembering how she had felt on that deserted stretch of pathway beside the green water of the canal. How easy it would be: just one little push, a splash, and it would be over. No one to hear, no one to help.

And they—Ron and Nancy—had been going to Torcello.

It was the missing piece of the puzzle that she'd been searching for.

How, though, she asked herself, could he hope to get away with it? The body had been found; sooner or later it would be identified. Even if it wasn't, how could he explain his wife's disappearance?

That wouldn't be impossible, she argued with herself. The desk clerk at the hotel had seen him leave with his wife's suitcase, had heard the explanation of her absence. Perhaps he could tell people at home, wherever home was, that his wife had left him, had run away with another man. They might believe it.

She was being fanciful, Callie said to herself sternly. The man was probably, at this moment, sitting with his wife in the first-class compartment.

Suddenly it became very important to find out. She needed to see Nancy, to assure herself that the woman was all right.

The instant that the seatbelt light went out, Callie scrambled over Marco's legs with an embarrassed apology, slung her handbag over her shoulder and rushed up the aisle towards the first-class compartment.

But others, equally eager to disembark, blocked her way, standing in the aisles to retrieve their carry-ons from the overhead bins, then making slow progress up the aisle. By the time Callie reached the first-class section at the front of the plane, it was empty of passengers.

She moved swiftly out of the gate and down the corridors towards Immigration, following the signs and the people, still determined but losing hope as she arrived at the huge Immigration hall where people queued to have their passports examined.

The queues snaked back and forth, but there was no sign of Ron and Nancy; if, indeed, they'd been in first class, they were probably already through into the baggage hall. Their luggage would come through first, and they'd be through Customs and out of the airport before she'd even cleared Immigration.

The woman in front of her in the queue stepped up to the desk when her turn came. She was, Callie noticed, wearing a headscarf and a large pair of dark glasses.

The immigration officer flipped open the passport, gave it no more than a cursory look, then stamped it and handed it back to her. 'There you are, Mrs. Hawkins," he said, waving her through.

Callie gasped and stared at the rapidly retreating back. The woman was definitely not Nancy: she was tall, leggy, young.

It was Gabriela, without any doubt this time.

Perversely, the immigration officer lingered over Callie's passport, scrutinizing first her photo and then her face, before taking his time in finding a page and stamping it. When eventually he proffered the passport, she snatched it from his hand and took off in the direction in which Gabriela had gone, towards the baggage hall.

Callie found the carousel which was designated for the Venice flight; there was no sign of Gabriela, and the luggage was disgorging with frustrating slowness.

Across the carousel she saw Marco, waiting expectantly for his luggage, but she looked away quickly. It wouldn't do for him to catch her staring at him. And besides, there were other, more important, things to think about.

Gabriela, travelling on Mrs. Hawkins's—Nancy's—passport. What did it mean? What could it mean, other than the obvious?

Her bag came gliding by on the conveyor belt; she grabbed it, threw it on a trolley, and headed for the Blue Channel.

She would never know now, she told herself as she emerged into the crowded terminal. If Ron *had* pushed Nancy into the green water of the canal on Torcello, he would very likely get away with it. There was nothing she could do about it now.

She could scarcely go to the police and tell them of her suspicions, with nothing more to go on than a few overheard conversations, a tiny item in a newspaper, and the name Hawkins—she didn't even know his real first name, and it almost certainly wasn't Ron. The police would laugh her out of the station.

And then she saw them. They were behind a smoked glass panel that screened a fast food restaurant-cum-coffee bar from the terminal. Gabriela had shed her headscarf and her dark glasses. Ron held her close in an intimate embrace, their bodies and their lips pressed together, his hands entwined in her black hair.

For an instant Callie watched them. "She who has eyes," she whispered to herself. Then she spun around, just as Marco—Marco, a member of the Metropolitan Police—came through from the baggage hall into the terminal, pushing a trolley. Without giving herself so much as an instant to think about it, she rushed up to him, registering at the back of her mind his delighted smile just before she spoke. She would think about that later; now there were more urgent matters to deal with. "There's something I want to tell you about," she gasped. "Something you might not believe ..."

✝

†HE KΠÍGH†'S COΠFESSIOΠ

P. C. DOHERTY

OH DAY OF WRATH!

OH DAY OF MOURNING!

HEAVEN AND EARTH IN ASHES BURNING!

THE KΠÍGHT PAUSED OΠ THE STEPS leading up to the cathedral. He stared narrow-eyed at the tympanum above the main doorway. The carving depicted a stern-faced Christ, flaming sword in one hand, in the other, the orb of power surmounted by a cross. The sculptor had carved Christ the Judge, coming at the end of time when, as the apostle said, "Heaven and earth would dissolve into fire!" That most dreadful of days when the sun would be darkened, the moon and stars fall from heaven, and all creation rocked to its very foundations. The beggars, squatting on the steps, minus hands, arms or legs, gathered their evil-smelling rags and left their favorite spot to crawl down, moaning and banging their clack dishes. The knight looked as if he was a crusader, who had taken the cross and fought the infidels around the Middle Sea. They whined for alms. The knight opened his purse, scattered a few coins on the steps and returned to his lonely vigil. He stood, one hand on the hilt of his sword, the other gently tapping silver-studded gauntlets against his leather, sleeveless cote-hardie which hung down just beneath his knee. One beggar, who'd managed to get close, squinted up at the stranger. More perceptive than his comrades, the beggar thought the knight had the same severe face as that of Christ carved in stone above him. Steel-grey hair, parted down the middle, fell to his shoulders. His clipped moustache and beard were flecked with silver, the sunburnt face rather gaunt whilst his high cheekbones and deep-set eyes gave the stranger a haunted look.

The knight was dressed handsomely enough: a quilted jerkin of burgundy beneath the coat, open at the neck to display the collar of a white linen shirt: his dark-blue hose, of pure wool, were pushed into high-heeled riding boots on which silver carved spurs clinked at his every movement. The beggar noticed the finely embroidered war belt, strapped round his slim waist, with decorated scabbards for the long sword and a stabbing dirk. The beggar squinted behind the knight: the stranger carried no saddlebags and the beggar couldn't see the whereabouts of any horse or sumpter pony.

"Master, have you travelled far?" he croaked.

The knight just kept staring at the carving as if fascinated by the monkey-faced demons and the depraved, staring eyes of the damned who, guarded by angels, crouched submissively to the left of Christ.

"Have you come for the Maundy Service ceremony?"

"I have." The knight's voice was soft.

The beggar couldn't believe his good fortune. A silver coin appeared between the knight's smooth, dark fingers. The beggar's dish shot forward to gratefully receive such an offering.

"You've come for the Maundy ceremony?" the beggar whined. He screwed up his good eye: he hoped the knight wouldn't notice the awful pitted marks on his pox-riddled cheeks. "Will the bishop wash your feet as Christ did those of the Apostles?"

"He will wash my feet," the knight replied.

"And I suppose you've paid good gold and silver for the privilege!"

Try as he might, the beggar couldn't disguise the contempt in his voice. A mighty prelate, the friend of princes, kings, and emperors, Bishop Otto was well known for his love of clinking gold. Every Maundy Thursday, just before Easter, the bishop would sing a solemn High Mass. During the service he'd wash the feet of twelve men, who'd paid good silver for the privilege. Christ himself had done the same but freely, humbly, submissively to show how, even though he was the master, he was the servant of all, setting an example for his followers. Christ had definitely failed with Bishop Otto, the beggar mused staring up at the knight. Bishop Otto was a shepherd more interested in the fleece than the flock. A cleric who had risen far and fast and now clothed his corpulent body with the finest silks and warmest wool. He had built himself a palace in the grounds beyond the cathedral where he feasted and dined like the

wealthy Lazarus from Christ's own parable. A bishop who, at a snap of his
be-ringed fingers, could summon up a retinue of fifty knights and three
hundred well-armed mounted men, not to mention a legion of retainers
and servants. The beggar, who'd lost a hand in a hideous siege so many
years ago, moved slightly sideways as a powerful merchant swept up the
steps.

"And will he hear your confession?"

The knight said something in Latin.

"What was that?" The beggar cupped one swollen ear in his good
hand. "What was that sir? I don't understand Latin."

The knight glanced down, eyes crinkling in amusement.

"Oh yes, he will hear my confession."

Days later the beggar would recount this meeting, in hushed, hoarse
tones, a cold shiver of fear prickling his sweaty back.

"I tell you," he'd later confess to other members of the begging fra-
ternity, "on that terrible Thursday it was like looking into the face of the
good Lord Jesus himself. Dark, swarthy, and lined his face was, but his
lips were full and his eyes, although hard and piercing as a falcon's,
became soft as a maid's."

Of course his companions laughed at him, yet the beggar persisted.

"I tell you," he'd screech. "The knight had the same face as I have seen
on the picture of Christ in Judgement, dark and brooding!"

No one believed him, and no one was interested in his story. Indeed,
why should Christ come to Bishop Otto's cathedral city? A place of
wickedness, of subtle corruption that polluted the council chambers, the
churches, in truth anything associated with Bishop Otto.

"I wish you well, sir," the beggar whispered. "The bishop will shrive
you."

"No, sir," the knight replied. "Christ the searcher of hearts will shrive
me!"

Grasping the hilt of his sword, spurs clinking, the knight walked up
the steps and through the cavernous doorway. The cathedral was a beautiful, somber place with a soaring, vaulted roof. Squat, fat pillars along
each side of the majestic nave guarded transepts cloaked in shadows.
Here and there a burst of sunlight as the stained glass windows, depicting countless scenes from the Bible, caught the sun of that Maundy
Thursday and splashed it along the smooth-edged paving stones. For a
while, the knight just stood inside the doorway admiring the elaborately
carved rood screen which divided the sanctuary and choir from the rest
of the church. Beyond the rood screen stood the high altar: because this

was a most solemn moment of Lent, its white Purbeck marble was covered in a purple and gold cloth. Lent was also the fasting season, so no sanctuary candles were lit, but the air still smelt sweet with the fragrance of beeswax and the purest incense money could buy.

The knight stepped forward and leaned against a pillar. Now his eyes were growing accustomed to the gloom, he could make out all the statues which, because of the season, were covered by somber cloths, be it the Virgin and Child in the Lady Chapel to the left of the high altar or those in the small chantry chapels, one of which stood just to his left. Every icon, crucifix, and statue was veiled and would remain so until Bishop Otto intoned the "Gloria in Excelsis" at the Easter vigil during the early hours of Sunday morning. The thought seemed to amuse the knight. He smiled and stepped away from the pillar, tucking his gauntlets into his war belt. A servant came hurrying up, dressed in the green and gold of Bishop Otto's livery.

"Sir, you are not allowed in here. We are preparing the church for the Maundy Mass. Bishop Otto will also be hearing the confessions of those whose feet he will . . ."

The servant stopped his gabbling as the knight drew from the sleeve of his doublet a small, cream-colored parchment.

"Oh, I see! I see!" The servant smiled falsely and bowed. "You are one of the chosen?"

"I paid good silver," the knight replied stepping forward. "His lordship the bishop has graciously agreed: I am to be one of the twelve whose feet he will wash and whose confession he will soon hear as preparation for that solemn ceremony."

"Of course! Of course!" the man stuttered. "And what is your name?"

"My name, sir," the knight put away the scroll of parchment, "is Joseph, Sir Joseph of Arimathea." He laughed softly at the consternation on the retainer's face.

"You don't think that's my name? I am a knight who fights for Christ's faithful on earth. You know the custom. When you take up such a calling, you give up your name and identity and pick the title of one of Christ's followers. I have chosen Joseph of Arimathea, the man who asked for Christ's body to be taken down from the cross."

"Of course, I understand." The liveried servant bowed again. "I saw your name on the lists. Come this way, sir! Come this way! We have to be so careful. So careful," he muttered as the knight followed him up the nave. "We have so many beggars and troublemakers, the importunate, the petitioners. . . ."

"Where will the bishop hear my confession?"

The servant paused then led him across into the transept where a small chantry chapel stood against the wall of the cathedral, its other three sides bounded by soaring wooden screens. Incidents from the Bible were carved along each side: Noah falling asleep after he had left the ark: David fighting Goliath: Satan taunting Job. The servant allowed the knight to study the carvings before opening the door to the small chantry chapel. The stone floor inside had been covered with a thick, soft Turkish carpet whilst the entire chapel was divided by a purple and gold cloth that hung from a copper bar resting on the wooden screens at either end. The middle of the cloth had been carefully cut out and replaced with a piece of white gauze, before this was a prie-dieu. The knight, without being asked, knelt down on the prie-dieu and stared through the white gauze. He could make out the far wall of the cathedral on the other side. He smelt the fragrance from the perfume pots placed in the bishop's makeshift confessional. He peered more closely and glimpsed the pomanders resting on the table before the carved, high-backed chair where the bishop would sit to hear the confessions of the chosen few.

"His lordship will begin confessions," the servant bleated, "two hours before Mass."

"May I see where he will sit?" the knight asked.

The servant was about to refuse, then smiled at the glint of silver coin held between the knight's fingers.

"Of course sir, of course you may."

He took the coin and lifted the edge of the purple-gold cloth. The knight stepped around: this half of the chantry chapel contained the altar. The knight marvelled at how the bishop had prepared every luxury for himself: the throne-like chair was quilted and cushioned, a footstool peeped from beneath the table, on which stood a crucifix, two pomanders, a silver gilt-chased goblet, and a gold-embossed jug of wine. All was prepared as the knight had been informed by other penitents from previous years. He walked up and down, touching and lifting certain items.

"How long will the confessions last?"

The servant pointed to an iron spigot beside the table, the candle fixed on it was carefully ringed with twelve lines.

"Each penitent," the servant explained, "will be allowed the time the candle burns from one line down to the next, no more than two hours in all. His lordship is insistent on this. He is very busy, his duties are onerous."

"Yes," the knight replied. "I understand what you say."

He stood as if fascinated by a painting to the right of the window above the altar: Judas Iscariot, a bag of gold in one hand, a halter in the other, was climbing a tree to hang himself. At the foot of the tree, and from between its branches, glared the demonic red faces of devils waiting to collect his soul.

"Rather gruesome, yes?"

The servant impatiently tapped his foot against the carpet. He didn't want the knight to linger here so long, after all the bishop's chamberlain, or one of his guards, might come along.

"Sir, we have some white wine and comfits for you in the sacristy."

"Of course you have."

The servant lifted the curtain and went out. He reached the door to the chantry chapel before realizing the knight had not followed: he hurried back to find Sir Joseph struggling to free the edge of his spur from the thick carpet beside the table.

"I am sorry." The knight smiled apologetically.

He gave another tug, his spur broke free, and the knight followed the servant out. They went through the rood screen, across the marble-floored sanctuary and into the large sacristy. The other penitents were now gathering, being served Rhenish wine and dishes of spiced comfits by Bishop Otto's servants. The knight stood for a while. The rest appeared self-conscious. As customary, none of them were residents of the city but powerful lords of the soil or merchants from beyond its walls: they had paid for the privilege of allowing the bishop to wash their feet and hear their confessions beforehand.

The knight took a chair and sipped quietly at his wine. He watched the light in the windows fade and listened to the tolling of the great bell of the cathedral marking the hours. Other members of the bishop's household appeared, sacristans and clerks. Two knights from his retinue came and stood in the doorway of the sacristy studying the faces of the would-be penitents: they were making sure there was no one whom they recognized as having a grudge or grievance against their lord. Again the bell in the cathedral began to toll, candles were lit, and the knight heard the great doors of the cathedral being closed. The time for shriving was fast approaching.

The penitents were called to order. The bishop's chamberlain, a thin, scrawny-faced man, dressed like a figure of death in a black robe that spanned neck to toe, swept into the sacristy. A silver crucifix hung round his neck, rings of office glistened on his fingers.

"Gentlemen." He clapped his hands softly. "Gentlemen," he repeated, a forced smile on his sour face. "You have gathered here so his lordship Bishop Otto may shrive you in the chantry chapel of St. Matthias. You will wait outside, kneeling on the prie-dieus provided. You only enter when each penitent has left."

"There will be no guards?" a haughty merchant demanded. "I don't want someone near the door listening to my confession!"

"Of course not," the chamberlain soothed. "You will meet his lordship by himself, confess your sins, receive absolution." He shrugged, a rather pretty gesture. "Where you go afterwards is your concern: one of the side chapels, you may return here, or perhaps take the evening air before High Mass begins. However," he lifted a finger in warning, "you must be back here when the bishop vests for Mass. Oh yes . . ."

He paused at the tinkling bell and hastily stepped aside as a cowled figure carrying a crucifix solemnly entered the large oak-paneled sacristy. Behind him processioned two boys carrying lighted tapers and a young deacon, dressed in a snowy-white alb, swinging a thurible where the charcoal crackled, sending out gusts of fragrant incense. Two more retainers followed and then Bishop Otto himself, garbed in purple from head to toe. He entered the sacristy, hands extended, as if about to receive the plaudits of all his flock. The chamberlain snapped his fingers. Everyone, except the members of the bishop's retinue, fell to their knees. The knight lifted his head. Bishop Otto was smiling benevolently round, a patronizing smile, reserved for public appearances, intended to show his care and concern for those he was supposed to serve and lead. A fine man, Bishop Otto, with his light olive-skinned face all freshly shaved and perfumed. His snow-white hair was swept carefully forward, the purple skull cap positioned ever so elegantly, the white lacy cloth, beneath the silk, frothed around his throat. The bishop's hands came together as if in prayer. He studied each of the penitents who had paid for the privilege of meeting him. The smile disappeared. The smooth olive-skinned face was impassive, as his black eyes, hard as glass, moved round the sacristy. He glanced at the knight, looked him up and down and dismissed him without demur. The knight stared down at Bishop Otto's gold-gilt sandals. He observed the costly rings on each finger, the silver chain on the bishop's left wrist and how the pectoral cross, which swung from an ivory chain, looked to be pure gold.

"My children." The bishop's voice was low and throaty. "My children, you are most welcome here. The chamberlain has already explained the order of the service so we shall begin now. Your turn will be decided by casting lots."

The chamberlain carried round a bronze bowl containing scraps of parchment. The knight took his and opened it; he would be third. Once this was finished, the bishop vested for the service. He donned a snow-white surplice and took a silver-edged purple stole from a casket, kissed the cross in the center and wrapped it round his neck. Bishop Otto then sketched a blessing and, preceded by his entourage, processioned out of the sacristy to take his place behind the screen in the chapel of St. Matthias.

The penitents now rose: they shuffled their feet in embarrassment and stared sheepishly at each other. The men had come to the cathedral because of their sins, heinous offenses that could only be absolved by Bishop Otto, who had obtained special canonical power and indulgences from Rome to absolve certain offenses. The bishop's servants moved amongst the penitents explaining how, perhaps, at the end of the service, the penitents could show their gratitude to his lordship in a more practical manner, like an offering to the cathedral? The group of penitents, apart from the knight, clustered like a group of schoolboys, laughing nervously and nodding in agreement.

The chamberlain returned to take the numbers. The penitents were instructed to line up in order, then were led from the sacristy into the darkened nave. The knight glanced around. Daylight had faded and the nave felt gloomy and cavernous, their footsteps echoed like the beat of a distant drum. They walked mournfully, like a line of felons being escorted to the scaffold. The chantry chapel of St. Matthias was now ringed by beeswax candles. Further along, on either side, armed retainers of the bishop were betrayed by candlelight in the glint of steel or gleam of a blade or hilt of a sword. The prie-dieus were ready, arranged in rows of three. The penitents knelt on the cushioned rests. Some put their faces in their hands, others threaded Ave beads nervously through their fingers. The knight, however, knelt upright, hands joined, staring fixedly at the door of the chantry chapel.

The confessions began. The first two penitents were dealt with. Eventually it was the knight's turn; he rose, bowed towards the high altar and entered the perfumed warmness of the chantry chapel of St. Matthias. He knelt on the prie-dieu and stared through the gauze. He could make out the plump, rounded features of the bishop: his stubby nose, pursed lips, the ringed fingers as he rested his head in his hands ready to listen to the next confession.

The knight continued to stare through the linen cloth. He sniffed and caught the fragrant smell from the copper-topped, glowing brazier on which the servants had sprinkled crushed herbs. The knight maintained his silence, waiting for the bishop to turn; the cleric did so, a gesture of annoyance.

"Well, my son, what are you waiting for?"

The knight breathed in and smiled at the rich smell of wine on the bishop's breath.

"I am sorry, my lord." He muttered.

"That is why you are here, my son." Bishop Otto's tone was pompous, redolent with false charity and compassion. "We are all sinners before the Lord. Now, I will hear your confession. *In Nomine Patris et Filii . . .*"

The bishop began the rite. The knight closed his eyes.

"Bless me, Father, for I have sinned. It is a month since I was last shrived—"

"A month?" the bishop broke in. "Only a month? The men who come here have not been shriven for many a year!"

"My lord, I am a crusader. I have taken vows of poverty, chastity, and obedience."

"Of course, of course," the bishop hastily replied. "I had forgotten. You have taken the name of Joseph of Arimathea, the devout Jew who shrouded Christ's corpse? Have you looked after the body of Christ, sir knight, or have you, by thought, word, and action, torn at his sacred flesh, re-opened his blessed wounds?"

"My lord, I have sinned." The knight agreed. "And, to quote the psalmist, my sins are always before me. I constantly repeat the words of the Psalm: 'Have mercy on me, Oh God, have mercy on me and, in your infinite compassion, blot out my offence. Truly my sins I know . . .'"

"Yes, yes," the bishop interrupted. "But what sins?"

"My lord, first I must tell you a story which has haunted my soul for many a year."

"Continue, my son."

The knight paused at the clink of a ring against the goblet. He saw the bishop take a generous slurp from his deep-bowled cup. The chantry chapel had fallen silent, even sounds from beyond the door had subsided. Nothing but the spluttering of the beeswax candles fixed in the iron spigots around the walls, their flames dancing in the draughts which seeped through cracks and crevices.

"My son?" The bishop was now cradling the goblet, leaning towards the white gauze.

The knight could glimpse the anger in this haughty prelate's face.

"My lord, I shall be brief. Many years ago, in a city like this, near a cathedral like this, lived a young lawyer: a sprightly fellow with bright eyes and keen wits. A man who loved life; he could dance a merry jig or sweetly sing any carol you named."

"And you murdered him?" The bishop couldn't help intervening.

"No, my lord, I did not murder him. This lawyer had a passion for justice: for the poor worms, those of our brothers who live in the gutter and eke out the hard bread of existence."

"He was a rebel?"

"No, my lord, a just man. He defended the rights of the artisans against the wealthy burghers and guildsmen. He presented their cases, defended their claims and would only accept a jug of beer in payment. A man much loved, my lord . . ."

"And what happened to him?"

"He was taken up by the powerful guildsmen of the city and imprisoned in the darkest dungeon of that city's castle. They called it the Trinity Chamber."

The knight ignored Bishop Otto's gasp of astonishment.

"I have heard of this," the bishop murmured.

"A large dungeon," the knight continued matter-of-factly, "with hard, granite stone floors, walls, and ceiling, a barred window high in the outside wall allowed in some light."

"This lawyer was ill-used?"

"No, my lord, the Trinity Chamber, though a dungeon, is comfortable and clean: no cracks for rats or mice. I have spoken to the gaoler: fresh rushes covered the floor, a cot bed with unsoiled linen sheets. It possessed a table, stool, and chair. The lawyer was not ill-used, well, at least, not physically. The guildsmen questioned him day and night but they could find no case against him."

"And how is this a sin?" The bishop spoke abruptly.

"Hush, my lord! In a short while I shall make sense. As the gospel says: 'That which is hidden in darkness will be revealed for all to see.'"

The knight paused. The bishop eagerly sipped his wine.

"Now, the lawyer had friends in the city who appealed to the emperor. He issued a writ, demanding this advocate be released no later than Maundy Thursday, three days before Easter. The guild master received this writ, ceased his questioning, but he decided to enforce the writ to the very letter. He had received it at least a week before the prisoner was to be freed but he let him languish."

"Did this lawyer know he was to be released?"

"No, not really, my lord. Anyway, on Spy Wednesday, the night before his release was to take place, the captain of the guard aroused the constable of the castle and brought him down to the Trinity Chamber. They could not believe what they saw in the poor light through the grille on the heavy oaken door, the young lawyer sprawled on the floor, a thin, Italianate stiletto thrust deep into his heart."

"So it was suicide?" Bishop Otto fought to keep his voice steady.

"Well, that was the verdict of the coroner."

"But how?" the bishop asked.

"Yes, my lord, that's the great mystery. The Trinity Chamber was well guarded: two soldiers outside and more, both at the end of the passageway and at the top of the steps which led down to the dungeons. No one could have squeezed through that window." The knight half-laughed. "Even a squirrel would have found it difficult. The coroner examined the Trinity Chamber most carefully, but vainly, for any secret passageways. The guards took solemn oaths that no stranger had entered that cell whilst the Constable went on oath to explain how the Trinity Chamber took its name because its heavy oaken door had three locks. Each could only be opened by a different key. He held one, the captain of the guard held another, whilst the third was held by the guild master. At no time did any one man hold all three keys."

"But how did the dagger get into the cell? Had someone smuggled it in? Did the lawyer have one when he was taken up and arrested.

"No, my lord. The prisoner never carried sword or dagger. He was a man of peace, whilst all visitors to the cell—and they were very few— were most scrupulously searched."

"Indeed, my son, this is a mystery." Bishop Otto whispered. "But where is the offence? What is to be absolved except the sin of suicide?"

"But, my lord," the knight replied. "Why should a young lawyer, in love with life, on the verge of being released, take his own life? And how did he obtain possession of such a dagger?"

"Did the guards notice anything untoward? Signs of struggle in the cell?"

"No, they did not. They found the corpse once darkness had fallen: the prisoner had extinguished the small oil lamp he was allowed and they thought he had gone to sleep. Only when one lifted up a lantern and peered through the grille did they notice the corpse."

The knight sensed the bishop's growing agitation but held his peace. Bishop Otto could not disrupt this confession and the only way out of the chantry chapel was the door behind the knight. The bishop took another gulp of wine and sighed throatily.

"And the prisoner, how was he in the days before his sudden and mysterious death?"

"Very quiet, my lord. The guards, however, were changed constantly: none of them developed a relationship with him. They were paid mercenaries and did their task as they had on many an occasion."

"And what visitors did the prisoner receive?"

"None were allowed from the city."

"Then this is strange. . . ?"

"Yes, my lord, it is."

The knight shifted his gaze to the candle flame; white beeswax ran down like translucent pearls towards the black iron holders. In the church outside the choir began to prepare for the evening service.

"*Salve me Domine et monstra mihi faciem tuam*; Save me, Lord, and show your face to me."

The knight closed his eyes and repeated the words.

"Here we have," the Bishop remarked, "a hideous death: a man stabbed through the heart, yet no secret doorway or passageway existed. No one could enter that cell without the permission of two others."

The bishop paused. The knight knew what the bishop wanted to ask.

"I, er . . . ?"

"Yes, my lord?"

Behind the curtain the bishop tried to control his own fear: this ritual had changed! He was no longer listening to the knight's confession; it was almost as if his visitor was preparing to listen to his.

"He had one visitor," the knight continued evenly. "The guild master had a chaplain who often visited the prisoner to provide spiritual comfort. He would take the guild master's key and open one lock whilst the constable of the castle and the captain of the guard opened the other two. Once inside, the doors were locked until the chaplain demanded to leave. Apparently this chaplain"—the bishop now hid his face behind his hand—"carried a brass crucifix. He would place it on a ledge and light a taper on either side. He would then sit and whisper words of ghostly comfort. The mercenaries, of course, respecting such a meeting, gave the prisoner and the chaplain privacy."

"And was this chaplain questioned?"

"Oh yes, my lord. He, too, was perplexed and puzzled. He could not understand why the young lawyer had taken his own life! He claimed he had given him great news—that he was soon to be released."

"Then why?" The bishop's hand fell away.

"My lord, I went to that castle. I talked to everyone I could. One fact emerges. The only people who were informed about the emperor's writ, before the lawyer's death, were the guild master . . ."

"And his chaplain?" the bishop added.

"Yes, my lord, the chaplain."

"And you questioned others?"

"Those whom I could find, my lord. I reached the conclusion, after years of reflection, that the lawyer was not murdered, not in the legal sense, but he did commit suicide."

The knight paused at the clatter of the wine jug against the globe.

"I knew that young lawyer," the knight rasped. "He was my younger brother, Robert, a man full of life with a passionate desire to see justice done. We were, my lord, like two peas from the same pod: the loving sons of doting parents, privileged and rich. We wanted to spend our lives either for the gospel or for others."

The knight paused and stared at a wall painting of Judas the traitor hanging himself.

"I took the cross whilst Robert decided to follow the law. We went our separate paths. However, when we were young, my brother and I witnessed an execution: a thief who was hanged. The execution was bungled. A hideous, ghastly sight: a man's face turned purple as he slowly choked to death at the end of a rope.

"My brother later confessed that he had constant nightmares about it. He had a horror of death by hanging! Now, this is what happened." The knight cupped his hand to his mouth. "My brother was taken up and imprisoned. He was questioned and threatened. The emperor's writ arrived, but the guild master and his chaplain decided to keep this information to themselves. Instead, the guild master secretly instructed his chaplain to visit the prisoner and tell him that he'd be tried and hanged. I suspect the guild master had learnt about my brother's secret nightmares."

"Oh no!" The bishop groaned.

"The chaplain, that creature of the night, with a soul as dark as hell, eager for preferment, accepted this task gladly. He entered that cell and, under the cloak and guise of his office, frightened my brother. He did not tell him about the writ but warned him of his impending death, describing in detail how the execution would be carried out."

"But surely the lawyer would protest? The guards would have known?"

"Would they, my lord? Here was a young lawyer cut off from his friends, unjustly arrested and imprisoned, questioned and interrogated, then left to his own thoughts and dark dreams. Into the cell creeps our Judas priest, quietly advising the prisoner not to protest; how he was doing his best to soften the wrath of the guild master but, look, he had smuggled in a dagger, hidden in the hollow brass crucifix he brought."

"How do you know that?" the bishop stuttered.

"My lord, I've told you. I visited that castle. In its small stone chapel stands a brass crucifix; it is hollow, cylindrical. The top of the cross can be screwed off, inside nothing more than a long empty tube. A dagger, a stiletto of the Italian style with no cross hilt, could be inserted. The old sacristan claimed that the hollow tube had been fashioned to hold charcoal and incense. I went out and bought such a dagger in the marketplace. I returned to the chapel and found it easy to place it inside." The knight paused. "My brother was murdered. Oh, he took his own life but in God's eyes he was murdered." The knight wetted his lips. "Imagine it: a young man, with a morbid fear of hanging, left alone in a dark cell, deprived of all company and friendship. He believes he has been deserted by his friends. He has no knowledge of the emperor's writ, of his impending release. Instead, the Judas priest tells him the opposite, about a swift trial and summary punishment, to be hanged from a gibbet. Why should he doubt the words of a zealous priest?"

Bishop Otto hastily filled his goblet and slurped noisily.

"The young lawyer, terrified out of his wits, begs for help, he'll do anything to avoid that. So the Judas priest, as a kindness, offers to help but demands it be kept secret. The lawyer agrees and the dagger is brought. Come, come, my lord! My brother was not the first prisoner to take his own life in order to escape a hanging and, I suspect, he will not be the last. I wonder," the knight mused, "if he had not taken his own life and been found with that dagger, would some other pretext have been found to kill him?" The knight pressed his face up against the white gauze. "You, my lord, were the assassin, the Judas priest. You carry my brother's blood on your hands, his life on your conscience! His soul still pleads for justice before God Almighty!"

"How dare you," the bishop rasped, glaring through the white gauze.

"How dare I, my lord? Quite easily. You know the story well, you were the chaplain! You were the Judas priest who, for thirty pieces of silver, the prospects of preferment, forced a man to take his own life. Like Judas you should hang as the sky above you turns black with the birds of the air coming to pluck your soft flesh."

The bishop turned to fill his goblet. He found it hard to hold the cup. He heard a sound and turned quickly. The space beyond the white gauze was now empty whilst the chantry door was closing. The bishop sat as if carved out of stone: heart beating, mind teeming with terror. He dared not jump up. How could he accuse such a man? What had been said here

was covered by the seal of confession. People would wonder. Anyway, the
door was already opening and the fourth penitent was kneeling at the
prie-dieu, eyes gazing expectantly. The bishop placed the goblet on the
table and rubbed his stomach. Perhaps it was just a dream? His fingers
kneaded his soft stomach to ease the shooting pains.

"Yes, my son." His words were forced. The bishop swallowed the foul-
tasting bile at the back of his throat.

Outside the knight had left immediately, not pausing to kneel or say
a prayer. He went out through the main door where the bishop's servants
and guards clustered. He swung his cloak round his shoulders and fastened the clasps and, grasping the hilt of his sword, clattered down the
steps. He stopped and smiled up at the starlit sky. Who could say what
had happened? Bishop Otto's servants might check that jug and goblet
but they'd keep quiet for had not they been responsible for that? The beggar, whom he had encountered earlier in the day, still crouched in the
shadows.

"Did you receive absolution, sir?"

The beggar edged forward, his shrivelled features, in the light of the
dirty tallow candle he held, looked like those of a gargoyle.

The knight opened his purse and placed a silver coin in the astonished man's hand.

"No, sir." He smiled down at the beggar. "I did not seek absolution
but justice!"

And then he was gone across the deserted forecourt, disappearing as
mysteriously as he had arrived.

The beggar could only crouch in amazement and stare at the silver
piece. He would always remember that Maundy Thursday. The mysterious knight, cloaked and cowled, entering the cathedral and leaving so
abruptly. Yet that was only the beginning of the drama. Hadn't bishop
Otto been taken suddenly ill as he vested for High Mass, clutching and
clasping at his stomach and chest? He had collapsed to the ground in a
dead swoon, his plump, smooth face turned haggard, a white froth stain-
ing his lips. How his fat body had jerked, arms flailing as his retainers
tried to help. No one could understand his dying words. Why he kept
crying out, "Absolve me! Absolve me, Domine! Absolve me, oh Lord,
absolve me!"

And everyone wondered, *From what*?

✝

The Shorn Lamb
A Father Dowling Mystery

Ralph McInerny

I

April was the kindest month in Fox River, Illinois, and no more so than in St. Hilary's parish. Wintry blasts had given way to the warmer winds of spring, seemingly endless snowfall gave way to April showers, crocus and forsythia lent living color to a world that for months had been a melancholy grey. And high above, like a rare star, the sun shone. In the rectory, Marie Murkin, the housekeeper, could be heard singing her version of *Pennies from Heaven*. In his study, enveloped in clouds of pipe smoke, Roger Dowling, the pastor of St. Hilary's, his office and rosary said, had settled back for an afternoon of uninterrupted reading. He was frowning over Peter Ackroyd's life of Saint Thomas More when Marie's singing ceased and she passed the study on her way to answer the front doorbell. Father Dowling's concentration on Ackroyd's learned if tin-eared narration of the martyred Lord Chancellor wavered as the sound of voices in the front hall came to him. There was a lull and then Marie appeared in the door of the study.

"A Professor William Caspar insists on seeing you."

"Insists?"

"I told him you were busy."

"Marie! Show him in."

"Don't say I didn't warn you."

"When was that?"

But she was gone, soon to be replaced by a large, untidy man with a beard that might have been an argument for mandatory shaving. His tweed sport jacket was open, doubtless because he could never have buttoned it over the enormous belly that was emphasized by the green turtleneck sweater he wore.

"Reverend Dowling?"

"Roger Dowling." He rose and, after a moment's hesitation, put out his hand. The visitor looked at it and then grasped it firmly.

"William Caspar. I teach history at the Fort Elbow branch."

"What period?"

"Usually afternoons."

Professorial wit? "I am reading Ackroyd's life of More."

"Don't know it," Caspar said, taking the chair Father Dowling indicated. "I want to talk about apparitions."

"Ah. Which one?"

"The one in Skokie."

"Skokie!"

Caspar nodded. "I have to tell you that I am an agnostic at best. If I had the leisure I would write a book debunking the Shroud of Turin."

"That might take more than leisure."

"But this business in Skokie has the ring of the genuine to me."

"Tell me about it."

Caspar studied the priest. "You want me to tell you about it."

It took some time to convince his visitor that he had never heard of any apparition in Skokie, that it was not something the priests of the Archdiocese had been briefed about, and that he was under no obligation to take seriously anyone's claim to have been visited by the Blessed Virgin.

"St. Bartholomew. Quinn says that Bartholomew, one of the Apostles, visits him frequently and tells him all sorts of things."

"What sorts of things?"

"That's what I want to find out. I thought any priest would be thoroughly informed on the matter."

Father Dowling was asking himself what, beyond the fact that he was one of the apostles, he knew of St. Bartholomew. He had the vague memory that he was buried in a chapel on the Isola Teverina in Rome, but he would have to look that up. He was fairly certain that St. Bartholomew had kept strict celestial silence during the two millennia of the Christian era. That he should suddenly start chatting with a logician named Quinn in Skokie seemed out of character.

"A logician."

"He's a colleague of mine. A lapsed Catholic."

"Who has apparitions."

"He doesn't call them that. He says they're just conversations. But what he passed on to me from Bartholomew has left me shaken."

"St. Bartholomew sent a message to you through Quinn?"

Caspar nodded. His chin was tucked in and his beard lay tangled on his chest. "Things no one could possibly know. Certainly not Quinn."

"Could you give me an inkling?"

"Things in my childhood. Things I doubt I ever told anyone. They seemed meant to establish his bona fides. And then he predicted my death."

Father Dowling was tempted to say that anyone's death could be safely predicted, but Caspar seemed to sense his skepticism. "He gave me less than a year, Reverend."

"I don't wonder that you're upset."

"Upset? I'm not upset. But I want to know more."

"Is the predicted date soon?"

Caspar covered his bearded mouth and for the first time noticed the walls lined with books. But he was not distracted. "I am pledged not to reveal it."

"What more would you like to know beyond the day and the hour?"

"I want to know who is going to kill me."

Father Dowling was not a suspicious man, but he was a realist. Professor Caspar, a self-described agnostic, came to him with an extraordinary story about a logician named Quinn in Skokie who allegedly held regular conversations with St. Bartholomew. Among the revelations was that William Caspar was going to be killed. Of course the thought occurred that an elaborate practical joke was being played on him, an effort to plumb the credulity of a Catholic priest. But William Caspar spoke so ingenuously and with such eager urgency, he was either a consummate actor or was saying what he believed to be the truth.

"You teach history?"

Caspar reacted impatiently to the question. "I want to talk about St. Bartholomew's prediction that someone is going to kill me."

"Who would want to kill you?"

Caspar combed his beard with stuffy fingers. "You don't know what it's like teaching in a place like the Fox River campus. The students!" He flipped his beard and his eyes rolled upward.

"Pretty bad?"

"Of course they're stupid. Why else would they be enrolled there? They come into college with minds like blank slates. No, that's not true. They've been educated by MTV and rap artists. They sit in class with earphones clamped to their heads listening to God knows what. And they all want A's. I've been threatened."

"You didn't need a revelation to know that."

Caspar closed his eyes in thought. "Some disgruntled student? Of course. And then there are my colleagues."

"One of them might kill you?"

"Oh yes. If they could get away with it."

"Quinn?"

"No! He is my closest friend." A pause. "Male friend."

"Ah."

"There's Betty."

"A potential assassin?"

Caspar laughed a great booming laugh. "I intended to ask her to marry me."

"Something happened?"

"What we've been talking about. How could I marry her knowing that I am shortly going to be killed?"

"What is it you want me to do?"

"Could Bartholomew be wrong?"

"Perhaps the question should be: Could your friend Quinn be wrong in what he says Bartholomew told him."

Caspar thought about that. "Not when he tells me Bartholomew mentioned things in my past that no one could possibly know."

"You're sure about that? How well does Quinn know you?"

"As I said, he is my best friend."

"And you never mentioned these memories to him."

"Never."

It was Father Dowling's turn to fall silent. After a moment he said, "Did Quinn say why you were being warned?"

"So I could protect myself, I guess."

"And make a liar out of St. Bartholomew?"

"Look, Father, I've had all these debates with myself. Would you talk to Quinn?"

"And say what?"

"Put these kinds of questions to him. Am I doomed?"

"Surely you've asked Quinn these things."

"He says he will only tell me what he has been told to. He isn't going to debate with Bartholomew."

"So what would be the point of my seeing him?"

"You're a priest. Quinn is a Catholic. Or at least he used to be. He'll tell you things he wouldn't tell me."

And so it was that Father Dowling agreed to go to Skokie and talk with Quinn the logician.

2

Bruno Quinn had set out to be a mathematician but his interests led him into the ever more abstract and less practical realm of theoretical logic. He had set out from set theory and ended by constructing formulae that required many unintelligible pages to interpret. He was famous. That he should have ended up on the faculty of the Fox River campus of the state university would have seemed to anyone else either a tragedy or a farce, but such judgments imply a contrast between his present situation and another possible one. Where were the students who could understand him? Where were the colleagues who might stimulate his thinking? He was as well off where he was as anywhere else. The pay was risible, but his wants were minuscule, the teaching far from onerous, enabling him to spend more time at his Skokie home than in his campus office.

Quinn appeared in the doorway looking like a shaved egg in a gym suit. Huge unlaced running shoes, the baggy pants and hooded top of the gym suit, and then the head devoid of any hair, save for the eyebrows. Glasses hung from his neck. He peered at his caller.

"Is that a Roman collar?"

"It is."

"Are you the priest Caspar spoke to?"

"I am."

"Poor fellow. Come in."

The living room was all but bare, and the next room as well, what would have served as a dining room. It was occupied by a trestle table on which stood a computer and piles of paper. A blackboard leaned against the built-in cabinet meant to hold dishes. Quinn pushed a wheeled chair toward Father Dowling. He caught it or it would have gone on into the living room.

"The house is settling," Quinn said. "It tilts. What nonsense has Caspar been telling you?"

"Do you have conversations with St. Bartholomew?"

"Conversations?" The skinned head shook. "He talks, I listen."

"What about?"

"Much of it is confidential."

"Just for you?"

"That's right. He has an amazing understanding of mathematics, not that that should surprise. I have come to see how little we know, comparatively. I am to him as a kid in kindergarten is to me."

"You talk mathematics?"

"It's not quite talk. It's like hearing formulas spoken as if they were a primary language. No sound is needed."

"How long has this been going on?"

"It started when I took Bartholomew for my confirmation name."

"But that must be . . ."

"Thirty-one years ago. From time to time, I would pray to him and ask a favor. They were always granted but I never said thank you, pretending they would have happened anyway. A year ago, he started to talk to me."

"And mentioned William Caspar?"

"Is that what he said?"

"And that you passed on to him the information that he would be killed."

"He actually told you that?"

"Isn't it true?"

"Of course not. Father, the man is insanely jealous because Bartholomew won't talk to him. I asked him what his confirmation name was, but he was never confirmed. You know he's not Catholic."

"But you are?"

"Not as thoroughly as I should be. As Bartholomew never fails to remind me."

"William Caspar did not seem deluded when he spoke to me. Of course, just speaking of such communications would make him seem deluded to most people."

"He teaches history."

This seemed diversionary, but Quinn went on to ask Father Dowling to see the essential triviality of the historian's pursuit. "Zillions of things have happened and history tells of an insignificant fraction of them and presumes to speak of the meaning of the past. Clearly fraudulent."

"Do you know Betty?"

"What about her?" Quinn had taken a stool behind the trestle table. "What did he say about my fiancée?"

✞

Father Dowling was not by nature a suspicious man, but the feeling he had had when speaking with William Caspar returned, and far more intensely. A game was being played and he was the butt of it. Why? Had he been picked at random, one priest as good as another to demonstrate whatever this elaborate joke was meant to demonstrate? He rose from his chair and pushed it toward Quinn, but it stopped before it reached him.

"It's uphill in this direction."

"Thank you for taking the time to see me."

"You're leaving?"

No need to add to Quinn's fun. He walked through the empty room to the front door. He turned when he opened it, but Quinn seemed engrossed in his computer. Father Dowling went out to his car and drove back to the rectory telling himself that for a priest to be trustful was not a fault and to believe what people tell him was not a flaw. But he felt like a fool.

✞

"Father," Marie Murkin said when he looked into the kitchen the following morning. "It was just on the news."

"What was that, Marie?"

"That bearded fellow who came the other day? Someone killed him."

3

To anyone who had known him alive, William Caspar would have been unrecognizable, not because he was dead, but because his beard had been shaved off and on his head were random tufts of hair left from an obviously hasty and amateur haircut. The body was found in the early morning by the manager of Captain Hook's, a driving range on the edge of Fox River. A ball was teed up on the rubber pad, the driver was clutched in the dead hand of the late professor of history. The corpse was wearing a jogging suit.

"What was the cause of death?" Captain Phil Keegan asked Dr. Lubins, the coroner.

"There are several possibilities."

"That's a pretty nasty lump on the back of his head."

"That might have been it. But he was roughed up beforehand. What do you think of that haircut?"

"Nowadays it's hard to tell when a butcher job like that is intended."

The conversation went on a few feet from where the body lay. Several practice tees away Cy Horvath was in conversation with Dr. Pippen, Lubins's assistant.

At that point in the investigation it was still not known that the body was that of a professor at the local campus of the state university. Cy found this out when he checked the only car parked at the driving range.

The history department was located on the eleventh floor of the former office building that housed the bulk of the Fox River campus. A young man in a pink sweater, pale blue glasses, and unreal yellow hair looked up when Cy entered.

"Are you Armstrong?"

The response was a giggle. "I am Joey, the secretary. You wish to see the chairperson?"

"Yes."

"Your name?"

But at that point a woman emerged from the inner office.

"I am Professor Armstrong," she said, looking at Cy appraisingly. She was a striking woman, fortyish, ash blonde hair, piercing eyes, the body of a goddess. "Betty Armstrong."

"Lieutenant Horvath. William Caspar is a member of your department?"

She blushed. She glanced at the secretary who tossed his tinted hair. Joey clearly did not like to be preempted. "Come in."

When they were in her office, she shut the door. "What about William Caspar?"

"He's dead."

"Oh my God." She put out her hand to steady herself and Cy grasped her elbow and led her to a chair.

"He was found dead at a driving range. . . ."

"Captain Hook's."

"You know it."

"I had been giving him instructions. We often went there. What happened to him?"

Professor Armstrong had been taken aback by the news that her colleague had been found dead at Captain Hook's Driving Range but hers was not the reaction of a woman whose fiancé had just been killed.

"You were showing him how to golf?"

"It was an impossible task." On the bookcase behind her there were several golf trophies on display, as well as a picture of the Madonna. Cy went to inspect the trophies.

"Obviously you're some golfer."

"I've been at it all my life."

"Nice picture."

She glanced at the Madonna. "Our Lady of Fatima."

"Ah."

"Have you ever been there? Fatima?"

"Where is it?"

"Portugal. I was cured there."

"Cured?"

"Of asthma. I tell you because you noticed the picture."

"A miracle?"

"I think so."

Cy had been told of the professor who claimed to be on speaking terms with one of the apostles. And here was the chair of a department talking about a miraculous cure at Fatima.

"Do you know Professor Quinn?"

"What does he have to do with this?"

"I'll be talking to him later. He and the deceased were close."

"They were both a little odd."

"Oh?"

She smiled. "Not that."

"You mean chatting with St. Bartholomew?"

"Isn't that ridiculous? Bruno says he has a message he is supposed to relay to me."

"He had one for Caspar too. The message was that he was going to be killed."

"That's ridiculous!"

"You and Caspar weren't engaged, were you?"

"Engaged!" She made a face. "I'm engaged all right. To Bob Lester."

Betty Armstrong was a widow, having married an elderly colleague when she was a new member of the staff. She and Lester would marry when the spring semester was over. Bob Lester was the golf coach.

4

Bob Lester worked as assistant pro at Calumet, a municipal course, to supplement his income. Part-time during the year, full-time in the summer. This meant he was a clerk in the golf shop, sold tickets, rented carts, and whiled away the day with a wonderful view of the course.

"I get in nine holes early and usually eighteen at the end of the day."

Lester seemed to be explaining why he was so modestly employed. "Is that all you do, coach the golf team?" Given the Illinois winter, there had to be another part-time job.

"I'm in the math department."

"With Quinn?"

"Quinn! How do you know him?"

Lester had a thin waist and great chest expansion. Golden hair lay upon his bronzed forearms and he might have been frowning against the sun.

"He said he was Betty Armstrong's fiancé."

Lester laughed disdainfully. "You ever meet Quinn?"

"Not yet."

Lester shook his head, but his smile was indulgent. "Quinn and a member of Betty's department both had a crush on her."

"William Caspar?"

"Another yoyo."

"He was found dead this morning at Captain Hook's Driving Range."

"No!"

"Wearing a jogging costume but with a golf club in his hand."

"Good Lord. Who did it, Quinn?"

"Betty Armstrong said she was giving Caspar golf lessons."

"She's too good for her own good. She thought regular exercise, being outside, would get his mind off her."

When Cy arrived downtown, Phil Keegan had a very bald man in tow. "This is Bruno Quinn, Cy. He's agreed to identify the body."

"I can't believe what I've been hearing," the mathematician said. "Who would want to hurt Bill Caspar?"

Cy took the muttering mathematician to the morgue where Pippen pulled out a drawer and displayed the body of William Caspar. Quinn let out a yelp.

"What happened to his beard? What happened to his head?"

"You identify him as William Caspar?"

"This is desecration!" Quinn was leaning over the body. He fell silent, then straightened up. "No wonder he wore a beard."

"Want to tell me about him?"

"He was my best friend."

Pippen went across the street with them where over Guinness they listened to Quinn's eulogy for his slain friend.

"Who do you think did it, Quinn?"

The mathematician looked sharply at Cy. "You suspect me, don't you?"

"Should I?"

"When did this happen?"

Pippen answered. "Time of death was in the early morning hours."

"I have no alibi," Quinn cried. "I live alone. I can come and go at will. Where was he killed?"

"The body was found at Captain Hook's Driving Range."

Quinn was puzzled. "But he knew how to drive."

"Golf."

"Golf! That's right. He thought if he learned how to play it would impress Betty. What a fool."

"Isn't she a golfer?"

"Mere diversion. The woman has soul. Have you heard of Fatima?"

Quinn launched into an account of private revelations, Lourdes, Fatima, others.

"You're quite an authority. Do you believe in miracles?"

"Of course." His eyes darted to Pippen. "In a sense."

"Someone told me you talk to St. Bartholomew regularly."

A toothy bald man laughing has a Halloween effect. "I told William that and he believed me."

"Just a joke?"

"No, no. I wouldn't joke about such things. Who am I to say that something cannot happen when perfectly sane people insist it has?"

"Like a cure for asthma?"

"She told you!"

"It came out. What is your relation to Betty Armstrong?"

"My relation?"

"Are you engaged to her or anything?"

Quinn's eyes rolled upward and then closed. He sighed. "I devoutly hope to be."

"Do you know Bob Lester?"

"Totally unworthy of her! They say he is a mathematician. Ha! He didn't know who Goedel was when I mentioned him."

"Q.E.D.?" Pippen said.

"Exactly."

☩

"Who's Goedel?" Cy asked when Quinn left and they were alone in the booth.

"I never wear one. Do you suspect him?"

"Quinn? Who knows? Want another?"

"Better not."

Was she suggesting that, weakened by alcohol, her will to resist would dissolve? This was a question Cy did not allow to form in his mind. His innocent flirtation with Pippen depended on its being innocent.

Cy returned to the office where Phil Keegan was floating the possibility that the blow on Caspar's head had been self-inflicted.

"Everything I hear about this guy suggests a total lack of coordination. He would be a menace on a golf course. To himself as well as others."

Phil got up to illustrate, using the club that had been found with the body and had been processed through the lab. Cy moved back and Gloria, his secretary, cleared out of the room. Phil did it in slow motion, showing how a wild back swing could bring the head of the club to the point behind the ear where Caspar had been struck.

"Is that a left-handed club?" Cy asked.

"What difference does that make? You see what I'm saying."

Cy took the club and looked at it.

"Phil, this is a left-handed lady's two-wood."

5

Father Dowling had mixed feelings about the way the alleged apparition had dropped out of the investigation. William Caspar had come to him with the story of St. Bartholomew, the apostle appearing to his friend Quinn and predicting that he would be shortly killed.

"That's pretty close to a death threat," Phil said.

"Caspar took it quite seriously."

So had Father Dowling, in another sense. He found it offensive that someone should jest about communicating with St. Bartholomew and then attribute a death threat to the apostle. Of course Quinn knew that Caspar had told Father Dowling of the alleged prophesy.

"He told Cy it was just a joke on Caspar."

Was that possible? These two absurd men had been vying for the favors of Betty Armstrong who was engaged to a third man, Bob Lester. Betty professed to have been cured of asthma through the intercession of Our Lady of Fatima. Were the conversations with St. Bartholomew concocted to establish a spiritual link with Professor Armstrong?

The golf club that had dealt the fatal blow to William Caspar—as Dr. Pippen now attested—was from the golf bag of Betty Armstrong. Father Dowling went with Phil Keegan to the eleventh floor office of the chair of history. A yellow-haired young man reacted like Dracula to the cross when he saw Father Dowling. He could not take his eyes from the collar.

"She in?" Phil asked.

The yellow head nodded. Father Dowling thought of Cymbeline. "Golden lads and lasses must, like chimney sweepers come to dust."

"You must have known Caspar," Phil said to the young man.

"As little as possible."

"Why so?"

Blue eyes rolled upward. "A boor and a bully."

Betty Armstrong's door opened. Her eyes went immediately to the club Phil was holding. "Is that my two-wood?"

"I was about to ask you the same question."

She took the club and backed into her office, Phil following. Joey scooted into the hallway as if afraid to be left alone with Father Dowling. "Did you notice his hair? If I say anything about it, it's considered harassment." She looked at the club.

"I should tell you that this club was the weapon that killed William Caspar."

She pushed it from her, handing it back to Phil.

"It's been missing from my bag." She went to a closet and opened it, bringing out a blue and white leather bag. Three knitted head covers adorned the driver, three and four woods. The irons clanked as she pulled the bag into view. "See. Only three woods. Of course they're metal."

"Of course."

"Is that where you keep your clubs?"

She gave Father Dowling a look. "I brought them up from when the cab dropped me here. Usually they are in the trunk of my car."

The cab had brought her from the airport two days before when she returned from a conference in Lousiville.

"Who knew they were here?"

"It was no secret." She pointed at a plastic target in the corner. "I practice putting here to calm my nerves."

There was a putter in the closet, but since her bag had been there as well she had been using a putter from the bag that looked like a flatiron. It occurred to Father Dowling that anyone looking for a weapon in that golf bag would have chosen the putter. Or one of the irons. But a two-wood?

"Are these the clubs you used when you gave Caspar instructions at Captain Hook's?"

She shook her head. "The clubs supplied at the range were good enough for him. Besides, these are women's clubs."

"Who could have taken the club from your bag?"

"Oh, it wasn't there."

"What?"

"When it was brought up from the cab I noticed the two-wood was missing."

"And you had the clubs with you in Louisville?"

"I got in two rounds."

"Where is the mathematics department?"

"On the ninth floor."

From Armstrong's office they descended to the ninth floor where Phil asked a woman with extremely thick glasses if Professor Quinn had been in the office two days ago.

"He never comes in."

"Never."

"Seldom."

"When was he last in?"

"Did you say two days ago?"

"Yes."

A slow smile threatened to crack her face. "I was out with the flu."

No one had sat in for her. Against one wall there were mailboxes for the staff. Most of them were jammed with junk mail, book catalogs, newsletters, administrative communications. The box under the name Bruno Quinn was clean as a whistle.

"Looks like he was in to check his mail."

✝

The direction of Phil's thinking was clear later when they sat at a table in the St. Hilary's rectory.

"Jealous rivals," he said, savoring Marie's mince pie. The housekeeper had joined them for dessert, and nodded approval of Phil's account.

The bald mathematician and the hirsute historian had both been smitten by Betty Armstrong. She had been giving golf instructions to Caspar, which might have been construed by Quinn as an advantage for his rival. He himself had sought to endear himself to Betty Armstrong by claiming mystical communications with one of the apostles. The golf lessons tipped the balance in Caspar's favor, or so thought Bruno Quinn. He followed his rival to Captain Hook's where Caspar had gone to practice and struck him with the club he had stolen from Armstrong's bag before it got to the closet in her office.

"But Caspar was holding the club, Phil."

"He grabbed it away from his assailant," Marie offered.

Her assistance brought doubt into Phil's eyes. The phone rang and Marie went into the kitchen to answer it. A moment later, she returned, her face ashen.

"That was Lieutenant Horvath. Bruno Quinn has just been taken to emergency. Someone attacked him."

6

Bruno Quinn seemed to have been attacked from behind, struck a blow that might have cracked his egg-like skull. But it was the tufts of hair glued to his pate that struck Cy Horvath when he pulled aside the curtain and looked down at the fallen mathematician. His eyes were open but dull.

"Tell me about it."

"Tell you what? I answered the door, there was no one there, I stepped outside and . . ." His eyes closed in pain.

The apparent weapon was found in the front yard of a house two doors from Bruno Quinn's—a putter with a flat and massive head. Cy nodded when this information was given to him but continued with Bruno.

"Did you call 911?"

"How could I?"

A call had been made, telling of a man lying on the front steps of a house in Skokie. A cautious neighbor, a passerby with a cell phone, any-one. Not quite. The Skokie 911 board recorded the number from which calls originated. The call had come from a pay phone at the 7-Eleven a block away from Quinn's house. The man who had been on duty the night before was at home. Sleeping, as he angrily explained to Cy when he came to the door.

"Just a couple of questions."

"I'll never get back to sleep." The man had streaks of red and purple in his hair. And red in his eyes.

"Someone made a call from the payphone in the 7-Eleven this morn-ing at one-thirty."

"Yeah."

"You didn't notice . . ."

Cy knew the answer before he got the question out. He would have apologized for waking the clerk up but the door was closing on him.

"No luck?" Pippen asked, when he got into the car. She had come along to get away from Lubins, her boss.

"I didn't expect any."

Pippen knew about routine. Ninety percent of what one did turned out to be pointless. It must be like that for her when she did autopsies. Reminding himself of her work was meant to diminish her attractiveness.

"Where to?"

"Calumet Golf Course."

Bob Lester was busy in the golf shop when they got there, and the sight of Cy did not spur him to hurry. Finally he ran out of customers and came toward them.

"Does Betty Armstrong keep her clubs here?"

"She has a locker, sure."

"I'd like to see it."

Lester bristled at the suggestion but then he remembered that Cy was a police detective. Without a word, he led them to the locker rooms, the men's on one side, the women's on the other. He turned to Pippen.

"I can't go in there. Hers is locker twenty-nine."

Pippen asked Cy what she was looking for.

"See if there's a putter in the bag."

"How did you know that?" Lester asked, before Pippen went into the women's locker room.

"Know what?"

"That Betty's putter is missing. I brought her clubs here from the campus and when I took them out of the trunk I saw that the putter was missing. Why are you looking for it?"

Cy decided not to provide Bob Lester with the occasion to feign surprise. Pippen returned to say there was no putter in the bag. In the car, Cy was relieved when Betty Armstrong answered her phone.

"Is your putter in your office?"

"Who is this?"

"Sorry. Lieutenant Horvath."

"My putter? I keep a putter here, for practice."

"The one you play with?"

"That's in my bag."

"Sure?"

"Of course I'm sure. And my bag is in my locker at the Calument Golf Course."

"Taken there by Bob Lester?"

"You seem to have answers before you ask the questions."

The putter had been in her bag, her bag had been taken to her locker at Calumet by Bob Lester, the putter had been used to put a dint in Bruno Quinn's head, mimicking how Walter Caspar had been killed. The two men had been in pursuit of Betty Armstrong, who was engaged to Bob Lester. . . .

"Maybe," Cy said.

7

When Betty Armstrong showed up at the St. Hilary's rectory, Marie Murkin led her down the hall to the study immediately, fighting the urge to quiz the visitor before turning her over to the pastor.

"Father Dowling, I have to talk with you."

"Please sit down. Would you shut the door, Marie?"

Betty Armstrong did not wait for the door to close. "They think Bob killed William Caspar. They think he struck Bruno Quinn."

"Obviously you don't."

"Of course I don't. Bob is the gentlest person in the world."

"I look forward to meeting him."

"Would you talk to the police?"

Father Dowling tried not to show amusement at the assumption that all he need do was say the word and a police investigation would stop.

"There are certain things they will want to know, Betty. Bob Lester did have access to your golf bag."

"Anyone could have walked into that locker room and stolen my putter."

"And the two-wood that killed Caspar?"

She fell silent, her eyes darting about in search of an answer. Then she burst into tears. Father Dowling was sorry he had asked Marie to shut the study door.

"I'm sorry. I'm as bad as Joey."

"Your secretary."

She nodded, then smiled. "So sensitive." She grew serious. "Father, I know Bob did not do these things. I don't care what accusations are made, he is incapable of such actions."

"Then of course the police must find the one who is."

Her eyes narrowed. "I have a very good hunch who it is. And he will never be suspected."

"And who is that?"

She leaned forward and whispered, "Bruno Quinn." She sat back, waiting for his reaction. "Think of it. He killed William because of the absurd notion that they were rivals for my hand. Now, to protect himself, he simulates an attack on himself."

"With your putter?"

She smiled grimly. "Joey has the answer to that."

"Oh?"

"He says he saw Bruno come out of my office, concealing something, and sidling into the hallway."

Father Dowling handed Marie a note and then returned with Betty Armstrong to her office on the eleventh floor. Joey was at his computer, but he quickly switched screens when his boss came in. He showed the same uneasiness as before at the sight of a priest.

"Joey, tell Father Dowling what you told me."

"Why don't just Joey and I talk about it, Betty?"

"Good, good." She disappeared into her office, closing the door behind her. Father Dowling took one of the chairs in the outer office and looked about the room. He said to the ceiling, "Tell me about William Caspar."

"It's Quinn who took the clubs."

He nodded. "I suppose you saw Caspar regularly."

"I couldn't avoid it! He came to check his mail. And to sneak a peek at Betty. Can you imagine that clod thinking he had a chance with her?"

"Did you tease him about it?"

Joey's eyes rounded. "I didn't dare." He ran a hand through his bright yellow hair. The ringlet in his nose sparkled.

"So it was a one-way street."

"What do you mean?"

"Shaving off his beard and giving him that crude haircut were big mistakes, Joey. Why would the one who killed Caspar do such things? They weren't the deeds of a supposed rival. They spoke of revenge."

"That's nonsense."

"Daily taunting became too severe a burden, didn't it?"

"Did Betty tell you this?" He cast a betrayed look at the closed door of the inner office.

"No, you did. By shaving and barbering Caspar and gluing tufts of hair on the bald head of Bruno Quinn. Did Quinn tease you too?"

"I don't have to answer these questions."

"Joey, you can't avoid them. Do you feel any remorse. . . ?"

"No!" He jumped to his feet. He stopped before Father Dowling and, his eyes half shut, hissed, "I'm glad. But no one can prove anything."

The door opened and Cy Horvath came in. He nodded to Roger Dowling and blocked the exit as Joey tried to hurry past him.

"Let's have a little talk," he said, taking Joey's upper arm.

Joey kicked out at Cy's ankle, but Cy moved out of range with what might have been a dance step. A moment later, he had Joey in a chair. The defiant look left the yellow-haired secretary and he bowed his head and wept. Father Dowling left Cy to his melancholy task.

8

Betty Armstrong wanted Father Dowling to preside when she married Bob Lester on the practice putting green at Calumet Club but since neither she nor Bob were Catholic, and weddings other than in church were frowned on anyway, he was able to beg off graciously. Marie attended and returned a little lightheaded with champagne and with a glowing account of the affair. Phil Keegan and the pastor were following a ball game but lent her half an ear.

"Bruno Quinn said it was too bad Joey couldn't be there." Marie paused. "As a bridesmaid!"

Phil snorted.

Just such teasing taunts had triggered the death of William Caspar. Betty Armstrong told of her colleague's incessant allusions to Joey's dyed hair, the ring in his nose, the diamond earring.

"I warned him," she added. "But obviously not enough."

It had begun with an astonishing claim that Bruno Quinn was in communication with St. Bartholomew who told him of the impending death of William Caspar. Never kid a kidder. The historian proved totally credulous of this fabricated story, given apparent credence by items Quinn had found in the memoirs Caspar fitfully kept and stored on his hard drive. Breaking into his friend's computer was child's play for Quinn, and he had astonished Caspar with revelations about his youth. When Caspar was found dead at Captain Hook's Driving Range, it was only natural to think Quinn had something to do with it. But the true explanation had been hidden on the margin of events—the all too visible but still over-lookable secretary to Betty Armstrong. Day after day, week after week, he had been subjected to the cruel teasing of William Caspar. When he learned of Caspar's early morning bouts at the driving range, he saw his opportunity.

"Why did you use one of Betty Armstrong's clubs?"

Joey never gave a satisfactory answer to that question. Or to his use of the putter. Joey, it seemed, had brought Betty's clubs up from the cab when she returned from Louisville and taken them down to Bob Lester when he was transferring them to Betty's locker at Calumet.

"Because they were there."

The knitted cover to Betty's two-wood was found in the back seat of Joey's car, apparently tossed there before he crept toward William Caspar, flailing away at practice balls. He had put the murder weapon into the dead hands of his victim. The putter he had removed when he took Betty's clubs down to Bob Lester.

Hadn't he seen that this would seem to implicate Bob Lester?

"He was devoted to her! They made a lovely couple."

And so they had, on the practice putting green at Calumet. Marie cut out the picture that appeared the following morning. She shook her head at what she took to be a misspelling in the caption. Profs Putt Happiness First. Father Dowling suppressed a groan. Puns, like teasing, bring murderous thoughts.

†

Contributors

PETER TREMAYNE is the pseudonym of Peter Berresford Ellis, a Celtic scholar who lives in London, England. He conceived the idea for Sister Fidelma, a seventh century Celtic lawyer, to demonstrate that women could be legal advocates under the Irish system of law. Sister Fidelma has since appeared in eight novels, the most recent being *The Monk Who Vanished*, and many short stories which have been collected in the anthology *Hemlock at Vespers and Other Sister Fidelma Mysteries*. He has also written, under his own name, more than twenty-five books on history, biography, and Irish and Celtic mythology, including *Celtic Women: Women in Celtic Society and Literature* and *Celt and Greek: Celts in the Hellenic World*.

ED GORMAN has been called "one of the most original crime writers around" by *Kirkus* and "a powerful storyteller" by Charles Champlin of the *Los Angeles Times*. He works in horror and westerns as well as crime and has written many excellent short stories. To date there have been six Gorman collections, three of which are straight crime, and the most recent of which is *Such a Good Girl and Other Stories*. He is probably best known for his Sam McCain series, set in the small-town Iowa of the 1950s. ("Good and evil clash with the same heartbreaking results as Lawrence Block or Elmore Leonard.") He has also written a number of thrillers, including *The Marilyn Tapes* and *Black River Falls*, the latest being *The Poker Club*.

ANNE PERRY writes, "I was born in Blackheath, London, in 1938. From an early age, I enjoyed reading, and two of my favorite authors were Lewis Carroll and Charles Kingsley. It was always my desire to write, but it took twenty years before I produced a book which was accepted for publication. That was *The Cater Street Hangman*, which came out in 1979. I chose the Victorian era by accident, but I am happy to stay with it, because it was a remarkable time in British history, full of extremes, of poverty and wealth, social change, expansion of empire, and challenging ideas. In all levels of society there were the good and the bad, the happy and the miserable." Here she takes a break from the Victorian Age to focus on the Middle Ages with her usual craftsmanship and style.

MALACHI SAXON was born in 1944 in London, England, and studied medicine, as well as philosophy and psychology, in Oxford. He went to Rhodesia in Africa and after serving in the army, worked at a variety of medical posts, including lecturing on anatomy at the University. Now retired, he lives in the Scottish Highlands with his wife and children. Principal sport is rifle shooting, having won the top prize, the President's Medal, in Zimbabwe. Lately, however, he spends more time playing golf to keep his son, a budding Tiger Woods, company.

EDWARD D. HOCH is past president of Mystery Writers of America, winner of its 2001 Grand Master award and its Edgar award for best short story of 1968. He has published nearly 850 short stories as well as anthologies, collections, and novels. He has been Guest of Honor at the annual Bouchercon mystery convention and received its Anthony Award for best short story. In 2001 he received the convention's Lifetime Achievement Award. In 2000 he received The Eye, the life achievement award of the Private Eye Writers of America. He resides in Rochester, New York, with his wife, Patricia.

LILLIAN STEWART CARL writes what she calls "gonzo mythology" fantasy novels, as well as mystery and romantic suspense novels. While growing up in Missouri and Ohio, she began writing at an early age, and she has continued all her life, even while traveling to Europe, Great Britain, the Middle East, and India, among other places. He novels include *Dust to Dust, Shadow Dancers*, and *Wings of Power*. Her short fiction has appeared in *Alternate Generals; Past Lives, Present Tense; Murder Most Medieval;* and *Death by Horoscope*. She lives in Carrollton, Texas, with her husband.

CHUCK MEYER was a mystery writer cleverly disguised as an Episcopalian priest. He was the author of twelve books, including murder mysteries, humor, and titles on death and grieving. In the course of his lifetime, he wrote numerous magazine articles and conducted hundreds of speaking engagements each year. He graduated from Earlham College and Union Theological Seminary and got his practical education working in a New York prison and Texas jail. He created the Reverend Lucas Holt mystery series, which features a middle-aged chaplain turned Episcopal parish priest in Austin, Texas, who solves crimes with the aid of reformed ex-cons collectively known as the God Squad. Until his untimely death in 2000, he was Vice-President of Operations and chaplain at St. David's Hospital in Austin, Texas.

STEPHEN DENTINGER's first story appeared in the March 1956 issue of *Smashing Detective Stories*. Since then his fiction has been published in *Ellery Queen's Mystery Magazine*, *Alfred Hitchcock's Mystery Magazine*, *The Saint Magazine*, *Mike Shayne Mystery Magazine*, *The Magazine of Horror*, and a number of anthologies. He resides with his wife in upstate New York and is a familiar figure at the annual Bouchercons and other mystery gatherings. He recently took part in a panel on historical mysteries at the Bloody Words mystery conference in Toronto.

MONICA QUILL is the pseudonym of Ralph McInerny.

MARGARET FRAZER's medieval murder mystery series featuring Dame Frevisse, a great-niece of Geoffrey Chaucer, now spans eleven novels, with Edgar Award nominations for *The Servant's Tale* and *The Prioress' Tale*. The most recent, *The Clerk's Tale*, was published this year. Her short story "Neither Pity, Love, Nor Fear" won the Herodotus Award and more of her short fiction has appeared in *Murder Most Medieval* and *Much Ado About Murder*. She lives in Minnesota and is at work on more Dame Frevisse novels.

KATE GALLISON is the creator of two series characters who couldn't be more different. Nick Magaracz is a private detective who works in New Jersey, while her other, longer-running series features Mother Lavinia Grey, an Episcopal priest who also lives and sleuths in New Jersey. Recent novels include *Grave Misgivings, Hasty Retreat*, and *Unholy Angels*. She has worked at several careers before turning to writing, including computer specialist and bill collector.

Michael Jecks worked as a computer salesman until 1994, when an industry sales slump forced him to consider a new career. He wrote *The Last Templar*, the first of nine medieval mystery novels, found an agent, and then a publisher who offered him a three-book deal. Of his novels, he says, "I guess I'm like many people who love books—for many years I thought I should try writing, but with a mortgage to support there never seemed to be time. My stories are based on extensive research, which has persuaded me that people haven't changed at all in 700 years. The same motivations lead to murder: jealousy, infidelity, greed, and so on. I try to show where our ancestors were different. How did the law work, how did people generally view government and justice? How did they live? It's not easy to show what life was really like, but it's a challenge I enjoy." Recent novels in his Medieval West County series include *The Abbot's Gibbet* and *Belladonna at Belstone*.

Kate Charles, a former Chairman of the British Crime Writers' Association, is known for her Book of Psalms mystery series, set against the rich background of the Church of England. Her latest book, *Cruel Habitations,* is one of three stand-alone suspense novels, also drawing on the Anglican Church and her experience as a parish administrator.

Paul Doherty is the author of many historical novels and mysteries, all of which have been widely praised in both the United Kingdom and America. His books have been published by Robert Hale, Headline, and Constable Robinson in the British Commonwealth, and by St. Martin's Press in America. He studied history at Liverpool and Oxford Universities and gained a doctorate at Oxford for his thesis on Edward II and Isabella. He is headmaster of a school in London and lives with his wife and family near Epping Forest.

Author and editor Ralph McInerny has long been acknowledged as one of the most vital voices in lay Catholic activities in America. He is co-founder and co-publisher of *CRISIS*, a widely read journal of Catholic opinion, while finding time to teach Medieval Studies at Notre Dame University and write several series of mystery novels, one of which, *The Father Dowling Mysteries*, ran on network television for several seasons and can now be seen on cable. Scholars are rarely entertainers, but Ralph McInerny, as himself and under his pseudonym Monica Quill, has been both for many years.

COPYRIGHTS AND PERMISSIONS